Come in at the Door

T0288155

My lord is so high, you can't go over him,

My lord is so wide, you can't go 'round him,

My lord is so deep, you can't go under him,

You must come in at the door."

Negro Spiritual

Come in at the Door
by William March

The University of Alabama Press • Tuscaloosa

THE LIBRARY
OF ALABAMA
CLASSICS

The University of Alabama Press
Tuscaloosa, Alabama 35487-0380
uapress.ua.edu

COME IN AT THE DOOR. Copyright 1934, 1962 by W. E. Campbell, LLC
The University of Alabama Press
All rights reserved.

Originally published 1934 by H. Smith and R. Haas

Inquiries about reproducing material from this work should be addressed to
the University of Alabama Press.

Manufactured in the United States of America
Cover design: Emma Sovich
∞

The paper on which this book is printed meets the minimum requirements
of American National Standard for Information Sciences—Permanence of Paper
for Printed Library Materials, ANSI Z39.48-1984.

Library of Congress Cataloging-in-Publication Data

March, William, 1893–1954.
Come in at the door / William March.
pages ; cm — (Library of Alabama Classics series)
ISBN 978-0-8173-5811-2 (pbk. : alk. paper) — ISBN 978-0-8173-8831-7 (ebook)
1. Delta (Miss. : Region)—Fiction. I. Title.
PS3505.A53157C57 2014
813'.52—dc23
2014024849

To

Susy March Campbell

with much affection

The Whisperer

THERE was once a man who had been sick for a long time. When he was better, his brothers lifted him in their arms and carried him to the roof where they had fixed a chair for him; where he could rest quietly in the soft, spring sunshine. Occasionally one of the family or some old friend came to visit him, but mostly he lay alone, relaxed and indolent under the mild sky; staring at his hands resting before him on the blanket, as if there were a message in their wasted meagerness. Occasionally he would lift his arm and pass his fingers hesitantly across his cheeks, closing his eyes and remaining so inert that one would not have thought him alive at all.

Pain had sharpened the senses of this man. He had been so close to death that his mind still held some of the things he had seen: his mind was like a ball of white light which burned purely and gave no heat. It was so sure, and so clear, that it no longer belonged to his tired body; it was something entirely apart from his body: an instrument which understood things that lay beyond the power of reason.

When he was tired of looking at the sky, this sick man would turn his head a little and watch people leaning anxiously out of windows or moving below him on the street. It seemed to him that all people were disturbed and hurrying, as if engaged in secret errands which must be accomplished quickly. Sometimes he would pick out one figure and follow that figure as long as he could, trying to guess from gestures, or actions, the motives which made it do the irrational, unpredictable things which it did. Then, defeated of knowledge, he would sigh and lie back again. He thought: "There is no order and no plan in living: people merely run about, looking into hidden corners. They touch for an instant and examine one another with their eyes, seeking for something; then, not having found it, they pass on. They are like ants that meet on a smooth path and rub their heads together."

And so the sick man played with his fancies, his mouth opened a little, the pulse in his wrist beating faintly. All at once he had a curious thought about the restless people before him: it seemed to him, at that moment, that when God created mankind He had woven a thread for each soul to be born and had hidden these threads cunningly. But He did not tell man, clearly, that a thread lay hidden for him: He had only given him the wish to seek something, a vague thing which he could not even name.

The sick man was still thinking those thoughts when his mother came up to see him, bringing his medicine and a bowl of broth. When he had eaten, he told her what he had discovered and his mother listened patiently, as if he were still a little boy.

"But does no man find his right thread at last?" she asked.

The sick man was silent for a moment, his lids half closed, but at last he spoke: "It is not enough for a man merely to find his thread, for he must also unravel his thread from all others, once he has found it, and he must follow it to its end. . . . And how can a man do this when his thread is full of knots and his fingers are too stiff to untie them? How can a man follow his thread when other feet have broken it, and the pieces have blown away?"

The man lay back and began to cry, the tips of his fingers resting together. His mother wiped his face with her handkerchief and straightened his rug for him.

"You are sick," she said, touching his forehead with her hands. "When you are well again, you will not remember these terrifying things."

From the Diary of Sarah Tarleton

May 14, 1902. *My dear niece, Ellen Decatur Tarleton, married today the man of her choice, Mr. Robert Chester Hurry. The ceremony was performed at home and the whole house was decorated with vines and spring flowers. The bride was given away by her father and the groom was attended by my nephew, Bushrod. The bride's young sister, Bessie, served as flower girl, looking very sweet and innocent as she scattered blossoms along the path which led to the improvised altar. After the ceremony the blissful pair drove to Reedyville, where they entrained for their new home.*

Go, happy couple, and ride the Horses of Courage and Love across the Restless Sea of Life! We have not lost a daughter; we have gained a son! Our best wishes for your health and happiness go with you.

August 5, 1904. *Today there came a telegram announcing the birth of a fine 9 pound boy to my niece, Ellen Hurry. Mother and baby are both resting well. Our congratulations and good wishes to you, my darling niece and nephew, on this happy occasion. May the life of your son be long and happy and free from sorrow. Preserved 35 quarts of figs today. Fruit this year very abundant.*

1

THAT summer, during the long, hot afternoons, Mitty would often take the young boy by the hand and together they would go to the river to get sand for the kitchen floor. When they reached it, Mitty would sit against a sweetgum tree and fan herself with her apron, and the boy would rest his head in her lap, or sit upright against her shoulder, tracing patterns in the dust with his fingers.

To Chester, at eight, the world consisted of his father's farm, as a center, with Athlestan, the County seat, to the north, and the old Bragdon place a mile southward. To the west groves of pines, purplish-green and as level as water against the sky, stretched as far as eyes could see. To the east there were cotton fields, or fields of peanuts, and still farther on, beyond the cultivated land, was the river before which they now rested, a sluggish, unhurried river, colored like coffee with cream stirred into it.

The river flowed slowly, between yellow bluffs, high and concave, on which grew honeysuckle and wild pea vines. In some places the river broke into eddies, but where Mitty and the boy rested its movement was imperceptible, seemingly without motion: it flowed straight and flat before them. A mile to the north it turned gently in a golden curve and its source was lost to sight between the thick growing trees; toward the south it bent gradually eastward and was more agitated here, breaking up into minor whirlpools, with yellow foam on them. In these eddies stick and bits of broken refuse whirled about.

Years ago, before the railroads had come, shallow-draft river boats carrying passengers and collecting freight had steamed up the river. In those days wharves at which the boats might tie up safely had been built, and the farmers would haul down their cotton and pile it on the yellow banks near the wharves to await such steamers. When at last the boat arrived, the place, which before had seemed deserted and void of all life, took on sudden activity. But all this had happened in the past; it was part of a past which the boy could not remember or visualize. The river was quiet now. The boats and the activity were all gone. Even the wharves had rotted and were falling away.

Below Mitty and the boy the remnants of such a wharf persisted,—a few canted, unsteady posts with rotting planks. Water birds with calculating eyes rested on these pilings, watching the water patiently or rubbing their beaks against the oil sacs at the end of their spines and ruffling their feathers out as if a strong wind had disarrayed them for a moment. Occasionally a gull or a pelican blown inland from the Gulf sat there and surveyed the sluggish river with a distasteful, uncomprehending expression; flapping; stretching its body upward; clinging to its perch with sharp claws as if nailed there, and screaming its lonely, unbearably pure call. Mitty and Chester would often sit quietly, as they sat today on the bluff above the rotted landing, and watch the colored river and the strange, unhappy birds blown inland from the sea.

Mitty's world was larger than the boy's, and her memory of it was longer. She talked of places and things which he had never known: of Reedyville, Pigeon Creek or the Tallon homestead. They were all situated in a land called Pearl County and Chester could never hear enough about them. . . . And so Mitty would sit by the river fanning herself and talking of the past.

"Tell me about my mother," he would ask. "Tell me about my mother and my Grandfather Tarleton, too!"

Then Mitty would chuckle indulgently. She was an erect woman with a black skin as soft against the hand as velvet: a skin so completely and so deeply black that it seemed frosted with a lighter color, as the black skin of a muscadine appears silver in some lights. She walked with a flowing swing from her hips, her arms held tidily to her sides, her head thrown back at an exact angle, her chin slightly raised and held there poised as if she balanced, eternally, something precious upon her skull.

But in spite of her black skin and her short, nappy hair, her features were delicate and high-bred. Her nose was thin, high bridged and faintly curved; her eyes were heavy lidded and half closed as a rule. She sat fanning herself and glancing up the river, paying little attention to the boy's questions; then, finally, when he thought that she would not answer him at all, she began to talk.

"Your mamma died when you was a baby in long dresses," she said. "She taken sick on a Sunday and she was laid out for dead before the next Sunday come 'round." Mitty leaned backwards against the sweetgum tree and listened to the drone of insects about them, and the muffled tapping of birds. . . . "Your mamma was a gentle little thing, baby. She had blue eyes and the yallowest hair. She crimped her hair on pins at night, and fluffed it out like. Her skin was whiter than buttermilk." Mitty glanced down at her own arms, turning her wrists upward, and laughed: "He-e-e-e-e!" on a soft, ascending scale, as if she found her blackness amusing.

Chester waited until her laughter had died and she was wiping her eyes with her handkerchief. "All the Tarletons are *light* skinned, but your mamma was the lightest skinned of all. She was the very lightest skinned one!"

"Tell me about how you and mamma were born on the same day."

13

"Why, honey, I've told you that story more times than one; I done told you every word of that story, and often, too."

"Tell it to me again, Mitty!"

"Got to be a-gittin' down to the bar and dig sand. Got to be a-gittin' back to the house and start supper going."

"Mitty—please!" He rose to his knees and put his arms around her neck, hugging her close. "Tell it again, Mitty! Tell it to me one more time!"

"All right, baby. All right, sugarpie. . . . Mitty can't say no to nothin' her baby asks, when he sweet-talk her that way. . . ."

She sat for a moment staring at the sluggish river, watching a log floating slowly down stream. "Your mamma and me was born on the same day, all right: that much of the story is *sho*. . . . I was born in the morning, and your mamma was born about sundown. The next day they taken the baby and give her to my own mamma to nurse, because your Grandma Tarleton didn't have nourishment for none of her children after your Aunt Lillian was born, and my mamma had enough for two, and to spare. . . . Leastways that's what she told us when we was little girls playing together." Mitty became silent. She was seeing pictures which Chester could not share. He knew that, somehow, and waited until she resumed.

"When your mamma started to school, she wouldn't learn out of her books 'lessen I learned with her. So your Aunt Sarah Tarleton had to teach us both." Mitty slapped her leg: "Lord!" she said, as if delighted; "Lord God! Lord God!" and swayed back and forth laughing.

Chester looked up quickly: "Baptiste can read, too. Baptiste can read better than any white man."

Mitty's laughter stopped. "What make you say that?" Then, without waiting for an answer: "I expect Baptiste tell you that himself."

"Yes, ma'am."

Mitty drew down her lips in disgust. "That yaller nigger!" She spat, as if repeating his name had soiled her lips. "That yaller nigger! Putting a high mark of respect on hisself; trying to pass hisself off for a Frenchman." Her face set sullenly. She got up, jerking the boy upright. "Come on, boy! Come on, white boy, let's get our sand and get back to the house!"

But Chester held onto her hand and would not move.

"Mitty, please!"

"Why don't you ask Baptiste to tell you 'bout your mamma and your Grandpappa Tarleton and your Uncle Bushrod and all iffen he so smart? What make you fool with a black, ignorant nigger like I is?"

"I like you best, Mitty."

But Mitty continued in an aggrieved voice. "I got an education, too. Miss Sarah taught me the same as she taught your mamma. I can talk proper, too, iffen I wanted to demean myself. I could pass myself off for white, too, iffen I wanted to do that." She looked at her blackness and her anger vanished. She laughed again, explosively, at the idea of her being taken for white.

"Tell me about how mamma used to look."

And Mitty said: "Your mamma was the very sweetest thing in this world. She had long yaller hair which she wore banged and hanging down her back. Some thought she was thin and puny like, but she run and frisked about like a hoppergrass. We were like sisters together: We played together all our lives, never having ere a secret from each other. Oh, but she was the prettiest thing! All the white gentlemen come to spark her after she come back, but she wouldn't have nothing to do with ere a boy or man of them. Then your pappa come courting her too, and she liked him better than the others; but she said she wouldn't marry him or no other gentleman unlessen I went to live with her." Again Mitty became silent. She looked with half-closed eyes at the trunk of a tree which had lost its footing and was leaning down the yellow bluff, its branches almost touching the water. "That's all there is to the story, baby." She lifted her bosom and raised her arms outward, letting them fall to her sides again. "Your mamma said she wouldn't marry no man or go nowheres without taking me with her, and here I is."

"Talk about my grandfather and my Uncle Bushrod."

"Now, baby!—Now, baby! You's the provokinest baby ever I seen; I done told you all about them a dozen times or more." But at last she gave in: "There was a big family of us Tarletons when your mamma and me was little girls, but they're all dead now, or married and scattered. . . . They're all married and scattered now, except your grandfather and your great aunt, Sarah, and your Uncle Bushrod and your Aunt Bessie."

They sat for a time silent after that and then Chester asked: "Why don't pappa take me to see them sometimes?"

Mitty shook her head. "There ain't no accounting for your pappa, baby.—He's an uncertain man."

She arose and picked up the basket which she had brought with her. She balanced herself on her toes, stretched herself widely and yawned, lifting her arms in a sudden back-flung movement which was more beautiful than the artifice of any dancer. "We'd better git our sand, baby, and git back to the house."

An old road, abandoned now and grown over with wire-grass and vines, led downward to the river where the skeleton of the rotting wharf stood.

Mitty said: "Be careful, baby, where you step! There might be a moccasin lying in that tall grass." Chester crowded closer to her skirts, but he did not answer. Together they walked down the slope that led to the river bank.

When boats ran up and down the river the sand bars which blocked it had been dredged away or channels cut through them; but now, after years of quietness, with life gone from the river, the bars had all come back. One had formed just behind the old wharf. It stretched from the bank to the center of the stream and it was shaped like a man's thumb, bent backward a little at the joint. The bar gleamed new and unsoiled and the August afternoon sun had put a shimmer above it.

Mitty and the boy reached the bar and began scooping up the sand, emptying it into the basket she had brought. The sand here was not white and dead, like sand that fringed the Gulf, but was richer in color: a pale gold, of the texture and shade of yellow cornmeal. It was soft to the fingers and soft to the feet, and Chester lay stretched on the bar letting the yellow sand run through his fists, from one to the other, like an hour glass.

For a few minutes Mitty worked silently, her back bending forward as she scooped up the gleaming sand. Then she stopped for a moment, wiped her forehead with her sleeve and gazed at the winding, yellowish river; at the green growth that crowded its banks. The trees which were tallest were so dark against the sky that they seemed at this distance not green at all, but rather the rich purple of Cæsars. They lay like an even river along the horizon, outlining the other greens beneath them and separating those shades from the mild blue of heaven. Below this wide ribbon of purple were layers and circles and half-moons of other greens; green with more blue than yellow in it and green with more yellow than blue. There were bright, lacquered greens so hard and brilliant that they seemed made of metal, and there were soft greens that were silver when winds lifted them upward. These shades were all blended and tied together in a pattern of color that stretched downward like a wedge to the yellow, gnawing river.

Mitty knelt on the bar and stared at the loveliness before her, a white cup limp in her black, unmoving hands. She raised her chin upward a little:

17

"This here place is as pretty a place to be in as ever I seen since I followed your mamma from Pearl County."

Chester did not answer, he was thinking his own thoughts. He turned over and the sand in his fist ran out slowly in a tiny, three-cornered stream. He lay on his back in silence. "I never saw my grandfather or my Uncle Bushrod or Aunt Sarah, did I, Mitty?"

"No, baby. No, baby, I expect not."

"Why don't they come to see us? Why don't they come to see us, if Pappa won't go to see them?"

"That I don't rightly know. That I can't answer."

Chester sat up on the bar. His face was set in a hard, mature line. "I hate him," he said quietly.

"Baby!" said Mitty in a shocked voice. "Don't talk like that!"

"I don't care," said Chester. "He's always—" But he stopped, unable to put into his words his vague discontent.

Mitty sighed. "Nobody but God Almighty is accomplished to judge. Your pappa has been a good father to you in lots of ways that you don't know nothing about."

Chester got up and stood on the sand, his feet braced and wide apart. "What makes him act the way he does? What makes him treat me like he does?"

"You'll understand when you're older, baby. You're too little to understand now."

Chester stared at the sun until the green trees and the yellow river wavered and ran together in wild confusion. He sat again on the sand and closed his eyes. When he opened them once more two water birds flew slowly up the river, crimson against the green of the far bank. "I wish he was dead," he muttered, his words intended for his own ears alone. "I wish he was dead and already buried!"

But Mitty had heard him. She dropped her basket and made a strange noise. She drew a circle from right to left, quickly, and

18

began breaking twigs and placing them in a pattern outside the circle, whispering words to herself and swaying sidewise.

When she had finished she seemed tired. She lay upon the sand so long that Chester became alarmed. He crept up and tried to put his arms around her, but Mitty shoved him away. "Don't you ever put a deathmouth on your pappa again! . . . Don't ever do that as long as you live!"

She got up angrily and lifted the filled basket to her head, balancing it there as she walked across the sand. Chester got up in fright and ran toward her, catching at her hand, but she paid no attention to him.

"Get away from me, white boy! Don't ever speak to me again." She muttered sullenly to herself and shook her shoulders, walking up the incline with long strides, her head balanced precisely; but when they reached the top of the bluff, she stopped, knelt beside the boy and put her arms about him. "How do you think your mamma up in heaven feels when she hears you talking thataway? How does she feel to have shame put on her amongst God's other sweet angels?"

Chester stood quietly, feeling her arms about him.

"I won't put a deathmouth on him again, if you say not to." But to himself he thought stubbornly: "I wish he was dead, though. I don't care what she says."

Mitty put down her basket and held him close to her bosom. "Baby!—Baby!" she whispered in despair. "I don't know what's come over you lately." She sat down on the bank and held him in her lap, singing songs to him.

Finally she squinted her eyes and looked up at the sun. She had spent more time than she had intended beside the river. It was already past time for starting supper. She got up abruptly, balanced her basket again and began to hurry with her long, flowing stride, her head poised at its exact, queenly angle, and Chester trotted by her side.

"Why don't Grandfather Tarleton or Uncle Bushrod come to see *us*, then?" asked Chester.

But Mitty did not answer him. She hurried more and more until Chester was panting from his effort to keep abreast of her. Their way led, finally, through Talcott's lane. From it they could see Robert Hurry plowing in the north field. In another field, which bordered the lane, were two other men: they were Jim and Baptiste, the farm hands. Jim did not pause in his work, unconscious that they were passing, but Baptiste seemed to know, somehow, the exact instant they emerged from the wood and came into view, as if he had been watching for a long time. He waved his hand gayly and called, *"Bonjour, Chester—Bonjour!"* Chester started to wave his own hand, and to call back, but Mitty jerked him roughly and he almost lost his balance. Baptiste came over to the fence and leaned upon it, and Mitty looked coldly at his smiling, light face; at his straight, brown hair; his yellow-irised, beautiful eyes, which were a little too liquid, a little too heavily lashed.

"Talk like a nigger, you nigger!" she said.

But Baptiste only laughed at her. As she moved off he called gently: *"Au revoir, Madame Hurry,"* then, mockingly, he added: *"Au revoir, mon charmant lis blanc!"*

Chester laughed appreciatively, but Mitty jerked him again and pulled at his hand. She hurried forward with her erect queenly gait, but Chester looked back over his shoulder and smiled at Baptiste until they passed the bend in the lane which hid the field. Once in her kitchen, Mitty built a fire in the stove and put on pots of water to boil.

"Hurry, baby. Hurry and bring Mitty in some stove wood. . . . Your pappa don't like to wait for his supper."

But Chester was still convulsed with Baptiste's witticism. He said: "Baptiste called you his charming white lily." He lay on the floor and laughed, rolling from side to side in his mirth.

"Bring me in some stove wood, baby," said Mitty patiently, her eyes veiled and cunning all of a sudden. "Come on, sugar-pie: help old Mitty get supper." She walked to the stove and rattled the door to the fire box. "I nursed you ever since you was born, honey. I taken care of you 'cause you're Ellen's own baby." Her voice was hurt and pleading. . . . "And now that yaller, lyin' Baptiste tryin' to turn you against me. Now that Baptiste make you mock me."

From the Diary of Sarah Tarleton

November 10, 1904. *I will never forgive That Man for what he has done as long as I live! Never! The thing is unbelievable. I cannot even now, as I write, take in the fact that my niece Ellen died a week ago and has been buried. Why didn't he notify us? Why didn't he give us the opportunity of looking once more on her dear face? I cannot understand it. The whole thing seems like a dream. Perhaps we would have never known at all if we had depended on him for information. And now all we know are the few facts in Mitty's letter. Mitty says that she was happy and never complained, but then it was always her nature to be loyal to those she loved and to make the best of things. Oh, That Man! How could he do such a thing? How could he? How could he?*

November 12, 1904. *Lillian and her husband Evan Chapman came over from Reedyville. They had a long family talk and want to take Ellen's baby to bring up as their own. Lillian is writing That Man today offering to take the child to raise and to provide for him as if he were her own.*

November 30, 1904. *Lillian Chapman has received an answer to her offer to take her sister's baby. It was not from That Man. He did not even trouble to write. It was from a firm of lawyers, in Athlestan, and they told her briefly to mind her own business. Wrote Mitty a long letter today. Thank God that she is there. She can be depended on to do her duty.*

2

THE house, a weather-beaten, rambling affair, was set on a rise in the ground. It was surrounded by shrubs and creepers which, after generations of cultivation, had become an individual wilderness again. Steps led upward to a sagging veranda in which holes had rotted, but the wooden pillars supporting the balcony were still firm and undecayed on their foundations of brick. Shutters guarded the windows facing south but they had been nailed fast against hurricanes which occasionally blew inland from the Gulf.

At one time the family had owned much land, had dwelt in security, easily and well, but that was a long time ago. Later generations of the Hurrys had lived first by selling the timber from the land they owned and then, gradually, the land itself, parcel by parcel, until now there was little left except the old house and the immediate fields that surrounded it. There was an atmosphere of defeat and decayed grandeur about the place. It stood there on a small knoll stained and barren, huddling against itself, hiding its poverty in the growth of trees and shrubbery which surrounded it.

After Mitty had supper under way she sent Chester to his room to prepare himself properly for the meal. It annoyed Robert to see his son with dirty face and hands. Chester washed himself carefully, standing on tiptoes to reach the flowered, slightly lopsided bowl. Then he combed out his straight, light hair and parted it as evenly as he could, holding his head to one side to catch his image in the flawed mirror. In the mirror he saw, also, a framed picture of his mother reflected. The picture was on the opposite wall, to the right of his bed. He turned away from the mirror, his hair half combed, and went to the wall where the picture was, and stood there, the brush dangling limply at his side, while he studied again her undecided, delicate features. He did not remember his mother, of course, although often he tried to believe that he did. Only Mitty connected him with her; only Mitty bridged the gap between them. As he stood there thinking, he felt suddenly that he wanted to cry, not understanding the reason back of his emotion; but he turned away again, angrily, and finished brushing his hair.

The room was furnished sparsely, but it was very clean. Farther down the hall Mitty herself slept. She had always slept in the house, as if she were a member of the family and not one of the servants. Facing the front of the house was Robert Hurry's room, a place where Chester was not permitted to go.

The boy had finished his preparations for supper. He sat by the window and waited. Presently he heard Mitty calling him from below. He got up nervously and hurried down the stairs, hoping that he would reach the table before his father, frightened vaguely at what his father would say to him.

The family had not used the big dining room for many years. It was now bare of furniture and lay shrouded in dust and darkness and meals were served on a table in the kitchen. Robert Hurry was already eating when his son entered and sat opposite him. The boy came in silently and did not raise his eyes. If he kept his head lowered and his eyes averted he could pretend that his father was not there at all.

Robert Hurry was about thirty-five years old in those days. He was thin and dark and his teeth were decaying and in need of attention. His skin was tanned through constant exposure to the elements and there were deep lines drawn outward from his nostrils. He rarely looked at people and when some old acquaintance spoke to him on the road he would mumble something and turn his head away. When he spoke his voice was unexpectedly harsh.

He was the last of a family whose gentility had worn it out. His mother, a gaunt, feverish woman wasted with disease, had planned since his early childhood that he go to college and study law, and by pinching and saving she had finally made it possible for him to do that. He consented to her plans because he had no strength to oppose her, but he had no aptitude for books, and he had felt lost and out of place at the university. To himself he seemed inept and countrified. He had little money to spend and he felt his isolation from his fellows. Few people knew him by sight and still fewer by name. He spent his time lounging in pool rooms or drinking, when he had money, in cheap undercover saloons, cutting as many classes as he dared. On one occasion he took up with a tent show and followed it around for a few weeks. He had some vague idea of getting away from the university, of breaking loose from everything that he had ever known. He wrote his mother telling her this; but when he got her letter he went back to school and studied furiously for a month or so, making up all the work that he had missed.

In his senior year he met Ellen Tarleton, a girl in one of the lower classes. For a time he did not believe it possible that Ellen could actually be seeking him out, but he noticed that he always met her, as if by accident, when he went to the university post office or when he crossed the campus. At first he was annoyed at her persistence, but later he came to accept her as a matter of fact, a thing not to be escaped, like his mother.

There was no understanding between them when he finished and took his degree. He had not even kissed her or held her hand, but he promised to write to her after he returned home. This he did, his letters beginning, very carefully, "My dear

Friend," and closing, "Sincerely yours, Robert Chester Hurry."

After graduation he returned home. The place was even shabbier and more forlorn than he had remembered it, but he returned to it with a sense of relief. He knew even then that he would not leave it again. The idea of pleading a case in court or facing people in a crowded room frightened him. He did not tell his mother this: he lacked the courage after the sacrifices that she had made for him. He said nothing at all and she did not question him about his plans. He would listen, nodding his head, while she talked of the past glories of the family: of the generals, the bishop and the governor which had come out of it; vigorous people who could manage not only their own destinies but the destinies of others. He would make no comment while his mother talked, but thought: "She's telling me all this to spur me on, but it is no use. I can't do it. There's no use in trying." Then he would feel sorry for his mother, pitying her shabbiness. She never definitely mentioned her wishes but it was understood between them that after his period of "rest" had passed he would go away from the old place to establish anew, against an alien background, the glories of his family.

One day Robert spoke to her about Ellen Tarleton and his mother had said half resentfully: "Who is she? Who is this girl? You've never told me of her before."

He had explained, but Mrs. Hurry had got up and walked out of the room. In the door she paused: "When you're at the top of your profession you can marry anybody you wish," she said. "Don't waste your time on this silly, country belle."

Robert did not answer his mother. He did not mention the matter again, but he continued to write Ellen each Sunday; and when his mother died the following winter, he went to see her. They became definitely engaged on that visit and a few months later they married.

He felt a new power, a new importance came over him and

he worked steadily. He studied agriculture and thought of farming on a scientific and an intensive scale. It was the first time in his life that he had ever been happy. Ellen had been quite happy, too: of that he was certain. After her death, he had relapsed into his old lethargy, but of recent years a harshness had come over him. He avoided contact with the world as much as possible. When he had to face it his manner was suspicious and snarling.

For a time Robert and his son sat in silence, with Mitty serving them in equal silence. Then Robert spoke: "When supper is ready, I want you to be here."

Chester said: "I came as quick as ere I could."

"I don't care to have any excuses."

"Yes, sir," said Chester. He looked down at his plate. He did not raise his eyes again until the meal was finished.

Later Robert sat on the decaying porch and smoked his pipe. The sun had set and the sky behind the even horizon of the pine grove was rich in pinks, grays and greens, colors blended together so imperceptibly that it was not possible to say when one shade left off and the other began. He sat there in silence, drawing on his pipe and staring at the sky as if he expected to find words written there for his guidance. Presently he called to his son. Chester came to the door, hanging back sullenly.

"Sit down, son," said Robert.

The boy seated himself on the steps, his body rigid and unresponsive, but he would not look at his father. They sat thus until the last color died out in the sky and there was a level grayness everywhere. There was a sound of crickets in the grass and the sad hum of pine trees moving in a slight wind. A moth flew out of the trees toward the decaying house, bumping against its windows, seeking light.

"Come over here, son," said Robert.

Chester rose and went to him. He lowered his head, but Robert lifted his chin, and looked into his son's light eyes. He shoved him away. "Go to bed," he said harshly. "Go to bed!"

Chester went back to the kitchen and sat down on a stool. Mitty was drying the last of her pans. She hung up her cloth and came over to the boy. She put her arms about him and held him to her. "Now, sugarpie! . . . Now, Baby! Your pappa don't mean any harm." But Chester sat cold and unresponsive. Mitty sighed a little. "Come on, Chester, let's go to bed." Quietly the boy got up and walked toward the stairs, and Mitty followed him. He undressed and got into bed and Mitty sat by him, holding his hand.

When he was asleep she came downstairs and finished tidying up her kitchen, humming to herself, her wet arms gleaming like metal in the lamplight. She finished, at length, and went out on to the porch. "Mr. Robert," she began; "it's past nine o'clock. You better get some rest iffen you and Jim going to cut cord wood tomorrow morning."

Robert looked at her vaguely, as if he had not understood her words. He said: "Why has God cursed this house? Why has He taken everything away from me?"

Mitty came over to him. "Come on, Mr. Robert, and go to bed. Don't think about them things any more."

"She was so delicate and so gentle. She was too precious for this world."

"You better go to bed now. You want to get up in the morning."

Robert rose and put his arms about her, his body resting against hers. She held him close to her and stroked back his hair. She looked anxiously over his head. "I'll fix you a nice hot bath in the kitchen: I got plenty of hot water."

They went back to the kitchen and Mitty dragged in a wooden tub and began filling it from the boiler. When Robert had undressed and was in the water she came over to him, as if he, too, were a little boy, and began scrubbing his neck and ears with a soapy wash-rag. He sat in silence, patiently; then he spoke: "I miss her more every hour that passes."

"Don't grieve so about Ellen, because she's happy at this moment with all her new friends, and all her loved ones, in heaven."

"Do you believe that? Do you believe in a heaven and that she's there?"

Mitty laughed indulgently. "Sho I believe that! Sho I do: because it's the truth. . . . Right at this minute Ellen is flying about the throne of God Almighty. . . . Her hair is hanging down her back but as she flies about the wind from her wings fans it up a little. She's smiling to herself because she just sung a psalm to the Lord God Jehovah, and He's mighty pleased."

Mitty straightened her back and stood silent for a moment, the limp wash-rag, still in her hands, dripping water on the floor. "She has on a robe of white muslin, with diamonds and rubies sewed in the hem. In her hair is a wreath of pink roses, picked before sunup, with dew on them yet. . . . She is the purest of all God's angels; she is the sweetest one!"

Mitty laughed her rich, contented laugh. She bent over and began to rub his back with the wash-rag, but Robert stood up in the tub and put his wet arms about her.

Mitty said, patiently: "Now, Mr. Robert, don't do that. Don't do that please, sir."

But Robert paid no attention to her protests. He held her tighter in his arms and Mitty did not struggle. Instead she closed her eyes and an expression of cunning came over her delicate, black features.

"It makes Ellen unhappy to see us grieve," she said softly. "We mustn't do that no more. . . . Right at this moment she's thinking about us and looking down from the throne of God watching us; watching us and waiting our coming."

Suddenly Robert shoved Mitty away from him with such violence that she staggered backward and almost lost her balance. He began to curse her in a low, whispered voice. "You black wench! . . . Do you think I'd touch you?"

"Dry yourself and come on to bed," said Mitty. "Come on to bed and get some sleep. You and Jim got to get up early tomorrow morning."

When he had gone to bed she went back to the kitchen and mopped up the water which had dripped onto the floor. She picked up the tub and carried it slowly out of the kitchen door, down the walk, where she emptied it. By the fence she saw Baptiste standing, his arms resting on the rails.

"Good evening, Madame Hurry!" he said mockingly.

Mitty stood looking at him, her face without expression. "How come you watch things that ain't ere a bit of your business?" she asked.

Baptiste laughed a little, his full sensuous lips drawn into a little point. "How is your bathing establishment getting along?" he asked gayly. "How are you making out with it?" Mitty started to answer him, but she did not. Instead, she turned away and went back to her kitchen, putting things in readiness for breakfast the next morning.

3

BACK of the Hurry house and a little to the right was the cabin in which Jim lived with Hattie, his wife. Jim had lived on the Hurry place all his life and Hattie had been there since Jim married her, twenty years before. They both worked in the fields when there was work to be done, but they received no wages for what they did. It would never have occurred to them to ask for wages, just as it would never have occurred to Robert to offer them money. They were a part of the land, a part of the family, and they took their luck with it.

In the old days before Robert Hurry had married and when his mother was still alive things had been better for them. The old woman gave them money at Christmas and in the spring to spend, not a great deal, but sufficient to enable Hattie to buy a bit of finery now and then, a velvet hat with a flowing ostrich plume, for instance, or a set of red beads.

But this had all happened before Mitty had come to the place to live and had peremptorily taken charge of it. She gave no gifts, and made it understood at once that none might be expected.

"That Mitty sho a close trader," said Hattie; "she sho ain't gwiner give nothin' away." But there was no resentment in her statement.

"She say she got to save money to git the house painted and the fences fixed," said Jim.

"What she want to do that for?" asked Hattie. "What she keer? Ain't gwiner help none to have the place painted fur as

I kin see." They would look at each other and laugh for no reason at all, shaking their heads at Mitty's stupidity.

To one side of Jim's house was the cabin where Baptiste lived. He had turned up one day about three months before, his belongings tied in a red handkerchief. He was hungry and Mitty had fed him in the kitchen, watching him all the time to see that he did not steal anything. She fed him grudgingly. There was something about him that she did not like, an instinctive, deep-seated aversion which she could not have explained.

After he had finished his meal Baptiste offered to cut stove wood for her. While he was working, Robert Hurry came up and started talking to him. After a moment he looked at Baptiste more closely. Baptiste was talking deferentially, but extremely well; he seemed to know a great deal about many things. Robert Hurry began to feel stimulated all of a sudden and to laugh, and Baptiste laughed with him, cordial but a little subservient, with that calculated friendliness of despised people whose wits have been sharpened against despair.

Then, somehow, Robert found himself talking about his days at the university. He talked excitedly, eagerly, for the first time in many months; and Baptiste, alternately chopping wood, and alternately resting on his ax to listen, was appreciative and attentive. Robert talked on and on, delighted with the stranger; but back of his pleasure was a voice which kept saying: "This man is not your equal. You shouldn't treat him as such."

At last he said, somewhat stiffly: "You have a very good mind. A very good mind indeed for a negro."

"Thank you, sir," replied Baptiste. He leaned backward against his ax. "You were speaking of your law studies a few moments ago. Do you remember offhand the Parsons Case? . . . I have never quite understood it. I've often wondered about it."

"Why, that's simple," said Robert. "That's quite simple." He began to talk again. He talked for a long time, illustrating his

32

lecture by drawing rough pictures on the ground. "How did you ever hear of the Parsons Case? Have you studied law?"

"Oh, no!" answered Baptiste, his light, amber face a humble map of denial. "Oh, no, sir. I never had that opportunity. But I've read a little law by myself."

Robert was interested in this man and he began to ask him questions about himself. Baptiste thought he was about twenty-three years old. He had been born up the river above New Orleans.

"But how did you get your education?"

"I haven't very much," said Baptiste. "I went to sea when I was about fifteen. I've seen a lot of places of course, and then, too, I've read some and listened to people." He lowered his head as if slightly embarrassed. "I've always listened when educated men like yourself talked. I've learned a great deal that way." He looked up timidly, his wide, hazel eyes a little imploring, as if he were afraid that he had presumed too greatly.

Robert laughed and turned away, slightly embarrassed. "I doubt that," he said genially. "I doubt that very much." All at once he remembered his superior station. His manner became less cordial. "When you have finished, come in the house; I want to talk to you further." In his mind there was already a half-formed plan. Chester was getting big enough to go to school, and there was a possibility that this light-skinned man would be a good tutor for him. But when Baptiste stood before him, he changed his plan abruptly. He would wait and see how this man turned out.

He said: "How would you like to stay here for a while and work? How would you like to do farm work?"

Baptiste looked at him gravely, more respectfully even, as if there were already a new relationship between them. He was a well-built, muscular man, but there was a refinement, an inap-

33

propriate daintiness about him that was difficult to isolate or identify.

"I'd like that very much. I've done hard work. I was raised on a plantation."

"All right. All right, we'll consider that settled."

Baptiste turned to go.

"There are a great many books still in the house. You can take anything to read that you want."

"Thank you," said Baptiste. "You are very kind."

Mitty watched him go out of the door, her hands folded under her apron. She came into the room and spoke to Robert. "What that yaller nigger doing in here?"

"He's going to work for me," said Robert. He opened and shut a dry inkwell, not facing her: "We need another man this year. There's too much work for Hattie and Jim to do alone."

Mitty remained silent, watching him shrewdly; and suddenly Robert was furious because the things he said were not true and because he realized Mitty knew that he lied.

"Get back to your kitchen!" he said harshly.

"Yes, sir," said Mitty in a sullen voice.

At first Baptiste put himself out to be pleasant to Mitty, but she refused to have anything to do with him. When he saw it was impossible to make friends with her, his manner gradually changed: he began to put on superior airs, and to patronize her.

Chester was not fond of Baptiste in the same way that he was fond of Hattie and Jim. His feeling for the new hand was more complex, more difficult to define. They had many talks together, and Baptiste began at once to teach him French. He was greatly pleased because the boy learned so rapidly.

Baptiste had many tales to tell of foreign ports and foreign lands where strange races, some of the cannibals, lived. He talked of islands shaped like crescent moons which enclosed purple bays. There were brown men who lived on those islands, men who wore their hair long, like women, and who braided red and yellow flowers into it. All day they lay sheltered under straw dwellings, eating and drinking to their hearts' content; but at night time they came out of their houses to sit by the beach and to sing songs of love.

"I had a wife on one of those islands," said Baptiste. "She was the daughter of a king. She loved me because my skin was so white: all the poor natives worshiped me because I was the first white man they had ever seen and they thought I was a god. They brought me the finest parts of the roast meat, the most delicate fish that came out of the sea.

"My queen and I lived in a dwelling place made of soft grass, and before our door the finest musicians and the sweetest singers played and sang sad melodies. . . . In the day time we sat there with arms about each other watching the blue sea, with white waves that ran toward the shore, one line after the other, forever and ever."

But Chester was bored with the long descriptions with which Baptiste decorated his stories. He leaned forward: "Didn't anything *happen* to you on your island? Didn't you kill wild animals or go to war, or anything like that?"

Baptiste smiled indulgently: "Why, of course I did. I was the mightiest warrior of them all. That's why the old king, who gave me his beautiful daughter, asked me to take his place on the throne. They were simple, brown people, but I taught them much. I taught them how to make gunpowder and cannons; and with those things we destroyed their enemies, a race of wild men, black cannibals, who ate up their neighbors."

"How do you make gunpowder, Baptiste?"

But Baptiste looked mysterious and shook his head.

"Never you mind about that. Little boys shouldn't know such things."

"But how did you learn to make it?"

"Never you mind! Never you mind! I know how to do a lot of things I'm not telling about."

Jim spoke up: "Baptiste know how to do fancy work like a gal. Baptiste know how to hemstitch pillows and center pieces!"

"Do you?" asked Chester doubtfully. "Do you know how to do that?"

"It's possible," said Baptiste in his precise, stilted voice. "It's possible." He laughed gently and winked. "Colored people are as simple as children. . . . They exaggerate, do they not?" He brought Hattie into his confidence by looking over the boy's head, and raising his eyebrows in his most winning manner.

"Sho!" said Hattie in delight, nodding her head. "That sho is right, Baptiste. Don't pay no mind to old Jim."

But these subtleties were lost on the young boy. "Tell me some more about your island. What happened finally?"

Baptiste became grave. "I left at last. I gave up my brown wife and my throne: I told them that I must go back to my own people. When I got into the war canoe that was to take me away, all my subjects were there to bid me good-by. They stood on the shore and sang the parting song: the saddest song in all the world; but my little wife, the king's daughter, when she saw that I was really about to leave her, threw herself from the cliff and was killed before my eyes. As I was rowed away from the land I saw my subjects covering her body with red and yellow flowers. That was the last sight I had and it was a sad one."

Baptiste looked up, tears in his beautiful, hazel eyes. "And so perished my true wife, the daughter of a king."

Jim laughed until he had to hold his sides. Jim was given to sudden, unexpected laughter which left him helpless. The sight of a frizzly chicken walking through the yard or a dog stopping suddenly to chew a flea out of his tail would send him into shouts of uncontrollable laughter which had to run its full course. "Never heard of no king's daughter marrying a nigger. Never heard tell of that."

"You, Jim!—Let Baptiste alone," said Hattie. "How do you know what a king's daughter done done?"

"You see?" said Baptiste patiently, and a little hurt. "You see how it is?"

"Sho," said Hattie soberly. "That sho is right, Baptiste."

Chester would listen by the hour to these stories. He tried to picture the strange lands which Baptiste described, but he was never entirely successful.

"Talk some more French, Baptiste," he would ask.

"What good would that do? Nobody could understand me."

"I bet you can't talk it," said Jim. "I bet you just say you can and ain't nobody here to 'spute you."

"Oh, you think I can't talk my own native tongue?"

Jim threw back his long, anvil-shaped head and began to shout. "Baptiste passes hisself off for a Frenchman! Baptiste passes hisself off for a white man!"

Baptiste sighed, and turned his head away.

"Let him alone, Jim!" said Hattie.

Jim slapped his legs and rocked from side to side. "That's sho a new one on me! Never heard tell of a nigger Frenchman befo'."

Baptiste got up with dignity and walked out of Jim's cabin. "You see!" said Hattie. "You done made Baptiste mad."

"I don't care," said Jim, helpless with mirth. "I don't care nothing about making that French nigger mad." But when his laughter had subsided, he got up and went over to Baptiste's cabin, to bring him back.

When Mitty came from her kitchen and called out to Chester that it was his bed time, the boy was always unwilling to leave. Finally she would have to come down and get him. At such times she would speak politely to Hattie and Jim, but she would ignore Baptiste. And Baptiste would stand watching her with amused, half-closed eyes. When she left he would say gravely: "Good night, Madame Hurry. I trust you get enough sleep to-night."

But Mitty would look at him sullenly and not answer.

Later, when she was putting Chester to bed, and he tried to repeat some of the stories that Baptiste had told, she would shake her head contemptuously. "That yaller nigger!" she would say. "He ain't been nowhere and he ain't seen nothing. The only boat he ever seen been tied up to the wharf in New Orleans, or running up and down the river."

Mitty had hoped that Baptiste would soon tire of the place and that he would go away one day as suddenly as he had come, but such was not the case. Baptiste continued to make himself comfortable in his cabin. He was a good workman, better by far than Jim or Hattie, and there was no complaint to find in him. As the weeks went by Mitty disliked him more than ever, but there was nothing that she could put into words. She wanted Robert Hurry to run him off the place and was always grumbling vaguely about him, but Robert paid no attention to her. He often stopped and talked to Baptiste. Occasionally he even asked him into the house for a talk.

"Why don't you go up north or some place where nobody cares what your color is?"

"I don't know, sir."

Robert sat looking at him. "You have a very fine mind: you must know that. You could make something out of yourself in the north."

Baptiste raised his hand and rubbed his cheek with his long, delicately modeled forefinger. He crushed his hands together nervously, his fingers interlacing. "I have tried to get away," he said, "but I can't do it. Something always makes me come back

to where I was born. I don't care what strangers think of me. I want the respect of my own people."

Robert took a book from the shelf and handed it to him. "Read this, and let me know what you think of it."

Baptiste bowed and walked toward the door, but Robert stopped him. "How would you like to stay on here this winter and teach my son?"

"Very much," said Baptiste.

"He's growing up like a savage," said Robert. "He talks like a nigger. He knows nothing at all."

"He's very bright, though," said Baptiste. "I've been teaching him French."

"I want you to start with him just as soon as the cotton is picked. There are schoolbooks in the house somewhere; but if you need anything else, let me know."

"Very well, sir. Whenever you think best."

After Baptiste had gone, Robert went out to the porch to smoke his pipe and to think. There was a faint, almost imperceptible chill in the air. The insects, which had sung all summer, were quiet now, as if they felt cold weather coming and were alarmed. Only frogs in the creek across the road croaked occasionally.

When it was time for him to go to bed, Mitty came out and sat on the steps, wiping her arms on her apron. "It feels chilly like."

But Robert was still thinking of Baptiste. He laughed harshly —he laughed rarely—and stood up. Mitty got up too, following him into the house. He came into the kitchen and sat down. There was still fire in the stove and Mitty opened the lid and put in more wood. In a moment it caught and blazed up. She opened the door to the fire box and a red light flowed across the room, touching the wall and running up it a little. Mitty seated herself on the bench back of the stove and closed her eyes.

"Would you like to have a fresh cup of coffee befo' you go to bed, Robert?"

Robert shook his head in vague denial.

"It won't be no trouble to make. I got me a pot of hot water all ready."

Mitty got up and began to rearrange her fire. She put on a pot of grits to soak and weighted the lid down. She turned her head sidewise and looked at Robert sitting on his chair. His head had fallen slightly forward, as if he had gone to sleep.

When Mitty had completed her plans for breakfast, he spoke: "Baptiste is going to stay on the place all winter. I want him to teach Chester to read and write."

Mitty turned quickly: "How come you done that without asking me?"

Robert got up trembling, and began to talk in a loud voice: "Who do you think you are, you black wench? You'd better learn your place!"

Mitty straightened up and looked at him. "You going to get yourself upset again. You going to make yourself sick." Her voice was calm, matter of fact.

"I'm still the master of this house!" said Robert in a suddenly weak voice. "I do what I damned well please."

"Sho you do!" agreed Mitty sweetly. "Sho you do, Robert."

Robert sat back in his chair, and rubbed his hands over his face. Mitty came over to him, lifting him up. "Lean on me, just lean on me, and don't you bother none."

Robert remained silent. "Now! Now!" said Mitty, "you come on to bed. I'll make you nice and comfortable and then I'll bring you a hot toddy. You just leave everything to Mitty. . . ."

Together they walked up the stairs. Mitty laughed disarmingly: "What make you think I don't like Baptiste?" she asked ingenuously. "I sho do like Baptiste. . . . We just spending too much money, that's all."

After Robert had gone to bed, Mitty came back to her kitchen and sat again by the stove. She rolled her eyes upward toward the ceiling. A moment later her hands relaxed and a strange complacent expression came over her face.

The Whisperer

THE carnival came to town each year at spring, when the weather was warmer, and for a week the old ball park was transformed into a strident fairyland. Between the tents and the platforms were streets in which grass, not yet destroyed by curious feet, still grew; but where there was no grass sawdust had been sprinkled to hide the earth. At night the park was brilliant with lights set against reflectors. Barkers shouted before their individual attractions. Bands played and automatic pianos, a little off key, ground out sentimental songs. The crowds elbowed and jostled each other, craning their necks and talking excitedly, eager to see everything.

One night a man and his sweetheart stopped before one of the tents and looked at a canvas sign covered with red and blue symbols. Over the flap that led to the interior of the booth was a sign:

THE MAGIC MIRROR

WHICH TELLS ALL THINGS

They looked at each other, laughed and entered the tent. A man, unbelievably old and wrinkled, was seated before a small table. He was playing with a gray kitten, and at first he did not look up.

"What do you want to know?" he asked.

He looked down again and rubbed the ears of the kitten with a motion incredibly light and delicate.

The girl spoke: "Tell us what our life together will be."

The old man reached in the folds of his garment and took out a copper disc which was somewhat dull and glazed over with his own greasy fingers.

"My magic mirror was found in the tomb of a great Assyrian King. Scientists are puzzled before its wonderful qualities. They cannot explain why I see in it the future of all things that now live: the annihilation of all existing worlds, the defeat of space and time."

The young man nudged his sweetheart and winked. "You can cut out the ballyhoo and get down to business."

The magician lifted the small, unpolished disc and stared into it, moving his old head back and forth. He spoke to the girl: "Your question is too dangerous. You must ask me something else."

But the young couple were arrogant in their love and unafraid. They insisted that he tell them the truth and the old man began to talk in a voice slow and monotonous. When he had finished, the young couple went outside and walked beyond the limits of the carnival toward a grove of oak trees.

The man said angrily: "It's a fake. I don't believe a word of it."

And the girl answered: "He told nothing but lies. Our love is greater than the love of other people. It will never change. We will always be as happy as we are now. Nothing can destroy our love."

They sat upon a bench in the darkness, smelling the sweet smell of the night, looking up at the purple skies, at the millions of stars set there in calm brilliance; and again they felt the strange, beautiful desire for each other which they had recently discovered. They drew closer, their arms about each other, their lips together. They whispered words of love and were content.

Behind them, and far away, the carnival was in full swing, but the blare of the metallic pianos, the shouts and the trampling of feet against the grass, were things which concerned them not at all, could never concern them. Of this they were sure.

From the Diary of Sarah Tarleton

September 1, 1912. *Bessie left today for Reedyville to resume her studies in the high school there. Have been busy sewing for the past few weeks getting her ready, making school dresses, party dresses, nice underwear, etcetera, etcetera. She is a junior this year and naturally many social functions will demand her attendance. We all hope she will continue her brilliant scholastic record, but I am afraid she is getting boys on her mind. Ah, well! I suppose that is to be expected in a sixteen-year-old girl.*

October 6, 1912. *Bushrod is laid up in bed with La Grippe. We had a cold spell a few days ago, but now the weather is warm again. Have rubbed him with turpentine and mutton suet. What he needs is a good physic, in my opinion, but he is stubborn when he is sick, although a fine, sweet-tempered man on other occasions, and it is difficult to manage him. Must go now and see if he wants anything. A thought for today:*

> *Not like an o'erpowering general in array*
> *O gold and purple conquering some land;*
> *But I can live my life from day to day*
> *In quietness and help my fellow man.*

4

CHESTER's lessons with Baptiste began early in October. A first, unexpected and early frost had already fallen, but it had turned warm again. The cotton had been picked and the brown, dry stalks stood dead in the fields. The trees were turning, and there were now yellow and red patches against the deep evergreens. The fields and the stretches of meadow were yellow, brown or hazily purple, with stretches of bright green isolate and out of place amongst the colors of Autumn.

When Chester had finished his breakfast he went at once to Baptiste's cabin. It was not quite cold enough for a fire, but Baptiste had one going and awaited his pupil with conscious dignity. From the Hurrys' attic he had brought down an old-fashioned blackboard and many dog's-eared schoolbooks, and he stood now with his plump body blocking the fire. He greeted Chester gravely, as if he had never seen him before, and almost immediately the lessons began.

"Your father wants me to continue teaching you French," said Baptiste in his exact, stilted voice. "French is the language that gentlemen use when they converse with each other. We must now learn to read and write it also."

Chester nodded eagerly: "All right, Baptiste, all right."

Baptiste looked grave for a moment, closing his eyes and puffing out his full lips as if about to make some delicate decision. "My name is Simon Laroque Baptiste. Perhaps you had better call me Professor Simon during classes;" but at once his rounded body became apprehensive. He stretched out his hands and rolled his soft eyes. "This is to be only during lesson hours. Afterwards you may call me anything you wish."

But Chester had not challenged his right to be addressed as a superior: "All right, Professor Simon," he replied.

"The first thing," said Baptiste in a positive voice, "the first thing you must learn is to *speak* like a gentleman. You must stop speaking like a colored boy."

Baptiste went to the blackboard and began to write. "Do you know your letters? Can you count?"

Chester shook his head and said no.

"Very well, then," said Baptiste; "we will start at the very beginning."

When the first lesson was over Baptiste and the boy went for a walk through the brightly-colored woods and Baptiste explained the mysteries of addition and subtraction. Then gradually they became silent.

In the wood they seemed removed and detached from any living thing. It was so still that their very passing agitated a little the calm air and brought down about their heads bright leaves, already frost touched, already loosened from their stems, which awaited only the breeze of their passing, their most uncalculated touch, to break from the stem that bore them and fall downward, spinning a little, drifting a little, to the deeply carpeted ground. They lay brilliant and conspicuous against the brown mold on which they rested, touching the earth gently, not a part of it yet.

As they walked silently the boy reached out and took Baptiste's hand in his own, feeling very close to him all of a sudden. He wanted to say something to Baptiste, to express some vague thought, but he could not. He could only press himself closer to Baptiste, to lean against him almost. Then he began to kick with his feet the deep layers of dead leaves over which they walked. On top the leaves were pale brown, lighter than snuff;

but underneath they were heavy and clogged with moisture, sodden and dead, as if in becoming a part of the earth they must again take the earth's color.

"Be careful, Chester," said Baptiste. "You'll get your feet wet."

At last they passed through the wood and came to an old field, worn out and abandoned, in which wire-grass and weeds grew. The rails which had once enclosed it had rotted away or had been pulled down. At the edge of the field, near where they stood, was a persimmon tree loaded with ripe, lavender fruit, and Baptiste began climbing it. When he had filled his hat he came down again and they sat under the tree eating and talking.

A covey of quail, walking with exact, delicate steps, passed near them across the open space between the woods and the field, opening and closing their bright eyes. They were plump and beautifully colored and they walked with coquettish sedateness, lifting their feet daintily, holding them suspended for an instant, and then putting them down again. They paused for a moment to regard Baptiste and the boy, their throats stretched toward them a little, and then, unalarmed, they went on with their feeding, seeking in the grass or under the drifted leaves for insects and for blown seed. There was a male bird colored more deeply, with more vivid shades of brown, than his hens. He would turn his head from side to side to watch the strangers, then he would retreat suddenly with mincing, skipping steps. As Chester looked at him he thought that the bird was a little like Baptiste, but he did not say anything, afraid that even the sound of his voice would frighten the covey away.

For a while the birds fed quietly, but without warning, and all at the exact instant, they took fright. They arose in the air with a quick, terrified whirring of wings, with the speed of a bullet almost, and with a bullet's certainty of course. In a moment they had disappeared into the rank, high underbrush five hundred yards away.

"What scared them, Baptiste? We didn't move or do anything."

"I don't know, but obviously it was something."

"Maybe it was the Lord that told them to fly away. Maybe He told them that a bird dog was nearabout."

"I doubt that. I doubt it very much." He hummed a few bars of a song under his breath. "Do you believe those things that Mitty tells you about God and heaven and angels?"

"Why, yes! Of course I do!"

Baptiste smiled sadly: "What makes you believe it? What makes you believe nigger talk?"

"I believe it because it's the truth. I believe it because Mitty says it's true."

Baptiste sighed deeply, but he did not say anything.

Chester, too, was silent, turning these new thoughts over in his mind. "Then it ain't true: all the things Mitty tell me ain't true?"

"*Aren't,*" corrected Baptiste patiently.

Chester sat with a solemn face but at last he laughed appreciatively. "You're just playing a joke, Baptiste; but you can't fool me."

"All right, then," said Baptiste good-naturedly. He took off his cap and smoothed back his straight, light brown hair. He drew his lips together into a tiny pout. "Think that if you like. . . . I certainly don't want to be the one to destroy your primitive faith." He stood up. "We'd better be getting back home again. We've got a two-hour walk before us."

Chester followed him through the brilliant wood, eating the last of the persimmons. "Tell me about your travels over the world," he begged. "Tell me again about the time you were ruler of the island and married the king's daughter."

But Baptiste shook his head. "I don't feel like telling a story. Maybe I'll tell you one tonight."

49

When they came out of the woods onto the Athlestan road and approached the house, Hattie saw them and came to meet them. The lower part of Hattie's body appeared as if it had been put through a series of rollers, and pressed flat. Her legs were thin and shapeless, like laths, and her high, prominent buttocks seemed to possess only the dimension of width. She wiped her hands on her apron and spoke: "Mitty mad as the devil. She say how come you taken Chester off the place without asking her if you could."

Baptiste smiled: "Tell Madame Hurry to devote her energies to her cooking and her *other* duties."

Hattie, who rarely understood the big words that Baptiste used, laughed a little. She was boiling clothes in a smoke-stained, iron washpot. She stuck in an old broomstick and stirred the boiling clothes for a minute.

In a moment she turned to her empty cabin, as if speaking to somebody in it: "Baptiste sho is a biggety man," she said in a delighted voice. "He's the most biggety one."

But Baptiste shrugged his shoulders. He spoke to Chester: "You'd better go over and see what Madame Hurry wants."

Mitty was waiting for the boy in the kitchen. "What make you go off without telling Mitty?" she began in a hurt voice. "What make you do that, baby?" Chester hung up his coat and his cap but he didn't answer her.

"What make you treat Mitty the way you do?" she asked humbly. "What make you treat Mitty so mean, baby?"

"I'm not a baby! I'm learning to read and write; I'm learning arithmetic and to speak French, too!"

"Oh, you is?" asked Mitty in a high, sarcastic voice. "Oh, is that so?"

"Yes," said Chester eagerly. "Professor Simon is teaching me everything."

"Who that teaching you?"

"Professor Simon. That's what he says I must call him when I'm studying."

"That yaller nigger!" said Mitty. "That yaller nigger setting a high mark of respect on hisself."

"Do you want me to say the words for tree and water and sky in French?"

"I don't care nothing 'bout them words."

Then a moment later: "What you want to learn them words for?"

"Why, I want to be a great man received at all the courts of Europe. You got to know French, so Professor Simon says, if you're going to be a gentleman."

"Does Baptiste set hisself up for a gentleman?" asked Mitty with heavy sarcasm.

"Of course not," said Chester in surprise. "Baptiste is a colored man. Only white people can be gentlemen." Then he added generously: "If Baptiste wasn't a colored man he'd be a gentleman, I bet."

Mitty looked up, a hurt expression on her face: "You sho do like that Baptiste, baby. He's done taken you away from me, I expect. I done lost my baby. . . . I don't care about myself; it's your mamma I'm thinking about. Her and me was born on the same day. We was more like sisters than anything else. I don't care none for myself, but I hate to see you make your mamma unhappy."

"I haven't done anything to her."

Mitty looked at him shrewdly: "Yes, you have, too. You already showed plain enough you like that Baptiste better than you do us. You done showed that plain. . . . There your sweet mamma is, 'shamed amongst the angels of God, crying against her white wings and saying: 'Little Chester done turned against me and Mitty! . . . Little Chester done turned against us!' "

Chester came over to her somewhat self-consciously and put

51

his arms about her, and Mitty lifted him up and rocked him back and forth. "There now, baby," she whispered. "There now, sugarpie."

Later when supper was over, Chester asked permission to go to see Hattie and Jim.

"Haven't you been there all day?" asked Robert harshly. "What do you want to go again for?"

Chester looked down at his feet and would not answer.

"Chester better go to bed early," said Mitty sullenly. "He's all wore out with studying. Chester ain't looking well. He'd better go to bed right after supper."

Robert looked up at Mitty. He started to speak to her but changed his mind. He spoke instead to his son: "All right, you can go for a little while, but I want you to come when Mitty calls you this time. You may as well make up your mind that you've got to do what you're told."

5

When Chester arrived at Jim's cabin Hattie had already finished supper and Baptiste was helping her with the dishes. Jim had built up a big fire in the fireplace and was lying stretched out in front of it playing with a young coon which he had caught and tamed. There was really no need for such a big fire except that it gave a good light and made the cabin more cheerful. There was a faint, bracing crispness in the air and a full moon was riding, remote and cold, among banked clouds. Its light lay evenly over the fields, revealing the dead, upstanding stalks and the crisp, frost-bitten leaves that drooped from them. It touched the tops of the pine trees, still green and unbroken, washing their level darkness with a pale, amber light.

Chester came in the open door and sat down on a stool, his back resting against the woodbox. The young coon rolled over and over on the floor with Jim, baring its teeth as it scampered and making playful taps at Jim's face with its velvet paws. The coon's eyes were bright and friendly, and the firelight brought out the white and the reddish-brown markings of its body. Jim lay shouting with delight at its antics. When he was quiet, Chester could hear Baptiste talking with Hattie in his precise, clear voice.

Presently they were through with the dishes, and Hattie was wiping her damp arms on her apron. She came to where Jim lay sprawled in front of the fire, his body blocking it. She shoved him a little with her foot. "Git up from there, nigger; git up and give the rest of us some fire."

Jim got up and stretched himself, and as he did so the young coon, as lively as a kitten, sprang for his shoelaces and untied them with its teeth. Jim lay back against the wall, helpless in his mirth. "Look at that coon, Hattie! Look at that coon!—He done try to take off my shoes."

Hattie turned quickly and flung out her arms. "Scat! Scat, coon!" At her words the young animal lifted its brush tail high in the air and ran across the floor, disappearing under the bed. Cautiously it stuck its head out and licked its paws, regarding Hattie gravely all the time, its sharp eyes shining and mischievous.

Baptiste shook his head in humorous despair. "You negroes are as simple as children. No wonder that whites take advantage of you."

"That Baptiste," said Jim, still laughing. "That long-gone white boy."

"Shut up, Jim," said Hattie. "Shut up and let Baptiste talk iffen he wants to." She spoke more loudly, in the general direction of the bed. "You coon! What you doing there? You chew up my hat again and I'm gwine whup you."

Baptiste spoke: "Nobody would know I was colored, if I didn't admit it." He turned to Hattie. "You would have taken me for a white man, wouldn't you, if you had met me among white people? You wouldn't have known the difference, would you?"

"I expect not. I expect not, Baptiste." She yawned, exposing her soiled, gold teeth. "What you care for? What you bothering yourself with that truck for?"

Baptiste continued: "Did it ever occur to you that I might be the illegitimate son of white people, turned over to the woman I thought was my mother, to raise?"

Hattie rose and began stirring the logs which were dying down a little, bending from her hips, her wide, flat bottocks high in the air. "I expect that might happen, but it's unlikely."

"It isn't unlikely at all. It's very plausible, as a matter of fact."
Hattie threw on another log and sat down.

"What's the illegitimate son of white people?" asked Chester, speaking to Hattie.

"I don't know," replied Hattie, confused and a little ashamed before Baptiste, because of her lack of education. "Where your manners at, Chester," she said sternly; "where your manners to be asking a question like that?"

"What does it mean, Baptiste?"

"It means bastard," said Baptiste quietly.

"Oh," said Chester. He looked steadily into the fire, turning over in his mind this new angle of Baptiste's past. They were all silent until the young coon stuck his muzzle from under the bed, erecting his tail and flipping it from side to side, rustling the shuck mattress above him.

"Make him come over to me, Jim," begged Chester.

"I can't make that coon do nothin' he don't want to do," said Jim. "He ain't well trained yet."

"Call him, baby, and maybe he'll come," said Hattie. "Call him gentle like."

"It's not absurd at all," said Baptiste. "I've read of many cases like that."

"What's his name, Jim?" asked Chester.

"Buck," said Jim. "I just call him Buck, and sometime he comes, but in general he don't pay no attention to me."

"Here, Buck! Here, Buck!" said Chester, snapping his fingers.

"It happens all the time. . . . There's an unmarried mother and a baby and a fine family to protect. What else is to be done?"

"Here, Buck! Here, Buck!" said Chester, but softly, so that Baptiste's story would not be interrupted.

Baptiste talked earnestly for a long time, his face eager and held forward, his delicate hands raised upward. When he had finished, Jim lay on his back and spoke to the rafters above him. "That lyin' Baptiste," he said pleasantly. "That long-gone, lyin' boy."

In the silence that followed there came the rustling of a starched dress and a slight cough outside the open door.

"Who that there?" asked Hattie quickly.

Mitty stepped into the room. She was confused and slightly insolent, knowing that she had been caught eavesdropping. She ignored the group. "Come on, Chester; I come to take you home. It's bedtime, baby."

Baptiste half closed his amber eyes. A contemptuous smile clung to his lips. "I hope you enjoyed my story, Madame."

Mitty did not answer him. She caught Chester by the hand and jerked him toward her. "Come on, baby. Come on, when Mitty tells you to!"

Chester pulled away from her. He went over to Baptiste and whispered in his ear. "I'll be down early tomorrow. You can tell me the rest of the story then, Professor Simon."

Baptiste, too, got up, disengaging the boy's hand. "You had better go, now, because Madame Hurry is anxious to get to bed." He looked at Hattie and Jim and then laughed a little, insolently. But Hattie and Jim pretended not to have heard.

Mitty stared at him steadily, her eyes veiled and furious. She shoved Chester toward the door. When she reached it she stood a moment, irresolute, before speaking to Jim:

"Jim, walk on up to the house with us. I done seen something in the bushes coming down that scared me."

"Shucks, Mitty, ain't nothing going to hurt you 'tween here and the house."

"I'm scared," said Mitty, shivering a little. "I'm scared to go back by myself."

"Mitty seen a dog in the bushes maybe," said Hattie.

"Didn't look like ere a dog to me."

Jim got up good naturedly and began lacing his shoes. "All right, then. I'll walk a pieceways with you."

When they were well away from the cabin, Mitty spoke to Chester. "Run on ahead a piece, baby; Jim and me wants to talk."

When Jim came back to the cabin Hattie looked at him suspiciously. "What that Mitty want to talk to you about? She wasn't scared to walk that pieceways back to the house. That Mitty ain't scared of nothing."

Jim stood with his thick lips opened, his triangular nose splayed against his face. With his anvil head and his flat features he resembled one of those cocoanut shells carved to resemble a human head by some primitive artist.

"Mitty saw you and Baptiste fixing to run off together."

Hattie looked at the corner of the room where the coon lay curled up on a crocus sack. "So *that* what she say?"

She spoke to Baptiste. "Mitty told Jim that you and me fixing to take up together. . . . You hear that?"

But Baptiste, still occupied with his own thoughts, smiled, got up and went to the cabin. When he reached it, he lay fully clothed on his bed, the shuck mattress rustling beneath his weight. He spoke aloud to himself: "Everything that I say is a lie. I can't tell anything but lies. . . . That's a strange thing."

A feeling of unrest came over him, a deep uneasiness, a despair which had no roots in reason. He thought, turning from side to side on the rough mattress: "I shouldn't have stopped at this place. I should have kept on. I might, even now, have found what I am seeking if I had kept on. . . ."

Then he thought: "Mr. Hurry treats me well: what else could I expect from him?" For a long time he lay staring into the darkness, baffled, puzzled before the complexity of his own being.

Toward morning he went to sleep.

From the Diary of Sarah Tarleton

November 2, 1912. *Today is the 8th anniversary of the death of my beloved niece Ellen Hurry. I shall think of her all day and how she lies alone in a strange land away from those who loved her. I hope that Mitty also remembers this day and sees that her grave is decorated with autumn leaves and flowers. That selfish unfeeling man would never think of such a thing, but we will not forget.*

November 8, 1912. *Attended a meeting of the Pearl County Ladies Auxiliary this afternoon at the Tallon home. Fifteen ladies were present and several instructive papers were read regarding conditions in foreign fields. Mrs. Tallon and I were laughing together regarding Bessie's infatuation for Bradford Tallon and vice versa. They are young and I think their budding romance is very sweet.*

6

October passed quickly and November began with frost. In the fields the dry, barren cotton stalks bent in the wind, with tufts of white still clinging to their tops where delayed bolls had opened up after the pickers had passed through. Then rain came and beat on the bolls and turned the clinging cotton to a drenched grayness. The long grass that grew in abandoned fields, along the roadside, across the meadows that stretched beyond the road, had turned brown, and in the hazy light of Fall the countryside took on a lavender cast.

Chester was making progress with his studies, and Baptiste told Robert Hurry that he was a fine pupil.

"He learns very quickly, Mr. Hurry. He takes to his books."

But Robert seemed already to have forgotten that he had asked Baptiste to instruct the boy. He looked at the light-colored man before him as if he did not understand his words. Robert had grown more silent, more remote, as the Summer had passed. He rubbed his hand over his face in a rough gesture, as if to brush away something that lay between his eyes and the world about him. Then he grunted, turned, and went toward the barn.

"He has no respect for me," thought Baptiste. "I'm nothing to him. . . . Why did he lead me on? Why did he offer me so much?"

That afternoon he and Chester took a walk through the fields and down the red road. They walked for two miles until at last they came to the Bragdon place. The house had burned many years before and only a few columns, charred with fire and blackened by smoke, remained.

It was a favorite destination for their walks, and as the boy rummaged about among the fallen bricks and turned over with his foot pieces of charred wood, Baptiste sat silent, his face in his hands. "It's time for me to leave this place," he was thinking. "I do not know what I wanted, but whatever it is, I shall not have it now." He spoke to Chester: "Here's a strange thing, here's a strange thing, indeed."

"What is it, Baptiste? What have you found?"

"It's not that at all. It's only a little thing which happened to me one day when I first came to work for your father, but I've never understood it." His eyes lifted and his brows came together as if he were puzzled. "One day when I was plowing alone in the north field I turned up a little man not much longer than my thumb." Baptiste stretched out his plump, beautiful hands, his thumbs held rigid, that Chester might see the size of the man he had found. "He was a very little man and he was sleeping in the nest of a field mouse, all curled up, with his knees resting under his chin."

Chester came up excitedly. "What did you do with him, Baptiste? What became of him?"

"He woke up, when I held him in my hand, and stretched himself, and he jumped up and down and started swearing at me. He shook his fist in my face and stamped his foot against my palm, but I just laughed at him; and when he saw I wasn't going to harm him, he laughed a little himself."

"But where is he now, Baptiste?"

Baptiste was thoughtful. The dreaming, far-away look came into his full, amber eyes. "He was asleep for the winter, Chester, and the night air would have been too cold for him; so I wrapped him up in my handkerchief and made him a new nest,

60

and buried him under the dewberry bushes. Nothing could harm him there, I knew."

"Let's go dig him up again, Baptiste. Let's go look at him."

But Baptiste seemed hurt. "I'm really surprised at you, Chester," he said mildly. "I'm surprised that you should suggest such a thing."

"Can't we dig him up in the Spring when the weather gets warmer? . . . I'd like to have him to play with. We can build a house for him, and put a fence around it so the cats can't get him."

Baptiste didn't answer for a while. He was thinking: "Why do I continue to stay here? I shall not find what I am seeking here. It's time for me to be going away again. . . ." He spoke: "I won't be here in the Spring. I'll be far away by that time." He had not meant to say the words, but now that he had spoken them, he knew that they were true.

For a moment Chester sat silent, unable to take in the full significance of Baptiste's words. "Do you mean you're going to leave us?"

Baptiste nodded his head: "I must be getting on."

"Would you leave me, too?"

"Yes," said Baptiste. "Oh, yes."

Chester turned over with his foot a charred beam which had lain for a long time. Under it he saw a few thin, tenuous roots, web-like and intricate, and as pale and lacking in life as the roots of plants that grow on the bottom of the sea. There were also four black beetles and a long, lace-like centipede, all dormant and sluggish against the cold earth. The underside of the wood was patterned by nacre in wavering, iridescent lines, with shallow designs etched in the wood's surface by the mouths of hungry insects. He picked up a stick and touched lightly the centipede and the beetles, and they moved a little, but stopped again, half dead from the faint chill.

Chester said: "You aren't really going to leave. You're just saying that."

"It is the truth," said Baptiste. "I must be going on. I can't stay here always."

Chester poked idly at the insects before him, guiding their movements, stirring their sluggishness to life again. "Then take me with you wherever you go."

"I can't do that. I can't do that and you know it."

A strange feeling of fury came over the boy. He lifted his stick and began crushing the insects before him, carefully, methodically, each in its turn. The centipede drew to a ball convulsively and fell on its back, its legs waving in wild agony upward and downward, each leg, even in death, working exactly, like a delicate mechanism, inward and outward, freely, without touching and without hindering one another, until at last the waving legs became quiet from the body outward, only the tips beating a little.

Baptiste had got up. "We better be getting back. We'll say the names of everything we pass in French. That'll help you to remember them better."

Chester said with shy, uncomprehending bitterness: "If you liked me, you wouldn't want to go away."

"I must go away. It's something I can't control."

"I wouldn't go away and leave you."

"You'll soon forget me, little Chester. You'll forget me in no time at all."

"Go away then, nigger; go on away, if you want to!"

"I shall leave right after Christmas," said Baptiste, as if to himself. "I'll start the new year a long way from here."

Chester came into the house and Mitty spoke to him: "If your shoes are muddy, better come in here by the fire and dry them out." He sat by the stove, his feet stretched to the heat.

"How come you home so early? How come you ain't gone

down to see Professor Seemo?" She spoke in a slightly hurt and slightly sarcastic voice. "How come you and him ain't together?"

Chester had a quick impulse to tell her that Baptiste was leaving, but he changed his mind. He thought: "He's going away and leave me. He'll be talking to other people before long. Maybe he'll be telling them stories about me. Maybe he'll be making them laugh with stories about us." A hot feeling of resentment came over him.

"I don't care anything about that yaller nigger. I don't care if I never see him again."

Mitty stared in surprise. "What that you say, baby?" she asked, unable to believe the words she had heard. Chester threw himself on the floor and Mitty bent down and took him in her arms. "Baby!" she said in a soft, delighted voice. "Baby!"

She sat down in a chair and rocked the boy back and forth. "A big boy eight years old," she chanted, "but he likes to have old Mitty rock him. Yes, sir, he sho do. He sho do like to have his Mitty rock him." Her breasts, as big and as rounded as cabbages, bulged her dress and the boy rested his head against their softness, smelling the sharp smell of her body.

Quickly she stopped: "What Baptiste done to you, honey, to make you turn agin him thataway?"

Chester pressed his face more tightly against her. "Nothing!" His voice came out muffled and indistinct, unwillingly, as if there were something he wanted to conceal. "Nothing."

But Mitty was not convinced. She lifted his face away from her bosom and looked into his wet eyes. "What he done to my baby?" she insisted. "What he done done?"

This time Chester would not answer at all. He only trembled and pressed closer to her again.

"Tell Mitty, sugarpie; Mitty won't tell ere a soul iffen you tell her."

She waited for his answer, but the boy would not speak. She

put him on his feet, got up and walked carelessly about the room, cooking her supper. From her place by the stove she spoke, her voice light and conversational. "Did that Professor Seemo ever put his hands on you, baby?"

Chester thought a moment, his own mind working quickly, surprised a little at the question, not seeing the direction of her thought, and Mitty laughed gayly, taking his answer for granted. "What else he do? . . . I bet he talk to you about a lot of dirty mess." She nodded her head. "I bet he do that, don't he, sugar-pie?" She wrinkled up her face and winked, as if there were some dark secret between Baptiste and the boy which she understood and acquiesced in.

"Yes," he said finally, "he did that."

Mitty was bustling about her stove not looking at the still figure of the boy. "When was the first time he put his hands on you, baby?" Her voice was as casual as if she asked the time of day. "Was it the time he took you in swimming at the branch? Was that the time, baby?"

And all at once Chester understood the full import of her words, the implications behind them. A quick fury came over him. He got up from the bench and walked to the window, debating his answer. He saw Baptiste come out of his cabin and sit on his steps, cleaning his shoes. It was then that Chester spoke with downcast eyes, as if he were loath to tell what he did. Later he began to cry, but Mitty persisted in her questions. She took him in her lap, stroking his hair and drying his eyes. "My baby!" she said. "My pore motherless little baby!" Her eyes rolled from side to side. "I'll fix Professor Seemo," she said angrily. "I'll fix him so he won't ever bother my baby again."

7

THE next morning, when Chester had finished his breakfast and was ready to go to Baptiste's cabin for his lessons, Mitty came over to him and spoke gently. "There's something I want you to do for me, baby, but I don't want you to tell nobody about it."

"I won't tell, Mitty. What is it?"

"You take some of the combings from his head, but don't let him see you do it. You hide the combings away and bring 'em to me when you come up for dinner."

"What are you going to do? Are you going to put a conjur' on Baptiste?"

"Never you mind, sugarpie." Her chocolate-colored eyes rolled upward toward her brows, her thin, highly-bridged nose incongruous against the polished black of her skin. "Never you mind, baby. Just do what I tell you."

"I won't get the combings unless you tell me what you're going to do." His voice was stubborn, suspicious, but at once he remembered Baptiste's departure, that Baptiste was soon to abandon him. "I don't care if you put a conjur' on him!" he said angrily. "I don't care what you do to that nigger!"

"Baby!" exclaimed Mitty in delight. "Baby!" She smiled happily, as she used to smile before Baptiste came on the place to live. She put her arms about the boy and tried to press him to her, but Chester jerked away roughly.

"You're going to put a conjur' on him, ain't you?"

"Yes, baby."

"Will it make him stay here?"

Mitty thought a moment and laughed her soft ascending laugh. "I expect he won't get far, sugarpie!" She laughed again at her joke, "He-e-e-e!" her voice rising even and clear.

She buttoned the boy's jacket and pulled his cap down. "Hurry," she said; "hurry up or you'll be late for school." She saw that Robert had come into the room. He held a shotgun in his hand, balancing it; then he broke it and peered down the barrel, his vague eyes held close.

"Run along, baby. Run along and study hard. I'm going to fix something good for dinner if you be's a good boy. I'm going to cook something good that you like."

When the boy had gone, Robert spoke: "I'm going to go over near Bragdon's and shoot doves."

"Go ahead. Go ahead. . . . What I care?"

But Robert looked down, ashamed slightly. "I haven't got any shells."

Mitty turned and began to wash dishes, her face set stubbornly. "Why don't you go fishing, then?"

"Let me have some money to buy shells!" But Robert's voice though loud, carried no conviction, as if he knew beforehand that he would not get what he wanted. "Now, Mr. Robert," explained Mitty in a soothing voice; "us ain't got any money to be spending for shells."

"Let me have the money for shells," he said weakly.

"How we going buy fertilizer next spring? How we going to get the house painted? How we going to fix the place up if you go spending all the money for shells?"

Robert said: "It's my money. I'll do what I please with it."

And Mitty answered: "I'm saving up to buy me some fine Leghorn hens. I'm going to buy chicken wire and fence a place off. We can sell pigs and make something thataway, too."

Robert began to shout and curse her, but Mitty went on with her dishes. She spoke soothingly: "I don't begrudge you shells.

66

I don't want nothing for myself, and you know it, but we got to be thinking about little Chester. What's going to become of him?"

Robert sat down, the shotgun across his lap. "All right, Mitty. I guess I couldn't get along without you."

Mitty was delighted: "Sho you couldn't! Sho you couldn't." She put her arms into the dish pan, turning her highly-bred, delicate profile toward him. "I ain't a mean woman," she explained. "I wouldn't deny you nothing, iffen we had it." She rattled the lids on her stove importantly. "We ain't got no business paying that sorry Baptiste. We ought to save that money, too."

"I don't pay him much," said Robert. "I pay him little enough."

"Go down to the river," said Mitty; "maybe you can catch a channel cat."

That afternoon Chester brought back with him several strands of hair which he had taken from Baptiste's celluloid comb. Mitty took them eagerly. She sat down on the floor, her legs spread wide, and held the combings in her hand, and Chester sat beside her. "This is the first part of the conjur'," she said. "This is the very first thing to do." She took the fine, light brown hairs, as straight as the hair of any white man, and arranged them on her palm until they were one even strand; and all the time she was arranging the hair, and later knotting it into the resemblance of a hangman's noose, she was muttering strange, powerful words which Chester did not understand.

When the knot was completed, and the first words said, she took the boy by the hand and together they went to the ravine, near where the branch flowed and Mitty gathered in her apron an assortment of roots, feathers and odds and ends. She pored over them for a long time, selecting, discarding and then changing her mind. Finally she added two twisted roots, shaped strangely, and tied the sack together.

It was then that she went into the yard and threw corn to the chickens, calling: "Chick! Chick! Chick! Chick-oo! Chickoo!" The fowls ran toward her, their wings spread wide, their long, flexible necks all stretched downward in a close circle, gobbling up the thrown corn and Mitty watched them, turning her head so that she might see each of the chickens. When she had made up her mind, she stooped downward and seized by his legs a young, lemon-colored cockerel. The young cock jumped and tried to get away, but Mitty held him in the hollow of her arm and stroked his neck until he became quiet and lay passive against her breast.

It was almost dark when they came back to the house, but Mitty did not light her lamps or light her fires. She had more important matters on her mind. She tied the cock's legs together and he lay before her on the floor sleepily, his wings flapping a little, his eyes closing and unclosing slowly, ponderously.

Again Mitty began to speak her strange words, passing her hands above the unresisting cock until the fowl ceased to be a young cockerel in her eyes, and became, instead, Baptiste, bound and helpless.

"How you like Madame Hurry now, nigger?" she asked. "How you like your friend, Madame Mitty Hurry?" Unhurriedly she took up a knife and pressed it against the cock's throat, cutting it. She held the throat of the cock over a tin pot and his blood flowed into it. The dying cock struggled and made a faint noise and tried to get away, tried insistently, but more and more feebly, as Mitty held him in the crook of her arm. "I sho am sorry to do this to you," she said, "but it ain't ere a bit of my fault. It ain't no fault of mine. It wouldn't be right to hold it against me, neither. . . ."

"What kind of a conjur' are you putting on Baptiste?" asked the boy.

"Never mind," said Mitty. "Never mind."

A little before midnight Mitty and Chester went to Baptiste's cabin. There was a full moon that night and a chill, tugging wind. The bare trees leaned forward slightly against its force and then rose again. Mitty got down on her knees and unhurriedly dug a hole in front of Baptiste's doorstep, as if there were no chance of him waking, piling the earth neatly beside the hole she had made. The two of them squatted there for a long time, looking at each other. Chester leaned forward and Mitty whispered in his ear. "This is the part you got to do. When the moon goes back of the clouds again, put the sack in the hole and cover it up quick."

And Chester put in the sack which contained Baptiste's death and covered it with the cool, loose earth.

Mitty got up triumphantly and strode toward the house, her head held high, her thighs moving in long swings.

"Professor Seemo won't bother us much longer," she said. She raised her thin, high-bridged nose. "He-e-e-e! That Professor Seemo done got his clock slowed down."

"When will it work, Mitty?"

But Mitty laughed complacently. "Just you wait, baby, just you wait and see for yourself."

She went with him up the stairs, walking carefully, one hand holding the heavy railing, the other grasping the boy's hand. Chester spoke to her, but Mitty held up her finger. "Sh-h-h!" she warned. "Sh-h-h! Your pappa might wake up."

They reached the boy's room and entered it cautiously. Mitty closed the door and helped him undress. Through the window the countryside lay complacent under the moon. A cow mooed

69

twice with a sad voice, then mooed again steadily with a sound lost and unsubstantial.

Chester was in bed now, huddling under the cover, and Mitty bent over to kiss him good night.

"I hope the conjur' works quick," he said bitterly. "I hope you made it good and strong."

Mitty squeezed his cheeks together with her fine, black hand until his lips were a puckered rosette, gray in the moonlight. She kissed him again quickly. "There's a mean streak in you, sugarpie, and I don't know where you get it, either. It sho don't come from the Tarletons." She patted his hand complacently. "It must come from the Hurrys, but there's a mean streak in you just as sho as you're born!"

She tiptoed out of the room, and down the wide hall, but when she passed Robert's door it opened and he stood before her, his hair ruffled up, sleep still in his eyes.

"What are you doing up at this time of night?"

Mitty's eyes widened. "I ain't doing nothing." Then innocently: "It ain't so late."

Hurry said: "I dreamed of her again. I saw her face as plainly as I see yours."

"Go back to bed, Robert. You got to get your rest." She turned away, but stopped again. "Did you catch ere a fish in the river?"

"No."

Mitty laughed a little, delighted with herself. "You couldn't hit a dove neither," she said contemptuously.

The Whisperer

WHEN they were relieved by fresh troops the men fell back to the wood and dug in. They set about cleaning their rifles and bayonets, rubbing them with oil. Some of them, more energetic than their comrades, got water from old shell holes and washed their clothes, their naked shoulders shivering a little in the damp wood, but most of the men slept on the ground, relaxed and widely sprawled.

The top sergeant came and called the names of six men who were to go on a burial detail. The men selected slung rifles over their shoulders and started out, stopping at the galley where the supply sergeant issued spades and picks.

A little later they were walking in the wheat fields through which they had recently fought, fields trampled and flat now, looking for dead men. They worked steadily, burying the men that they found and marking each grave, talking only occasionally. Then, when it was beginning to get dark, they reached the shelled town where they had been fighting the day before and were about to turn back, their work completed, when Jim stopped.

71

"There's a man under that beam."

He stepped across the fallen wall and looked at the man's face.

"Who is it?" asked the sergeant.

"It's Johnny."

The entire detail gathered to look at the dead man. The beam had fallen across his legs, crushing them, but even before that he was dead from a wound in his belly. His tunic was opened and his hand held something which was fastened around his neck on a silver chain, an object pressed against his lips.

"What is it? What has he got in his hand?"

Jim said: "It's a crucifix. It's the crucifix that the old woman at Ancemont gave him."

The sergeant nodded his head. "I remember it. She gave it to him the night we shoved off."

They lifted the beam from his body and buried him in a grassy spot beside the road.

On the way back to the wood Jimmy thought of the dead soldier with the crucifix held to his lips. The thing had taken hold of his imagination. It seemed to him very beautiful. He thought: "I'm going to write Johnny's folks and tell them how he died."

The next afternoon he wrote his letter. He told of the incident of the cross, of the old peasant woman who had given it to the boy and the way she had cried and kissed him when he left the village. He told about finding the body, and how Johnny had pressed the crucifix to his lips as he lay dying. They had buried him the way that he had died; his hands folded upon his breast, the cross still resting against his lips.

Weeks later he got an answer to his letter. The family thanked him for the trouble he had taken in writing to them: That was kind, and they appreciated it. But they were sure he was mistaken as to the identity of the man he had buried. Their son was not a Catholic.

8

CHESTER sat before the blackboard, thinking: "The conjur' will start working pretty soon. If I watch his face, I'll see it the minute it starts." He gazed steadily at Baptiste, his round, gray eyes innocent and clear, his lips already shaped in denial. But Baptiste went on talking about continents and oceans and rivers, drawing upon his blackboard to illustrate a point, unaware that his pupil heard no word that he spoke.

Chester interrupted him. "How do you feel, Professor Simon?" His voice was anxious, waiting, as if Baptiste's health was a thing inexplicable.

Baptiste turned, the crayon in his hand. "I feel very well; I feel very well indeed, thank you." His face was surprised, questioning. "What made you ask me that, Chester?"

But Chester did not answer. He looked out of Baptiste's window at the brown countryside, shimmering in the clear, Autumn light.

Baptiste went back to the blackboard. "There must have been some reason for your question. You wouldn't ask me that out of a clear sky, in that peculiar way."

Chester shook his head. "I just asked you, that's all."

Baptiste looked at him a moment. "You're a strange white boy, Chester." He began explaining about Asia, Africa and the island continent, Australia. He talked on and on, his voice steady and soothing.

From his seat by the window, Chester saw Mitty come out of her kitchen and walk down the path that led to Jim's cabin.

She walked slowly, deep in thought, her head lowered slightly. Hattie was seated on a bench in the sunlight sewing patches of colored cloth together. She looked up, surprised at Mitty's approach, and began to pick up the scattered cloth, but Mitty stopped her. "Go on with your quilt, Hattie. I don't aim to stay more than a minute." She looked quickly about, peering into the cabin. "Where Jim at?"

"I don't know. He went off with the dogs som'ers."

At the sound of Hattie's voice the young coon came rushing out of the cabin into the bright November sunlight, rolling over and over on the ground, picking up a feather, and trying to hold it balanced between his forefeet.

Mitty sat on the bench beside Hattie. "I don't like that yaller Baptiste, and you know it, Hattie," she began.

"I knows that well, and so do he."

"Passing hisself off for a Frenchman," said Mitty; "telling lies every time he opens up his lying mouth."

"Baptiste don't mean nothing by his talk. There ain't no harm in the boy."

"Maybe not. Maybe not." Mitty raised her skirt and rubbed the belly of the coon with the tip of her shoe, and the young animal seized it playfully in his half-formed teeth, sniffing her leg with his nose. She lifted him into her lap and scratched his head.

"There's something I got to tell you about Baptiste. My duty as a Christian woman makes me tell it whether I want to or not. I got to tell this or it would hant me." She stopped, a look of fear on her black face.

Hattie put down her sewing and leaned forward, her lips drawn back, the soiled gold in her mouth gleaming dully. "What that, Mitty? What you know?"

"I know this—" She nodded her head several times. "I know this, all right. . . . Last night, and the night before that, there

75

was something shaped like a boar shoat with a man's head on it rooting 'round Baptiste's door, fumbling at his window. Whatever it was, it was dead, because I could see the cabin clear through it. It clum up the side of the wall with hands and feet shaped like a possum's and look down the chimney. It kept running round and round the cabin, grunting and making funny noises."

Hattie's eyes rolled back and she licked her lips. Her voice was high when she spoke: "What you expect it was, Mitty?"

"I don't rightly know, but it was a hant of some kind. Whatever it was, it dug a hole in the ground before Baptiste's doorstep and put something in it. That much I seen from my window. That much I do know."

Hattie spoke in a whisper: "Somebody put a conjur' on Baptiste. What he gwine do, Mitty? What that boy gwine do to break it?"

Mitty shook her head: "It look like a death conjur' to me. It's something I don't know ere a thing about."

She got up, sighing virtuously: "I had to tell you what I seen, Hattie, so you can tell Baptiste. Maybe he can break the conjur'. Maybe so, I don't know."

"That's real sweet of you, sister Mitty, to tell what you done seen. It's real sweet of you after the way Baptiste treat you, putting a bad mouth on your name."

"Baptiste just a young, crazy-acting boy," said Mitty tolerantly. "He'll learn better. I don't bear him no ill mind." She walked back to the house, her head held high, her long legs swinging lightly from her hips with effortless ease. The young coon ran after her for a little way, springing at her skirts, tapping at them with its velvet paws and making playful rushes at her.

"Do!" said Mitty. She laughed, "He-e-e-e-e!" and rocked back and forth in her mirth.

When she had gone Hattie sat quiet in the sunlight fumbling

with her patchwork. Time passed more quickly than she thought. It was almost noon before she remembered that she had not started dinner. She got up and went into the house, piling pine knots on the embers that lay in the fireplace. She began to mix bread with her bare hands and put it in a skillet to bake. She hurried with her cooking, but dinner was not ready when Jim returned with the dogs. He had caught two swamp rabbits and while he skinned and cut them up Hattie told him what Mitty had seen. Jim scratched his anvil-like head, unable to reason, or to cope with this situation.

"Mitty say it's a death wish. She say it so bad, she never heard tell of one like it before."

"Lord God!" said Jim in a frightened voice. "Lord God Almighty!"

Baptiste came at one o'clock for his dinner. He seemed very happy, playing with the coon, laughing and telling stories. Jim and Hattie watched him out of the corners of their eyes, a fearful, respectful look on their faces.

When dinner was on the table, Hattie sat down with them, but she avoided looking at Baptiste directly, turning her head away when he spoke or staring at him with frightened curiosity when she thought she was not observed.

"What's the matter with me, anyway?" asked Baptiste. "Everybody stares as if they never saw me before." He got up from the table and went to the fragment of mirror which hung on the wall near the bed. He touched his cheeks with his delicate hands, pressing upon them, pulling the under lids of his eyes down. "Chester looked at me all morning in a funny way. What's the matter? What's it all about?"

Hattie said: "Get that conjur' broke just as quick as you can. There's a woman at Athlestan can break it. Get it broke right now before it gets too strong to break."

"What are you talking about, Hattie?" He glanced at her in amazement. "What in the world are you talking about?"

"Somebody put a death conjur' on you." Jim's face was grave and a little frightened. "Somebody done death-wished you, Baptiste."

Baptiste shrugged and raised his hands outward, superior, deeply amused. "Well! . . . Well, of all absurdities!"

Hattie began to talk earnestly, telling him what Mitty had seen, but Baptiste would not take her seriously. "Why a boar with 'possum hands and a man's face?" he asked. He got up from the table, angry all of a sudden. "Don't talk about such childish things! Don't talk nigger talk to me!" He stood in the room, his pale face flushed a little. "Tell Mitty to mind her own affairs. If she's trying to frighten me she's wasting her time."

He got up and went back to his cabin. That afternoon he waited for Chester to come back, but the boy did not return, so Baptiste took a walk by himself through the woods. But the story Mitty had told stuck in his mind. "She must have seen *something*," he thought. He shook his head in denial. "Nigger talk! Nigger fears! . . . I thought I was above all that."

When he returned through the fields he saw Hattie still sitting on the bench before her cabin. She got up and came to meet him. "How you feel, Baptiste?"

Baptiste said, a little too positively: "I never felt better in my life. I don't want to hear any more talk about this."

"Go see that moojer woman at Athlestan. Go see her right away before that spell takes on good."

"Do you really believe in such things?"

"Go see that woman," insisted Hattie stubbornly. "Go see that woman, is what I say."

Jim came out and sat on the block before the door: "You better listen to what Hattie say. You better dig up that conjur' before it gets a good hold on you!" But Baptiste went back to his cabin, his plump, rounded body swaying a little from the hips. "You negroes!" he said tolerantly. "You negroes!"

It was almost dark and there were vague, diffused colors against the sky. There was a haze hanging around the trees as if mist from the sea had blown in; as if, far away, grass were burning in abandoned fields and smoke had settled on the world. He stood at his cabin door, his hand on the catch, listening. In a moment he went inside and lighted his lamp and built a fire in his fireplace.

He thought: "Of course the whole thing is absurd. Nobody would want to put a conjur' on me, unless it was Mitty herself." He leaned forward on hands and knees, blowing on the fire he had kindled. At once he sprang up. "I'm talking like a nigger," he said angrily. "I'm talking as if I believed in such a thing." He got out one of the law books he was studying and began to read it, but his mind could not take in the meaning of the words. He thought: "I'll get out of here tonight while there's time." He got up and began to gather his things together, but sat down again immediately. He spoke aloud, contemptuously: "She can't run me away. I'll stay as long as I choose." He began to feel exuberant, light.

He took off his clothes, finally, and lay on his bed, but he could not sleep. There was a soft touching of bare branches against the walls of his cabin, the stirring of animals, distant sounds of which he had never before been conscious. He thought he could hear a whispering outside. He got up and went to his door, looking out, but there was nothing there. Then he thought: "Whatever it was has hidden back of the cabin." He ran quickly to surprise the thing that he had heard, but there was nothing. He stood there in the cold air for a long time, his head canted to one side, listening, before he lay again on his bed; but the vision of a pattering monster that climbed walls and peered down chimneys persisted. He laughed at his fears, but he could not quiet them.

At last he got up. There was a feeling of relief in his mind as he knelt before his step and began to dig with eager fingers in the earth. He found the sack almost immediately and took it into his cabin, examining it in the lamp light.

He began to laugh nervously, in relief. "This is unbelievable! . . . Only a tobacco sack filled with odds and ends." He threw the sack into one corner of the room, blew out his light again, and slept soundly until morning.

9

BAPTISTE came into Hattie's kitchen, the sack twirling on his finger. The morning was overcast. There were low, scudding clouds across the sky, driven before the wind like herds of gray swine and like swine grouped close in terror. It had begun to rain before daybreak, and it looked as if it would keep up all day. There was a wet, musty odor in the cabin: a smell of sweat, mildew and wood decaying. Jim sat in a cane-bottom chair, his head against the wall, and Hattie moved slowly back and forth between her stove and the table on which she was placing breakfast. She moved indolently, as if half asleep, her high, fanlike buttocks lifting upward as she bent over to lift the iron skillet from the fire.

When she turned and saw the sack looped around Baptiste's finger she made a quick, frightened noise, her hands raised as if a robber faced her, backing toward the farther-most corner of the cabin.

"What that you got? What that you got, boy?"

Jim had risen in his fright and stood just outside the cabin door, peering in at Baptiste.

"This?" asked Baptiste indulgently; "this is the conjur' that frightened you two."

"Throw it in the fire, quick!" said Jim. "Throw it in the fire before something happens!"

Baptiste began to feel superior, master of himself again, slightly swaggering, slightly contemptuous. His fears of the night before had gone.

"How can an old tobacco sack with a few feathers and bones in it hurt anybody?"

"Throw it in the fire!" said Jim. "Throw it in the fire!"

"It's childish to think that a tobacco sack can hurt anybody," continued Baptiste. A wave of nervous power passed over him. He turned toward the door: "Touch the sack, Jim; touch it! You'll see that it can't hurt you."

But Jim's face broke up and ceased to be a face. It became all terror and all wildness to escape. He ran backwards clumsily. His eyes were like two stones held in his face by the muscles of his brows. His hands were raised upward and rigid, bent forward at the joints like the paws of a performing black poodle. He peddled backward furiously, afraid to turn his face away; but when he saw that Baptiste had stopped at the door, he, too, stood still, his eyes stretched wide, his breath coming quickly.

"Don't you tech me with that sack, nigger!" he said in a voice as small and as terrified as that of a little boy.

Baptiste spoke in a mild, wheedling tone. "There's nothing to hurt you, Jim: how can you be hurt by a sack and a few feathers?"

He turned to Hattie: "You aren't afraid of the sack, are you? You're not as foolish as Jim, are you?"

Hattie said nothing. She stood with her mouth slightly opened, her stained, unpolished gold teeth dull against her skin, almost the same color of her skin. One hand rested flat and splayed out against the wall, the other was held forward, curved slightly in a stilted, calculated pose as if she stood waiting for her partner, the instant before she began to dance.

Baptiste took a step toward her. "You're not afraid of the sack are you, Hattie?" He walked slowly toward her, his lips smiling ingratiatingly as one smiles at a stubborn child, the sack dangling on his finger. "Show Jim that the sack can't hurt him."

But Hattie's outcurved, coquettish arm straightened to the

table and fumbled for the bread-knife. When she felt it in her hand, her fingers gripping the handle, her passivity vanished.

"Tech me with that sack, boy! Tech me with it and see what I do!"

"Hattie! Hattie!" cried Baptiste in an amazed, despairing voice. "Hattie, I'm surprised at you."

"Just tech me!" said Hattie ominously. "Just try to tech me, that's all."

Outside the door Jim stood in the rain, unaware of it. His clothes were already soaked, adhering to his body, and water trickled down his cheeks and into the tops of his shoes. The grayness of the morning had increased and there was a fine mist over everything. Clouds stretched down upon the earth, lying close to the land, flattening and blurring everything into the same unaccented grayness. On the Athlestan road to the left someone shouted to a team of oxen and cracked a rawhide whip.

Baptiste became grave all of a sudden. "I'll burn the sack if you really feel that way, Hattie."

He turned to Jim standing in the rain, meaning to reassure him; but before he could speak an inexplicable feeling of terror came over him, terror which started at his heart and spread over his body evenly in slow, breath-taking waves. He made a strange noise in his throat, turned suddenly and threw the sack into the fire. He stood rubbing his hands together, as if some particle of the sack clung to them; he rubbed his hands against the sides of his pants over and over, until they were heated from the friction and began to burn him.

"What am I going to do, Hattie? What am I going to do now?"

When the sack was entirely consumed, Hattie answered. "There's a moojer woman lives out from Athlestan a piece. Better go see what she kin do. Better go befo' it's too late."

Jim came into the cabin and stood before the fire, his clothes steaming in the heat. "Don't you never try to tech me with a conjur'. Don't you never do that again."

"Come on and eat breakfuss," said Hattie.

They seated themselves at the table and Hattie put food on their plates.

"You better do like Hattie tells you. You better go see that moojer woman, and quick, too."

"No!" said Baptiste stubbornly. "I won't do that."

Suddenly he felt sick, as if a hand had reached into him and had seized his stomach with icy fingers, squeezing it into a tight, wet ball and releasing it. The sight of the food on his plate nauseated him. He pushed it away and got up from the table.

"You better eat your breakfuss, Baptiste," said Hattie. "You going to need all your strength." Her voice, now that danger to herself was past, had become tender, compassionate. "Eat just a little bit, Baptiste," she urged. "Try to eat some, anyway."

"Go on and eat something," said Jim. "Go on, Baptiste, and eat."

But Baptiste shook his head. He walked to the fire, his hands pressed against his lips, and sat on the floor beside the hearth. His face was empty of all blood: it was as dead and dull as unglazed, yellow paper. Sweat broke on his forehead, running down his temples. The insides of his hands were dripping with sweat: they were weak and passive, without any will of their own. He closed his eyes and lay back, trembling a little. He thought: "It's strange that I feel that way. It's strange that this has taken a hold on me, because I don't believe in conjurs and ghosts and things like that." Then came that deeper fear which is older than thought and which challenges it. "How do I know that there's nothing in conjurs? What does anybody really know about such things?"

"Come on, Baptiste," said Hattie. "Drink a cup of coffee. Leastways you can do that."

Baptiste thought: "Nigger talk. Nigger thinking. I don't believe in it."

Jim had finished eating and was standing in the door watching the gray, slow rain. "Here comes Mitty," he said. "She's coming down here."

"Get up, Baptiste," said Hattie, quickly. "Get up and sit in the chair. Don't let Mitty see you scared."

Baptiste got up. "I'm not scared," he whispered through bloodless lips; "my stomach is a little upset, that's all."

He took out his tobacco and rolled himself a cigarette, shaping it carefully. He licked the white paper, his full, voluptuous eyes glancing upward over the cylinder at the vacant doorway. In a moment Mitty stood there stamping her feet on the threshold, shaking her wet shoulders. She seemed surprised to see Baptiste. She stared at him carefully, critically.

"Hattie, what all's the matter with Professor Seemo? He look sick. He look downright sick to me."

"Baptiste got his stomach upsot."

"U-u-u-m! . . . He sho do look bad!"

"There's nothing the matter with me, Madame Hurry. Please don't distress yourself."

But Mitty pretended not to have heard him. She was speaking to Hattie. "This rainy day a good time to clean up that old attic room. A good time to pull down them cobwebs and sweep. Thought you might come up and help me do it." But before Hattie could answer Mitty nudged Jim in the ribs. "So Professor Seemo sick at his stomach? He can't eat no breakfuss, is that right?" She laughed lightly, gayly, her long ascending laugh. "Maybe somebody done bigged him. Maybe some gentleman taken him for a gal and bigged him."

"Now, Mitty," said Hattie. "Now, Mitty, please, ma'am, don't tease Baptiste."

Baptiste got up unsteadily and again terror and nausea flowed

85

through his body. He felt weak and his legs seemed too frail to support. He walked into the rain, toward his own cabin, not glancing back; but when he reached the lean-to where Hattie had her washing pot he stopped, placed his head against the side of the wall and began to vomit, his body torn with convulsive motions, the sound of his retching coming shrilly through the still air.

Mitty stood in the door watching him. "Baptiste been bigged just as sho as you born! Some gentleman seen him doing fancy work and taken him for a gal!" She slapped her strong arms against her thighs with a flop. "He-e-e-e!" she laughed in a long, ascending scale. And then again: "He-e-e-e!"

"Now, Mitty," said Hattie; "now, Mitty, don't tease him." She ran out in the rain toward Baptiste, but he stood up at her approach and walked away unsteadily. He went back to his cabin and lay on his shuck mattress, staring upward at the ceiling, listening to the rain swishing against the roof. He got up, at last, feeling stronger, and put the blackboard in its place. He straightened up his cabin and built a fire. He sat down again and waited for Chester, but the boy did not come. Instead, Robert Hurry entered. "Mitty says you're sick," he began. His vague eyes looked about the place, resting on everything and seeing nothing. "What's the matter with you?"

"My stomach is a little upset; I think that's all."

"If you don't feel better by tomorrow I'll send you to Athlestan to see a doctor." Robert seemed embarrassed, out of place. He went to the fire and stirred it, but he realized that he should not be serving his inferiors and he turned away, self-conscious and slightly angry. "I think Chester better not come down until you're feeling all right. You may have something contagious."

Baptiste put away the blackboard and the schoolbooks and lay again on his bed. He let the fire die down to embers and at last go out.

10

BAPTISTE could not have said whether or not he had slept the following night; he had no certainty of sleep, but there was a sort of awakening the next morning: a slow return to the actual things of the earth. For a while he lay at peace, somnolent, staring at the rafters above him, listening to the faint rustling of shucks as he turned from side to side. He lay that way for a few minutes, his hands raised as if he contemplated prayer, his delicate fingers touching cathedral-wise above his belly, his elbows drawn close to his body, pressing it, as if his body had suddenly become very precious to him. Regretfully he got out of bed, standing naked on the bare floor, his yellow body trembling. He reached for his shirt and his faded overalls but the floor lifted with him and tilted sidewise and he lay back half clothed on the bed again. He was still lying there when Hattie rapped on his one, tiny window.

"Baptiste!" she called. "Baptiste!" She opened the door of the cabin and peered in at him. She came quickly toward him, her flopping, nigger shoes scraping over the floor with the sound of sandpaper being rubbed, her flat, lath-like legs sticking upward from them.

"It's started," he said. "The spell has started." There was no color, and no inflection in his voice at all: it was all one tone, all one key.

Hattie got a rag and soaked it in water, washing his face gently. She held a glass of milk to his lips, his head steady in the crook of her arm, and Baptiste drank; but when she took her arm from beneath him, his head fell back on the pillow and rested there twisted at an angle, his chin lowered as if he could no longer raise it.

"There ain't nothing to worry about. You got plenty time to go see that moojer woman."

Baptiste's eyes were closed. It seemed as if he had not heard. He raised his hands upward and pressed down on his face. "Where does she live?"

"She lives where the road forks at the north end of town," said Hattie. "Come on, get dressed and go see her. No use acting this way."

"Where does she live?" asked Baptiste stupidly. "Where does she live, Hattie?" Hattie began to shake him. "I done told you that. I done told you where she live at!" She pulled him upright. "Ask anybody in Athlestan. They can tell you where she live at."

When Hattie had gone, he finished dressing and went outside. The sun was out; the rain had stopped. He sat quietly before his cabin in the sunlight, feeling the chill, bracing air on his cheeks. To the right Jim was cutting wood, grunting each time the ax fell, and near him the young coon scampered about on the ground, twitching his nose and waving his ringed, bushy tail. At length Baptiste saw Robert come out of the house and go toward the barn and he got up and walked toward him. He stood in the barn door until Robert turned and acknowledged his presence.

"What do you want, Baptiste?"

"I'm feeling worse. I want to go to that doctor."

Robert was somewhat surprised. "Are you sick? You should have told me. I'm sorry to hear that." He took down an old bridle, shook it and hung it on its nail again. "I'll give you a note to Dr. Carew. He doesn't treat colored people as a rule but I've known him a long time. We were in college together."

Baptiste followed him into the house and stood waiting while Robert wrote a note to the doctor. He put it into the pocket of his jumper and turned to go, but Robert stopped him.

"I remember an interesting case we had in law school. It was Saxon vs. the Acme Carbonic Gas and Bottling Corporation, as I recall it now; anyway the facts were these: A belt broke at the plant one afternoon and was flapping about endangering lives. Saxon, an employee of the company, went over to shut off the power and in doing so he was knocked down and injured. The Court ruled that he had assumed the risk of his act and that he could not recover damages from his employers."

Baptiste closed his eyes. "I'm sick," he thought. "I'm very sick."

"I've got the case in a textbook on damages somewhere. I'll look it up for you."

"Thank you," said Baptiste. "Thank you very much." He rested his head against the door and pressed his trembling hands together.

"There was a dissenting opinion by Judge Mayhew who maintained that shutting off the power was an act in line with an employee's duty and that since he was acting in line of duty an action lay against the Acme Corporation."

Robert quit talking and looked at the man before him. "Tell Dr. Carew to send me a bill for your visit," he said gruffly. "Tell him you are one of my farm hands."

Baptiste nodded, murmured something and went out of the room. He stood for a moment on the brick walk that led toward the road before he hurried away with his quick, nervous steps, his body swaying a little. He walked rapidly, neither looking to the right nor the left, not speaking to people. At noon he reached the town. He found the doctor's office and mounted the stairs that led upward from the sidewalk.

Baptiste reached the top step and sat down upon it. It was

dark in the corridor but behind him a little light filtered through a window set high in the grimy wall. He pressed his face into his hands again and sat there silent until terror came over him once more. He sprang up and ran down the stairs toward the patch of sunlight that lay across the sidewalk, his shoes clattering against the bareness of the boards.

He came to the house of the moojer woman and stopped there. The house was built high on brick foundations, against a slight rise in the ground. The pillars on one side were lower than on the other, to equalize the slope of the land, giving the place the appearance of resting on uneven stilts. The moojer woman came to her door, hearing the noise the gate made, and called: "Who dat? Who dat coming in at my gate?"

She peered at Baptiste with sharp, brilliant eyes, her head tied up in a colored handkerchief. Baptiste came up the steps and she opened the door for him. There was a musty smell inside the house, like starch which has soured blended with the odor of old books. At the windows were buckets filled with earth with geraniums and begonias blooming in them. The woman went over to her flowers and examined them critically, pinching off with her finger a yellowing leaf or a withered bloom.

"Set down, boy. Set down and tell me what you come for." Then, without turning, she said: "Don't be scared. Being scared won't help none."

She came toward him and sat down, her hands clasped together between her knees. Swollen veins bulged upward on her hands like tiny mountain ranges. Her knuckles, too, were swollen and her little fingers were bent into perpetual half circles with disease. Her hands were dark brown, but between her fingers her skin was pinkish and unhealthily white, as if she had recently shed in patches.

She reached out and took Baptiste's hand. "Tell me what all you come for. Go ahead and tell me."

Baptiste began to talk. He told of the conjur', of finding the sack, and the moojer woman sat staring above his head, her face without expression.

When he was half through his recital she turned to someone in the rear: "Phe-e-e-nie! You, Pheenie!"

A half-grown girl came into the room and Baptiste stopped talking, waiting for her to go away. "Go ahead!" said the moojer woman. "Go ahead, boy—I kin hear you."

To the girl she said: "Time to feed them mockin' birds. Time to give 'em dere aigs."

"Yassum," said Pheenie. "Yassum, I done fixed hit."

She took down the cages and put them on the table and fed the gluttonous birds with a mixture of mashed egg yolks and meal. They fluttered about making an excited noise, and grasped the spoon in their hungry beaks. "Lord God!" said Pheenie. "What make you so hongry? You don't do nothing to get hongry for."

The moojer woman began to twitch, her lips drawn back into a snarl, her eyes remote from the world. She said: "It's a death wish and hit was done at night in the dark. The moon was back of a cloud when hit was done and I can't see the face of the one dat deathwished you."

Baptiste caught his breath harshly.

"Was it a man or a woman who did it?"

"It was a *kind* of a man," said the woman. "It was a little bitsy man. It look like a shorty to me."

Baptiste got up. "Help me!" he said in terror. "Help me!"

"Can't see who done it," said the woman petulantly. "Can't see who deathwished you."

She looked up at the birds in their cage above her, sticking her lips out a little. "Tweet! Tweet!" she said. "Tweet! Tweet! Tweet!" But the gorged birds stared at her, a hostile look in their eyes, and would not sing.

She turned back to Baptiste. "I can't help you none, boy."

Baptiste got up and walked away, and the woman went back to her plants, examining buds, breaking off old blossoms. She had already forgotten him, with that stolid imperviousness to despair which those whose business it is to watch the agony of others must possess.

As Baptiste walked the road again a feeling of peace came over him, a sense of inevitability. He walked slowly, kicking up with his feet the red dust of the road, glancing at the growth that surrounded the road, brown and dead now with occasional patches of green in it.

Presently he saw a wagon pulled by an ewe-necked horse approaching, a wagon badly in need of axle grease whose wheels creaked in four different keys like a quartette of guinea hens quarreling together. One of the rear wheels seemed a little larger than the others or more flattened on one side, and, as it turned, that end of the wagon lifted upward and settled down with a slight thud.

In the wagon on cane chairs were two negro girls dressed in cheap, gaudy colors and saturated with strong perfume through which the musk of their own bodies came out modified and minimized slightly. They sat prim in their finery, their buttocks and their breasts vibrating to the jolts of the vehicle.

Baptiste stood in the road and hailed the wagon. It stopped with the warped side of the wheel in the air, the rear of the wagon raised a little. He spoke to the driver casually, calmly: "I've been conjured."

And the man looked at him with his wary eyes, the eyes of a small animal surveying what he suspects to be a trap. "Who done it?"

"I don't know. The woman couldn't see his face, but it was a small man. I was just wondering if you knew such a person around here. . . . A hunchback, or a dwarf maybe?"

"No, suh," said the man with emphasis. "No, suh!"

One of the girls spoke: "Dere's a dwarf on Mr. Eldridge's place, over by Three Tree Branch. I seen him one day."

The driver spoke angrily. "Keep your mouf shet! Keep your mouf shet, gal."

"Yassuh!" said the girl submissively. "Yassuh!"

Baptiste released his hold on the bridle. "That's all I wanted to know. Thank you very much."

The old negro slapped his horse with slack reins and the wagon started forward again, creaking and tilting a little and creaking again on a lower note. The young girls turned their necks, as if their bodies worked on the same strings, their eyes widened identically, their heads at the same angle. They stared at Baptiste until they saw him leap the ditch and run into the woods; then they both laughed, doubled up in their chairs.

In the wood Baptiste walked aimlessly. He took out his pocket knife and cut himself a hickory sapling and sat down on the earth, trimming the sapling into a club, feeling its weight carefully. Late in the afternoon he came back to the Hurry place. Chester saw him turn in from the road and ran toward him, but Mitty, who had been watching the boy, called from her kitchen door in a shrill voice, "You, Chester! You stay indoors like your pappa told you!"

Baptiste threw himself on the ground and began to cry. He lay there in the tall grass, pressing his palms against his temples, making a whimpering sound. "Something terrible is going to happen," he whispered; "something terrible."

Hattie came over to him.

"Go away! . . . Go away, Hattie!" His voice, when he spoke, was calm, matter of fact, as if he had resigned himself to what awaited him; and Hattie knew, then, that the woman in Athles-

93

tan had not been able to help him. She leaned over him, her thin buttocks rising above her waist like stuffed pillows flattened with long use, and all at once terror flowed outward from Baptiste's heart like waves that run from the center of water into which a stone has been flung; circle after circle of agitation, widening and flowing outward, until each is lost against the shore; until the pool, being all commotion, all unrest, seems undisturbed under the completeness of its agitation.

From the Diary of Sarah Tarleton

December 2nd, 1912. *There's talk again about the Hodge Brothers building their sawmill. They've been buying options on timber all through the country. Old man Tallon has given an option on his timber rights and so have the Cornells and the Wrenns. Bushrod says he'll never sell his as long as he lives. Nobody knows where the mill will go up but we all know that it will bring prosperity to this county.*

Lillian Chapman drove over from Reedyville today in her fine Ford car. She is learning to drive and she wanted me to ride down the road a little ways to prove her skill. She took Bessie and Bushrod instead and I watched the store while they were gone. Autos are getting to be common now, but I'll never trust myself in one of them. If our Merciful Heavenly Father had wanted people to ride about in such things he would have created them as he created horses or other animals for men's use.

December 8th, 1912. *They butchered at the Tallons yesterday and Mrs. Tallon sent over a pork loin by Bradford. Neighborly and sweet, I thought.*

December 22nd, 1912. *Things in the store very rushing with Christmas approaching. Both Frank and I have been helping Bushrod as there are too many people for him to wait on alone. The Yuletide season always fills me with sadness. I think of my dear, dead parents and those far away happy days of my youth, and tears well upward into my eyes. Must go press out Bessie's silk dress. She is singing tonight at a Church social at Addie Wrenn's.*

11

CHESTER remained in his room, as Mitty had instructed him. Occasionally he played with the toys which Jim and Baptiste had made for him, but mostly he sat at his window which overlooked the cabins. At ten o'clock that morning he saw Baptiste come out and stand in the sunlight. He wore no hat and the wind lifted his brown, straight hair occasionally. He stood rigidly, his pale face held upward to the sun; then, without warning he began to sing, shaking his head back and forth. There was no tune for the sounds which came from his throat and no actual words for his meaning. He began to run around his cabin, faster and faster, making all the time a strange, moaning noise.

Hattie and Jim were watching him with frightened expressions, and from her kitchen window, behind her curtains, Mitty also watched.

Hattie spoke pleadingly: "Baptiste! Baptiste! Don't let that conjur' better you! Don't give in!"

Baptiste stopped and looked at her. His amber eyes blazed with madness. They were ringed about with purple shadows and were puffed out a little. His skin seemed dull and lifeless, the color of yellow mold that attaches itself to trees which have lain fallen for a long time. He took a few mincing steps toward Hattie and bowed. Hattie stood her ground, but Jim retreated and picked up a club. "Come away from there, Hattie."

"I ain't afraid," answered Hattie. "I ain't afraid of Baptiste."

"Will you dance this waltz with me?"

"Baptiste! Baptiste! Don't give up! Don't let that conjur' beat you!" She walked over to him. "Listen!" she begged; "listen to what I say—"

At that moment Baptiste raised his arm upward, his body twitching, and began to shout with a sound as lost and as terrible as the hollow baying that rushes from the throat of a hound. He ran into his cabin and picked up the hickory club he had cut. He came again out of the door, glancing back over his shoulders as if pursued, and began running through the high wire grass. He reached the fence and vaulted it, pausing to look over his shoulders, and stood for a moment on the Athlestan road, as if undecided what to do next.

Mitty pulled back her curtains and watched him until he disappeared. "Well, that's the last of Baptiste," she said. "That's the last we'll ever see of that boy. He-e-e-e! He's long gone to Montgomery by now."

But Mitty was incorrect in this, for Baptiste, when he reached the road that forked off toward the Eldridge place, turned and followed that road. He walked into the underbrush and hid himself in a growth of gall berry bushes that grew near by, peering out, waiting. He lay that way for a long time, his club clutched in his hand. The sky was coldly, brilliantly blue with a rim of white clouds across it. The sun was warm, for December, but a wind, with a faint nip in it blew at intervals, stirring the bushes and flattening the rank weeds.

And so Baptiste lay in his place of concealment, watching the road with furious, frightened eyes. At last he saw approaching from the direction of the Eldridge place, a grotesque, dwarflike creature. He walked slowly, on legs thick and bowed, his stuffed, shapeless arms hanging from his shoulders like the toy arms of a doll. He did not seem to be a man at all, but rather a mechanism set in motion by springs and regulated by wheels. He walked the middle of the deserted road, his curved, sawdust legs giving a little under the weight of his heavy body, and

Baptiste got up from where he had lain. He leaped the ditch and stood in front of the stranger, blocking his way.

The dwarf stopped and looked to left and right, but there was no immediate fear in his face. His eyes bulged and pressed outward and his jaw was perpetually thrust forward. He resembled, vaguely, a fish with immense, protuberant eyes; a toy dog with a concave face and wrinkled, aged brows. His skin was black with a luster that was almost purple.

The dwarf spoke: "What you want?"

His voice was deep. It rumbled, rich and orchestral, like the notes of an organ vibrating in an empty church. He stood looking at Baptiste, a suspicious expression in his eyes. "Don't stop me, nigger; don't block my path."

Baptiste said: "What have I done to you? Why did you want to conjure me?"

"I ain't conjured you," answered the dwarf. "I don't know who you is."

"I'll pay you to let me go. I've got some money. I'll pay you what you want."

The dwarf shoved at Baptiste with his jointless, toylike arms. He turned and tried to run down the road, in the direction from which he had come, his bowed, grotesque legs working with slow and concentrated fright, but Baptiste, without running at all, walking with long strides only, kept abreast of him, talking to him, pleading with him in his soft voice.

The dwarf stopped again, knowing himself to be helpless, and looked up and down the road, but there was no one in sight. His lips pulled back and showed his outthrust lower teeth. He boomed again in his rich, beautiful voice: "I ain't bothered you none! I ain't bothered you none, and you know it!"

"Break your conjur'," pleaded Baptiste. "Break it, because I can't stand this much longer."

Then the dwarf rushed at Baptiste with his stuffed arms,

which seemed without joints or articulation; he thrashed furiously in the air with his arms, a whirlwind of terror and impotence; and Baptiste held him off with his club. The dwarf leaned against the club, whirling his arms in space and rolling his eyes wildly. He cried again in terror, his chest rising and falling, his organlike voice rolling magnificently across the fields and upward toward the quiet sky.

"Break your conjur'," said Baptiste.

But the dwarf pulled away from the club and ran clumsily across the road, as if he would hide in the underbrush. Baptiste watched him, the club balanced in his hand; then he took three skipping, mincing steps, raised his club and brought it down full force upon the fleeing negro's head.

The dwarf fell by the roadside and lay there, his lumpy body twitching a little, his eyes wide opened. Baptiste stood over him and raised the club above his shoulders, balancing himself carefully; and again it crashed against the dwarf's skull. He began to shower blows on the prostrate man, missing his body entirely more times than not.

When Baptiste was exhausted he sat down by the road and rolled a cigarette. An overpowering languor came over him. He thought: "I have not slept for six days, but now I can sleep."

He stretched out full length beside the man he had killed, the bloody club between them. There was a feeling of jubilance flowing through his body, exhaustion as exquisite as pain. The joints of his knees ached and his arms still tingled a little from the vibration of his club on the dead man's skull. Slowly his eyes closed and his mouth opened and the half-consumed cigarette fell from his lips and burned itself out on the ground.

He was still sleeping profoundly when the sheriff of the county put him under arrest.

That night Mitty was very gay after dinner. While Robert

was on the porch, she picked the boy up and held him in her arms. She sat on the kitchen bench and sighed her contentment. Chester pressed his face closer against her warm, soft breast and Mitty smoothed out his hair. "Everything going to be nice again with that Baptiste gone," she said. "Everything going to be just like it was."

"What is getting hanged like, Mitty?" he asked absently.

"Old Mitty tell her baby a story," she answered. "I'll tell him a story 'bout his mamma and his Grandfather Tarleton, and his Uncle Bushrod. . . ." She paused a moment, listening, until her keen ears caught the rhythmic creak of Robert Hurry's old rocking chair.

"Your mamma and me was born on the same day," she whispered. "I was born in the morning and your mamma was born about sundown. She had long yaller hair which she wore banged like. She was a sweet thing. She was the sweetest one."

The Whisperer

THE woman of whom I shall tell you had been blessed beyond the lot of most mortals: she had comfort, contentment and intelligence; but as if those things were not enough, she had been given, also, a beauty so perfect and so rare that all men bowed before it.

She lived in a house over which wisteria grew like knotted ropes. There was a wide porch in front and it was here that this great beauty received her admirers. They came each night and sat, content merely to look at her, to listen to her voice. There were many men who loved her, but she refused them all, one after the other. Later, when they had married other women less lovely, and were happy, they came to see her as before, and they were received, as a queen receives. . . . And so the woman lived on, taking no lover, marrying no man, giving her beauty to all men equally.

But one spring day, as she looked into her mirror, she saw that her cheeks were beginning to fade, that her throat was losing its firmness a little and she was terrified at what time might do to her. That night she said that she was not well and received in her small parlor, and with the lights dimmed a little, with rouge on her cheeks and lips, she was lovelier than before.

After that she would never go into the cruel sunlight again, and later she would not stir from the house even. She settled down onto her couch and became an invalid. All day she read that she might talk brilliantly, and practiced before her mirror that she might be gracious and charming. As the years passed her worshipers died or drifted away until at last there were left only six old men who remembered her; but those men came regularly to see her, and sat in her bed chamber. (For she lay in bed always, now, a thin barrier of gauze between her and her court with two rose-colored lights, set exactly, to illumine her face in just such a way. . . .)

She died when she was past sixty, in her sleep, without pain, and the six old men heard of it and came, before she was cold, to see her body for the last time. She lay on her bed, near the window, through which the bright sunlight flowed. But there was no rouge to cover her wrinkles now, and no flesh-tinted bandages to hold her sagged throat upward. Her golden wig had been taken away and her harsh, old woman's hair was pulled backward from her forehead and fixed into a gray, tight knot. (She had not anticipated death, and had not prepared for it, and it had caught her unaware.)

But she was never to know that, of course; nor was she ever to know that her struggle against time was senseless, her effort and her life wasted; for she had failed to realize that the eyes of her lovers must grow dim as inevitably as her beauty must pass.

The six old men grouped about her, feeling lost and forlorn. For many years they had not seen her face clearly. They bent now above the bier, peering at her, touching her mottled, claw-like hands. "You lovely thing," they whispered in wonder to this dead, shrunken old woman. "You lovely, lovely thing!"

12

MITTY rose early and began putting the house in order. It was still two hours before daybreak and there was a late moon hanging low above the rim of the pines. "Wake up, sugarpie," she said; "it's the morning of Baptiste's hanging. When you get dressed come down to the kitchen and eat some breakfast."

Jim helped them into the surrey and Mitty took the reins in her hands, slapping the mule smartly on its rump. "Get up, mule!" she said impatiently; "get up! . . . We'll get there just about right, baby; we'll get there in plenty time." But Chester's head had slipped down and rested against her warm thighs, and he had gone to sleep again.

Toward daybreak they arrived at Athlestan. It was still dark without even a touch of relieving grayness. The shops and the business offices which faced the courthouse were all shuttered: there was no sign of life on the street. The courthouse was in the center of the small town; back of it was the jail, a four-story building of red brick, towered and crenelated like some medieval castle, and with windows barred in thick iron. There was a walled-in passageway which ran from the jail to the courthouse, and behind the jail was the paved yard where prisoners exercised. In this yard the hanging was to take place.

It was a full hour before the execution but already a crowd had gathered, people petulant and sleepy, who yawned from time to time. The negroes present in the yard stood apart from the whites, against the side of the far wall. They laughed and rolled their eyes excitedly and chattered together.

It was still night, but morning was not far away. In the sky a moon hung low, near to setting. The countryside was washed with the liquidity of the late, low-hanging moon. There was a feeling of wetness in the air and the washed smell of early morning. On the pavement, the dew lay heavily underfoot. It had collected in globules on the branches of trees and on the underside of leaves where it clung and lengthened, like the nose of a hound, until swollen too heavy to hang longer. There was, also, in the gutters of the jail a hushed, precise sound of dampness congealing and flowing, and dripping, finally, a long way on to tin. . . .

Gradually the moon faded and set and for a while there was nothing in the sky except three stars, remote and far away. The jail, the courthouse and the adjoining square seemed strange in this even darkness. . . . Then a cock, startlingly near, began to crow in a strident voice. He was answered by another cock farther off. Behind the livery stable on Front Street a third cock joined in. Soon there was a bedlam of crowing cocks, some far away, with voices like faded threads against the horizon, some immediately near and lusty. They crew triumphantly, answering each other and being answered in a pattern which never completely varied and which was never entirely the same, as if these minutes before the dawn were their own and in them they possessed power. Gradually the crowing ceased and the sky lightened and for a time there was again the unaccented sound of water dripping from eaves. . . .

Mitty took the boy's hand and led him to the section reserved for white people. She put her arm over his shoulder and whispered to him occasionally, to establish the fact that they were together. But nobody disputed Mitty's right to stand in front of the gallows with the white people of the town.

The sun was touching the top of the earth now with rich colors: salmon, yellow and red; the walled yard came into gradual distinctness. The yard seemed strange in the vague light of morning. Upon its thick walls bottles had been set in the cement and then broken: the silhouette of the broken bottles in the half light made it seem as if a great army with raised lances had come to Baptiste's hanging, and stood waiting outside the wall. The dew which had fallen all night clung also to the broken bottles and the red brick walls, and dripped downward in small streams. Even the new, unseasoned pine timber which formed the scaffold was damp with the dew.

The scaffold had been built the day before and Baptiste, from the barred space of his cell, had watched the workmen building it. With every beat of the hammers, with every whine of the saws, his heart had tightened to his terror, his throat had constricted, his lips dried; and he lay on his cot and moaned, thinking of his end. Then he would determine not to listen to the hammers any more. He would get up and sit on his stool and face the bare wall; he would put his fingers into his ears to shut out the nearness of his doom; but invariably the sound of hammers would break through; invariably he would feel the harsh rope about his neck, his feet beating empty air. Sweat would come upon his forehead finally and run down into his eyes and his open mouth. Then he would jump up in terror and press his yellow face against the bars and watch the carpenters at work. Between the tight bars of the window he would stick out his yellow arm and wave it back and forth with a constant, meaningless gesture. . . . "Don't!" he would whisper. "Don't finish it, white folks! Don't finish it!"

But the carpenters paid no attention to Baptiste's plea. They went on calmly with their work, spitting, scratching their hinder parts and occasionally squinting up at the sun. They had worked carefully and they had built the scaffold solidly and high. It was built close to the north side of the wall where the L began. To its left was the gate that opened from the street and through which supplies for the jail were received; to its right was a peach tree, grown, no doubt, from a seed carelessly thrown, whose branches were now heavy with pink blossoms.

The audience gathered for the hanging became impatient after a while. They looked at their watches and stamped their feet, until, at last, the door in the rear of the jail opened and the sheriff of the county with his two deputies came out. Between the deputies, and completely supported by them, was the slack body of Baptiste. He was leaning backward at a terrified angle; his face and hands were of the same even ashiness, and he heaved his chest upward, sucking the clear air into his lungs as if he realized that soon, now, air would be shut from his blood forever. His hands were tied behind his back with heavy cord. He kept rubbing his wrists together with a persistent, minor gesture. His shirt was not buttoned and his shoelaces not tied as if he thought, at the last, that there was no need for such things. When Baptiste came out of the door his eyes were closed, but he opened them when he heard the lock snap behind him and felt the deputies stop, as they faced the scaffold, only a few yards away.

The sheriff, walking ahead, had already reached the steps and was mounting them. He turned and motioned to the deputies and Baptiste braced himself and stood upright, supported by their arms. Then he collapsed suddenly and lay without sound on the brick-paved yard. The deputies lifted him up, but when they took away their hands Baptiste fell forward again, this time striking with his shoulders the steps that led upward to the gallows. The patient, soft-spoken deputies lifted him once more, talking to him all the time, but he would have fallen again; so they carried him to the scaffold in their arms. Baptiste did not resist the deputies—his terror was too deep for resistance—he lay passive and shivering, his gray lips pulled back from his teeth as if the muscles of his cheeks had locked that way, and he made a quiet sound which resembled the mewing of a kitten.

Then, at last, the deputies got him upon the scaffold and held him upright, and Baptiste stared at the people below him with blind eyes; smiled at them with bloodless lips. The sheriff spoke to him: "If there's anything you want to say, you better say it now." Baptiste did not answer for he had not heard—words no longer registered on his brain—but his knees bent forward and folded under him and he fell down again. When the deputies raised him up and turned him toward the crowd he was still smiling his terrible, bloodless smile, but the mewing sound had become louder and more intaken.

Almost immediately the hangman came forward with a black hood, from which draw strings dangled. He put the bag over Baptiste's head and tied the strings loosely. Baptiste stood upon the trap, held up by the two deputies, the noose fastened about his neck and the sheriff came forward and addressed the people below him. "This man, Simon Baptiste, killed another negro, an innocent man, in cold blood—without any reason. He had a fair trial and was convicted fairly. Let his hanging be a lesson to you people who hear me today."

When the sheriff stopped speaking, he raised his hand. The deputies released Baptiste and stepped backward, and a moment later the trap was sprung and Baptiste shot, feet first, into space. But the hangman, being young and inexperienced, had not got the noose adjusted correctly and Baptiste's neck was not broken when the trap was sprung. He struggled in agony at the end of the rope, contorting his body so that he swung rapidly from one side of the yard to the other and spun slantwise, like a spent top, making all the time a high, gurgling sound. He struggled for a long time at the end of the rope, trying to break the cords that bound his wrists; lunging out with his feet and kicking the sides of the gallows; swinging dizzily and striking the peach tree with his body, until, at last, the rope caught in the branches of the tree and fouled there, and Baptiste spun about at the end of the rope, kicking and lunging and making a strangled noise. As he thrashed about under the tree, showers of petals fell from its branches and onto the ground.

He became quieter after a while, exhausted with his struggle, and hung limply at the end of the rope. Spasms of pain passed over his body and he shuddered at quick intervals. He resembled nothing so much as a mule twitching its hide to rid itself of flies. . . . But even after he became quiet he kept trying to free his hands so that he might take hold of the rope and relieve the pressure on his throat. Finally he did manage to free his hands, but he was too near death then to catch the rope above his head. He could only lift his hands upward and wave them back and forth, his palms opening and shutting. He died with his yellow hands groping for the rope. His hands were like the splayed claws of a dead hawk. They were rigid and curved with pain.

For a moment there was silence while Baptiste, unresistant now, swung back and forth, a gentle weight, and the agitated tree dropped its blossoms in flurries like pink, intermittent snow, and then the watching negroes, as if upon a prearranged signal, began an old song:

> "My lord is so high, you can't go over him,
> My lord is so wide, you can't go 'round him,
> My lord is so deep, you can't go under him,
> You must come in at the door."

The sheriff ran down the steps from the scaffold toward the singing negroes: "You negroes, hush!" he said in a scolding voice. "You hush, or I'll lock you all up!" The negroes ceased, all on the same note, rolled their eyes and flattened against the wall.

The hanging was over and people were already moving off. The sun was well up by this time and the color of dawn had gone away, absorbed in the morning sky, which was deeply blue —a perfect vault of unshaded blue—with clouds across it. Outside, in the public square, a dog barked; birds began to twitter in the trees that lined Front Street. A wagon creaked on a regular beat. The town was coming awake gradually. There was a banging of doors and distant laughter. Smoke curled upward from chimneys and there was a smell of bacon frying. But Mitty was not conscious of these sounds and smells of early morning: She stood there watching the body of Baptiste, a strange, complacent look in her eyes.

At some time during his struggles his unlaced shoes had fallen off and lay on the paved court beneath him, one turned sidewise and one standing straight up. For a moment Mitty regarded the cracked, patent leather shoes with their cloth tops and then her eyes lifted slowly until they rested on the stiff feet of the dead man. She saw, then, that he had worn for his hanging white socks which had been darned with strands of colored silk woven criss-cross into intricate patterns. She put out her hand slowly, as if she would touch the darned places, but she drew it back and stood quiet. . . . Suddenly she had a picture of Baptiste in his cell, his yellow face bending earnestly over his needlework, and she held her sides with her hands and laughed with her lips and the muscles of her face, but no sound came from her throat.

Later she turned to look for Chester, wondering how he had managed to slip away from her protecting arm, but she could not find him. She peered about the courtyard, seeking him. A yellow woman, seeing her fright, spoke to her: "If you's lookin' for the little white boy, he run out when Baptiste raise his hands. He run thru the passageway, to'd the co'thouse." Mitty hurried away after the boy. She found him in the surrey, awaiting her, sitting quietly.

She became gay all of a sudden: "Come on, baby," she said; "the sto's will all open up fo' long, and I'm going to buy my sugarpie a pretty to take home. . . . Come on, see if I don't!— I'm going buy my sweetheart a pretty just as sho as you born!" . . . But Chester would not answer. He drew away from her in sudden fright, careful that no part of his body should touch her. A moment later he leaned out of the surrey and began to vomit.

Hattie met them at the road. She had been standing there for a long time waiting, anxious to hear the details of Baptiste's hanging. She looked quickly at Chester, but he would not look at her. His face was white and there was a sick, frightened expression in his eyes.

"What's the matter, baby?" she asked. "What Mitty done to you?"

"I ain't done nothing," said Mitty in a high, deprecatory voice. "I ain't done nothing, but little Chester feeling sick-like. I expect he ate something in Athlestan that upsot him." Then, turning to him, she added sternly. "Here, boy, get down, we home again."

Chester got out of the surrey and stood before the two women. Then without speaking he turned and walked away. "You, Chester," called Mitty; "don't you go far: Hattie say she got dinner most ready."

"I got something you like, too," said Hattie, nodding in a mysterious manner. "I got something I cooked special for you."

But the boy did not answer or look around. He walked away from the house in the direction of the old Bragdon place.

Hattie said meditatingly: "That boy look sick to me!"

"He'll be all right before night," said Mitty. "He done ate something, I expect." Hattie drove the mule into the barn and began to unhitch while Mitty stood and told her of the hanging.

13

THE first leaves, tender and very young, were coming upon the trees, and greenness flowed over the land as gently and as evenly as water. Dogwoods were blooming: white, metallic blossoms with a green tint at the edge of their petals, as if they did not know, as yet, whether they were leaves or flowers. Along the Athlestan road, and in the corners of fields, dewberry bushes were covered with frail flowers, pink and white, which fell from their stems when touched.

Chester walked through the wood and across an old pasture, sat down, and looked about him. Far away he could see his father and Jim busy at spring plowing, turning the earth in long, straight furrows. As he watched, Jim became amused suddenly at something he had seen or something which Robert Hurry had said to him. He doubled up, clutching his belly with his folded arms, and through the clear air Chester could hear the faint remnant of his mirth. A feeling of anger came over the boy, a deep, unreasoning hatred against his father. He got up and walked away. Later he went back to the house, where Mitty was waiting for him. Mitty began at once to scold him for being late, but when she saw his face she stopped and tried to take him in her arms. "Everything going to be like it was before, honey." She held her delicate, curved nose high, her nostrils opening and closing. "Everything going to be better without that old Baptiste hanging 'round the place," she said.

But Chester pulled away from her, and went to his room. He lay on his bed and looked out of the window at the crêpe myrtle trees in flower, watching the wind move the new leaves of the trees. Every sight that he saw, every sound that he heard, reminded him of Baptiste, and in his mind, back of every emotion, beyond every thought, was the sight of Baptiste twisting at the end of the rope; the bitter consciousness that he, and he alone, was responsible for Baptiste's death. The things he had told Mitty had all been lies.

Mitty came into the room, a tray in her hands. "I done fixed you a good dinner," she said. Chester shook his head and turned his face to the wall and Mitty stood above him, coaxing and threatening by turns, but the boy would not speak to her. She put the tray on a table and went out, an anxious look in her eyes.

She came to the kitchen where Hattie was. "I don't know what ails little Chester . . ." she began.

"You shouldn't a-taken him to see Baptiste get hanged. I told you not to do dat."

"You tend to your own business, woman," said Mitty coldly; "you tend to your business, and I'll take care of mine!" She spoke again, in a placating voice: "Ain't nothing the matter with Chester. He'll be all right by morning. He'll forget all about it befor' morning."

But such was not the case. That night the child began to shiver, as if he had a chill, and in the afternoon Robert Hurry fetched Dr. Carew from Athlestan. But Chester did not know all this. His first clear thought was several days later, his first sight was a strange man bending over his bed. His father and Mitty were both in the room, watching him anxiously, and when he saw his father he began to cry and to beat against the bedclothes: "Go away!" he said in a weak voice. "Go away! Go away!"

Robert came over to him, a puzzled look on his vague, weak face. "It's me, Chester!" he said gently. "It's me, son!" But Chester pulled the clothing over his head and began to cry louder, terrified, trembling under the cover, and all at once Robert became very humble. He said: "I'm your father. You aren't afraid of me, are you? I wouldn't do anything to hurt you, son."

Chester called out in an agonized voice: "Mitty! Mitty! don't let him touch me!"

Robert stood still, a strange, uncomprehending expression on his face, and Dr. Carew touched his arm. "You'd better leave him alone for the time being, Bob. He's still a little delirious."

After Robert had gone out of the room, Mitty walked to the bed and spoke coaxingly. "The doctor done sent your pappa away. There ain't nothing to be afraid of, baby." Then in a voice half pleading, half triumphant: "My baby don't want nobody around him but his Mitty, do he? . . . He don't want to have nothing to do with nobody, except his Mitty!"

Dr. Carew spoke: "What happened to this child, anyway?"

And Mitty stared up innocently: "I don't rightly know, sir. I expect he just ate something what upsot him."

Dr. Carew started to answer, but changed his mind. He laughed shortly. "So he just ate something what upsot him!" he said humorously, mimicking Mitty's voice.

"Yes, sir."

"That's very interesting, I'm sure. A very interesting diagnosis, indeed."

He came over to the boy. "You feeling better now, son?"

"Yes, sir."

Dr. Carew stood holding the boy's wrist, his pleasant face grave and a little worried. He shrugged his shoulders helplessly.

"All right," he said at last; "be a good boy and get well quickly." A moment later he went out of the room.

Robert Hurry was sitting on the porch staring straight ahead at the level pines, unmoving and eternally green against the sky, and Dr. Carew stood in the doorway regarding him curiously, fingering his watch chain, his eyes half closed. Then he came quietly and sat on the steps beside his friend. Robert brushed his face roughly, disturbed and somewhat pathetic in his uncomprehending dismay.

"I don't understand this at all. . . . If I had treated the boy badly—if I had been unkind to him, or anything like that. . . . But I haven't, John. I've done the very best that I could for him. No man could have been a better father than I have tried to be." He stopped, puzzled, his weak mouth half opened. . . . "I don't understand it," he repeated helplessly; "why should he be afraid of me?"

Dr. Carew lifted his heavy watch fob and held it on his palm, as if calculating its exact weight. "When Chester is stronger, you'd better send him away for a while."

Hurry turned quickly and looked at him. "What good would that do? What's the matter with this place?"

"You're paying me to give you advice. Whether or not you take it is your business."

Robert was silent, staring at the even row of pines before he spoke. "I love the boy a great deal: you don't know how it hurts me to see him act as if—" He stopped. "All right, John," he said. "All right, I'll do what you say."

A few weeks later he wrote to his father-in-law asking if his son could visit there for the summer, and almost immediately he got a reply from Sarah Tarleton saying that Bushrod would be in Athlestan the following week, and, if it were convenient, he would stop by the farm and take the boy back with him.

Mitty broke the news to Chester. "You going to see your grandpappa and your Aunt Sarah and all the Tarletons," she announced. "Your pappa going to send you to stay in Pearl County for two or three months."

Chester was still weak from his illness, but he jumped up eagerly. "When do I start? When can I go?"

Mitty laughed, her lips twisted in self-pity: "You seem mighty proud to leave old Mitty, after all she done for her baby. You seem mighty proud to go."

On the day Bushrod was expected Mitty dressed the boy in his best. She had cut his hair the night before and had scrubbed his neck and ears until they glistened. He stood waiting on the porch for his uncle, his clothing packed in an old cloth valise with broken straps, and Mitty sat on the step beside him, glancing anxiously at the road. A clean handkerchief covered her plaited hair and she was wearing a heavily starched blue and white calico dress which crackled when she moved. All this was in honor of Bushrod Tarleton, of course. Mitty considered the Tarletons people worthy of one's best.

When they had almost given him up, Bushrod appeared. He was driving a rig which he had hired from the livery stable in Athlestan. He turned off from the road and approached the house. He wrapped the reins around the cup which held the buggy whip and sat for a moment looking about him. "Well, if it ain't Mitty!" he exclaimed, as if surprised to find her there. "How are you, Mitty?"

"How do, Bushrod. It sho been a long time since I seen you." She bustled about like a young girl and giggled in delight. "Go ahead, Chester," she said excitedly. "Go ahead and shake hands with your Uncle Bush."

Bushrod was a man of middle height, very solidly, very compactly built. His shoulders were broad, his hips flat and his buttocks small and rounded. Chester looked at him critically, but he had not as yet raised his eyes to his uncle's face. When he did, Bushrod's eyes held him: they were the bluest and the kindliest eyes he had ever seen. Bushrod began to laugh and rub his hands together, and his eyes narrowed to bands of light as brilliant and as warm as blue flowers. His teeth glistened, white and beautiful against his tanned skin. He had jumped out of the buggy and walked over to Mitty and the boy. Without embarrassment, without self-consciousness, as if he lived in this house, he sat down on the steps and put his arm around Chester. "How old are you?" he asked.

"I'm eight." Suddenly a feeling of warmth flowed through him. "I'm eight years old going on nine."

Bushrod held him at arm's length, while Chester stood patiently under the scrutiny, a little flattered to be the center of this group, and yet not knowing exactly what to do.

"He looks a little like Ellie around the eyes," said Bushrod reflectively.

"He do look some like Ellie," agreed Mitty contentedly; "but I always say he favors you the most. There's something about Chester at times that makes me think of you when you was a little boy."

Bushrod examined the boy again, his blue eyes narrowed, his lips pursed out. "Well, I guess you're right. I guess you're right at that, Mitty."

Presently Mitty disappeared into the house and Chester and his uncle sat alone on the porch. Chester had got up, automatically, to follow her, but Mitty told him that he must stay and talk to his uncle. This was not difficult for Bushrod talked on and on in his friendly way. He asked the boy many questions about the farm and Chester answered as well as he could. Inside Mitty could be heard moving about and setting the table, and after an interval she came upon the porch again. "Come in, Mr. Bushrod, you and Chester, too, and see what I done fixed."

Bush removed his hat and his coat and washed himself in the kitchen. He came out refreshed, rubbing his hands briskly.

"Where is your father? Where's Bob gone to?"

"I don't know."

"He round somewhere," said Mitty casually; "but don't you all wait for him. You go on and eat it while it's hot." Bush seated himself across the table from Chester and Mitty served them, keeping up a loud flow of conversation regarding the old times. When the meal was finished, Chester and his uncle came again and sat upon the porch. Bushrod kept glancing at his watch.

"It looks like Robert isn't coming."

"He must have went off somewhere; I don't know what happened to him," said Mitty apologetically. "I don't know where he done gone to."

"Well," said Bushrod, "I guess Chester and I had better be moving along, if we want to get to Athlestan in time to catch our train." He got up from his chair and walked to the buggy, Mitty and Chester behind him. They reached the gate and looked to the north, and there, before their eyes, was Robert Hurry plowing steadily.

Chester felt ashamed before his uncle. His face twisted up and he turned his head away. "He didn't even come up to tell me good-by," he thought.

Almost immediately, Mitty was kissing him. "Have a nice time, sugarpie, but come back soon."

Bushrod was seated in the buggy, the reins in his hands, and Mitty lifted Chester up beside him. She stood by the wheel, her black head held high, making her voice casual.

"Remember to be a good boy, Chester, and always mind what your mamma's people tell you."

Bushrod took up the buggy whip and flicked the roan mare and they began to move off down the sandy road. Chester put his knees on the buggy seat and waved to Mitty. He felt frightened and lost all of a sudden. "Good-by! Good-by!" he called, in an anguished voice.

Through the isinglass slit in the back of the buggy he saw Mitty come running after them for a little way. Then, as if realizing that she must let him go, she sat down by the side of the road and threw her apron over her face. She rocked her body from side to side, making no sound, while above her head, high up against the blue sky, a circle of buzzards, toylike, shrunken with distance, wheeled and glided. Chester watched her diminishing figure as long as he could, but presently they forked off at Talcott's lane and the hedge hid her from view.

"When I was your age," said Bushrod, "I liked to go swimming in the branch. I bet you like to go swimming too."

14

THE Tarletons, although they also farmed on a small scale, were known in Pearl County chiefly as merchants. Their store was situated at the point where the county road, which ran straight to Reedyville, crossed the road that led to Morgan Center. Back of the store was the yellow, two-story frame house where the family lived. It was set in a thicket of scrub oaks and wild plum trees which had been cut back so that the view of the Reedyville highway might not be obscured. There was a small farm behind the house, but the family raised only enough corn for their stock and only enough vegetables for their own consumption. It was from the store, situated so advantageously at the crossroads, that they derived their living. The store had been opened by Frank Tarleton as a young man, but in later years he had turned it over to his son, Bushrod, since he was the only one of the boys who remained at home. For his part, Frank looked after the farm and puttered about at his ease.

When Chester arrived with his uncle that April afternoon, he found the rest of the family assembled, waiting for him. Bushrod swung him down from the buggy and stood holding his hand. "Well, here we are at last. I hope you like the place, Chester."

Miss Sarah Tarleton came up and kissed him vigorously. She turned him around, inspecting him, her wide, protuberant eyes serious behind their spectacles. "He certainly resembles Ellie. There's no doubt about that."

She was a small, calm woman, inclined to be stout. Her face

was broad and serious, her nose somewhat flat at its base. She moved slowly, ponderously, her pale eyes forever earnest and kindly behind the thick lenses which she wore. Before she had come to live with her brother, she had taught school at Morgan Center and she still retained much of her professional manner.

"This is your grandfather," said Bushrod.

"Howdy, Chester; howdy, son?" said Frank. "We want you to know we all welcome you to our home."

But Sarah was turning the boy around again, inspecting him from all angles. She made sympathetic, surprised noises with her tongue. "So pale and thin!" she remarked in a distressed voice. "So peaked!" She brushed back her graying hair. "What have they been doing to you, anyway?"

"You'll like it here when you get used to it," continued Bushrod. "You'll be a little homesick at first, but that'll wear off."

Sarah got up from her knees and shook her head angrily. "We haven't any reason to expect anything from That Man, but I did think Mitty would take better care of you than she has."

"Now, Sally," said Frank in his mild, nasal voice. "Don't turn the boy against his own flesh and blood."

Sarah puckered up her lips and closed her eyes for a moment, considering deeply. She nodded her head, as if realizing the injustice of such a thing. "I apologize. I apologize for my thoughtless words."

Chester said: "I've been sick; Mitty said I almost died."

Bushrod laughed his gay laugh, his blue eyes crinkled up, his white teeth glistening. "Well, what of it? Everybody gets sick at one time or another. We'll fatten you up in no time at all."

Frank Tarleton said: "We better go on indoors and give Chester a chance to get settled down." He spat, squinted up at the sun and began to twist his drooping, somewhat soiled mustache.

When he was settled in his room and had bathed and changed his clothes, Chester came on the porch and sat beside his grandfather. Bushrod had gone to the store and Sarah was preparing supper. To the left of the house fig trees were growing, and behind them the wild plum thicket, now in full bloom, was an island of beaten, unsoiled foam. The trees were like white clouds which had fallen to earth, resting lightly upon the land; they filled the air with a sweet, sharp perfume.

Frank Tarleton sat smoking silently, a little embarrassed in the presence of his grandson, not quite knowing what to say. He was tall and spare, stooped a little, crippled a little with rheumatism, but still vigorous. His neck was wasted and spotted with brown, his long, grayish mustache was soiled with tobacco. There was a faint odor about him of leather and dry, decaying wood. He wore, generally, a high starched collar, but no necktie.

It was Chester who spoke first. "Where is Bessie? Mitty said that I had an Aunt Bessie, too."

"Bessie's in school. She's living with her sister in Reedyville and going to high school."

"Oh!"

"She'll be back home some time next month. She comes home for the summer vacation." Frank looked above the plum thicket toward the road. "I haven't been able to do much for my children, but I've given them all a good education, if they'd take it. Education is a wonderful thing to have, son."

"Yes, sir," agreed Chester. He was not really listening to his grandfather. His eyes were on the back of the store and he was thinking of Bushrod, wondering if it would be polite if he got up and joined his uncle. But Frank, now that he was started on his favorite subject, talked on and on. Gradually the sun sank and it began to grow dark. Across the road, and beyond the fields, the sky was luminous and deeply pink, as if a light shone behind it, coloring it with the fire in opals. A hush settled over the place. The flowering plums were not white now; they had taken on a faint lavender cast. Frank droned steadily in his thin, reedy voice and inside the house Sarah was singing hymns as she moved about. From the kitchen there came a hiss and sputtering and the comforting smell of ham frying.

After a while Sarah came onto the porch, peering into the dusk with her bulging, short-sighted eyes. She said: "I thought Bush was out here with you two. I declare, I could vow I heard him talking." She rolled down her sleeves and straightened her apron. "Run down to the road like a good boy, Chester, and tell your uncle that supper's on the table."

When they were seated, Sarah asked a blessing over the food, but Bushrod would not close his eyes or lower his head. He did not believe in religion and made no secret of the fact. This distressed Sarah a great deal, and she often upbraided him for his lack of faith, but Bushrod would put his arms about her and hug her tightly, his eyes laughing and crinkled to a thin slit of blue, and in the end Sarah would have to laugh herself. She would take off her spectacles and reset them more firmly. "Oh, I'd be afraid to say the things you do," she would answer. "I'd be afraid our Loving Father in Heaven would strike me dead."

But this would always set Bush to laughing more. He would glance up at his father and wink, and Frank would smile a little, twist his stringy mustache and reply in his mild, apologetic voice: "Don't tease your Aunt Sally, son. Always respect the opinion of others."

Bush would answer, "I'm a practical man. I don't believe in anything I can't see and touch."

But this night Bush remained silent and after a while Aunt Sarah looked up from her prayer and unfolded her napkin. She spoke first to Chester: "I opened up a jar of fig preserves. Most boys like them on hot biscuits;" and the family began to eat bountifully, in silence.

Toward the end of the meal Sarah spoke again. "I got a letter from Bessie this morning. She's crazy to met you, Chester. She

123

wanted to come over and spend Saturday and Sunday with us, but she's got to study for her examinations next month."

"Oh, well," said Frank. "She'll be home for the vacation, anyway, in a few weeks."

"Bessie is making a fine record in school," said Sarah with deep pride. "She's a born scholar."

Frank answered, his mouth full of ham and hot bread: "I aimed to give all my children the best education possible. I made up my mind to do that when I first married."

At last the meal was over and Sarah began clearing the table.

The parlor, used less frequently now, since the family was smaller, was a big room which was always shuttered, with shades always down. Bushrod walked in and lit the lamp, and Sarah came in behind him and seated herself carefully on a blue plush chair. "I'll let the dishes go until morning. A body doesn't meet a grandnephew every day, I expect!"

Frank sat down by the lamp and put on his spectacles. He took up a copy of the Reedyville paper and began to read it. Bush was on the piano stool, turning himself around idly, occasionally striking a chord.

"Don't, for heaven sake, do that, Bush!" said Aunt Sarah mildly. "It makes me dizzy just to watch you. . . . Of course if you want to *play* the piano, I have no objection to that."

She took up a wicker basket and inspected her darning. She stuck her hand into the foot of a sock, holding it close to her near-sighted eyes, looking for holes. She said: "I'd better tell you something about the Tarleton family, I expect, so you can get us all straight in your mind."

Across the room Frank was also speaking. "I see by the Reedyville *Times* that the Hodge brothers are going to put up a sawmill."

"It's about time," said Bushrod. "They've been talking about it long enough."

Aunt Sarah was not listening, she was thinking her own thoughts, collecting her data and organizing it efficiently. She spoke: "Your grandmother died when Bessie was a little girl. There was something the matter with her kidneys: they didn't function properly. It was a great loss. It was a great loss to us all."

Frank picked up the paper again and began to read: "Those interested in the progress of Pearl County will be delighted to hear that our progressive citizens, Mr. Thompson Hodge, and his brother, Mr. Russell Hodge, who have been quietly taking options on timber in this vicinity, have decided to go ahead with their project, having obtained the backing of Powerful Financial Interests in the East."

Bushrod laughed as if greatly amused, and in the silence that followed Aunt Sarah, now busy darning, could be heard once more: "The oldest of the Tarleton children is Jesse Randolph. He studied medicine and is practicing in Atlanta. He's a specialist in children's diseases. We see very little of him nowadays, but he's very happily married and doing well—"

Chester interrupted her. "Then there was a boy named Arnold who died as a baby. . . . Aunt Lillian Chapman comes in next. She lives in Reedyville and Uncle Evan is in the furniture business."

Sarah said: "Why, where in the world did you learn all that?"

"Mitty told me."

Aunt Sarah smiled complacently. "Mitty is a great help. Mitty has been a great comfort to us. I have always prided myself on my knowledge of character. I don't know how I do it, but I'm never wrong about a person, and I knew from the first that Mitty could be relied upon. Something in my heart always told me that she was gold of the purest ray serene."

Frank continued his reading and Bushrod listened, his blue eyes bright and amused.

"Ground will be broken immediately and the plant will be erected as quickly as possible. In addition to the mill, a town will be laid out and houses built for the employees."

"To be called 'Hodgevill,' I'll bet a pretty," said Bushrod laughing and winking at Chester, as if he understood all about the Hodge Brothers and their vanities.

"We're a closely knit family," continued Sarah. "We have our internal differences, but we always stick together."

Frank held the paper farther from him. Then he, too, laughed. "You're pretty nearly right at that, Bush. . . . They're calling it *Hodgetown,* although the paper goes on to say that the Hodge Brothers didn't want their names to appear, and consented only because their many friends demanded it."

Sarah looked up from her work, interested at last: "The Wrenns, the Outerbridges and the Cornells have all given options on their timber." She pursed out her lips and took a few quick stitches with her needle. "I was over at the Tallons' place a night or so ago and they were talking about the mill. Mr. Tallon was drinking a little. He said he was ready to sell out to the Hodge Brothers when they were ready to buy."

"I'm keeping *my* timber," said Bushrod. "I wouldn't sell it for any price. First thing you know, there won't be a tree left standing in the county."

"Well, people have got to have houses to live in," said Sarah. "They've got to get timber from somewhere."

"They won't get ere a stick of mine!"

"Maybe they don't want your timber, son," said Frank. "Maybe they're not figuring on buying it."

"I happen to know differently. They didn't come direct to me, but Ed Wrenn was asking me what I'd take for it, and I told him it wasn't for sale at any price."

The boy sat through this conversation, understanding little of it. He began to feel lonely and to wish he were home again. He thought of Mitty, Hattie, Jim and of another face he couldn't quite remember. He wanted, all at once, to be alone and he was glad when Aunt Sarah told him it was time for him to go to bed. She lighted a lamp and guided him upstairs. After she had turned down the covers for him, she kissed him quickly, reminded him to say his prayers, and left. Frank and Bushrod were yawning and stretching themselves when she returned to the living room. They, too, were ready to go to bed.

"Don't wait up for me," said Sarah. "I've got three whole days to catch up in my diary. I won't go to bed for an hour yet." She went over to her desk and unlocked it, took out a book and began to make entries in her minute, copy-book hand.

For a long time the boy lay in bed turning from side to side, feeling strange and out of place. Then, before he knew it, he was asleep: but almost at once he awoke in terror, his hands trembling. He lay there shivering in the dark until the door opened and his uncle came in. Bush sat on the side of the bed and spoke reassuringly, as if he understood Chester's distress. "You wouldn't believe what a big baby I was. Why, when I went away to University I was almost a grown man, but I was so homesick at first I said I was going to take the next train back to Pearl County. I didn't though, and before a week had passed I liked it fine at the University."

Chester felt comforted. He reached out and took his uncle's hand, holding it tightly in the dark. Bushrod said: "I want you to come down to the store tomorrow and help me sell goods. . . . What do you say to that?"

From the Diary of Sarah Tarleton

April 2nd, 1913. *Will wonders never cease! I no longer have the capacity for experiencing surprise! Frank got a letter today from That Man, saying that Chester had been sick for the past few weeks and asking if he could visit us during his convalescence. What has occasioned this sudden change of heart on his part? It is the first time since his marriage that he has recognized our existence. Naturally we are all delighted. I have replied for Frank saying that Bushrod would call by for the boy inasmuch as business would take him to Athlestan in a few days, an untruth, but a harmless one, for which I hope the Divine Master will forgive me.*

April 10th, 1913. *Bushrod arrived this afternoon with Chester. He is a strange, silent boy with light hair and eyes. He is pale and very thin, but that of course is because of his sickness. He looks somewhat like Bushrod did at his age, but he isn't the handsome child that Bushrod was. He looks more like my younger brother, Edward Charles (named for his grandfather on his mother's side), who died with breakbone fever at the age of fifteen. I can understand Chester's silence and inattention, because he must feel strange and out of place at first. The thing I can't understand is the peculiar habit he has of occasionally clutching at his throat with his fingers and then raising his arms in the air. He did that several times without being aware of it. He must be broken of this habit before it grows on him.*

15

DURING the days that followed Chester was homesick for Mitty, Hattie and Jim. He thought a great deal about his father's house, remembering the river and the fields. He would stand still and think: "This is Monday, and it is nine o'clock in the morning. Mitty is scouring her table or sweeping around the steps with a brushbroom. . . . Jim is cutting wood and Hattie is sorting clothes and putting them in the iron pot to boil. The coon is jumping about, chained to a post. He's so big now that he must be tied up, or he'd run off into the woods." Then a wave of hot sickness would come over him. He would stand silent in the kitchen where he was helping Aunt Sarah with the dishes, his mouth slightly opened, his eyes veiled and far away. After Sarah had spoken to him several times and had received no answer she would say, half laughingly, half in earnest:

"I declare, Chester, you don't pay the least attention to what I say. I might as well be talking to a block of wood."

Chester would come back to reality with a start and finish the dishes rapidly. After a while Aunt Sarah would add: "I apologize for my rudeness, Chester."

Then, as Chester remained silent, she would continue patiently. "What do you say now, Chester? What do you say when a person apologizes?"

"I don't know."

"You must say, 'Your apologies are accepted, madam!'" prompted Aunt Sarah.

"Yes, ma'am."

"A gentleman or a lady must always speak good English and must always be polite," she continued in her precise voice, giving each syllable its proper value, eliding nothing. . . . "Education is a great thing."

The boy would put down the dishcloth and look outside at the young cotton with its bright, polished leaves, bathed now in the light of the sun; or across the road where meadows lay covered with pink and yellow flowers, lifting upward toward the horizon like colored swells of water. He was anxious to be in the store with his Uncle Bushrod, sitting beside him, or listening to the occasional brisk city drummers with their stories of far places, which he never hoped to see. Then he would sigh, for he knew that this was impossible until his lessons with Sarah had been done.

On the day following his arrival she had asked him about his education and was shocked to find that he knew so little. "A big boy going on nine years of age!" she said, her hands raised upward, her bulging eyes bent toward him. "A big boy like that!" She had settled her glasses firmly, the puffs of flesh beneath her light, nearsighted eyes twitching at this unbelievable thing. That afternoon she had started teaching him. "You are already two years behind," she said. "We must face that fact. We must study harder and make it up."

But Chester said nothing.

"You don't want to grow up in ignorance, do you?" she asked mildly.

"No, ma'am."

"And you don't want to be in a class with six-year-old children, do you, if your father sends you to school in Athlestan next fall?"

Aunt Sarah undertook his education as a duty, not really expecting to accomplish much, but she was surprised at the way he learned. She began to regard him with new respect. To her brother she said: "That child has a good mind, believe it or not. He really has!" She said it emphatically, as if she expected her words to be challenged. She nodded her head in her professional, school-teacher manner. "He applies himself with diligence to every task that he undertakes."

She did not know, of course, that Chester studied so conscientiously because he knew that as soon as the lessons were completed he was free to go to the store and sit with his Uncle Bushrod, to listen to him talk or help him serve his customers.

At the time Chester came to live in Pearl County Bushrod was a man of about thirty. He had finished high school in Reedyville and had gone to the state university, but he had not taken his degree. He returned in the middle of his junior year. At first nobody knew his reason and he refused to discuss the matter. He talked with his father regarding his prospects and Frank told him that he would turn the store over to him, and, later on, the farm, with the understanding that Bessie, or any of the other children were to live there, too, if they so desired. Bush agreed to this gladly. When the matter was settled, a few days later, he went to Reedyville and married Ruby Bogen, who was already notorious for her love affairs and whom he had known since his high school days.

His sister, Lillian Chapman, had bitterly opposed the match and had done what she could to prevent it. She considered it her duty, as a sister, to talk to Bush. She got him alone in her parlor finally, and seated herself beside him.

"You don't understand this sort of girl. You're making a terrible mistake, Bushrod!"

"All right," said Bush cheerfully. "It's my mistake."

Lillian got up angrily and paced the floor. "I won't let you disgrace the family this way. I won't let you get tangled up in such a mess."

But Bush only smiled at her, his deep blue eyes crinkled up

and bright. "Don't get yourself all steamed up, Lilly. Keep your pants on."

"Do you realize that she's had an affair—" Then she stopped and laughed bitterly. "You could hardly call them *affairs:* that's too dignified!—She's slept with half the men in this town. . . . The clerk at the Magnolia Hotel even calls her up when a drummer wants to go out with somebody."

"I've talked to her. She's stopped all that."

"Don't you realize that she's only using you because the Vice Society is after her and are about to run her out of town? Haven't you got sense enough to know that that is the only reason she's marrying you?"

"I happen to love her," said Bush. "That's all." He got up to go.

Lillian, too, stood up, smoothing her elaborately coiffed, yellow hair, her eyes furious. "You'll regret this to your dying day. You'll wish you'd taken my advice."

"I don't think so." Bushrod paused at the door. "You'll see all the difference in the world in Ruby once she's married and settled down."

"She'll never change," said Lillian. "She's just a cheap little prostitute and always will be."

Lillian Chapman's predictions had all come true, and because they had, and because Bushrod had really known, in his heart, that they would, he disliked his older sister intensely, blaming her, in a vague way, for Ruby's derelictions. After his marriage Bushrod had brought his bride to live in the yellow house back of the store, but Ruby, used to the trivial vice of Reedyville, was not content. Almost at once she began to betray him with everybody in the county, having no sense of selection, no feeling of discrimination. Bushrod bore these things without comment, and the family did what they could to ignore them.

It was only Aunt Sarah who ever mentioned her. One night

when Ruby had walked out of the house to meet some lover who waited in a buggy at the crossroads, she had flung down her napkin and got up from the table. "How you can put up with that cheap, painted creature is beyond me, Bushrod! . . . Haven't you any pride? Don't you know that people are laughing at you behind your back?"

Frank Tarleton spoke gently: "That comes under the heading of Bushrod's business, not yours, Sally. It don't hurt you any, as I see it!"

"After all, Bushrod is my own flesh and blood. I'm only speaking for his own good."

Frank chewed for a moment, his tuft of soiled chin whiskers working gently upward and falling again. "Lots of trouble is caused that way, just the same."

Sarah sat down again, after a moment. When she was calmer, she spoke: "I apologize to Bushrod for saying those things about his wife."

"That's all right!" said Bushrod. "That's all right." He drank from his glass, his Adam's apple rising in his brown throat. "I'm a practical man, that's why I stand all this. I knew it would be this way before I married her. Lillian warned me enough about her." He continued bitterly. "I knew what she was. . . . I could get upset and shoot a man or so, I guess. Maybe I could shoot her, but what good would that do?"

Frank Tarleton sat twisting his mustache. "You're a full-grown man, son. You've got to figure it out for yourself."

"I've got to be *practical* about this thing," said Bushrod. "I want to be practical about everything."

He had never mentioned the fact, but the thing which hurt him even more than his wife's faithlessness was the knowledge that she talked about him to her lovers, or the people of the county, making fun of him. The things that she said often got back to him, but he let no one see his feelings.

133

And so things went on for a few months and then Ruby solved the problem for the Tarleton family. She did not return at all after one of her dates. Later it was found that she had gone to Birmingham with one of her old Reedyville lovers, a barber, and was living with him there.

After that the family never mentioned her to Bushrod and he never spoke of her again. It was as if she had never existed in his life at all.

From the Diary of Sarah Tarleton

May 26th, 1913. . . . *Already Chester is looking better, but he is still quiet and strange. I suppose that is just his nature. He is not a happy child. I have talked to him about the way he jerks his arms upward in the air and he has consented to let me tie his arms when he feels nervous, so he can't do it. I hope he will be benefited thereby. I have been making him some new shirts and underwear. Poor, neglected child, his wardrobe was very scanty. He never thanks me for anything that I do. He never thanks anybody or seems to appreciate anything. I don't think he is selfish. He is just without imagination. The fig trees are covered with green fruit. There will be a fine harvest next July.*

16

ONE afternoon after Chester had finished his assignment for the day and Aunt Sarah had heard his lessons, he sat on the back porch rocking idly in the hammock which Bushrod had made of barrel staves, graded carefully as to size. The air was close and sultry. No living thing moved across the meadow: no thing walked on the road. The leaves hung without motion, drooping a little in the still afternoon.

Bushrod and Frank were in the store taking an inventory and Aunt Sarah, her duties for that day done, was seated before her desk writing in her diary. As the boy sat in the hammock, propelling himself lazily with his foot, feeling drowsy and somnolent, his head nodded and fell forward and gradually the swing stopped and remained still. When he opened his eyes, he saw that black clouds had formed across the sky, close to the earth, and in a moment the slanted lances of rain fell downward, pattering sharply against the shingles, striking the red dust of the road with a soft, muffled sound. It rained heavily for a few minutes, but behind the drops the sun still shone, its light shining through the shower, turning the long, straight lines of rain to prisms which reflected all colors. Then the clouds blew away as quickly as they had come and there was only the placid dripping of eaves and the red, damp earth. In the sunlight the wet leaves glistened and sparkled and the earth seemed fresh again and newly made.

Chester got up and stood examining the countryside. Straight ahead and beyond the fields was the boundary of Bushrod's timber. There had never been an ax in this tract of virgin timber, nor had Bushrod ever permitted his trees to be boxed for turpentine.

Chester walked across the fields toward the trees, his eyes veiled and drawn inward, as if he were still asleep. When he reached the pines he walked more slowly, stopping occasionally to stare upward. It had not rained in the grove and the brown straw which covered the ground was dry and crisp against his bare feet. He dug his toes into the earth, under the straw, feeling the earth's coolness against his skin. . . .

He walked on and on through the wood, careless of direction, unconscious of his destination, until the pines began to thin a little and the light of the sun shone through, marking the carpet of straw with patterns of light. He saw before him a glade through which a creek flowed, a creek which widened at this point to a small, dark pool. It was surrounded on three sides with baytrees and shrubs, but on the side facing the boy there was a tiny beach of white sand.

He sat down at the edge of the grove and rested his back against a fallen log, looking about him. The rays of the sun slanted through the pines and lighted the glade until it swam unsteadily in a shimmering, golden mist. His eyes became heavy and he felt languid all at once.

It was dusky in the grove and the pine trees above his head made a sad, constant noise. The trees grew straight and close together, without branches or blemish. It seemed that the whole world was made of trees with only the cuplike glade to interrupt their even march. Everything had become remote and very still with that waiting quietness of cathedrals. Chester looked about him lazily, his eyes half shut. Then, in the dusk dark of the grove before him he saw three young angels, dressed in white robes, flying in and out among the trees, their spread wings fanning the air: they beat upward and downward slowly, without effort, and their whiteness was beautiful against the emerald needles of the pines.

The hair of each angel was of the same length, but the color of each was different: the hair of one was golden, the hair of the second was black, while the third had auburn hair. Then, laughing together, as if amazed at their daring, the three young angels flew into the open glade, where their wings were more free, and swam and dived in the golden light, rolling and turning about, chattering sweetly together as young girls will. They would fall apart, their arms waving up and down, their wings beating; then they would loop backward in an exact pattern and come together, their three heads touching, their arms folded to wide triangles, their backs arched a little, their white feet almost level with their heads. For a long time they played and laughed in the clear air, not knowing that they were watched, or not caring. Then, when they were a little tired, they flew to the top of a tall tree and sat side by side on the highest limb, half hid amongst the deep green of the needles. Their heads and their pure, young breasts touched. They circled each other with their arms. Their wings folded backward. They sang a song together.

Under the drowsiness of the song's beauty, Chester closed his eyes. His head nodded a little, but he did not go to sleep. The music became fainter and fainter and then ceased so gradually that no man could say when it ended. Chester opened his eyes, surprised at this absence of sound, but the angels were gone. There was only a dim echo of their song in the air and the last faint rustle of upspringing wings. Above the still, black pool were three dragon flies, rising and falling and floating suspended over the water.

Chester felt sad and alone because the angels had flown away and left him. He thought of Mitty, Hattie and Jim and wished he were back with them, but at once the idea of returning fright-

ened him, and he began to tremble. He slipped down to the
earth and pressed his face into the rough, pungent straw. He
picked up a fallen pine cone, brown and hard, and began pulling off its petals in the way Hattie did when she used to make
him dolls as a young boy.

Suddenly he sat upright, startled a little, and threw the pine
burr away. He turned his head, and there, leaning against a tree,
was a man he had never seen before. He studied the man's face
for a moment. At once he was reassured.

"Howdy do," he said politely. "This is my Uncle Bushrod's
land."

"What in the world are you crying about?" asked the stranger.

His voice was the merest thread of a voice. It was so faint, so
whispered, that Chester marveled, even at that moment, how it
carried across the space that separated them. It was hardly a
sound at all: it was less than the noise that the pines made, less
than the wash of the pool against its bank, but it came clear and
distinct, each word separate.

Chester said: "I'm lonely. I'm not used to this place."

The whisperer laughed, a soft, tender laugh.

"Why, everybody in the world is lonely. . . . Didn't you know
that?"

The boy looked down at his hands, turning this thought over
in his mind. "No, I didn't know that. . . . I just thought I was."
He looked at the whisperer shyly. The man seemed to have no
age, but there were tiny, thread-like wrinkles on his forehead
and about his lips. His eyes melted with light. They were brown
and very kind. He was dressed in a faded jumper coat and a pair
of brown cotton trousers, also faded unevenly in patches.

The whisperer walked toward the boy, seating himself beside
him on the log. Only a thin fringe of trees separated them from
the sun-drenched glade and the pool. Above the pool there grew
a tree loaded with berries so round and so polished that they

seemed fashioned of red glass. When the wind stirred, as it did at this moment, some of the berries dropped from the tree and fell into the water with a faint sound; they floated there on the water for a while, crimson and hard on the black water, until a faint current caught them and they moved away. . . .

"So you're lonely!" said the whisperer. "So that's what's the matter!"

"Yes, sir."

The whisperer thought a moment, his eyes very serious. "Perhaps you'd like me to tell you a story about a man who was lonelier than you?"

"Is it about a king or a young princess?"

The whisperer rubbed his cheek, deep in thought, and pursed his lips doubtfully. "I suppose it could be just as easily," he said as if not quite decided. He sat for a moment looking straight ahead. "All right, I'll tell you a story about a lonely king:"

Once upon a time there was a king who ruled over a great land. He was beautiful and just and good and under him his people were content. He wanted everyone to be happy, to enjoy each moment of life, and for that reason he had built throughout his kingdom palaces and circuses for his subjects' pleasure. About himself, for his delight, he gathered the most beautiful women of the land, and the wisest and most learned men were his companions. For this young king, although he did not know it at first, was afraid of loneliness and sought by every plan to defeat it.

And so for a while he lived, if not happily at least without sorrow and at peace listening to his singers and his musicians; learning wisdom from his prophets and wise men; sure of the unending caresses of his concubines, of the rich tenderness of his lovely queen.

But after a few years the young king wearied of all pleasure.

A feeling of melancholy settled over him. There was something else that he wanted beyond all the things that he had, but he could not name this thing nor could he even express his wish to another. For many days he sat in a darkened chamber thinking and during this time the pleasure palaces were closed, music was stilled in the kingdom, dancing was stopped. At last the young king came to a decision:

"I will send for my queen and talk to her, telling her of this unrest that lies inside me. She loves me and she will understand: her love will make her wise."

And so the queen came in and sat by her lord, holding his hand in her own. He began to talk to her, and the queen listened, but she could give him nothing except her love, and the young king saw that she was powerless to comprehend the longings in his heart.

When the queen had gone away the king got up and went to the window, looking out at the darkened pleasure palaces and the deserted pavilions, seeing his people walking about slowly, dressed in somber colors. "My queen, whom I love, and who loves me, with whom I have slept and whose body I have seen so intimately, is really a stranger to me. How can I know what thought is back of her smiling face when she holds my head in the crook of her arm? I know not the first thing about her. She is a complete stranger. . . ."

In his despair he sent for his chancellors and his prophets, one by one, but they had only dry wisdom for him. They nodded their heads and proposed profound spells and incantation, but the king saw through their impotence. Not one of them had understood the things he was trying to say. He dismissed them wearily and went back to his chambers. "During my entire life I have been surrounded by people: at all hours of the day and night there are people with me, or near me, awaiting my call, and yet I am completely alone. I have always been alone." When he realized this he lay upon a royal sofa and pressed his face into the down pillows, his heart dark and inconsolable. "The gods have cursed me above all men," he cried; "I am the most miserable of all creatures."

At last there was only one wise man in his kingdom to whom the young king had not talked: a recluse who lived alone at the top of a steep mountain and who dressed in rough goat skins. This man was revered throughout the land for his learning and his holiness and it was to him that the young king, dressed in sackcloth and walking on foot, made a pilgrimage.

The old hermit received the king in his cave. They sat upon the floor of dry, beaten earth, littered with the droppings of goats. The king spoke in surprise: "Why is it, reverend and wise man, that you prefer this cold, dirty cave, when you might have, if you wished it, the finest rooms in my palace? Why do you wear rags, when you could as easily go about in silks of the finest purple? Why are your arms and ears bare of adornment when they might be covered with gold and precious stones?"

For a moment the holy man did not speak, gazing half humorously at the petulant face of the young, disconsolate king. Then he half closed his eyes and smiled shrewdly. "I will tell you," he said. "I will tell you why I prefer this damp cave and then you will understand." He began to talk earnestly and the king listened to the hermit's words as others had listened to him. A puzzled look came into the king's face. He shook his head and raised his hands helplessly. "But I don't understand," he said at last; "I don't understand you at all. . . ." Then, for the first time in many weeks, the young king began to laugh. He rose from the littered floor and spoke to the hermit who was so wise. "I understand, now," he said; "I understand what you are trying to tell me. Loneliness is the natural lot of man: he can never share himself with another, although that is the thing he wants most to do."

The hermit answered: "Every man must walk alone. It is the bitter and the ultimate knowledge."

Quickly the young king went out of the cave and ran down the side of the mountain to the place where his retinue awaited him.

"I am restored to health," he said; "for a man is a fool if he repines over what cannot be helped. Let us dance and sing while we may. Let us pretend again that we love each other."

The whisperer stopped speaking and looked at the boy's puzzled face, at his wide eyes and the lock of pale hair falling across his forehead.

"Did you like the story?"

Chester shook his head.

The sun had almost set. It was getting darker amongst the trees, and the glade before them was washed now in the last, heavy light of the sun. The rays gilded the leaves on the shrubs and lay quivering in a red path across the black, silent pool.

The boy got up, knowing that he must hurry home for his supper. "I don't know what the story is about," he said apologetically. "I don't understand it."

The whisperer answered: "You will some day, you may be sure of that."

When Chester had walked a little way he turned. The whisperer was still seated on the log, breaking up twigs, tossing them into the air and catching them again before they fell.

17

AUNT SARAH was making split biscuits for supper, in honor of Bessie's arrival. She said, in a provoked voice: "What has become of that girl?" She went to the porch and called again. "Bess-e-e-e!" But there was no answer.

"I don't know what has got into Bessie. She shouldn't go off without saying anything, just at supper time."

"Oh, leave her alone, Aunt Sarah," said Bushrod mildly. "She'll show up."

Frank Tarleton said: "She's probably gone over to the Tallons' on the chance of running into Brad."

"I don't approve," said Sarah. "I want it understood that I don't approve."

"Well," said Bush, "she's going to see him whether you approve or not. You've got to be practical about this thing."

When supper was being placed on the table Bessie appeared and seated herself demurely. She was the youngest of the Tarletons, a gaunt, rather tall girl verging on womanhood.

"This is Chester," said Bushrod. "This is your nephew."

Frank laughed a little: "It seems funny for Bessie to have a nephew that big, doesn't it?"

"Let me alone," said Bessie; but she got up and shook hands with the boy gravely: "We trust your stay with us will be very pleasant."

Frank laughed again: "Well said, daughter," he remarked genially. "Well said!"

"Let me alone!" said Bessie.

Frank sighed and spoke to the table: "I don't know what's come over Bessie lately. She acts like we all hate the sight of her."

"All girls are high-strung and nervous at sixteen," remarked Sarah, nodding her head. "It's the most difficult period of their lives."

"Will you kindly leave me out of the conversation?" asked Bessie. "Can't you think of something else to talk about?"

She had grown up so rapidly that her arms and her legs seemed too long for her body. Her face was thin and skeletal, ending in a tiny, pointed chin, and her eyes seemed enormous in their sockets.

"Now, Bessie," said Bushrod, winking at her. "Don't go a-treatin' your own folks so sorry!"

"Why, Bushrod!" said Sarah in surprise. "From your speech nobody would imagine that you were a university man."

Bessie began to giggle nervously. "Bushrod can put on airs just so long and no longer. He can't keep it up."

She became gay all of a sudden. "If you want to know where I was this afternoon, I'll tell you. I walked over to see Mrs. Tallon. She's showing me how to do Mexican drawnwork. . . ." She turned to Chester and rolled her eyes, shrugging her shoulders in humorous helplessness.

"Nobody asked you where you'd been, daughter," said Frank quietly. "I haven't been able to do as much for my children as some men, but I haven't thwarted them in any way."

Bessie got up quickly and kissed her father, her arms tight about his neck. "Nobody can say anything mean about you when I'm around. Just let them try it, that's all!"

"For heaven sakes, Bessie," said Sally humorously. "Who has said anything about your father, I'd like to know."

Bushrod looked up, his eyes too innocent. "How was Bradford? I haven't seen that boy since the Sunday he drove by with Milly Cornells. They surely made a good-looking couple."

"Now, Bushrod," said Sarah. "Don't tease your little sister. She's only a child!"

"I'm seventeen years old!" said Bessie indignantly. "I'm not a child!"

"*Sixteen*, dear," remarked Aunt Sally patiently. "You won't be seventeen until August."

"I don't see any difference," said Bessie. "I can't see what difference that makes."

"It's time enough to think of boys after you have finished high school," continued Sarah. "There's plenty of time for those things later on."

Bessie jumped up: "Oh, come on, let's clean the table!"

"Don't bother," said Aunt Sarah. "I'll clean the table and wash the dishes. You go into the parlor and entertain the gentlemen. I'll be in later."

"All right," continued Bessie. "But don't say I didn't offer to help."

When they were all seated, Frank said: "Sing 'The Last Rose of Summer,' Bessie. I've been wanting to hear that again ever since you left." And since Bessie happened, at that moment, to be in a gracious mood, she consented. Bushrod got up, went to the piano and began an elaborate accompaniment with many trills. When he had finished, Bessie raised her chin and began to sing.

Her voice was not powerful, nor was it unusual in any way, but there was a fresh sweetness in it which was pleasing. She sang the song with much feeling, as if she, and she alone, could understand the melancholy dissolution of roses. She liked only sad songs in which lovers died, or were parted by cruel parents.

For the next few days Bessie ignored Chester, and then, suddenly, she became very affectionate toward him. She took him under her wing, as her special charge, taking him to see the various people who lived in the county. She was affectionate and gruff by turns, her attitude toward him depending upon the mood she was in.

One day they went to watch the workmen who were now busy building Hodgetown. They halted at Wrenn's creek which was being widened and dammed for a log-pond. Before them the carpenters were working like ants, as if they must get their task done as quickly as possible.

Chester, who had been silent, spoke suddenly: "What are you going to be when you get out of school?"

This day Bessie was in one of her genial moods: "I'm going to be a great opera singer! I'm going to tour the world and have royalty at my feet!"

"You can't sing good enough for that, can you?"

Bessie laughed indulgently. "Why, of course I can. Last winter I sang in the Methodist Choir and everybody said I had the sweetest natural soprano voice in town." She looked up, a satisfied smile on her lips. "Lillian is going to let me take lessons from a singing teacher after I'm seventeen. . . . You'll see. You'll see how famous I become!"

She sat idly poking about in the leaves with a stick she had picked up. "I'm taking French in school, but of course I've got to learn Italian and German, too, if I'm to be a singer. Maybe I'll have to learn Spanish, I don't know; but I will if I have to, never you fear." She added angrily: "If you go blabbing what I've told you about being a singer to pappa or Aunt Sarah, I'll, I'll . . ."

"I won't tell anybody."

He sat there quietly, his light, wide eyes remote and far away, staring at the frame houses that were rising in rows back of the mill, but not seeing them; listening to the shouts of the workmen and the muffled whine of the saws, but hearing no thing

147

except something far down and dim within him. He frowned and drew his lips tight, but he could not quite recall the thing he wanted. He could not entirely see it or clearly hear it.

"I can speak French, too."

Bessie laughed derisively. "Oh, you can, can you! Why, you haven't even been to school."

Chester sat silent, wondering if he had spoken the truth or if it were something that he had made up. Then, like a parrot, he began to say the sentences which Baptiste had taught him.

Bessie threw away the stick. "Why, where in the world did you learn that, Chester?"

He frowned and shook his head: "I don't know. Maybe I didn't learn it at all: Maybe I just *knew* it, like American!"

"Don't be silly! You *had* to learn it somewhere."

As they talked, Bessie kept looking over the boy's head, or glancing to right and left, as if she expected someone. When she heard a crunching on the pine straw behind her she suddenly became very animated and bright. She laughed gayly, for no reason at all, and Chester stared at her, as if she had lost her wits. She took the boy in her arms and began to stroke his hair. "Oh, you poor, motherless child. You poor little thing."

"Let me alone," said Chester, struggling out of her grasp. He knew that the exhibition of affection was for the benefit of the young man who stood behind them.

"Why, Brad!" said Bessie in wide-eyed surprise. "Why, Brad! What are you doing here?"

"Well, here I am. I don't suppose you'll mind if I sit down a spell."

"I don't own these woods, I'm sure," said Bessie. She raised her eyes archly. "You better ask the Hodge Brothers."

"I don't reckon they care much," said Brad. "I seen you all sitting here from across the creek. So when twelve o'clock came, I figured I'd run over and eat my dinner with you. Mamma put up plenty for me and I figured you might be hungry and eat some with me."

"That's very nice of you. But we brought lunch, too."

"All right, then," said Brad. "Let's all eat together."

Bessie thought a moment, as if debating the propriety of such a thing. "Very well," she said at last; "but Chester can witness that this wasn't any of my planning."

Bessie opened the two boxes and spread the cloth she had brought, laying the food upon it. As she worked, Brad picked up the boy and swung him in a wide circle.

"Well, how do you like it in Pearl County? How do you like living with your grandpa?"

"I like it all right."

"Brad! Brad!" said Bessie sharply. "Put Chester down. He's not strong. He's been sick."

"Oh, shucks! I'm not going to hurt him any!"

Brad Tallon, at twenty, was a powerfully built fellow with a thick neck and big, red hands. His face was broad, stupid and good-natured, and when he was amused he laughed and slapped his legs. He sat down and began eating rapidly, cramming food into his mouth in great chunks, talking all the time. Crumbs of bread dropped from the corners of his lips, but Brad picked them up and stuck them into his mouth again. There was a slight space between his two front teeth which somehow gave him a friendly expression.

Chester sat opposite him, a little shocked at such table manners, remembering all the things that Mitty had taught him; but Bessie, usually so sensitive and so delicate in such matters, watched Brad with adoring eyes, giggling constantly at his vulgar, vigorous humor.

When the meal was finished, Brad lay back against a tree and lit a cigarette. He had become silent and self-conscious all of a sudden. Bessie was busy putting back the dishes she had brought, and he kept looking from her to Chester.

"Why don't you run down to the branch and catch us some crawfish, sonny?"

Chester got up. "You come show me the way. You come show me how to catch them."

But Brad winked slyly. "They won't come out if I'm there. You won't catch ere a one with me there. Crawfish naturally hate the sight of me."

Chester turned to his aunt: "Can I go, Bessie? Can I go by myself?"

"This isn't any of my planning," said Bessie in triumph. "I haven't got anything to do with this at all."

Then Chester got up and ran toward the shallow stream, but, although he watched patiently for a long time, he could find no crayfish to catch.

Bessie continued to see Brad Tallon at every opportunity. There was no reason why she should not do so openly, but she preferred making a great mystery of the matter. Each night in her room, with her door carefully bolted against intrusion, although there was no one who would have cared to intrude, the family all being asleep, she wrote him a letter. When she had had her breakfast, she slipped away into the woods and hid those missives in a hollow stump. There was generally a letter for Bessie which Brad had left there on his way to work. Bessie would read these letters eagerly, giggling with excitement, glancing over her shoulder at Chester who had been posted as a sentinel. When she had learned by heart every word of it, she would tuck the letter in her flat, bony bosom, against her growing breasts. She would carry the letter about with her all day, a far away look in her eyes, a faint smile about her lips, composing the answer that she was to write that night.

And so the summer passed. Chester spent his mornings study-ing with Sarah, or with Bessie. In the afternoon he was in-variably with Bushrod, in the store. They rarely spoke to each other, but speech was not necessary. The boy was content merely to sit on the steps and watch the road, knowing that Bushrod was near by, or to listen to him selling something to one of his customers or exchanging local gossip.

But most of all he enjoyed the time after supper, the hour or two which preceded bedtime. They would all come into the parlor except Aunt Sarah who was busy with her dishes. Later she, too, would come in, her distorted eyes friendly behind the thick lenses, her broad face a little red from the heat of the dishwater. There was, generally, at such times, a faint smell of lye soap about her and a still fainter smell of hot biscuits and syrup. Frank would sit in his regular chair and read the paper and Aunt Sarah would sew or glance through some book cal-culated to improve her mind. Occasionally Bushrod would play the piano and Bessie, if she were in the proper mood, would sing.

One night Frank said to his daughter: "Sing 'Believe Me If All Those Endearing Young Charms;' I haven't heard that song in the Lord knows when."

Immediately Bushrod went to the piano, struck a chord and began a high-flown, elaborate accompaniment. Bessie adjusted her dress, raised her flat chest and began the song in her high, sweet voice, her head lowered and bent forward a little in the manner of opera singers whose photographs she had seen. When she had finished Frank said gravely: "I don't know ere a man in the world with such remarkable children. I'm proud of them all."

"They've all turned out well," said Sarah. "Jesse is doing splendidly in his practice and so is Thomas. . . . Lillian is certainly one of the intellectual leaders in Reedyville. There's no doubt about that, say what you will."

"Don't forget me!" said Bushrod laughingly, his eyes brilliant and blue between their narrowed lids. "Don't forget the leading merchant of Pearl County."

"Now, Bush!" said Sarah. "I wish you wouldn't make fun of everything I say."

Then a moment later, she too made a request: "Sing 'Hark, Hark, the Lark at Heaven's Gate Sings.' . . . That was dear mother's favorite song." And so Bessie would sing for her family or for the neighbors who often came to call. Sometimes Bushrod, after much coaxing, could be induced to recite scenes from classic dramas or poetry he had memorized.

He would stand quietly, his eyes closed, his voice low and unobtrusive.

> *"Why didst thou promise such a beauteous day*
> *And make me travel forth without my cloak,*
> *To let base clouds o'ertake me in my way,*
> *Hiding thy bravery in their rotten smoke?*
> *'Tis not enough that through the cloud thou break,*
> *To dry the rain on my storm-beaten face,*
> *For no man well of such a man can speak*
> *That heals the wound and cures not the disgrace:*
> *Nor can thy shame give physic to my grief;*
> *Though thou repent, yet I have still the loss:*
> *The offender's sorrow lends but weak relief*
> *To him that bears the strong offence's cross.*
> *Ah! but those tears are pearls which thy love sheds,*
> *And they are rich and ransom all ill deeds."*

Professor Drewery, who was greatly admired by Sarah for his learning and who called often, would speak with admiration:

"Your knowledge of Shakespeare is unusual, Bushrod. How do you find time to learn all those things?"

And Bushrod, a little self-conscious, would answer: "There's not much to do in the store in the mornings."

Frank said: "Bush would have made a fine scholar. It's too bad he wouldn't finish college. We hoped to make an English professor out of him."

"I learned all I wanted to know," said Bush. "I learned that art alone endures."

Then he looked about quickly, as if he had somehow betrayed himself.

"Education is the greatest thing in the world," said Frank. "Education is everything."

Sarah sighed gently, her bosom heaving upward: "I must take issue with that, for honor is finer. Honor is greater than everything else combined." At once there would begin an involved discussion between Professor Drewery and Aunt Sarah as to the value of abstract virtues. During these periods Chester would often go to sleep and Bushrod would take him upstairs and see that he went to bed.

And so the summer passed pleasantly. Bessie was sewing on new school dresses which she would wear in Reedyville. She had become very particular about her appearance and Aunt Sarah was often humorously provoked. "I declare, Bessie," she would say; "a person would think that you were about to be presented at the Court of St. James! . . . Who in the name of heaven is going to notice, or care if they do notice, whether a schoolgirl's dress is an inch too full or not?"

But Bessie would not give in, and in the end Aunt Sarah would have to rip out her work and do it over.

As these preparations for Bessie's departure continued, Chester became even quieter than he had been at first. He took long walks by himself and sat for hours in the place where the whisperer was. He avoided the family as much as he could. He did not even go into the store to be with Bushrod any more. Then a minor despair came over him, but there was no one he could talk to because there was nothing he could put into words. He knew only that the prospect of returning home frightened him in some manner that he could not understand. There was something that he could not bring into consciousness, and there was only this feeling that unseen, uncontrollable things would destroy him. Aunt Sarah discussed with her brother and Bushrod the change which had come over the boy, as the time drew near for him to return.

"I suppose he's just tired of us and wants to get home again."

"I don't know," said Bushrod doubtfully.

But Aunt Sarah stopped him. "I've been with children all my life, and I pride myself on the fact that I understand them thoroughly. The mistake people make is to believe that children think in the same manner as grown-ups. To understand children we must put ourselves in their places, make our minds simple, and—"

"All right, Aunt Sarah. I'm not going to argue with a graduate of a normal school."

And so Sarah mentioned casually, at breakfast the next morning, that she must be putting Chester's things in order again for his return. The boy made no answer, but a look of fear came over his face. He raised his hands upward and clutched at the air, his face white and strained.

"Why, what in the world, Chester!" asked Sarah in alarm. "What has come over you?"

Bushrod spoke quietly. "Are you sick, Chester? Aren't you feeling well?"

Chester shook his head. He pushed back his cup and lowered his face.

Bessie got up angrily. "You leave Chester alone! Why do you

keep bothering him?—Leave him alone! You're enough to drive *anybody* distracted."

Chester spoke to his uncle: "Don't let them send me back, Uncle Bush! Don't let them send me back!"

Frank Tarleton said: "Nobody's going to send you back if you don't want to go."

Later the boy went to the store to sit with Bushrod. After a short silence Bushrod asked: "Isn't your father good to you?"

"I don't know."

"Does he beat you, or anything like that?"

"No," said Chester.

"But there must be some reason. There must be some reason why you don't want to go back."

Chester remained silent, a puzzled look on his face. "I just don't want to go, that's all."

In the afternoon, while Bessie was hearing his lesson, the family had a long talk.

Bushrod said: "That boy has been badly treated just as sure as you're born. Something has happened to him, to scare him that way."

"Chester is a strange boy," said Aunt Sarah. "He's like That Man in many ways."

"Why don't you have a talk with him, Sally?" asked Frank. "Why don't you ask him what's troubling him?"

But Bushrod interrupted: "You wouldn't get it out of him. I've already tried, and so has Bessie."

"That's true," said Sarah thoughtfully.

"I'm not going to send him back there if he don't want to go," said Frank.

Sarah nodded her head vigorously. "That's exactly what I've been thinking."

And so the family debated for a long time. At first it was decided that Frank should write a letter to Robert Hurry and ask

155

if the boy could remain with them for the winter and go to school, but that plan was abandoned. "You can't explain things in a letter," protested Sarah. "The only way to do it is to see That Man face to face and explain things to him. I'll go myself and get it over with. I'll tell him the child is unhappy and doesn't want to come home. . . . And on the other hand we'll be delighted to keep him with us for the winter."

Bushrod rubbed his chin thoughtfully. "I wouldn't do that, Aunt Sarah. That'll only turn him against the plan. I'd tell him that Chester has made friends of his own age and wants to go to school. Tell him that he can come back any time that Robert writes."

"Well, possibly that would be better," said Sarah thoughtfully.

And so a few days later she made the trip.

She returned almost immediately. Her broad face was flushed angrily, her gray, nearsighted eyes furious. She went into another conference with Bushrod and Frank Tarleton. They sat in the parlor, with the door locked, but Bessie and Chester, listening outside, could occasionally hear Sarah's voice when her anger got the better of her, and she raised it a little.

"There can never be any *question* of him going back there again!" said Sarah. "Never! Never!" Her voice raised a little. "That Man has forfeited any claim that he might have on the child." There was silence; then she spoke again, her voice softer now, and a little more subdued: "There was no pretense, no effort to spare other people's feelings."

"What are they talking about?"

"Hush!" said Bessie.

"I didn't expect any better from That Man," said Sarah in a shocked voice, "but I thought Mitty would have more self-respect."

Bushrod's voice was raised angrily. "I'll fight him through

every court in this country before I'll let him have Chester again! By God, I'll see him in hell first!"

"There's no sense in swearing, son. There's no sense in swearing." Frank sat, twisting his mustache, his face distressed, not knowing quite what to do.

That night Bushrod told the boy that he was to remain with them, for the time being, at any rate. Professor Drewery was opening his school the next week, and it was arranged that Chester should go.

Chester was not quite sure what had happened, but he felt, somehow, that Bushrod, and Bushrod alone, had saved him from something terrible and menacing. His affection for his uncle increased, and for a time he dogged his steps, never letting him out of his sight. He began to copy Bush's walk and manner of speaking until Sarah would say laughingly: "I declare, Chester is getting so he even *looks like* Bush."

From the Diary of Sarah Tarleton

August 28, 1913. *This is a painful duty. I hardly know how to record the happenings of the last few days. I do not like to speak or think evilly of my fellow creatures, but That Man is beyond the pale. Yesterday I arrived in Athlestan on the local and hired a rig from the livery stable and was driven out to the Hurry place. It was early in the morning and no one was up. I went into the kitchen and made myself a pot of coffee as I didn't want to disturb anybody. At six o'clock I decided to wake Mitty. I tiptoed upstairs, not knowing the house, and stood wondering which door was hers. Then I heard an alarm clock go off in the room right in front of me and I heard Mitty speaking to somebody. As God is my witness, I thought no evil, even then. Then as I was just on the point of calling out to her I heard the voice of That Man. My blood froze in my veins. I threw the door open and there confronting my eyes was That Man and Mitty lying in bed together. She was wearing one of the beautiful nightgowns which I had made for my niece's trousseau so many years ago. That is the thing that hurt me most. I do not remember what I said, but may God forgive me for it. Then I walked downstairs with Mitty behind me crying and trying to explain that what she had done was not her fault. I went out of that house and walked all the way back to Athlestan. Today I reached home. Frank has written a letter to That Man stating that we will not give up Chester, of whom we are all so fond. Poor child! Poor child! We understand so much about him now which puzzled us before. If That Man tries to go to law, we will fight him* to the last ditch. *Wearing my dead niece's lace nightgown which I made with my own fingers! Oh, this thing is too unbelievable!*

September 2, 1913. *Old Mr. John Foster, who has been making his home for the past ten years with his daughter, Mrs. Lawrence Outerbridge, sustained a bad fall this morning. His right arm and his shoulder blade are broken, but every hope is held out for his recovery. Got Bessie off to school today. Lord, but that child is a trial. Everything must be just so, but she is sweet and thoughtful when she isn't in one of her moods. I had to laugh at Brad Tallon. He came over to see Bushrod, or so he said, and pretended not to know that Bessie was going to Reedyville. When Bush told him, he offered to drive her over, since Bush was so busy. Very sweet and thoughtful. I have no objection to Brad, except that he drinks and is a little wild. But then any man worth his salt sows his wild oats some time or another.*

18

A MILE and a half from the store was the school presided over by Professor Drewery. He was a thin, dried-up old bachelor with a fan of tiny purple veins radiating like a lavender mist across his cheeks. He stood upright, his small, cup-like belly thrust forward, his back stiff and unbending. He did not have many pupils, not more than fifteen or twenty at any one time, and he taught them all himself. He was greatly respected in Pearl County because of his learning and because he was what was called "a strict disciplinarian." He and Sarah Tarleton were good friends, and she asked him often for Sunday night supper. Sarah had told him about Chester and his studies, and Professor Drewery had examined him one night, asking him questions and nodding solemnly at his answers, his head inclined a little to one side. He told Sarah the boy was ready to go in the third grade and she was delighted. "If he can't keep up, just let me know," she had answered. "I'll arrange to teach him myself, after school, if he finds it too hard."

Professor Drewery, his mouth full of Sarah's hot biscuits, shook his whole dry body in denial. When he had swallowed, he spoke with heavy gallantry. "It is difficult to imagine the nephew of such an intelligent woman as yourself unable to keep abreast of his fellow pupils." Aunt Sarah stretched her protruding eyes a little wider and looked down at her plate. She considered Professor Drewery a brilliant conversationalist. She had planned taking Chester to school the first morning herself, but she found that the day clashed with the monthly meeting of her missionary society. She must spend the morning baking and getting things ready for the ladies when they arrived, so Bushrod took the boy instead. He came inside the schoolhouse and talked to Professor Drewery while Chester stood close to him, a little puzzled, a little undecided as to what was expected of him. Finally, Bushrod left and Chester was alone, and Professor Drewery showed him where he was to sit: he was to share a desk with a boy of his own age, Carl Graffenreid.

At recess his fellow scholars crowded about him. Some of them he had seen before with their parents at the store, but most of them were unknown to him. There were, for instance, the two youngest Tallon boys, Andrew and Jim, a year or two older than himself. Rafe Hall, the biggest boy in school, was about sixteen. He smoked cigarettes when Professor Drewery was not looking, and he talked about his sweethearts in a familiar, condescending way.

Rafe broke the silence: "I see Bush Tarleton brought you to school this morning. Looks to me like you'd be afraid to go around with him. Folks all say he's crazy as a loon."

Chester turned indignantly. "Uncle Bush is not crazy. He's got more sense than anybody, I guess."

"Oh, go on!" said Rafe tolerantly. "Bush Tarleton is as dizzy as a bat and everybody knows it." He spoke to Jim Tallon. "How about that, Jim? Ain't Bushrod crazy?"

Jim Tallon was a slender boy with dark eyes and skin. He was a year younger than his brother Andrew. He scraped his shoe in the dust, thinking, trying to be fair. "I expect he is; leastways that's what folks say."

There was silence, and then Herb Outerbridge spoke to Chester earnestly, as if it were important that he be convinced of his uncle's lack of reason: "How about his wife running off and leaving him? . . . I guess you know why she had to do that."

"I heard it was because Bush wanted her to take lessons on a cornet and Ruby wouldn't do it," said Sam Cornells.

Jim Tallon drew his delicate, black brows together. "I don't see anything crazy in that. Bush plays on the piano; maybe he figured they could have duets at night."

But Rafe Hall puffed his lips knowingly and winked at the smaller boys. "I guess that's not what they done at night! At least it ain't what Ruby done. She burnt 'em up. Ruby burnt a hole in the road." He laughed loudly, and Andrew Tallon laughed with him.

Andrew was larger and more compactly built than Jim. He resembled his brother Bradford. Except for the hideous cleft in his lip, with white bone showing through, he would have looked a great deal like him. When he spoke it was difficult to understand him. His voice was cloudy and hardly more intelligible than the grunting of a pig. But Jim could understand him always, and, by habit, repeated his words for the sake of others. He did so now.

"Andrew says that playing the cornet wasn't why Bush's wife left him."

Herb Outerbridge spoke: "Oh, you mean about the *pictures?* Oh, sure, everybody knows about that."

Harvey Cornells said: "I heard about that too. The Reverend McClung preached a sermon about Bushrod's pictures one time. He said nobody could blame a woman, no matter what she was, for leaving a man that had dirty pictures tattooed all over his body."

Andrew Tallon laughed his choking, cloudy laugh and slapped his leg with his hand. He began to speak rapidly in his grunting voice. "Bushrod went to see the Preacher the next day and throwed him in the watering trough for saying what he done."

"I sure would like to have seen that," said Sam Cornells. "I'd give a pretty to have seen that."

Rafe Hall took out his pocket knife and cleaned his finger nails, pronouncing the final judgment: "If Bush Tarleton ain't crazy, there's not a dog in Georgia."

Then the bell rang again and the boys went back into the schoolhouse.

That afternoon Jim and Andrew Tallon, since they lived in the same direction, walked most of the way with Chester. Jim said: "Brad and your Aunt Bessie are sweethearting, ain't they?"

"I don't know; maybe they are."

"Well, I know they are," said Jim. "Andrew and me know the place where they put their letters. We used to sneak off and read 'em before Bessie or Brad got there."

Andrew laughed his strangled laugh.

"You never read such stuff in your life," said Jim. "And if anything Brad is a bigger fool than Bessie."

But Chester was not interested in Bradford's and Bessie's love affair. He already knew all about that. He wanted to hear more of Bushrod and his tattooing. "What has Uncle Bushrod got tattooed on him?" he asked.

Jim told him what the county knew. It seemed that Bushrod was always drawing pictures of things which happened, and once a year he selected the picture he liked best and went to see a man in Baycity, an old sailor. While there the sailor tattooed on some part of Bush's body the design he had brought with him. The facts were undisputed, according to Jim. Some of the boys had come upon Bushrod one Sunday afternoon as he swam alone in Pearl River and had seen the pictures for themselves.

"Funny you ain't heard about it," grunted Andrew; "living right there in the house."

"What sort of pictures are they, Jim?"

"I don't know. I didn't see them, myself; but they tell me they are all smutty."

They had reached the place where the road to the Tallon place forked off from the main highway. The boys sat down for a while, interested in their conversation. It was September and the weather was still hot, the countryside dry and parched, and against the sky were white, massed clouds which moved with indolence down the horizon. The boys took off their shoes and dragged their bare feet through the dust. It was deep red and warm, and as soft and as yielding as rain water. They sat there for a time talking, but finally Andrew got up, stretching himself.

"We better be getting on home, Jim. Ma will be worried about us."

The Tallon boys walked down the smaller road toward the pines. When they reached the trees they both turned and waved solemnly, but Chester sat thinking, not seeing them. Even after they had disappeared among the trees and were lost to sight, he sat by the quiet road thinking. He scooped up, in his cupped palms, handsfull of the soft, smooth dust and trickled it over his feet until he had completely hidden them. . . . Across the road was an arch of earth thrown up by a burrowing mole. At once he went to it and scraped away the dirt with his hand, following the hole for a little way, but he could not locate the mole; it had burrowed, farther on, deeper into the earth, under a fallen log, and was lost to sight.

He was excited over what he had learned about Bushrod. Bush had taken on a new importance. He wanted to see the pictures for himself and he sat thinking, wondering how he could ask Bushrod to show them to him, but he could arrive at no conclusion. In his heart he was indignant that people should laugh at Bushrod, and call him crazy. He thought: "I'll tell Uncle Bush what they say, and he'll stop it all right," but almost at once he knew that he would not mention the matter to Bushrod or anybody else. He realized, even then, that Bush didn't care in the least what people thought or said about him.

At last, when it was almost dark, he got up, unaware how

quickly the afternoon had passed. Sarah was waiting for him at the gate. "Land *sakes,* Chester!" she cried. "Where on earth have you been? I thought you'd got lost."

"I was just sitting by the road. I wasn't doing anything wrong."

Aunt Sarah continued, clucking her tongue against the roof of her mouth: "Hurry now and wash your feet and hands and face. It's almost time for supper. . . . You'll worry me into my grave yet."

Bushrod came in from the store and he and Frank sat on the porch, smoking their pipes. Before them were seas of yellow flowers which ran evenly from the fields to the road, leaped it, and flowed again, and disappeared, finally, over a rise in the ground. In the fence corners were lantana bushes in bloom, with white, pink and yellow flowers all in the same cluster. . . . It was almost dark now and the first bull bats began to whirl in the air, poised and exact, cheeping hungrily after insects.

Frank Tarleton put down his paper and took off his glasses, wiping his eyes with a handkerchief. It had got too dark for him to read. He yawned and stretched and flung his arms out. "It seems mighty quiet here with Bessie gone; I'll be glad when that girl finishes school."

"Come to supper," said Aunt Sarah. "Come to supper, all."

And so the months passed quietly, with trivial incidents only. Chester had forgotten his father's home and he rarely thought of Mitty any more. Bessie had finished high school and had gone to the state university. She came back the first summer, a little more rounded, a little more womanly, but still taller and more angular than a woman should be. She liked it at the university. She was making all A's and was recognized, already, as an outstanding scholar. She had given up the idea of a career as a great opera singer. Her ambition, now, was to teach mathematics.

That summer she and Chester were together a great deal. Bessie had begun to regard him as something of a human being, now that he was twelve years old. One day they took a walk toward the west, in the direction of Outerbridge's farm. The ground was low in this section, and undrained, and they walked through the soggy land, which gave a little under their weight, until they came at last to a cypress swamp. It was dismal in this swamp and only sullen, dun-colored birds waded in the water or flapped slowly between the trees. There was water everywhere, and out of it great cypress butts, swollen like gourds unevenly inflated, curved upward past the level of the greenish tide; but above the point where the knees ended, the trunks of the cypresses compressed themselves into smooth, wooden cylinders and rose upward, hindered with small limbs only, to great heights. Suspended from branches and crushing the shrubs which grew on tufts of earth in the swamp, were streamers of gray moss hanging desolate and lax, moved by no wind.

Bessie sat upon a decaying tree which lay half in the water and half on the bank, and drew up her damp, muddy feet. She had been telling Chester about her experiences at the university, of her triumphs there, but now she was silent, as if she felt that her words were inappropriate in this dismal place. Behind her, in the swamp, a bird called across the water with a sound as harsh and as rusty as the clang of falling iron. She turned slightly and faced the lagoon, staring at it. It was stagnant and covered in places with scum and across its surface there moved globular masses not wholly vegetable nor yet quite sentient which propelled themselves somehow in this flat water with tentacles held outward to grasp.

"This place gives me the shivers," said Bessie. "I know it's silly and superstitious, but it does, just the same."

Chester came over and sat beside her. Far away, across the

marshy land, was a ramshackle cabin with smoke coming out of the sagging, clay chimney. "Who lives over there, Bessie?" But Bessie only shrugged her shoulders.

There grew in the marsh beside the lagoon small, red lilies; and farther on were strange things with wide-opened mouths, long throats and hungry stomachs. Insects buzzed about these plants, tricked by the smell of decay which they threw out, closer and closer, until they ventured too near. Then the lips of the plants sprung forward in a quick convulsion, and the insects were knocked downward and enmeshed forever among prehensile needles. They struggled and cried faintly but they passed, inevitably, down the long throat, from one spine to another, until they came at length into the bulging, complacent belly that awaited them.

Bessie spoke: "I haven't seen flycatchers as big as those for a long time."

But Chester got up and went over to the plants. He knelt and peered into their open mouths, smelling their charnel-like putrescence, watching the insects which struggled for freedom. He saw, then, that the throat of each plant was threaded through with red, intricate lines, as if these things were actually alive, with veins through which the blood of their victims flowed. He pulled back, dimly afraid.

Bessie, seeing his face, laughed and smoothed back her hair. "Why did we ever come out here in the first place? It seems as if we could have picked a better place than this."

They turned to go back. Chester spoke: "Bessie," he began, "tell me about Uncle Bush's wife."

Bessie thought a moment. "There isn't very much to tell. She was just a bum. What Bush saw in her is what I can't understand."

"Tell me about how he met her."

Bessie told him what she knew. Ruby had had a bad reputation even as a child—she explained how this information had come to her through her sister, Lillian Chapman. Her people were respectable enough, Bessie supposed; anyway, they had owned a butcher shop in Reedyville. Ruby was not even pretty, but men had always run after her and finally she became involved in an affair with a married man. She was loud-mouthed and common and smoked cigarettes openly. She was given to violent fits of rage.

Bessie had been about eight years old at the time of Bushrod's marriage, and curiously enough she had liked Ruby. Ruby had always been kind to her personally, and had made a great deal over her, but Aunt Sarah had prevented any intimacy between them. She had wondered why at the time and had thought Aunt Sarah unjust, but later, of course, she had understood. Even now her feeling for Ruby was friendly, rather than otherwise, although she understood the flaws in her character.

"When Bush and Ruby married the blow almost killed Lillian," said Bessie. "She took it as a slap in her face after the way she had worked to have Ruby run out of town. She has always believed that Ruby married him just to spite her."

Chester was thinking these things over, and Bessie continued: "Bushrod was considered one of the handsomest men in Pearl County and he might have had his pick of any nice girl he wanted. Why he chose Ruby Bogen is beyond me."

Bessie walked with her long, swinging stride, thinking out loud: "Poor old Bush! . . . Ruby certainly ruined his life. He gave up everything for her; he did everything she wanted; and he got nothing back."

"Aunt Sarah sure hates her."

Bessie shrugged her wide shoulders. "Let's hurry home. It's getting late." She raised her eyebrows and spoke in the new, superior voice which she had developed at college: "Aunt Sarah is quite laughable, don't you think?"

"I don't know." He had never thought of Aunt Sarah that way. It had never occurred to him not to take her seriously.

Bessie smiled tolerantly. "I find her *most* amusing," she said. "In fact I find the whole family droll."

From the Diary of Sarah Tarleton

April 10, 1917. This is the fourth anniversary of Chester's arrival. My, but time does go fast! It seems hardly yesterday since he came. He is growing up very quickly, like a weed, in fact. He is a good, steady boy and a comfort to all of us, but especially to his Uncle Bushrod. Not much news today. Jim and Andrew Tallon came by to see Chester this afternoon. It's a shame they don't do something about Andrew's harelip before it's too late. Had letter from Bessie. She is doing well at the university. There'll be another Phi Beta Kappa key in the family soon.

Thought for today:
> *"When dark clouds gather*
> *And down falls the rain*
> *Always remember*
> *The sun soon shines again."*

19

ONE Sunday, when Chester was fourteen, Frank Tarleton and
Aunt Sarah went to spend the afternoon with the Tallons. They
had hardly driven out of sight before it began to rain. Bushrod
came in from the porch dragging his chair, and sat in the dining
room where Chester was reading. He seemed preoccupied and a
little sad. His habitual, light, laughing manner was gone. He
picked up a book and began to read, and then put it down.
Chester, too, put down his book and sat waiting.

"You'll be going to high school next year in Reedyville. I'll
miss you while you're away."

"I'll miss you, too, Uncle Bush."

Bushrod got up and went to the piano. He played for a few
minutes and then returned to the room. He was restless and he
could not keep still. Abruptly he spoke: "Art is a great thing,
Chester. It's made by unhappy people for other people who are
unhappy." He sat down again, resting his hands on his knees.
He laughed a little, as if apologizing in advance for what he
was going to say. His large, perfect teeth were white against his
tanned face and his eyes were brilliant slits of blue. "That's practical," he said. "That's being practical about things."

"It must be fine to be a great artist," said Chester thoughtfully.
His voice was beginning to change a little and he was showing
the first, faint symptoms of approaching adolescence.

"Art is the only thing that has ever lasted in this world," said
Bushrod. "It is the only thing that will ever last." He sat thinking for a moment before he came to a decision: "I have never

spoken to you about my wife, but you're getting old enough to understand a lot of things."

Chester looked up eagerly, but he did not answer.

"I know how people talk," continued Bushrod, "and I know they've told you a lot of things about Ruby and me." He stopped helplessly. "I suppose it was funny, in a way. . . ."

But Chester interrupted him. "I never believed a word anybody said. I know whatever you did was right, Uncle Bush!"

Bush nodded his head gravely: "Thank you very much, Chester. I really appreciate that." He began to talk freely about Ruby, how he had met her and how he had fallen in love with her. "Of course that's all over long ago," he explained. "There was no sense in grieving, so I forgot her. That's the only practical way to look at things. I did the best I knew how. That's all anybody can do."

Behind him a clock ticked with a steady, faint sound. It was dim in the room and only a little light came from the gray skies. Sheets of rain, blown by the wind, swept over the fields, and the red road looked darker and richer in its wetness. But Bushrod was speaking again:

"Of course I wasn't as easy about it at first as I am now. I took it pretty hard when she ran away. I guess it hurt my pride more than anything else. I felt very sad and lonely and a little while after she had left, I took a trip. I had never been north and I wanted to see what the country was like, so I went. One day I was in Chicago and I took a walk through the streets. I didn't like it in Chicago. There were too many people and too much going on."

On the hearth Aunt Sarah's cat purred in contentment and the rain beat against the window in a steady, rhythmical swish; but Bushrod was not conscious of these things. A far-away look had come into his blue eyes. He was occupied with the tangle of his own past.

"I was walking along the lake front one day and I came to a big building, directly across the street. I didn't know what it was at first, in fact I thought it was the post-office, but later I found out it was an art museum. I stood still, to inspect it, and looked upward, and there, across the entrance to the building, I saw chiseled in big letters the following words:

ART ALONE ENDURES

"I looked at the words for a long time, not quite knowing what to make of them, and a peculiar, weak feeling came over me. I got the idea that those words were put there by a person who aimed to help others with their troubles, and that he knew, when he cut them in the stone, that some time a man like me would pass by and read them and be comforted."

Bushrod was again thoughtful. "Are you old enough to understand what I mean, Chester?"

"Yes," said Chester. "I think I know, Uncle Bush."

Bushrod drew his brows together, his face serious in the effort he was making to recall and to express in words the emotion he had felt at the moment of reading the inscription.

"I kept reading the words over and over: Art Alone Endures! . . . Art Alone Endures! . . . while people bumped into me and took me for a countryman just come to town." Bushrod's face relaxed and he laughed tolerantly at his own absurdity. "Well, if that wasn't exactly what I was, I'd like to know! . . . And so I stood there, with my mouth open, I guess, being pushed about and bumped into by all those people who were in such a hurry, but I didn't care; I didn't mind what they did or what they thought. For I had understood, all of a sudden, what art really was. I understood all about it. I remember a girl, wearing a red sweater, who passed. She had yellow, curly hair and the wind blew it about. She kept laughing and pushing her hair out of her eyes. She's a part of the picture, too, although I don't, to this day, know why.

"I came home after that and went to work again in the store, but I thought about the words I had seen for a long time. Then one day, while I was cutting off six yards of percale for Mrs. Ed Wrenn, I said, before I knew what I was doing: 'When a man writes a book or makes a statue or does anything like that, he is only taking something ugly out of himself and making it beautiful; then the thing which has been troubling him can't hurt him any more. That's obvious and practical.'"

Bushrod laughed reminiscently. "I'll never forget old Mrs. Wrenn's face. She looked away as if I were crazy." Bushrod became thoughtful for a moment. "Well, maybe I *am* crazy, like people say. How do I know?"

"I don't think you're crazy," said Chester. "I don't think that, Uncle Bush."

Bushrod nodded his head, for he was already speaking again. . . . "I kept thinking about what I had said to Mrs. Wrenn, and the more I thought about it, the more I believed it. . . . Of course I couldn't paint pictures or become a sculptor, but I figured out a way for myself, too! I figured if I had a picture of my trouble tattooed on my body it would be a part of me and then it couldn't hurt me any more."

He leaned forward, his fingers locked together, and spoke earnestly. "That sounds like I was working backward, but it really amounts to the same thing, when you get down to it. . . . So the next week I made a drawing of what I wanted and took it to Baycity. I figured since it was a seaport with lots of sailors that I'd find a man who could do the tattooing for me, and sure enough I did. He was a man named Jim Saltis and he lived over a ship chandler's place near the waterfront."

Bush picked up the cat and began to tickle her belly. "Well, that's all there is to it. . . . I just wanted to tell you this, now that you're growing up, so that you could see my side of the story. You're the first person I've ever told all this to."

Chester sat with his impassive face, but inwardly he was very excited. He said rapidly, his words stumbling over each other: "The people who think you're crazy don't know what they are talking about. Don't ever think that I believe it."

Bushrod got up and went to the window, looking out at the rain. "Good Lord! I don't care what folks say about me."

Chester wanted to see the tattooing, but he could think of no way to phrase his request. He sat there, unwilling that this opportunity should pass, and yet not knowing what to say. Bushrod solved the matter. He turned slowly from the window. "I've never showed the pictures to anybody, but I'll show them to you," and without waiting for a reply he added: "Come on up to my room, if you want to see them."

When they were there, Bush closed the door and took off his clothes, and Chester stared at his uncle's naked body. "Which was the first picture you thought of, Uncle Bush?"

Bushrod put his hand upon his wide, lean breast. "This was the first." It was a picture of a woman and a man running with locked arms over a small hill: it was Ruby and her barber, of course. Bushrod said: "It hurt me pretty bad when Ruby acted the way she did and then ran off and left me, but I don't care any more. It is all something that doesn't concern me any more. . . ." Below the running figures was Bushrod kneeling on the ground, tears streaming from his eyes, his hands stretched toward the retreating couple. A cornet was lying across his arms. For a time the boy examined the pictures, his eyes moving from one to the other while Bushrod stood turning his body this way and that, as if he were exhibiting a canvas of which he was very proud.

Below the running figures, Christ, with Bushrod's face, prayed on Gethsemane. Bushrod explained that the composite figure

175

was praying that He recover something which He had lost. He didn't quite know what the thing was he wanted, but He was asking His Father in Heaven to reveal it to him. From behind a rock the evil face of Judas sneered, and over both the praying figure and Judas was a sea gull with wide, steady wings.

"I always liked that one," said Bush, "but I haven't any idea what it means. Maybe that's why I like it." He turned sideways, so that the light would be right.

On his left arm there was a picture of his mother in her wedding veil, a bouquet of flowers in her hand, a wolf with snarling teeth at her feet. But the largest picture of all was on Bushrod's back. It was a cross outlined in blue, the beam lying stretched on his shoulders, the base touching the end of his spine. In the square of this cross, between the shoulder blades, was the figure of a man kneeling before another man who was blessing him, and at the foot of the cross were the words: Take My Cross Upon Ye and Learn of Me. . . .

On his buttocks were two objects which even Bushrod could not explain. They resembled large lettuces, one worked in red and the other in blue. Bushrod said that they were "mystic roses," but just what a mystic rose was, he could not say. All he knew was that it was a term used by Catholics. He had heard the expression somewhere and had like it, that was all.

There were other figures, but these were the ones that interested the boy most. When Bushrod had put on his clothes they went to the porch and sat there looking at the road. "It's funny that so many of the pictures are religious," said Bush, "because I'm not a religious man. I've often wondered about that."

The countryside was turning green again and in the corner of the yard the fig trees were lengthening their bareness with spurts of leaves not unfolded yet, tender and young, like clenched, green hands. The rain had stopped and the sun came out just in time to set again. The wet leaves glistened and in the last wan light the road was dark red and saturated. Bushrod smoked his pipe and the boy sat on the steps, slightly below him.

Bushrod said: "You ought to go and play with the other boys more. You shouldn't stay indoors as much as you do. You must get pretty lonely."

"I'm not lonely, Uncle Bush."

Bushrod smoked steadily. "Bessie finishes college pretty soon, now, and will be back with us for good. That'll make it more lively." He laughed indulgently. "That Bessie! There's no figuring her out. I never saw such a girl."

Chester laughed a little too, and then they both sat silent with their own thoughts.

There came a loud shout from the road. A buggy had driven up to the gate and stopped. Bush got up. "It's Holm Barrascale," he said. "He must want something out of the store." He stepped off the porch, the boy behind him, and walked to the waiting buggy.

Holm said: "My wife's been hankering all day for a piece of peanut candy. She wouldn't let me rest none until I promised to go git it for her."

Bush took out his keys and stepped onto the porch of the store.

"I sure hate to plague you on a Sunday," said Holm, "but when the old woman gits her head sot on anything there's no talking her out of it."

"That's all right," said Bush. "We're here to sell goods. We're practical people."

Bush wrapped up the candy, but Holm lingered before the counter, anxious to talk to somebody. "It looks like we're going to get drawed into this European war, sure. I don't see no way out of it."

But Bush did not answer. He was willing to accept the Barrascales as customers only. They were not his friends.

The sun had set now and there were long, spear-like clouds above the horizon, luminous and touched with fire. There were streamers of color across the sky, red and green and golden, which faded gradually into thinner and more delicate shades. "Do you ever hear from Ruby?" asked Chester. "What became of her?"

Bushrod said, after a long time: "The last I heard of her she was in New Orleans; in a sporting house, they said. There's no bitterness in my heart. I try to remember that Christ did not condemn the woman taken in adultery. . . . But I hate to think of Ruby leading that life. The man she run off with treated her pretty dirty."

Presently a buggy came into sight down the red, slippery road. It reached the store and Bush went down to open the gate. Sarah got out first with her plump spryness; her brother Frank, because of his rheumatism, a little more slowly. "Lord above!" she said, "what a rain. There's a washout down the road. I thought we'd never get around it."

"It rained right smart," said Bush. "That's a fact."

"Mrs. Tallon's very worried about Brad," continued Sarah. "It looks like war and he and a bunch of other boys want to go together. They all think it will be a lot of fun."

"Let's have ham and scrambled eggs for supper," said Frank. "I think I'd relish it."

20

THE next week Bessie came home unexpectedly. Lillian Chapman drove her over from Reedyville. When Bessie, with her suitcases, had got out of the car and stood by the road, Lillian backed and turned around, facing the direction from which she had come. Aunt Sarah, looking through the window, saw this. She knew from the jerking, vigorous way in which Lillian handled the automobile that she was angry. She saw the sisters talking together, Lillian calm and precise, Bessie making gestures with her angular arms. "What in the world?" gasped Sarah. "What in the world has happened now?"

She took off her apron and smoothed back her hair, which was becoming quite gray. She ran down the steps to the road, her eyes a little worried behind their thick lenses, the folds of flesh which sagged under her chin vibrating in her haste.

"Is there anything wrong?" she asked anxiously. "Is there anything the matter?"

Lillian answered in her calm, irritating voice. "You'd better ask *her*. You'd better hear what she has to say." She started the engine. "Maybe you can do something with her. I've tried, but I can't."

"If you really want to do something for me," said Bessie, "you can mind your own business."

"Bessie!" said Sarah reproachfully. "That's no way to talk to your elder sister who has only your good at heart, I'm sure." To Lillian she said: "Aren't you coming in? You're surely not going right back?"

"I've got to go to a meeting of the Civic Improvement Association this afternoon," said Lillian stiffly. "I'm going to be late as it is." She drove angrily down the red road, the car rocking from side to side.

Aunt Sarah and Bessie stood by the gate. "What have you and Lillian been quarreling about this time?"

"Nothing," said Bessie. "It's simply that Lillian can't keep her nose out of other people's affairs."

Aunt Sarah sighed and picked up one of the suitcases.

Bessie was a full-grown woman now. Her early slightness had disappeared, but she was still angular and sparsely built. She was still a little too vigorous, and a little too abrupt for a woman. She swung the other suitcase upward from the ground and took the one which Sarah held in her hand.

"I spent the night with Lillian and Evan. I thought that would look better than going to a hotel."

Bushrod came out of the store. "Bessie!" he cried. "What on earth did you leave the university for just when examinations are coming on?"

But Bessie did not answer. She strode, still swinging the heavy suitcases, up the long, brick walk. When she reached the house she put down her baggage and took off her hat. "Go get pappa!" she said. "I'm only going over this thing one time. I'm not going to explain separately to each member of the family." She went up to her old room, with Bushrod and Sarah behind her, and began calmly to wash her face.

Sarah spoke earnestly: "I've always made it a point in my life never to interfere in anybody's business, but I must say you shouldn't miss this time from school, Elizabeth, especially since you have made such a fine record so far."

But Bessie came downstairs again, as if she had not heard her aunt. She went into the parlor and raised all the blinds, allowing the bright, morning sunlight to enter. She seated herself at the piano and began to strike chords.

Bushrod scratched his head, but Sarah sat down with ponderous gravity and surveyed Bessie through her lenses, her broad, fine forehead wrinkled up in dismay. "Bessie, you are the most maddening person I have ever met," she said helplessly. "You actually are, beyond a doubt."

"Come on, Bessie, and tell us all about it," said Bush. "I've got to get back to the store. I've got work to do."

"Go get Pappa!" insisted Bessie; "I'll tell my story just one time." •

Frank Tarleton was mending a fence. His figure, beyond the green field, could be seen as he moved lazily about, puffing his pipe. Bush walked to the back door. "Pappa!" he called. "Pappa! Bessie's back!" At the mention of her name, Frank threw down his tools and came loping up to the house, limping a little on his rheumatic leg. When he was inside, and had kissed his daughter, the family seated themselves and Bessie stated her case.

"Remember I'm going to do what I say, no matter who tries to stop me. I'm twenty-one years old; please remember that and save your breath."

Frank said: "It's not necessary for you to take that attitude, Bessie. I haven't been as good a father as some men, maybe, but I've never tried to stop my children doing what they wanted to."

"I'm going to get married."

"Oh, sure!" said Frank. "We want you to get married when you've finished college and taken your degree. You got lots of time for that."

"I'm going to get married tomorrow."

"Well," said Aunt Sarah diplomatically, "it's pretty sudden, I must say. But suppose you tell us all about it."

"There's nothing to tell," said Bessie, shrugging her wide, spare shoulders. "I simply got a letter from Brad a few days ago asking me to marry him. He's going to enlist in the army next week. He's already given up his job at the sawmill. I haven't got any time to waste, that's all. He may be sent to France and get killed and I may never see him again."

"Oh, pshaw!" said Frank. "Is that all it is? Nothing's going to happen to Brad. Even if he does join up he'll stay right here in the United States somewhere."

A note of terror came into Bessie's matter-of-fact voice. "He won't though. He'll be sent across and he'll be killed. I know he will. I know it!"

She began to cry. "I talked to him all last night, trying to persuade him not to go, but he won't listen to me. He wouldn't pay any attention to what I said. He just laughed and held my hands and tried to kiss me."

"Bessie!" said Aunt Sarah. "Why, Bessie!— You're acting like a little girl."

"He wanted to get married last night in Reedyville, and I came very nearly doing it, too, but Lillian talked me out of it; she said I ought to see you all first. She said everybody would think that Brad had got me in trouble and *had* to marry me if we did it without telling anybody."

Bushrod laughed, his half-closed eyes blue and brilliant, tiny wrinkles radiating toward his temples. "Good old Lillian! Good old girl!"

"Oh, you can trust Lillian to keep the family shield from getting tarnished."

"Your sister is quite right," said Sarah. "I must agree with her completely."

Frank sat rubbing his wrinkled cheeks, his soiled, white chin whiskers thrust forward. "We all want you to marry Bradford if you love each other. We haven't any objection to Brad. Of course, he's wild and drinks and carouses a lot, but he'll settle down quick enough with a family on his hands to take care of. . . ."

Bessie said, somewhat primly through her tears: "I never mean to be a burden around Brad's neck."

But Frank had not finished: "Of course, we all want you to marry Brad if you love him, but not yet, baby."

"It would be a shame," said Sarah, "to leave school now, when you're doing so well. . . . We're only speaking for your own good, Elizabeth."

"What do you know about it? What do you know about love? I notice you never got married."

"All right. Look at it that way if you want to. But suppose you do marry Bradford. What good will it do you? He'll be sent to a training camp for a few months and you'll still be here. What will you gain?"

"I'll go to the training camp with him. I'll stay outside and he can come to see me when he gets off."

"They won't let you do that, daughter."

"I'd like to see somebody try to stop me!"

Sarah said: "Go ahead and marry Brad if you want to. But he'll be sorry afterwards, even if you aren't. Do you think a young soldier wants to have a wife hanging around all the time?"

"It will be plenty of time to think of marrying him when he comes back," said Frank.

"I'll marry him and stay here, then. I won't bother him if he doesn't want me. I'll marry him tonight. We'll have a few days together, anyway."

And so the conversation continued all that afternoon, back and forth, endlessly; but Bessie could not be moved. At the end of every argument she would say: "I'm going to marry him just the same." They were still talking when Chester came home from school. A little later the family, completely worn out, completely frustrated, left her alone and went about their business. Chester came into the parlor and sat down stolidly, regarding her with his quiet, unmoving eyes.

Bessie went to the piano and began to play again, ignoring his presence. Suddenly she turned and spoke: "I don't suppose *you* can think of any other reasons why I shouldn't marry Brad?"

Chester shook his head in his serious, literal way. "No," he answered.

"Well," said Bessie shrilly, "that's a relief. That takes a weight off my mind."

"When are you going to get married, Bessie?" She stopped playing and looked at him. "Oh, my God, its voice is changing! It's getting to be a man! Pretty soon it'll be grown up and involved in a mess like this, too."

"I don't think so."

"Of course not," said Bessie. "You're much too much like Bushrod. You've got so you even talk like him and look like him. There isn't a drop of sentiment in either of you. Both of you are stuffed with old rags." She put down the piano lid angrily and walked out of the room.

Brad was to come over for supper that night, but at seven o'clock he had not appeared and the family began without him. At nine he showed up with Len Williams and the two Cornells boys. They were all very drunk. Somewhere on their way they had picked up a band of negro musicians who played guitars and mouth-organs. The party halted at the fence and the negroes began a serenade. Bessie went to the window and watched them. She saw Brad open the gate and come staggering up the steps. He called her, but she stood silent in the room.

"You see," said Sarah. "He calls for his bride dead drunk. It would never work out. Let Brad go on off to war, if he wants to. When he gets back there will be plenty of time to get married."

Brad stumbed across the porch and hammered against the door. "Come on, Bessie! Let's go find a preacher!"

Frank and Bushrod came up. Bush opened the door and stood blocking it.

"Go home and sober up, Brad," said Frank gently. "Go home and get sober. . . . Come back tomorrow, if you want to, and we'll talk things over."

"I'm used to being treated like a gentleman," said Brad thickly. "I'm used to being asked inside, when I call on folks."

"You're not yourself, Bradford," said Aunt Sarah. "That's only the whiskey in you talking."

Brad paid no attention to her. "I know you don't want me to come in, but I came by for Bessie and I'm going in to see her whether you want me to or not." He pushed forward, but Bushrod raised his arm and held it rigid across the door, blocking his entrance.

"There's no harm in a man having a little fun, is there?" asked Brad sullenly.

He tried to elbow Bushrod aside, but Bush stiffened suddenly and shoved him, and Brad stumbled back to the steps. Bush followed him. "Don't ever try to come into a man's house when you're not wanted; you're liable to get killed that way." He stood facing Brad, his blue eyes cold and furious.

Sarah stood by the window, wringing her hands. "Oh, good heavens! . . . To have a scene like this for everybody in the country to talk about."

Brad, for some reason, sat on the steps and began to laugh. "Crazy Bushrod!" he said. "Crazy Bushrod!" He rocked back and forth in his mirth. He got up, weaving a little, as if he suddenly remembered the purpose of his visit. "Bessie!" he called. "Come on out, sugar."

Bessie came onto the porch and stood facing him. "Go away!" she said. "I never want to see hide or hair of you again."

Brad's friends laughed genially at his discomfiture, making loud remarks. Finally Brad straightened his tie and fixed his clothes with drunken dignity. "All right, honey," he said. "You were the one who hankered to get married, not me."

Then the musicians, to hide his embarrassment, struck up another tune and Brad and his friends went off down the road singing songs together.

"I'll never see him again," said Bessie. "Never again."

"Oh, sure you will," said Frank. "He'll be back before next fall, mark my words."

Bessie shook her head. "That was the last sight I'll ever have of him. Something tells me."

The Whisperer

EVEN after revolution came in this far country and the king, her father, and the queen, her mother, were imprisoned by their enemies, the little princess knew nothing of what had happened. She was a very young princess, as eager and as soft as a gray kitten. Her cheeks were smoother than satin, colored pink like rose petals, and her knees and elbows were still dimpled with the dimples of babyhood.

So sheltered and so gentle had her life been that she knew nothing of evil, nothing of pain, nothing of sorrow; and now nobody could tell her what her fate would be: she was so young and so lovely. Her eyes were blue with the sweetness of cornflowers, and her hair hung in a yellow fold about her shoulders. She surveyed the gray dungeon of her imprisonment, laughing with delight, as if the whole thing were a game, a sustained masque for her pleasure.

The queen, her mother, lifting the jeweled hem of her skirts that they might not be fouled by the filth of the prison, spoke to the young princess, smoothing back her hair with white, slender fingers: "Do not be frightened. This is a part of being a princess; it is a thing that all princesses must bear. It will not last long."

And the young princess clapped her hands and danced away, looking back over her shoulder. "I like it," she said gayly. "I will not be frightened."

Then the queen sighed and spoke to her consort, the king: "She must not know what awaits us. We must keep that from her."

And so many days passed, and then one night the queen spoke again to the princess: "The ceremony will take place to-morrow at day-break in the square. There will be a great crowd there, and cursing. There will be dogs barking and people leaning out from windows or sitting perched in trees and on stone walls. It may be there will be bands playing. . . . But do not be alarmed if the people seem unfriendly and shout at us. It is only a part of the ceremony."

The young princess said, very gravely: "I will not be afraid. I will not be frightened."

She was still grave with her young dignity when the jailer unlocked the prison cell and led them through stone passages to the place where the people awaited. At their appearance the crowd was silent for a moment, but when the king and the queen and little princess stood at last on the scaffold they began to shake their fists and to shout. The king and the queen looked steadily ahead, as if they did not hear the noise, but the little princess curtseyed to the cursing mob in the manner that she had been taught. She turned excitedly and caught her mother's ringed hand. "Did they all come to see me?" she asked in delight. "Did they really come to see me?"

The executioner stepped forward, rubbing his nose with one finger. The queen said haughtily: "The child first. The child will go first."

Turning to the princess who had never known pain, she said: "Go and put your head upon the block. The ceremony will begin now." And obediently the young princess put her head upon the block and gazed out laughingly at the mass of angry, distorted mouths that shouted for her blood and for the extinction of her line. She raised her hand and threw a kiss to her subjects. "Thank you! Thank you!" she said gayly. "Thank you so much for coming!"

Then the ax of the executioner made a swishing, half-circle in the air and descended, and the head of the young princess dropped from her body and rolled forward toward the bloody basket, the basket that awaits the head of all loveliness.

21

It was Chester's second year in high school and he was living with his aunt and uncle that winter. Bushrod came over to see him occasionally and wrote him long, weekly letters giving all the news of the family. It was thus that he heard of Brad Tallon's death. He had been killed in the Argonne early in November, but the family had only recently been notified. Bessie was taking the matter very hard. She blamed her family for having separated her from Brad and refused to live with them any more. Instead, she had gone to Atlanta to live with her brother Jesse, the doctor.

Chester showed the letter to Lillian. She read it through silently. "What Bessie needs is a good spanking." She sighed: "I guess it's pappa's and Aunt Sarah's fault, though. They always pampered her and Bushrod more than the others. This is what they get for their pains."

Lillian was quite a personage in Reedyville. She was president of the Browning Club and secretary of the Ladies Auxiliary. In addition, she served as a member of Mr. Palmiller's antivice society. She stood now putting her blonde hair in place, a superior, somewhat satisfied expression on her face. "Self-control is a lesson that we must all learn," she remarked. "It's the most important lesson in life."

At that moment Chester wanted to laugh, because his aunt reminded him so much of Miss Sarah, and he knew that nothing would make Lillian more furious than to be told that. He started to speak, but changed his mind.

190

Lillian looked critically at the thin, gangling boy before her. "Hold your shoulders straight," she said sharply. "Don't go about with your head hanging between your legs." Chester experienced a quick wave of dislike for his aunt. He walked upstairs and went into his own room. He got out one of his schoolbooks and began to study, but almost immediately he closed the book angrily. Below he could hear his aunt scolding the servant for something trivial which she had failed to do. Lillian was expecting visitors that afternoon, and things were not right.

He decided that he would write Bushrod a letter. He finished the letter, put it in an envelope and directed it. There came a knock on his door and he opened it. Lillian entered the room, a faint wave of expensive scent following her. She explained her visit. "The New Membership Committee of the Browning Club has called this afternoon and the ladies are downstairs in the parlor now."

"I'm not going to recite again. I'm not going to make a fool of myself for those old women to go off and laugh at."

Lillian raised her brows in a well-bred manner. "My dear child, you are very amusing. Nobody is going to laugh at you. They all admire you very much. Old Mrs. Wentworth particularly asked that you recite 'The Last Ride Together.'"

"Well, I won't do it!" But in his heart he knew that he would, that Lillian would find just the word, just the tone of voice to compel him to do what she wanted. He was sixteen and already resentful of the fact that he had little will of his own, that he generally did what people wanted him to do.

Lillian slid her bracelets farther up her arm. She sat down in a chair, as if very weary. "I'm sure you put me in a most embarrassing position, Chester. I told Mrs. Wentworth that you would be glad to recite the piece, not thinking for a minute that you were going to act this way. . . . How do you suppose

I'm going to feel when I tell them that you refuse your aunt as simple a thing as that?"

"I don't know how you'll feel," said Chester. He turned and walked to the window, looking out at the trees, just coming into leaf again.

Lillian took another tack: "Your Uncle Evan and I are doing what we can for you, dear. Of course we don't ask anything in return; we want you to do just as you please about things, of course."

There was a long silence. Chester turned from the window, miserable and somewhat ashamed.

"All right. I'll speak the piece."

Lillian embraced him. "I knew you would, you sweet boy. I knew you wouldn't be stubborn." She patted his cheek gently and straightened his tie. "Here, let me brush your hair for you." She smoothed back his limp, light hair and dusted his face with her powder puff. Her hands were trembling a little. "Say it dramatically," she whispered. "Relax your jaw and throat and throw the tone upward from the diaphragm, vibrating it in the frontal cavities."

"Let me alone," said Chester.

When they reached the door that led to the parlor, Lillian put her arm about her nephew and stood there posed for an instant. They were about the same height and she tried to draw his head down upon her shoulder, but Chester pulled away, red and embarrassed.

Around the room were grouped six ladies, all very earnest and most of them a little dowdy. Lillian said: "This is my young nephew, Robert Chester Hurry, Jr. He's living with Mr. Chapman and me while he attends high school." Then she made the introductions: "Mrs. Wentworth, Mrs. Charles Hemmes, Miss Juliet Piggott, Mrs. Porterfield, Mrs. Kenworthy and Miss Sadie Furness." Chester shook hands with each of the ladies in turn.

Old Mrs. Wentworth got up heavily, leaning on her cane. "Well, I'm very glad to meet you, young man. Your aunt must bring you over for dinner some night." She turned to Lillian: "I expect I'd better be getting on home," she continued in her deep, rumbling voice. "I don't like to leave Carrie alone by herself with nobody but old Maudie to look out for her."

"Oh, no, no!" said Lillian reproachfully. "Oh, no, not just yet, Miss Lida. Chester is going to recite for us. He's going to recite 'The Last Ride Together.'"

Mrs. Wentworth looked surprised, but very pleased. "That's my favorite poem," she said. "Well, that's very considerate of the young man."

Suddenly Chester's face turned red. He knew then that nobody had asked him to recite; Lillian had made the whole thing up. He wanted to go away, but Lillian had already taken him by the arm. "Stand over here, dear," she said; "over by the piano." She placed him carefully and turned his body so that the afternoon light struck the back of his head and illuminated his light hair. When she had him arranged to her satisfaction, she tiptoed to her seat and sat smiling at her guests.

In a moment Chester raised his head and began, and the seven ladies gazed at him admiringly, nodding their heads. When he had finished, there was a round of polite and somewhat surprised applause.

Miss Juliet Piggott, a large, stern woman, severely dressed, spoke enthusiastically: "That was beautifully rendered, young man. That was beautifully spoken, indeed."

"I think he has undoubted talent," said Lillian. "I think he ought to go on the stage."

They crowded about him and the boy accepted their congratulations. "I think it would be very nice if the young man would repeat the recitation for the entire club at our next meeting," said old Mrs. Porterfield.

"No!" said Chester in alarm. "Oh, no, I couldn't do that."

"He's a little timid," said Lillian in explanation. "Of course it's quite natural at his age."

"Oh, pshaw!" said Mrs. Porterfield. "Nobody is going to hurt you. They'll enjoy it very much."

Chester lifted his eyes to his aunt. She was regarding him approvingly. "You see!" her eyes seemed to say. "You see what a triumph I have arranged for you?"

Chester escaped from the parlor. As he went up the stairs toward his room he saw old Maria, the maid, enter with a tray of sandwiches and coffee. He paused by the railing and Lillian's voice came upward to him. . . . "He's the son of my sister who died. He's doing brilliantly in school. Very vague and impractical, like his father, though. But great natural talent for the stage, we all think." Chester sighed and went up the steps slowly. Lillian seemed to him somewhat pathetic and somewhat absurd. He went into his room and locked the door, sitting on the side of his bed. Bessie's words came back to him. "We're all a little cracked, and everybody laughs at us, really."

At that instant Chester felt very grown up and wise. "I'm superior to Aunt Lillian and the others," he thought, "because I know what we are, and they don't." He lay flat on his bed and began to twist his hands nervously.

Late that spring Bushrod drove over in his automobile to visit his nephew. They took a walk through the town and Bushrod seemed very gay and light-hearted. "You need a new suit," said Bush. "You're getting to be a man now, and you must dress better." He took Chester to a shop and outfitted him completely. Bush sat on a chair, smiling to himself, a look of pride in his eyes. "I want you to look as well as any boy in Reedyville. I want you to hold up your head with the best."

Chester said, a little cautiously: "It's costing a lot of money,

Uncle Bush. I don't want you to spend your money on me like this."

But Bush only chuckled. "I've got plenty put away. I've been saving my money all these years and the store's doing well. Don't you worry about that for a minute."

When Chester was dressed in his new clothes, he and Bushrod took a walk across the railroad tracks. After a while they came to a small butcher shop. "Some old friends of mine live here," said Bush. "I'll just stop in and speak to them." Behind the counter was a dingy-looking man wearing a soiled, blood-stained apron. He got up and shook hands with Bush cordially. He turned to the back of the shop and called out to someone above, and a moment later a fat woman appeared, her eyes swollen and heavy as if she had been asleep.

"Why, howdy do, Bushrod." Her voice was flat and a little nasal. "I'm glad to see you looking so well."

"I keep well," answered Bush. "I try to be practical and get plenty of exercise."

They all went into the living quarters above the shop and sat talking for a time. Chester was somewhat bored. He paid little attention to what they were saying. When the visit came to an end, the couple walked with Bush to the sidewalk and stood talking of impersonal things. Suddenly, the woman spoke in a bitter voice: "I don't know what she was thinking of to leave a good man like you who was willing to provide for her. . . . I don't know what she was thinking about!"

Chester was alert. He knew, then, that he was seeing Ruby's parents.

"Have you heard from her lately, Mrs. Bogen?"

"She's never written me a line, all these years," said the old, untidy woman. Tears came into her reddened eyes and she wiped them on her apron. "Never one word in all these years."

The soiled butcher looked stolidly up the street, as if he expected to see his daughter approaching. "If she came back on her bended knees starving and asked me for a bite of bread, I'd beat hell out of her and have her locked up as a whore."

"Sh-h," said Mrs. Bogen. "The young man—!"

"I don't care who hears me. That's what she is, and that's what she always was."

"Well," said Bush judiciously. "You have to take people as they are. You mustn't be so hard. You've got to be practical, Mr. Bogen."

They all shook hands again and Chester and Bushrod went back for supper at Lillian's.

When they were almost there, Chester broke the long silence. "What was there about Ruby that made you love her, Uncle Bush?"

Bush smiled reminiscently, his eyes blue and bright. "I couldn't tell you that to save my soul!"

"Is she very pretty, Uncle Bush?"

"I went into this thing with my eyes wide open, I'm not belly-aching about it," said Bush.

From the Diary of Sarah Tarleton

January 3rd, 1919. *The Tallons received official news today of Bradford's death. He was killed in action in the Argonne. My spirit goes out to them in their bereavement. My heart is broken for poor Bessie. She will take this very hard, hers being a devoted, intense nature. Poor child, she has not yet learned:*

> *"Each one must take his pain with chastened heart*
> *And bow his back in patience to the rod,*
> *And pray: 'Thou art all just, compassionate Thou art;*
> *Not mine but Thy own will be done, dear God!' "*

June 6th, 1919. *Bessie takes her degree (Bachelor of Science with honors) this week. She will not have us come to see her or to share in her triumph. She says that she will never return to Pearl County and that she never wants to see us again. She blames us for having separated her from Mr. Tallon. My nephew, Jesse, has written from Atlanta to say that Bessie is coming to live with him and his wife. She will obtain work in Atlanta, possibly she will teach in one of the high schools; possibly she will go to Columbia next year for her master's degree. Jesse has taken her side against us. He is very bitter, but God knows why. My conscience is perfectly clear. I have never interfered in anyone's business. That is not my nature.*

22

THE following summer Chester returned to the store. He had been away for three winters, and in that time he had changed. He had reached his full height but he was still thin, with big hands and feet. Reedyville had modified him a little, and approaching maturity had changed him in many ways. The first Saturday afternoon he helped Bush in the store and met all of his old friends again. Sarah had fixed all the dishes that he liked and fed him constantly. She made a great deal over him.

One quiet day Chester sat with his uncle outside the store on the bench which had been placed there. They had been talking of many things, and then, gradually, the conversation died. Before them a sow, with a litter of black and white pigs, wallowed in the dust and turned on her side, grunting contentedly. The pigs crowded over her body with their small, sharp feet and pulled at her teats greedily. It was very hot and very quiet. The smoke from the Hodgetown mill lay faint and undisturbed against the sky to the south. There was no figure moving on the road or against the landscape except an old man tacking patent medicine signs against the fence on the opposite side of the road.

At last Chester spoke: "There's something troubling my mind, Uncle Bush." He looked away, avoiding Bushrod's eyes.

Bush answered very quietly: "Why don't you tell me all about it?"

But Chester did not reply. He sighed helplessly and looked at his hands.

Bush continued: "Have you got into any sort of trouble? If you have you'd better tell me the straight of it. There's no sense in hiding such things."

Chester shook his head: "It's not anything like that."

He sat silent for a moment before he spoke in a slow, hesitant voice: "I want to be tattooed the way you are."

Bushrod laughed: "You just think so now. You won't later on when you think it over carefully."

"I have thought it over, Uncle Bush."

"People will laugh at you if they know it, and say you are crazy, just as they all say I am crazy."

"I don't care what people say," said Chester. "If people think you're crazy, I want them to think I'm crazy, too."

Bushrod looked across the shimmering fields, his blue eyes far away. "That's very nice of you, Chester. It pleases me to know you think so much of me."

There was another long silence: "The trouble is, I can't think of the picture I want tattooed on me, Uncle Bush. Sometimes I almost remember it, but it always fades out again."

Bush smoked his cigar placidly, releasing rings through his rounded lips. "I understand," he said. "I understand."

The sow, before them, grunted twice and turned heavily on her side. One of her litter was imprisoned under her. He squealed and pawed with his tiny, cloven feet but he could not free himself from the oppressive weight. The sow began also to squeal and to shake her ears, looking around angrily for enemies, and regarding, with concern, her imprisoned shoat. Bush jumped up from the porch and kicked the sow until she sprang up and freed the young pig. She stood there, her hide caked with mud which had dried brittle in the sun, her back bristled and arched, and grunted sullenly, but when the squeals of the young shoat were no longer in her ears, she selected another spot beside the road and lay once more in the dirt. Her hungry litter swarmed over her again, pulling at her soiled teats and grunting their delight.

Bush was back on the bench and he continued the interrupted conversation: "And you can't think of what it is that troubles you all the time? You can't remember it?"

"Sometimes I almost think of it, but not quite."

Bush sighed. "Well, maybe you'll think of it some day."

Waves of heat rose from the red road and trembled above the fields. There was no breath of wind and the pine trees were without motion, and silent. The sow, amid her swarming young, grunted lazily in her content, and from the house there came the sound of Sarah singing to herself as she washed the dinner dishes.

"If you really want to be tattooed, I'll not try to stop you. But you'd better wait until you finish high school. As soon as you do, I'll take you with me to Baycity and you can get your first piece of work done there."

Chester's face was puzzled, his eyebrows drawn together. He was trying to put his thoughts into words. "I only want to be tattooed one time; and I want that one picture over my heart."

"Well," exclaimed Bush in surprise, "well, you are a queer one, Chester."

"I don't want you to think that I'm criticizing your being tattooed so many times," said Chester. "It's not that at all, Uncle Bush."

"Oh, I'm not sensitive about those things. I know you aren't criticizing me. I know that, Chester."

"The picture I want must be beautiful and perfect."

"What sort of a picture is it?"

"I don't know, exactly. I can't see it clearly, Uncle Bush; but sometimes I wake up at night and know that I have dreamed the picture, although I can't remember what it is, except in the dream there is a sort of clock and a pendulum that swings back and forth and turns in a dizzy way. There is a big hawk with yellow claws flying over my head."

He paused self-consciously and looked at his uncle, but Bushrod was listening gravely. "That's a very strange dream," he said. "I don't think I ever heard one just like it."

Chester said: "Sometimes I'm afraid I'll never be able to remember the picture. When I wake up in the morning I say to myself: 'I'll think of the picture today, no matter what else I do,' but I never can."

"You'll think of it, all in good time," said Bush. "Don't worry about that." He tilted the bench back against the wall. "You're a better artist than I am, Chester. You've got a finer feeling than I have."

An automobile drove up and stopped, and Bushrod went into the store to serve his customers. When he came back onto the porch, Chester had gone. Bushrod, his hand held upward to shade his eyes, watched him as he disappeared down the road, red and dusty in the hot sun, with waves of heat rising and shimmering upward. He shook his head: "Chester is a queer one, all right," he thought. He realized that in spite of the affection which existed between them, in spite of the many talks they had had together, he knew nothing at all of what went on inside his nephew's mind. Chester had told him nothing. Sarah, he realized, considered the boy lacking in affection and unimaginative; Lillian had always thought him sullen and obstinate. Bushrod sighed. Chester was not quite any of these things. "Poor Chester," he said aloud. "He's going to have a hard time of it."

Chester walked the hot road, a strip of red between the everlasting green of the young pines. At a certain point, as if he knew this place exactly from long habit, he turned out from the road and walked among the trees. He was hidden from the road and he stood waiting to see if anybody had followed him, his lips opened, a curious expression on his face; but there was only the whistling of a redbird not far away. Reassured, he turned and walked deeper through the young pines and black jacks until he came to the place where Bushrod's timber began.

It was a magnificent forest of virgin trees, all apparently the same height, all apparently the same size. The bark of the trees was a deep, brownish purple, and the trees themselves rose straight upward without foliage or intervening branches until they spread outward, toward their tops, into a level green of massed needles. Chester walked between the trees, in the perpetual twilight of their shade, feeling the coolness there, listening to the sound that the wind made in their tops, a faint, murmuring sound of water.

Presently he came to the open space in the grove that he knew so well, the glade where the creek widened to a pool. He found the log against which he had rested so many times and lay back, his eyes far away and without focus. It had been eight years since he had left his father's house and his memory of it was already becoming dim. He tried to bring his father's face into his consciousness, but he could not. He could not even visualize Mitty clearly. He could see her features separately, one by one, but he could not fit them all together. Strangely, it was the young coon which Jim had once owned, that he remembered best of all.

He lay back waiting, but this day no young angels came out and flew between the trees, or dipped and circled in the open glade, nor would the whisperer appear again to comfort him. He wondered, a little puzzled, if he had ever seen the angels, or if he had ever heard the whisperer. Possibly the stories were things which he had made up himself, had come from some place in his being that he did not understand.

He lay thinking of those things, disappointed that the whisperer was not there, feeling lonely and a little hurt. Then, a moment later, he knew without turning that his friend was seated

202

beside him on the log. The soundless voice came to his ears. "I've missed you," it said. "You've been away a long time."

"I've been in school," said Chester.

The whisperer laughed, his face running to innumerable, minute wrinkles. "Do you still like to hear only stories about kings and princes?"

"There's something on my mind," said Chester, "but I can't express it in words."

"Shall I tell you the story of a man who was in the same fix, and what he discovered at last?"

"Yes," said Chester.

"This man was a writer," said the whisperer. "He had written a great many books which a great many people had read." The whisperer looked straight ahead, collecting his thoughts, organizing his story, and then he began to speak.

From the Diary of Sarah Tarleton

August 3, 1919. Bessie is no longer living with her brother. She quarreled with Jesse's wife constantly and they all decided that it would be better if she moved. Jesse says she has taken an apartment of her own. She has a new position as credit manager in Ewell's Department Store and is doing well. I've written her several times and so has her father, but she returns all our letters unopened. I can only hope that she will never be punished for breaking our hearts.

September 1, 1919. Bessie has left Atlanta and has gone to Columbia to work for her master's degree. She is specializing in social science. Jesse is financing her. It isn't necessary that I make my comment. My opinions are held lightly, it seems.

23

THE graduating class was large that year and the exercises were held in the old opera house on Porterfield Street. The orchestra struck up a march and the curtain was raised. Then the graduating class filed onto the stage from the wings of the theater, the boys from the right, the girls from the left, and, somewhat primly, somewhat self-consciously, they seated themselves in the chairs assigned to them. There was a burst of applause from the expectant audience and a craning of necks down the aisles, but at last the people settled down to comparative silence, whispering and rattling programs.

A young lady, the class poetess, came forward and recited the rhymed welcome which she had prepared for the occasion. She recited solemnly, earnestly, as if the fate of all nations depended upon her clear and unequivocal enunciation. Behind her, regarding her white lace dress, her classmates sat stiffly, aware of their sudden importance, conscious that somewhere, in the dim cavern of semi-darkness, certain eyes were focused on them in pride, and on them alone. They sat rigidly on their chairs, like the wooden figures in galleries at street carnivals, as if, at any moment, someone would hurl a baseball into their stiffness and that the figure so struck would sway backward from the hips and fold up with a faint creaking of hinges.

But the poetess was continuing. When she had finished, there was a round of applause, and she was recalled in triumph. Finally she had to recite the last three stanzas of her poem again.

Then the orchestra started up and the class arose and sang the school song, set to the tune of "Coming Through the Rye." Afterwards there was a short, uncomfortable silence until the principal of the school got up. He fumbled for his glasses, cleared his throat and stood diffident and confused before his audience: after the assured ease of the poetess his unhappiness seemed more than ever apparent. He stood looking out into the darkness, his eyes a little strained, his lips smiling with too great a determination, before he took from his pocket a notebook and consulted it. He began, then, in a nervous unnatural voice:

"Our valedictorian this year is Chester Hurry, son of the late Ellen Tarleton Hurry, also a graduate of this institution, and nephew of Mrs. Lillian Tarleton Chapman, one of our most important club women. In taking first honors this year he is carrying on the tradition for erudition and culture established in this school by his uncles and aunts, all of whom have made brilliant scholastic records in their time."

There came a faint, anonymous clapping from the left and Principal Hemmes waited a moment. The clapping was taken up all over the house, in a polite, uncertain way. From their seats in the third row Aunt Sarah, Bushrod and Frank Tarleton looked at each other with pride. Lillian Chapman, who sat with her husband in the row just in front of them, turned around and smiled.

"I was not a valedictorian," she whispered. "I was beaten by a quarter of one percent by a girl named Pearlie Whitmore."

"He's talking about Bessie!" said Bushrod.

When the applause had subsided, Professor Hemmes, after consulting his notes, continued:

"Unlike most of the pupils graduating here tonight, Mr. Hurry did not attend the grade schools in Reedyville: he came to us, a stranger in our midst, in order to enter high school. But during the four years in which he has been with us he has endeared himself, both to his teachers and his fellow pupils, by his sunny, cheerful disposition."

Bushrod looked at Chester and then down at his program. Something in Chester's set, serious face struck him as funny and he began to laugh to himself.

"I wouldn't call Chester sunny-natured or affectionate," whispered Lillian doubtfully.

But Aunt Sarah raised a finger to her lips and Lillian nudged her husband and settled back in her seat. . . .

"As is customary at exercises of this sort, our valedictorian has written an essay which he will now read. He has chosen for his title the words: "So Live That When Thy Summons Comes to Join.' . . . It is a mighty theme and one worthy of the talents of the young essayist."

"Bessie chose for her subject 'The Siege and Fall of Charleston, South Carolina, During the War Between the Northern and Southern States of America,'" said Lillian. "I helped her look up her references."

But Chester had risen from his seat and was advancing calmly to the exact center of the stage. He stood fumbling his manuscript, staring at it with his light, somewhat serious eyes. Almost at once he began to read.

Lillian said, not turning her head this time: "I think his suit is very becoming. Evan and I gave it to him as a graduation present."

But Frank Tarleton, leaning forward in his pride and eagerness, his hand cupped to his ear, did not hear his daughter's words.

At last Chester sat down in his chair and looked gravely at his hands. Twice he rose and bowed to the enthusiastic audience, which he saw but dimly behind the white glare of the footlights.

Afterwards there was another song and an address by Mr. Palmiller, chairman of the school board; and then Professor

Hemmes sat at a table on which the diplomas were piled, each rolled and tied neatly with white ribbon. He called the names alphabetically and, in response, each graduate arose and accepted the fruit of his work.

The Reverend Saul Butler closed the ceremony with a prayer which went on and on; but just when everyone thought it would never end, the preacher, knowing, by long years of practice, just how much a congregation may be tried, terminated it quickly, in the middle of a sentence almost. And the relatives and friends of the class pushed forward to congratulate the particular pupil in whom they were interested.

Chester stood in the center of his relatives. He was embarrassed and he wanted to get away.

"We are all mighty proud of you, son," said Frank. "We're all proud of the fine showing you've made."

"Chester is a credit to the family," stated Lillian. "He has an authentic talent for literary expression." She turned to Bushrod for support: "I think he's cut out to be an author, and I've been trying to persuade him to at least take a correspondence course in short story writing, if nothing else."

"Aw, shucks!" said Bushrod. "Let him alone, can't you?"

"Education is the only thing in the world worth while," said Frank. "Education is a great thing. Chester will make fine marks in college. I bet he does as well as Bessie."

"I'm not going to college," said Chester. "I'm not going, so there's no use to talk about it."

"Why, Chester!" said Sarah. "Your grandfather has always had his heart set on that."

"I'm not going, just the same."

"Let him alone," said Bushrod. "Quit bothering him, can't you?"

The family got into Evan Chapman's automobile and were driven to his home, where they were to spend the night. Bushrod and Chester were sharing a room, the house being crowded with so many guests, and at last they were together, in bed, with the lights out.

"I want you to know we're mighty proud of you," said Bush. He yawned and burrowed into his pillow.

Chester said: "Do you remember you promised to take me to Baycity with you when I finished high school?"

"Yes. Yes, I remember that. We'll go whenever you're ready. I wrote Jim Saltis the other day and told him to be expecting us soon."

Chester felt contented and at peace. He had known all along that Bushrod would not forget his promise. "Tell me about the new piece of work, Uncle Bush. What are you going to have done this time?"

Bushrod's voice was muffled and a little indistinct. "I'll show it to you when we get to Baycity. I'll let you watch Jim tattoo it on me. You and I won't have any secrets from each other."

Chester turned on his back and stared upward at the ceiling. Under the covering of the bed he could feel the warmth of Bushrod's body. He felt drowsy and very happy. He was drifting away into unconsciousness, aware dimly of noises outside the window, of somebody playing a radio across the street, of a garage door creaking and being slammed softly. Bush's voice roused him.

"Did you ever think of the piece you want tattooed over your heart?"

Chester was completely awake again. A feeling of despair came over him, a feeling which he could neither understand nor explain.

"I haven't thought of it yet. Sometimes I almost remember it, but it goes away again."

"It will come to you, don't worry," said Bushrod reassuringly. "It will come some day, Chester."

Then he sighed, turned over and went to sleep.

But Chester lay awake for a long time. When he knew that he was not going to sleep, he got up and sat in a chair by the window. The night was bland and sweet and a full moon was high in heaven. Its light lay on the roofs of the houses, above the uncaring, sleeping people. It poured through the open window, and across the floor, in a shy, wan stream. . . . Outside the air was rich with many scents mingled together. The leaves of shrubs rustled faintly and were silent.

Chester sat with his arms resting on the sill, his thin, immature face raised to the light. "It will come back to me some day," he thought. "Uncle Bush said that it would."

From the Diary of Sarah Tarleton

June 15th, 1922. *Chester and Bushrod got away today for Bay-*
city where they expect to remain a week. I declare, you'd think
they were going to China to become missionaries from all the
preparations and running about. Bushrod is going to have some
more tattooing done, I suppose. I've disguised it from myself all
those years but Bush is eccentric. *I suppose we may as well face*
that fact. But it is all harmless enough. I always say that he is his
own "worst enemy." The affection between him and Chester is
very beautiful: it is as if he had taken the place of his father.

24

THE rooming house of Jim Saltis occupied the second and third stories of an old, red brick building decorated with iron grille work and shuttered with long, green blinds. The iron work was rusty and had pulled away from the bricks at certain places, and the blinds themselves were old and sagging with slats from the shutters missing. A flight of steps led directly from the street and stopped in front of Jim's tiny office. Below, in the hallway, were photographs in a glass case of his art: bravura work in which serpents writhed over the nude bodies of women, or in which battleships, with smoke against the horizon, steamed down an ocean too rigid in its turbulence.

Jim was an old sailor who had retired from the sea for the easier life of running a rooming house. Between his work as a landlord and his work as a tattooer he managed to live comfortably. When Bushrod and Chester reached Baycity they went immediately to his place. Jim was expecting them and gave them a warm welcome.

"I got your letter, Bush, and I've been wondering what sort of a picture you got for me this time. I've been thinking and thinking."

Bushrod said: "I have a good one, I believe. I've got something very original."

"That's what Abbie told me. Abbie said, 'You can't ever figure out what Uncle Bushrod is going to think up. There's not any telling what he'll think of next.'"

Bushrod bowed with pleasure. "Be sure to thank the young lady for the compliment."

Jim preceded them into his parlor. He was red-faced and vigorous, and he moved quickly, as if perpetually obeying the orders of a superior.

"Hold on," said Bush. "I've forgotten to introduce Chester." Jim stopped and turned around.

"This is my nephew, Chester Hurry. He's just finished school and I brought him with me this time for a little trip. This is the first time he's been in the city."

Jim shook hands. "I hope you like it here. We've got all sorts of people in Baycity: good, bad and indifferent. You ought to find what you want, if you look hard enough."

"Thank you," said Chester. "I think I'm going to like it."

"That's fine! That's fine! . . . We always want our visitors to have a good time."

Jim's parlor was small and somewhat dark, but it was very clean and very neat. It contained an old set of velvet furniture with the wine-colored cloth worn away in places. There were pillows everywhere, pillows of every description and in every pattern: pillows shaped like lozenges, like half moons and like hearts. Some of these pillows had heavy fringes of lace, some were worked in beads and some were covered extravagantly with fruits and flowers in all colors.

"Sit down! Sit down!" urged Jim genially. "Sit down and take a load off your mind." He went to the window and drew back the pink curtains which were also fringed and which were embroidered with cornucopias of spilling, brilliantly colored fruit. More light came into the room brightening it.

Chester seated himself on a chair and rested his head against the embroidered linen scarf thrown over its back. Guiltily he removed the two pillows from behind his back and placed them on the velvet couch. Jim, who had seen his furtive act, smiled and winked in commiseration.

"Abbie is the greatest hand I ever seen to make sofa pillows and curtains. She's got the whole place cluttered up."

He addressed Bushrod. "Well, what's the picture going to be this time?"

Bush said: "I've got the drawing in my valise, but the rough idea is an ostrich with its neck in the sand in three separate loops. In the distance the ostrich's head sticks up again. He wants to look at something behind him, but he can't do it: there's so much sand on his neck he can't turn it any more."

Jim was enthusiastic about the picture. "I never done a ostrich, but it ought not to be hard. That's a good one, all right, Bush."

"I'll show you the drawing when I unpack my valise."

"You're going to stay with me this time, aren't you?"

"Oh, yes," answered Bush. "Oh, sure."

"Abbie's got your room ready for you. I'll just step out and tell her to fix up a place for the young man also."

"Chester can sleep with me if you're short of rooms."

"There's not any need for that," said Jim. "There's almost nobody in the house right now. I'll just step out and tell Abbie you're here; then you can go up to your rooms whenever you want to and freshen up. It'll only take a minute."

Jim parted the bead curtains and went out, closing the door behind him.

Bushrod looked at Chester and smiled. "Well, how do you like Baycity so far?"

"I like it all right," said Chester. He looked about him, his eyes taking in the details of the room. "Where does Mr. Saltis do his tattooing? He doesn't do it here, does he?"

"Oh, Lord, no!" said Bush. "I should say he doesn't." He chuckled: "I can just imagine what Abbie would say to him, if he did anything like that."

Bush walked about the room, looking again at its familiar pictures. "Jim can't deny Abbie anything she wants. . . . Well, I don't blame him much at that. She's the prettiest little thing you ever saw."

The door opened and Jim came back into the room. He had caught the last sentence. He said: "Are you telling the young fellow about Abbie?"

"Yes," said Bushrod. "I was telling him that I'd known Abbie since she was a little girl. I was telling him how pretty and sweet she is."

"She's a beauty, all right," said Jim. "God knows how she happened to be my daughter."

A few minutes later a young seaman, with his front teeth missing, came into the room and spoke to Jim. "Miss Abbie says the rooms are all ready and that I was to carry up the suitcases."

"They're all in the hall," said Bush. "Wait, I'll help you bring them up."

"That's all right, buddy," said the young sailor. "I've carried heavier things than that."

Bushrod and Chester followed him out of the room.

"Come down when you get washed up," urged Jim. "I want you to feel at home here. I want you to feel like a member of the family, not like you were renting rooms off me." He came behind them into the hall and walked with them up the steps to the next floor, where their rooms were.

"We'll start on that piece of work after dinner," he suggested. "That is if you want to."

"That's satisfactory," said Bushrod. "Any time that suits you, suits me, too. I haven't got anything to do for the next week except enjoy myself."

"I don't want to rush you," said Jim, "but I'm anxious to see that new picture of yours. I want to get to work on it."

One of the doors at the end of the long hall opened and Chester had a quick glimpse of a girl with golden curls. Immediately the door was closed half way. The girl made a small, piping noise, and began to giggle.

"Come on out, Abbie," said Jim. "Come on out and see Bushrod. He was asking about you the very first thing."

But Abbie continued to laugh. She covered her face with her lacy apron. "Go away!" she said. "Go away and let me pass! I look a sight. . . . I wouldn't have anybody see me this way for the world!" She lowered her apron for a moment and glanced at the four men in front of her. "Don't look at me, please!" she begged. She sidled against the wall, her face still covered, until she reached the stairs. Then she turned, still laughing, and ran downward.

There was a fatuous, devoted look on the face of the young sailor. He stood gaping after her, his mouth a little open.

"Take the bags in there," said Jim sharply. "Don't waste time, Sam."

Below Abbie could be heard singing, her voice gay and crystal and clear.

Chester spoke for the first time: "Is your wife dead, Mr. Saltis?"

And Jim looked at him, slightly surprised. "I haven't got a wife. I'm an old bachelor." He seemed to be turning the thought over in his mind, as if the situation required some explanation, but in the end he said nothing, letting his words stand as they were.

Later in the day Bushrod and Chester sat in Jim's bare workroom and before them was Jim Saltis himself, his inks and his needles near his right hand. He picked up Bush's drawing and examined it critically with calculating, professional eyes. Bushrod had taken off his pants and sat now in his shirt, his short drawers rolled up, exposing his hard, muscular thighs.

Jim said, somewhat doubtfully, tapping an unoccupied stretch

216

of flesh with his needle: "I don't know whether I can fit it all in that place or not." He pursed up his lips and frowned. "I'll have to shorten the neck of the bird or run it over on the other side of your leg. I've got to do one or the other."

"That wouldn't be right," replied Bush. "Why not run the neck all the way around the leg, dipping under the sand every few inches and let it come up again on the same side it started from? In that way you can have the ostrich facing itself, if you know what I mean."

"That's the ticket," said Jim enthusiastically. "That's the very idea."

He turned to Chester, who sat on a box watching: "I don't know what I'd do without your Uncle Bush. He's the only customer I got who takes an interest in tattooing as an art."

Bush smiled modestly: "Now, Jim," he said; "now, Jim!"

"It's the truth," said Jim positively. "It's the God's truth." He put down the needle and spoke directly to Chester. "Oh, I get a lot of people, sailors and such, who want a bit of work done now and then, but what do they want? . . . It's always the same with those fellows: it's always a full-rigged ship or an eagle, or a cooch dancer with tits and a belly button!"

Jim guffawed and slapped his leg. "You think I'm kidding, but it's the God's truth!" He took up a piece of carbon and began to outline, in widely spaced dots, the first part of the picture. He worked in silence for a little while, but he could not keep still very long. "How would it be to put a camel and a palm tree in the distance?"

"Oh, no! That wouldn't do at all."

"Why not?" demanded Jim. "What's wrong with that?"

"I can't explain it," said Bush, "but it wouldn't be right. That would spoil the whole idea."

"Just as you say," said Jim regretfully. "I won't argue the point."

217

After he had worked for an hour, there came a knock on the door.

"Who is it?" shouted Jim. Then, with no break in his words he continued: "Is that you, Abbie?"

"Yes," she said gayly. "Can I come in?"

"Sure!" said Jim. "Come on in."

Abbie came into the room, but when she saw Bush's bare thigh, she made a screaming, shocked noise and turned her head away. "Oh! I wouldn't have come in for the world, if I had known.—I wouldn't have!"

"It's all right, Abbie," said Jim, laughing and winking. "It's just plain skin like everybody else's." Bush put on his pants quickly and buttoned them up. When he had finished, Abbie turned and glanced roguishly through her laced fingers. She tilted back her head and laughed again. "You're a bad old thing, Uncle Bush. You ought to be arrested for shocking me that way." She kissed him lightly on the forehead, dancing away as if he meant to pursue her.

"Wait a minute," said Jim. "I want to make you acquainted with Mr. Chester Hurry. He's Bushrod's nephew."

Abbie turned sweetly and extended her hand and Chester went over to meet her. Abbie's face was round and soft and her yellow hair hung about it in curls. She had a tiny, somewhat flat nose and her wide opened, slightly protuberant eyes were light and also golden, almost the shade of her hair. She looked at Chester for a moment and then, when she saw the unmistakable look of admiration in his eyes, she glanced demurely at her hands. A moment later she looked up again somewhat timidly, and smiled in understanding, a smile for Chester alone, as if they already shared some secrets.

Bushrod was putting on his coat.

Abbie said: "Oh, I almost forgot what I came for! I've fixed some hot coffee and cakes on the dining room table. I thought

218

you might be getting hungry." She began to tickle her adoring father. "Hurry! Hurry!" she said. "Everything will get cold!" In addition to the coffee and the cookies there were tiny sandwiches cut also in a pattern of hearts and stars and half moons.

"Well," said Bush. "This is really a treat. I'm not used to so much attention."

"What you need is a wife to look after you," said Abbie. "You old bachelors make me tired."

"I've been married," said Bush quietly. "In fact I still am, so far as I know."

"Oh," said Abbie. "I forgot." She came to Bush in sympathy. "Oh, I beg your pardon. I really do."

Jim, who knew all of Bushrod's affairs, changed the subject at once. He nodded toward Chester. "How about this young fellow having a piece of work done, too, now that he's here?"

Bush explained, then, about the picture which Chester wanted: that he wanted one picture only, and how that one picture was to be placed over his heart.

"Sure," said Jim in a sympathetic manner. "I understand that part, all right; but what difference will it make if he has something else put on his back, say. One picture won't interfere with the other. You can't see them both at the same time."

"It wouldn't be the same thing," said Chester quietly.

"Well, maybe not," admitted Jim. . . . "But I can't see the difference, that's all." He put down his coffee cup and wiped his lips on one of Abbie's small, hand-made napkins.

"*I* understand what Mr. Hurry means," said Abbie. "I know just how he feels, and I think his wish is very beautiful!"

"Well," said Jim, winking at Bush. "Listen to Abbie's talking, won't you?"

Chester, at that moment, had a warm, deep feeling which he had never experienced before. He glanced at Abbie shyly, with a new interest. He discovered then that she was beautiful; that she was unlike any girl he had ever known before.

"I think Mr. Hurry is right in waiting until he's sure what the picture is. It's like something I saw once in the movies. I think it's very sweet and romantic."

Abbie got up and began to bustle about and scold. "You're not eating anything at all! I made these cakes with pecans especially for you, Uncle Bushrod. I knew you liked them so much, and now you won't even eat them!"

"My Lord!" said Bushrod, his blue eyes narrowed and very bright; "I've eaten at least a dozen."

"You're not eating anything at all," insisted Abbie in her sweet, childish way. "Don't try to tell me differently, because I've been watching you the whole time."

The Whisperer

OVER the town, through the streets, and into the houses themselves there drifted inescapably the smell of the stockyards: a sickening smell compounded of blood and rancid fat. It was August and it was so stifling, so oppressive, that the girl left the unwashed dishes lying in their grease and came to sit for a few moments on the porch.

Before her was a row of unpainted houses each precisely like its neighbor and each filled with people so alike that they might all have been cut with the same pair of scissors from the same piece of tin. Each house stared at the poverty of its neighbors across a street which was not really a street at all: it was only a width of sour earth pitted with mud holes and littered with rusting cans.

As the girl sat rocking, listening to the regular squeak of the chair, she raised her hands, still glazed a little from dishwater, and pressed them against her cheeks; but their faint smell of dishwater offended her and she lowered them in disgust. She got up, remembering that her sweetheart was coming to see her that night, and went into the house to prepare for him. She washed herself all over and changed completely, but almost before she had put on fresh clothes she could feel them sticking to her body. Sweat ran across her cheeks and down her back. She stood there in the room, her face twisted in disgust. Finally she picked up a bottle of violet perfume and touched the lobe of each ear with the stopper, but immediately she put down the bottle again: for the stink from the yards clung to everything, penetrated everything; it lay over the town and crowded into the houses like invisible, nauseating smoke; it was futile to combat its power with perfume, and she knew it.

She sighed and turned away, and at that moment she heard her sweetheart's step on the porch. She looked at herself in her mirror for a moment, hoping for reassurance, but her hair, which she had curled so carefully, was limp again and hanging disconsolately; her face was damp and shining and her neck reddened. She started to put powder on her face again, but angrily she threw down the puff. . . . She was still angry when she went on the porch and sat in the swing with her lover.

Across the street, in one of the houses, a child began to fret; and next door the man and his wife began again their unending, pointless quarrel. All down the street people sat on their porches and rocked, fanning themselves. The sky was close and no air moved: there was only the sickening smell of dried blood and boiling fat, of crowded, unwashed people, of stale garbage and sour fruit rinds.

But the man was not conscious of these smells. He sat in the swing looking at the girl, touching her hand clumsily, aware only of the drop of perfume which she had used. "You're like a field of violets with a wind blowing through it," he said shyly.

25

JIM SALTIS, taking more than ordinary pride in his work on Bushrod, proceeded slowly with the design, but at last it was finished. A few days remained before they were to return to Pearl County and Bushrod hired an automobile and took Chester on long trips about the town and through the countryside. They drove around the harbor and inspected the facilities or watched the loading of ships. Bushrod was very interested. He asked many questions and was always getting in the way of the stevedores.

As the day fixed for their departure got closer, Bushrod became preoccupied and a little absent in his manner. He did not want to return to the store and there was in his mind a half-formed plan to remain permanently in Baycity. There was nothing to prevent such a thing, if you come right down to it: His father, in spite of his rheumatism, could run the store with some assistance from Aunt Sarah, or, if that were too much for them, he could always hire Tom Outerbridge, who had helped out on occasions in the past. There was not much point in returning to Pearl County. He was missing all the excitement and all the gayety of life. He had ample money saved up to take care of himself and Chester for a long time, if they lived modestly. Chester was almost a man now. He wouldn't go to college or prepare himself for any special work or profession. There was nothing for him in Pearl County: he would merely drift on. About all he could ever expect was to farm or to get a job in the sawmill at Hodgetown. . . . Thus Bushrod reasoned and the more he thought of these things, the more the wish to remain in Baycity grew in his mind. He talked it over with Jim Saltis, whose opinion he trusted, and found that Jim shared his views.

That afternoon Bushrod and Chester took a walk and Bushrod stopped before a small, brick house, decorated intricately with iron grille work. He knew at once that this was the place where he wanted to live. He stood for a moment examining the sign on the door which indicated not only the vacancy of the house, but the fact that it was for sale, as well.

He spoke cautiously, feeling his way: "How would you like to live here in Baycity, Chester? Do you think you'd like it as well as Pearl County?"

He found, then, that the same idea was in Chester's mind. Bush was delighted. He stood laughing gayly, his eyes drawn to a blue, narrow line, his teeth white against the perpetual tan of his skin. "Well, think of that. . . . Think of both of us figuring on the same thing and neither wanting to speak about it first. By God, we might have gone back home and neither of us ever knew!"

Chester answered, in his serious way: "I want to get a job and go to work. I'm almost nineteen years old, and it's time I was making my own way. I've wasted enough time as it is."

"There's no need of you going to work, unless you really want to," said Bush. "I've plenty for us both, for the time being, at any rate."

"I want to go to work, Uncle Bush. I want to make my own way."

"That's a very fine spirit to show, Chester. . . . As a matter of fact I expect to get a job, too. I don't much care what it is just so long as it keeps me busy."

And so it happened that Bush bought the brick house and began to furnish it. Abbie was very helpful. She went about looking for bargains, haggling with shopkeepers. She was always very helpless and very pretty in her transactions, and she always got precisely what she wanted. Bush was surprised at her shrewdness. He put his arm about her and pulled her to him. He pressed down the end of her tiny, somewhat flattened nose, with his thumb: "I've seen some close traders in my life, but you take the cake. I'd hate to try to beat you swapping horses."

Abbie shook her curls and rolled her eyes upward. "Why, Uncle Bush!" she replied in her lisping, little-girl voice. "I think you're just laughing at me."

"Laughing, hell!" said Bush. "You could get the button off a rattlesnake's tail so quick he wouldn't miss it." He pinched her cheek genially and patted her head.

Jim smiled proudly. "Abbie may be only a sixteen-year-old girl but anybody that takes her for a fool will wake up and know better."

"Now, pappa!" protested Abbie, putting her hand over his mouth; "now, pappa!" She stuck out her index finger and folded the other fingers against her palm until her tiny, white hand resembled a pistol. She raised her thumb upward, as if she were pulling a trigger. "Bang! Bang!" she said, her eyes coy and innocent, her yellow curls tossing about. She came up to Bushrod. "I'll shoot you, too, Uncle Bush! . . . Bang! Bang!—now you're all dead, except Chester."

She danced away and Jim followed her figure with his adoring eyes. "It's not because Abbie's my own daughter," he remarked proudly, "but she's just about the sweetest little thing in this town. I never cared two bits for a hard woman. A woman's duty is to marry some good man, I've always said; and Abbie's going to make some man mighty happy one of these days. . . . Mighty happy!"

Bushrod nodded seriously. Abbie wasn't exactly the sort of

woman that he, himself, admired, but he could understand the admiration of others for her. He looked at Chester, silent and impassive, as usual, and saw the look of admiration in his nephew's eyes. He laughed deeply to himself. "All right," he thought. "Chester could do a lot worse."

A week later they were settled in the new house, but in the meantime Bushrod had been back to the farm and had told his family of his present plans. Aunt Sarah had said that she could run the store herself and had arranged to get a woman to cook and to do the housework. And so everything was now fixed and running along smoothly.

A few days after his nineteenth birthday, Chester went to work for a real estate and insurance company. He got the job through Evan Chapman, who was well acquainted with the members of the firm. His duties were not difficult. He liked the quiet routine of the work and was content. The months drifted by pleasantly. At nights he went to a business school or read at home. Sometimes he went out with one of the boys from the office to a dance or a movie and occasionally Jim Saltis and Abbie came to dinner, a dinner which Bushrod had prepared. Later they played cards, or listened to the radio.

Bushrod was learning to play the ocarina. He had seen one, in the window of a pawnbroker. He had not known, at first, quite what it was, but he had decided that he must learn to play it. Jim would sit and listen to the thin music, but Abbie and Chester would go away and talk together. As Chester became older, he began to see Bush with different eyes; he was already beginning to be a little ashamed of him, a little apologetic over his eccentricities. Bush was certainly strange, there was no doubt about that. He was always doing unexpected things, always expressing an opinion which nobody else shared. Chester had made friends with several young men in his office, but he was not quite willing to bring them home, although Bushrod often urged him to do so. He was afraid that they would make fun of Bush, that they would laugh at him behind his back. As the months passed he withdrew more and more into himself, but if Bushrod was conscious that the old spontaneity between them was gone, he said nothing. Bushrod was working now. He was manager of a small chain grocery store.

One night, the following summer, Chester and Abbie went out into the garden at the back of the house. There was a moon high in the sky and the iron grille threw involved shadows across the flag-paved walk. They sat on a bench and the thin wail of Bushrod's music came to their ears indistinctly. Chester spoke: "Do you think Uncle Bush is crazy?"

Abbie looked at him. Her eyes closed shrewdly. "Why of course I don't. What ever made you ask a question like that?"

She watched his face and saw the look of gratitude that came over it with her reassurance.

"Oh, I don't know. I just wondered what you and Jim really thought of us."

"Pappa thinks very highly of you both," said Abbie. "Very highly, indeed."

Chester reached out and took her hand in his own. "Back in Pearl County everybody said Uncle Bush was crazy because he was tattooed all over his body. Everybody laughed at him and made fun of him."

"Why, I never heard of such a thing!" said Abbie indignantly. "The very idea of saying such a thing." She disengaged her hand, reached out and caught at a swinging branch. She laughed quickly and shook her curls. "I'd like to be tattooed myself, but only common women who hang around the wharves are like that."

Chester was surprised. "What sort of women do you mean, Abbie?"

"Oh, you know: . . . Bad women, or girls like May who have sailors for regular sweethearts." Her eyes narrowed shrewdly. She tilted back her head. "You know," she repeated. "You know very well what I mean."

"But I don't know," said Chester earnestly.

Abbie turned away abruptly. "You're the funniest boy I ever met."

"What do they have tattooed on them?" he insisted.

But she looked upward at the moon and raised her arms, grasping for the branch again, her small, beautiful breasts outlined against her thin dress. "I don't know. Why do you ask me?" All her sweetness, her soft helplessness, was gone. Her voice was hard. The babyish lisp had disappeared. "Why don't you find it out for yourself?" she answered sullenly. "Why don't you find out for yourself if you're so interested?"

"Is May the woman who has a room on the third floor?"

"Maybe so. Maybe she is."

"What has May got tattooed on her?"

"I won't tell you!"

"But, Abbie, please do. I want to know."

"Oh, she's got a battleship, an anchor and chains, and her lover's name in a heart." Abbie stopped and turned on him furiously. "You think you're better than us, don't you? You think we're dirt because people like May live with us."

"I never meant anything like that, and you know it."

"You think I'm a bad girl like May and Virgie just because they live in our house. . . . Don't deny it, because that's just what you *do* think!"

"Abbie! Abbie! please don't act this way!"

"Do you think I like living near the wharves with sailors and women like May and the others? Do you think I like to have people look down on us the way they do?"

She covered her face with her hands and began to cry, and

before Chester knew what he was doing he had put his arms around her soft body. He held her protectingly. "I don't think that at all; you know I don't."

Abbie rested her head against his thin chest. Gradually her tears stopped. "You don't think I'm a common girl? You really don't despise me?"

When Chester could speak, at last, his voice trembled. "I think you're the most wonderful girl I ever met." He raised her chin and looked at her wet, starry eyes. He kissed her soft mouth gently.

Abbie became gay again. "Oh, you bad man!" she said severely. "You ought to be ashamed of yourself." She pulled away from him and retreated to the other side of the small court, but Chester followed her. "No! No!" said Abbie. "What sort of a girl do you think I am?"

"I think you're sweet and wonderful. You know I think that." Again he put his arms about her and Abbie laughed roguishly. "Just one more kiss. But it must be just a teensy-weensy one."

And so the months passed, and then, one day, an unexpected thing happened. It was the first of September and Chester had been working late that night, getting his accounts straight. It was ten o'clock when he got home and let himself in. He went back to the kitchen to get something to eat. Bushrod, hearing his step, came to meet him. His white, perfect teeth were exposed and his eyes were brilliant and blue with excitement.

"Ruby is here!" he said.

Chester looked at him stupidly. "Who is here?"

"Ruby!" said Bushrod. "My wife has come back."

He came into the dining room with Chester and sat opposite while Chester ate his supper. "She's been sick and she's down and out. I was the only person in the world she had to turn to."

Chester had a quick feeling of resentment, but he stifled it.

He looked at Bushrod's happy, excited face, at his blue, childish eyes.

"Oh!" he said.

"I'm sure glad to see her!" continued Bush. He picked up a fork and began to mark patterns on the cloth. "You don't know how happy it makes me to realize that Ruby turned to me in her trouble."

Chester chewed slowly for a few minutes. "How long does she expect to stay?"

Bushrod's face became grave. "She's going to stay always, I hope. . . . That was a strange question to ask, Chester: Where else would you expect her to stay?" He looked at Chester pathetically, pleadingly, as if imploring him not to make things difficult. His face fell a little. "I hope you two get along all right. I hope Ruby likes you."

Chester drained his glass of milk and put down his napkin, and automatically Bushrod picked up the soiled dishes and took them to the kitchen. When he returned, Chester had got up. "I'll see her in the morning, Uncle Bush. I'm tired now."

He went upstairs to his room but Bushrod followed him, talking happily. "I've already told Ruby that you were staying here and she doesn't object at all. Don't let that worry you, Chester."

Chester went into his room and shut the door. He thought: "So she doesn't object to my being here. Well, that's pretty nice of her!" He laughed angrily. "Pretty God damned nice, I call it." He sat down and turned on his reading light, but he could hear the drone of Bush talking endlessly in the adjoining room. Occasionally he could hear Ruby's voice. He sighed and put the book away. Later, in bed, he tried to visualize what Ruby looked like. Bush had often described her, but he could not bring any clear picture of her into his mind.

The next morning, while Bushrod was fixing their breakfast, Chester heard more about Ruby. After the barber had deserted her she had had a series of other friends, but things had been all right until she got sick. Finally, not knowing what else to do, she had written her mother and her mother had told her that Bushrod would take her back. So Ruby had spent the little money she had left on railroad fare and had returned to him. She had come back humbly, not quite knowing what Bush would say or do, expecting only that he would take care of her until she was able to continue her profession. But Bushrod's joy at seeing her again was boundless. Ruby had sat sullen and composed and in the end it was he who begged forgiveness.

"I cried when she came home," said Bush. "I couldn't help it. I was so glad to have her with me again." He put down the coffee pot. "There's something sweet about Ruby. There's something awfully sweet about her, when she wants to be."

Something in Bushrod's earnest stupidity struck Chester as funny. He wanted to laugh, but he did not. He felt, at that moment, tolerantly contemptuous of his uncle, much older than Bushrod, more of a man of the world. The thing seemed farcical.

"I suppose I'll have to call her Aunt Ruby, or isn't that necessary?" he said in an amused voice.

"Oh, I don't think so," said Bush hastily. "Just call her Ruby. I don't think she'll object." He was fixing a tray, arranging it neatly. "I made her promise to stay in bed and get some rest. She's still weak from her sickness. They didn't treat her very well in the hospital, she says."

There came a rustling of silk and a hoarse cough, and Ruby stood in the doorway. She was wearing a crimson kimono trimmed with lace which was somewhat soiled. She was heavily rouged. Her eyes were darkened and her lashes beaded extravagantly. Her hair was brittle and like wire. It stood about her head untidily, almost the color of straw, contrasting oddly with her small, black eyes and her swarthy neck and throat. She stood framed in the doorway for a moment. She yawned deeply. "Give me a cigarette, somebody." Chester handed her his pack and she took one without comment, lighted it and sat down at the table. Bushrod continued: "You shouldn't have got up, honey. You promised me to stay in bed." He stood holding the tray clumsily, not knowing what to do with it. But Ruby paid no attention to him. She had slept with him again and she was again sure of her power over him. Her contempt and her arrogance had come back. She inhaled the smoke deeply, looked out of the window and yawned once more.

From the Diary of Sarah Tarleton

August 15, 1923. *Spent a most pleasant week in Mobile with Bushrod and Chester. They are fixed up comfortably. I declare Bushrod is just like an old hen with one chicken, watching out for Chester. He would have made a fine father and it is too bad that his natural and praiseworthy desire for paternity has been frustrated.*

Chester has just gone to work for Hallman and Graham, owners of the Home Realty and Indemnity Company. His position is quite modest, but that is natural of course at first. I have no doubt but that his intelligence and the sterling qualities of his character will soon manifest themselves and that his employers will adequately reward his fidelity to their interests. I met a Miss Abbie Saltis in Baycity. It was she who helped Bushrod furnish the house. She is sweet and lovely. She made a great deal over Bushrod, but I pride myself on my ability to understand people and I believe her interest is in Chester! I joked him about it, but he became angry. He is a strange boy, so reserved and so entirely lacking in humor. Abbie has promised to be my correspondent and to tell me all the news. I have long since learned that I may expect no letters from Bushrod or Chester.

September 4, 1924. *Lillian called me up over long distance from Reedyville. She tells me that Ruby has gone back to Bushrod and is living with him openly. I hope that her information is not true, as Bushrod has already suffered enough at her hands. Lillian is writing him a letter, she feels that it is her duty to do so, warning him of Ruby and telling him again of her character and the loose life that she had led. Poor, poor Bushrod! And poor Chester, to be subjected to such influences.*

October 8, 1924. *To our great surprise we received a letter today from Bessie. Time has assuaged her sorrow and changed her attitude toward us. She is connected with some sort of a labor organization. She says she enjoys making speeches; but neither Frank nor I understand what she means. We trust that she is not doing anything immodest or unwomanly. Her letter was very sweet. She asked our forgiveness for all the harsh things which she has said. I shall start a long letter to her as soon as I have finished this entry.*

26

Ruby's first act as mistress of the house was to discharge the old woman who had cleaned the place and prepared the meals. Chester was somewhat annoyed, since he had hired the woman and was paying her himself, but Ruby was very voluble in her reasons: The woman didn't clean well; she was always prying into matters which didn't concern her, and, besides, she stole things from the kitchen. Ruby said that she would do the work herself. And so she took charge of the housekeeping in an indolent, slipshod way. But often she had headaches, or forgot dinner entirely, not being used to regularity and not understanding the wish for it in others. At such times Bushrod, slightly apologetic, but careful not to offend his wife, fixed something for himself and Chester after his return from the grocery store.

Chester was at home very little during these days. When he was, he avoided Ruby as much as possible, treating her with calculated courtesy. At first Ruby put herself out to attract him. She tried to please him: she was melting and provocative by turns, but when, at last, she understood the full degree of his cold dislike, her attitude changed. She began to do things and to say things deliberately to offend him. Toward Bushrod her attitude was more negative: She despised him and did not trouble to hide her feelings. It was about this time that she started drinking again, stealthily at first, but more boldly as the days passed. There was always a smell of whiskey about her. But she was more amiable when she was drunk, kinder to Bushrod in those moments. For a time (she was drinking heavily now) it was her humor to refuse Bushrod access to their joint room unless he paid in advance for the privilege of sleeping in his own bed. She would stand blocking the door, her black eyes small and avaricious, and bargain like a shrew for the price of her charms.

"Don't, darling!" Bushrod would say. "Please don't act like this."

Ruby would laugh drunkenly. "I'm not givin' *anything* away. Get that in your head, mister!"

And Chester, in the room adjoining, would turn over in bed, sickened a little; he would cover his ears or will that his mind not listen; but Ruby's strident voice would penetrate his consciousness. He would laugh bitterly. "Nobody will ever catch me in a trap like this. . . . Nobody."

One night Chester and Bushrod arrived home at the same time and stood at the door, each fumbling for his keys. When, at last, Bushrod opened the door and they entered the house, they were conscious of the sour smell of whiskey, against another and a more powerful smell. Chester went into the living room and switched on the lights, and there, before him, was Ruby stretched out on the sofa. She was wearing the kimono which she had worn at breakfast, and it was obvious that she had been drinking all day. She made a blurred, indistinct noise with her limp, wide-opened lips, as if she sought to blow bubbles.

Both men stood looking at her. They saw that she had vomited over the sofa and on the floor and lay, now, in the filth that she had made, her brittle, strawlike hair spread about her relaxed face.

The light bothered her. She raised her head slightly and opened her eyes, not quite remembering where she was. She smiled invitingly: "Come on to bed, big boy. Come on, I'll treat you right." She rolled her eyes from side to side and tried to sit up, the foulness of her breath reaching the nostrils of the two men, spots of her vomit dry on her chin.

"Kiss me!" she said in a wheedling tone. "Kiss me, big boy!"

Chester backed away. "How can you stand for this, Uncle Bush?" He walked across the room and pulled the shades down angrily. "How can you put up with this—this—"

Bush stood shamed and uncertain. "Lie down, Ruby. . . . You're not feeling well."

But Ruby got up, somewhat unsteadily, and shoved Bush aside. She stood with her legs wide apart, leaning against a chair for balance. She brushed her hair out of her eyes with a rough, vague movement of her two hands. Her eyes narrowed and she jutted her chin forward. She turned toward Chester and began to shout.

"You little bastard! You bastard you!"

Chester did not answer her. He spoke instead to Bushrod. "Why don't you throw her out in the street where she belongs?"

Ruby took a few steps toward him, her face working in fury. She stumbled and almost fell. "You get out yourself, you little punk! . . . If anybody gets out, it'll be you that gets out, not me!" She waved her arms and swore obscenely, her brittle hair tossing in her fury.

Bush took her arms and held them to her side. "Be quiet, for God's sake. You don't know what you're saying. The people next door can hear you. . . ."

"I've known pimps better than that little punk," she screamed. "Who the hell is he to try to turn my own husband against me?"

In the hall Chester put on his hat and coat and went out, slamming the door. He entered the first restaurant he came to and ordered dinner, but he could not eat the food put before him. He paid his check, got up and left. After that he walked about without plan or destination until he reached at last the wide, muddy river. It was dark, and he could see little, but there was

238

a fresh smell of salt in the air, a smell, too, of tar and bananas. A steamer came down the river accompanied by tugs. Her lights were all blazing and she sounded her whistle at regular intervals to warn other craft of her approach. The freighter passed close to where he stood, slowly, ponderously.

Chester spoke aloud: "I'm going to get out tonight. I'm moving to a hotel."

A wave of anger came over him. He walked home rapidly, entered, and walked upstairs. Bushrod had put Ruby to bed and had cleaned up the filth that she had made. He heard Chester on the stairs and followed him into his room. Chester neither looked at his uncle nor spoke to him. He got down his suitcases and began to pack his belongings.

Bush broke the silence. "I don't blame you for leaving, Chester, I want you to know that."

At the sound of Bush's voice, so hurt and so helpless, Chester felt his anger vanishing. "Why do you stand for this sort of thing, Uncle Bush?"

Bush sighed. "I don't know. God knows, I wish I did. I understand what she is better than anybody in the world. I've never been fooled by her."

"I can't figure you out, Uncle Bush. . . . It's all beyond me."

Bush said: "I'm only trying to be practical about this thing. I'm trying to see it from all angles, and be practical about it."

There was something pitiful in his abjectness. Chester stopped his packing and sat down on the side of the bed. He knew then that he could not desert Bushrod, no matter what happened. He couldn't leave him to face this emergency alone.

"I know I'm a fool," said Bush. "I know that people laugh at me or feel sorry for me, one thing or the other, but I can't help it."

Chester spoke: "If you want me to stay, I'll do the best I can."

"I'm going on forty-four years old," continued Bush. "Pretty soon I'll be an old man. If I don't get a little contentment out of life now, when can I expect to get it? . . . I've figured it all out: I'm happier with Ruby, even like she is, than I was during the time she was away from me. I just can't help that, Chester."

Chester put his hand on Bush's arm, in one of his rare gestures of affection. "You'd better stay in here with me tonight. We can talk things over in the morning."

Bush's face was pale and drawn. "You don't know how I despise myself. You don't know what a low opinion I have of myself."

"Let's forget that, Uncle Bush."

The next morning Ruby was sick. She groaned and rolled about in her bed. Before going to work, Bushrod went up again to see if she was all right. He had fixed breakfast for her and carried it to her on a tray, but Ruby couldn't eat it. She took his hand and kissed it humbly, her tears falling over his wrists. She was always sentimental after her drunkenness.

Bush supported her head with his arm and urged her to drink a little coffee, and Ruby, obedient and chastened now, swallowed at his command.

"Oh, God!" she groaned. "I wish I could die! . . . I wish I could die! . . . What would my dear father and mother think if they could see me in this fix?"

"Don't say those things, sweetheart. It's all past and over with now. Don't think of those things."

"No girl ever had a better home than I did. No one ever had a kinder father or a sweeter mother. . . . And to think of the way I've shamed them."

She began to cough, with long spasms that rose upward from her shuddering belly, until, at last, she lay back on the pillow exhausted. In the cruel light of morning she looked far older than her years: she was like an old woman blotched and soiled by time, with yellow, incongruously young hair frizzed about

240

her face. She closed her eyes, soft now in her suffering. She groaned and sighed feebly, wallowing in her humility: "I want to apologize to Chester for the things I said; I want to beg his pardon."

"That's all right, Ruby. It ain't necessary. Chester hasn't got any hard feelings against you."

"I want to beg his pardon! I want to get down on my knees."

She became so insistent that at last Bushrod did as he was told and called down to Chester below. He came to the room stiffly, yet determined to settle the point once and for all. He stood by the bed.

"I'll get down on my knees for you," said Ruby dramatically. "I'll get down on my knees, if that's what you want." Something struck her as funny and she began to laugh hysterically, her mouth wide opened; but almost at once she had another wave of nausea and she began to vomit the coffee she had drunk, while Bush held the slop jar to her mouth.

After that things were better for some weeks. The meals were better prepared and were served on time, but she ignored Chester completely, rarely speaking to him. When she did, she made no effort to hide her contempt, her black eyes hard, her tongue bitter. For the most part he stayed in his room and read, or went out with some of the men from his office. Occasionally he called on Jim Saltis and spent the evening there. He would sit in Jim's parlor, with Abbie across the table working on another of her sofa pillows, while Jim told of his old days, as a seaman. Sometimes Jim spoke of Bushrod, shaking his head sadly.

"Bush sure picked a bad one to tie up to. I don't know what he was thinking about. Being a sailor, I've seen some pretty bad ones in my life, but she's the worst I ever run across."

Chester did not follow those leads. His loyalty to Bush prevented him from discussing his affairs. He only looked across at Abbie with her fresh, immature beauty and waited until she raised her eyes and smiled at him.

And so things went along for a few weeks. One day Ruby asked her husband for money with which to buy clothes and the same afternoon she went shopping. She came home in a rare good humor and talked volubly of the bargains she had seen. Bush was delighted that she had begun to take an interest in her appearance again. He considered it a good sign, and hoped that things were going to be better for them; he hoped that their troubles were now over. He watched her while she stood in front of her mirror trying on her dresses, her face heavily rouged, her lips like scarlet fruit. She began, also, to buy gaudy jewelry and to wear it. For a while she was content, or appeared to be, with her shopping and her bargains, and then the quietness of her life bored her. She began to go out regularly in the afternoon, to make appointments with men she picked up on the streets. At first she was always home before her husband arrived, but since he said nothing to her, never questioned her acts, she gradually became bolder in her affairs. Automobiles would drive up to the house and call for her; often she would come home late at night, smelling strongly of whiskey, but giving no explanation of her absence.

She had made friends with a woman called Madame Rosa who ran an assignation house and who often called Ruby for one of her less particular clients. Ruby had plenty of money now. She spent her money indiscriminately. She was back in her natural profession and she was quite happy. It was about this time that she hired a young negro girl to wait on her and the two became fast friends. In the morning Ruby would read the papers, skipping everything except the society news, or play solitaire, while the maid put records on the victrola for her or gave her a massage. Often she had crying spells, when they were alone, and told the maid all of her affairs. Sometimes Madame Rosa came over in the afternoon, if business was slack, and the two sat quietly at home, drinking beer, or talking about their friends. But Ruby was not entirely satisfied. There was something else that she wanted.

27

Ruby had been living with her husband for more than three months. She was putting on weight and it was very becoming. Her face was not so thin and drawn as it had been. She was calmer and more contented for a while, and then, around Christmas time, she became restless again.

The approach of Christmas had always made her sentimental, and she talked a great deal about her childhood, how happy and carefree it had been. Often, for no apparent reason, she would cry while her maid was fixing her hair, or rubbing cold cream into her cheeks, but during this period she would not go out of the house without Bushrod, nor would she answer the 'phone when Madame Rosa called. One day she went downtown and had some visiting cards engraved. She showed them to Chester when he came home: Mrs. John Bushrod Tarleton.

"That looks pretty good on a visiting card. That's a swell name."

Chester examined the card and handed it back without comment.

"Say, what's the matter with you? What have you got against me?"

He looked at her steadily, his eyes cold and reserved. "What you do is your own business, Ruby. If it suits Uncle Bush, it's all right with me, too."

"You go around like you got a poker in your back."

Chester walked away and Ruby watched him going up the

stairs. Her face became set and hard. She brushed back her hair angrily. "All right. . . . All right, you little punk."

Two days later she anounced her intention of going to Reedyville to visit her parents for the holidays. Bush tried to dissuade her, but Ruby would not listen to him. She was very animated, now that her mind was made up. She looked over her extensive wardrobe and selected for the trip her flashiest dresses and hats. "I'll knock them dead, when they see me," she stated triumphantly. "I'll give them a surprise they won't forget soon." She had planned the whole thing: she would register at the Magnolia Hotel, taking the most expensive rooms available. Later she would call formally on everybody she had known. She would rent an automobile and drive her parents, in triumph, through the streets of the town that she had once been forced to leave. She would vindicate her early conduct. She would prove to Reedyville how wrong it was. She would overpower the sleepy place with her opulence and her charm.

Bush was perturbed. "I wouldn't do that, Ruby. You'll only get your feelings hurt."

"What do you mean, I'll get my feelings hurt?"

"You've forgotten how Reedyville is, honey."

But Ruby set her jaw in determination and shook back her yellow, straw-like hair. "I hope somebody tries to pull any stuff like that on me, that's all! What I'll tell them won't be anybody's business."

Bush pleaded with her, trying to talk her out of it, but in the end Ruby went, precisely as she had planned. Bushrod took her to the station and saw her safely aboard the train. When he came back to the store, he felt so badly that he had to go into the back room and lie down on the cot where his clerk slept. He had not been well for the past weeks. He felt nervous and apprehensive, as if something were about to happen, and his head ached most of the time. His throat was tight and constricted. He had hot flushes of blood to his head which left him feverish and weak and slightly nauseated. He was nervous all that day, and at night he talked things over with Chester. He sat at the table, but he could not eat. The thought of food repelled him.

"I didn't want Ruby to go. She's only asking for trouble." He leaned forward and rested his head on his folded arms.

"Don't let yourself get upset this way, Uncle Bush. It isn't worth it."

"It's foolish of me, I know, but I'm afraid she'll go off and leave me again."

Chester threw down his napkin and got up from the table in sudden, uncontrollable anger. "My God! . . . Haven't you got any pride? Don't you know that Ruby's just using you for what she can get out of you?"

Bush, to, got up. He tried to bluster, to speak indignantly, but there was nothing that he could say in his wife's defense. He stood there helplessly. He felt dizzy all at once and he sat down and looked at his plate, his eyes fixed and staring. "I haven't got any comeback, Chester. I guess what you say is all true."

There was a short embarrassed silence. "I'm sorry, Uncle Bush. I'm sorry for speaking the way I did."

"That's all right. I can see this thing from your viewpoint, too. I want to be practical about it."

That night Chester could not go to sleep. He thought for a long time about Bushrod and Ruby, wondering how the matter was finally to end. In spite of his dislike for her, his mind told him that she was not quite normal, that she was not quite adult and that she should not be judged as a mature person. During her absence he could get a better perspective on her, he could see that her fury, her drunkenness, her sentimentality were part of a pattern; they were things which Ruby could not escape. There was a kinder side to her. She could never pass a beggar without giving him money, she could never turn anybody away from the door without food. And, strangely enough, her friends all liked her and made a great deal over her. The whole extent of her fury was expended on Bushrod who alone was kind to her: that was the curious thing. Chester rolled from side to side, puzzled at these things. Then he remembered Bushrod's sick, worried face. Bush should go to see a doctor. He would suggest that, at breakfast in the morning. . . . At last, realizing that he could not sleep, he got up and put on his clothes, and let himself out of the house silently so as not to disturb Bushrod. It was December, but the air was as mild as spring and a salt breeze blew steadily from the Gulf.

For a moment he stood undecided at the gate before he turned and walked east, away from the harbor. He walked for a long time, his mind occupied with his own thoughts, hardly conscious of where his feet led him. Houses began to thin out, a few factories and warehouses appeared, and at last he was in open country.

He had been walking for hours, and he was very tired. To his right was a lane which led toward a dairy farm. There were lights burning in the house and a faint sound of milk pails being banged together. It was getting light in the east, but the sun had not yet risen. The fields on both sides of the lane were wet with a heavy fall of dew and the grass was cropped close by the teeth of cattle. In the center of the pasture a group of cows slept, huddled together. As Chester leaned over the fence, sleepy, his head nodding, he felt something wet and rough against his cheek and jumped back in alarm. But it was only a red and white calf that had licked his cheek, a calf with long, absurd legs which wabbled from side to side as it walked. The young calf braced itself, spread wide its fore legs and looked at Chester with soft, limitless eyes. It lifted its head and bawled, and the cows, huddled together, answered, lowing plaintively.

247

Chester reached over the fence and tried to touch the young calf but it turned quickly and fell to its knees. It ran stumbling to the center of the pasture, faced him and lifted its head again, but this time no sound came from its throat.

The noise of metal had ceased and out of the stillness an automobile engine was started with a roar. Chester turned and walked down the lane. Before he had reached the road, he heard the milk truck behind him. He stopped and waited, listening to it bumping over ruts, the filled cans rattling a little. When the truck reached the road, he would ask the driver to take him to town. The man looked at him curiously, somewhat suspiciously, and Chester felt that he should give some sort of explanation.

"I couldn't sleep, so I took a walk out here. I didn't realize how far I had come."

The driver was reassured. He moved over on the seat and Chester got in. The driver yawned. "I'm just the other way. It seems like I can't get *enough* sleep. . . . Christ! I can't get enough."

Bushrod's fears that Ruby might leave him again were quite groundless. She returned to Baycity on Christmas eve and came to the house in a cab without having announced her arrival. Chester and Bush were in the parlor fixing a Christmas tree. They had invited Jim and Abbie over for the evening. The taxi came to a stop in front of their door with a creaking of brakes and Chester looked out of the window. "Good Lord! It's Ruby back already." Bushrod was instantly beside him.

Ruby had got out of the cab and was paying the driver. It was obvious that she was a little tipsy. Bushrod went to the door to meet her and the taxi driver helped her up the steps. Her hair was disarranged and her hat crushed; the suit she wore was crumpled, as if she had slept in it. She looked foul and un-washed.

She came into the small living room, staggering slightly, and lay on the sofa. She raised her arms upward, her face twisted in rage, and began to shout obscenities. She cursed Reedyville and its people, one by one, filth belching upward from the cavern of her throat.

"Who is that bitch to treat me like I was dirt? She thinks she's better than I am, does she?"

"Hush, Ruby!" said Bush pleadingly. "Hush, darling."

But Ruby could not be silenced. "I went out there like a lady, as friendly as I could, but what did I get for my pains?" Ruby lay back on the sofa and rolled her head from side to side, crushing her hat even more.

"She slammed the door in my face, the dirty slut, that's what she did. She said she'd have me locked up as a common prostitute, and slammed the door in my face."

"Ruby, Ruby, they can hear you from the street."

"Let her alone, Uncle Bush. The neighbors ought to be used to it by this time."

"What I told her! . . . What I told her would fill a book. . . ." She began to laugh, her mouth lax and wide opened. It was difficult for her to stop laughing. "I got that bitch told, if I never do anything else. . . . My own sister-in-law treating me like dirt."

Chester and Bush looked at each other and immediately Bush turned his head away, his blue eyes worried and embarrassed. Chester laughed nervously. "I hope the Browning Club was meeting at the time and heard it. That'll be something for them to talk about."

"Ruby! Ruby! You shouldn't have done that, darling."

Ruby paid no attention to her husband's words. She opened her beaded bag and took out the engraved cards of which she had been so proud. They were all there; not one had been accepted. She threw the cards violently from her, scattering them on the floor, and got up and began stamping them with her feet. She tore off her hat and trod that, too, and her hair, tangled and uncombed, stood about her head like yellow, brittle wire.

"I wouldn't spit on them," she screamed. "I wouldn't spit on them if they came to me on their hands and knees."

Chester said: "I'd better call Jim and Abbie and tell them not to come over tonight."

"Baby! Baby!" said Bush, "you shouldn't have done that. You shouldn't have lost your temper." He went over and lifted her up, stretching her out on the sofa again.

Ruby had brought a bottle of whiskey in her bag and began to get drunk all over. Later she went into the hall and called Madame Rosa, whom she had not seen for several weeks, and after a while an automobile came by for her. Ruby went out the door reeling, still cursing under her breath.

She did not come home at all on Christmas day. She came the next morning, her eyes red and blurred, her voice thick. She took a hot bath, alternately crying and cursing at the negro girl who served her; but after she had changed her clothes and had had a few more drinks, she felt better. That afternoon Madame Rosa came to call with some friends. Ruby sent the maid out for more whiskey and shortly the party was in full swing.

It was still in progress when Chester came in. Ruby heard his step. She walked into the hall, where he was taking off his coat and gloves, and tried to persuade him to come in and meet her guests, but Chester shook her hand off roughly. A thick-set man with a large diamond on his little finger got up angrily and came over to interfere.

"You better watch your step," he said threateningly. "You better learn how to treat a lady." He pushed Chester against the wall and held him pinned there.

Ruby intervened. "Let the little punk alone, Charlie. If he don't want to associate with us, that's his loss."

The thick-set man, grumbling a little, went back to his seat. But the party was spoiled and a few minutes later Ruby and her guests got into automobiles and were driven away. "Let him alone," repeated Ruby, her eyes glazed and uncertain; "let the little pimp alone, Charlie. It's his loss, not ours."

Her spree lasted for eight days. At the end of that time she was taken to a hospital in alcoholic delirium. Bushrod visited her daily. One night he spoke gravely to Chester (They rarely spoke to each other any more.) : "I think I'd better get Ruby away from this town. I think that's what's the matter with her. She's running with the wrong crowd."

"Where are you figuring on going?"

"I think a long sea trip is the best thing. After that we can settle down somewhere else, and start all over again."

He looked at Chester with his mild, bright blue eyes, as if asking him not to offer any objections to the plan.

"That's all very well, but where'll you get the money?"

Bushrod spoke hesitantly: "I've decided to sell my timber. The Hodge Brothers are after it again and it'll bring a good price."

He began to gesture with his hands, to talk rapidly, plausibly, as if to forestall any objections which Chester might make. "I've been over it all with Ruby, and she's willing to go. She was very sweet about it. She realizes that she hasn't acted right, and promises to mend her ways."

Chester drew down his lips in disgust. He was familiar with Ruby's penitence and the value of her promises. He had a profound pity for Bushrod, knowing at that moment precisely what his life with her would be.

"I'm going to deed the house and furniture to you, Chester.

That's little enough to do for you after the way you've stuck by me."

"It isn't necessary, Uncle Bush."

"I know that. I know that, but I want to do it. You'll be falling in love and getting married in a few years yourself, and it will be nice for you to have a place of your own."

"I doubt that I'll ever get married. I think I've seen too much married life, as it is."

"You will, though," said Bush. "You'll change your mind when you meet the right girl."

A few days later Bush went to Reedyville to call on the attorneys for the Hodge Brothers, and, upon his return, Ruby was out of the hospital, looking better for her enforced rest.

He came into the house and put down his bag, swaying back and forth. He was so dizzy that he almost collapsed. He had to lay down for a while, and Ruby put ice caps on his head and gave him one of her headache tablets. After a while he got up, took a bath and changed his clothing. "I'm tired and rundown," he explained. "There's no excuse for my feeling so bad."

For some time his symptoms had been alarming him but he had spoken of them to nobody; his mind rejected the suspicions which were becoming more and more apparent, but this morning he did not go back to the store as he had intended. Instead, he went to the doctor and sat in the waiting room until his turn came.

The doctor was quiet, efficient, and not very communicative. Bush went out considerably reassured, so much so that he forgot for the next few days, in the excitement of going away, about himself, and how badly he felt.

They were leaving at five o'clock in the afternoon and Chester got off from his office to come to the train. When he arrived, Madame Rosa, Charlie, and a few of Ruby's other friends were also there, talking to her, but Bushrod stood away from them, entirely alone, not a part of the group, a lost, hurt look on his face, his blue eyes frightened and uncomprehending. Madame Rosa had sent Ruby a bouquet of roses and she stood now on the vestibule at the end of the train, the roses clutched sentimentally to her breast. She looked quite well and quite smart in her new tailored dress and her small, close-fitting hat with its half veil.

"Don't take any wooden nickels when you're drunk, Charlie."

Chester came up and touched his uncle's arm. "I want you to be happy, Uncle Bush. Forget all the things I said about Ruby. It was only because I was so fond of you."

Bush said: "I've put the house in your name. It's yours now. You'll find the deed in your bureau drawer, on top of your shirts."

"I didn't expect you to do that. It wasn't necessary."

"I wanted to do it," said Bush. "You wouldn't deny me that little pleasure, would you?"

"You'll be coming back before long. You'll want it yourself."

"I don't think so. This is the last time we'll ever see each other." He tried to smile reassuringly, but he did not succeed.

Madame Rosa and her friends were laughing and shouting advice, and Ruby blew kisses to them and nodded, amiable and sure of herself, her eyes insolent and veiled. As the conductor called all aboard, Bushrod reached in his pocket and took out a letter. He handed it to Chester. "I got this letter last night. Read it after the train pulls out." He looked down, avoiding his nephew's eyes. "I'm so ashamed," he said. "I want you to know that. I'm ashamed." He turned and walked into the car, a pitiful completely defeated figure.

Chester held the envelope in his hand while the train moved away slowly. He opened it, then, and took out the letter. It was from Bushrod's doctor, and it was only necessary that he read the first lines to understand its full import: "The laboratory report has just been received," it began. "I very much regret to advise you that you have a well-advanced case of syphilis."

He looked up quickly. Ruby was on the rear platform, blowing kisses to her friends.

From the Diary of Sarah Tarleton

March 8, 1925. *Today I had a long letter from Abbie. She has told me all about Bush and his wife. I hope that they can find happiness somewhere else. Abbie promises to keep her eye on Chester and to see that he is comfortable. She is a sweet, good girl.*

June 10, 1925. *Check up another triumph for the family. Lillian was today elected president of the Federated Women's Clubs of the state. It is a signal honor for the family. She sent me the clipping from the Reedyville paper. It was a long article with her picture, but not one of her best.*

October 23, 1925. *Oh, heavens and earth! Bessie has been arrested in New York by the police. I don't know the details, but it has something to do with a hosiery mill strike and carrying banners. The news came through Jesse's wife in Atlanta. Frank cannot be made to realize the gravity of the situation. I think he secretly delights in the fact that she flaunts law and order.*

28

CHESTER missed his uncle more than he had thought possible. He had again the old feeling of affection for Bushrod, but their rôles, in his mind, had now changed: he thought of himself, now, as the older, the more mature, person. Bushrod was the boy to be sympathized with and comforted. He would often think of Ruby and what she had done to his uncle; he would wonder where they were, what they were doing at that moment, and a wave of dislike would pass over him, until, at last, he would laugh at the stupidity of regrets, at the futility of his own emotions. Bessie had started writing to him, and he answered her letters regularly. Bessie's letters were always exciting and full of interesting things. She, too, laughed at everything. She would write pages about her life, her hopes and her loves, analyzing and refining, only to turn, before she was through, and destroy all she had done with bitterness or with ridicule. She was always vague as to just how she supported herself: she was always going from one job to the other. One time she worked in a department store, at another time she was a waitress, and still later she was a dentist's assistant. In between she wrote proletarian articles for small magazines, made inflammatory speeches and got herself in trouble with the police. Chester asked her many times if she needed money, but Bessie always said that she did not. She preferred to stand on her own feet and she would accept help from nobody: not even from her brother Jesse, with whom she was close, and who was a well-to-do man.

Once or twice, in the months that followed, Chester met

Abbie on the street and she stopped and talked to him, her hands fluttering about the lapels to his coat, her eyes rolling sweetly, but he was vague and evasive and got away from her as quickly as possible .He was afraid that Abbie and Jim laughed at Bushrod and himself and the thought irritated him. Abbie, at once shrewd and soft, understood his feeling. She would go home and sit quietly at her sewing, wondering how she could restore the old basis which had existed between them. And in the end Abbie took matters into her own capable hands and came to see him, accompanied by her father. They arrived one Sunday morning just after breakfast. Chester, still dressed in a bath robe, let them in and stood blinking stupidly while Abbie walked about the house, examining everything with practical eyes.

Jim said: "Abbie and I figured if you wouldn't come to see us, we'd come see you. If either one of us have done anything to make you sore, we want to put it right."

"This place is an awful mess," said Abbie truthfully. "All that woodwork ought to be cleaned with soap and water. . . . I never saw such a dirty sink."

"I'm not offended. Why, what ever put that idea in your head, Jim? I've just been pretty busy at the office."

"I don't know. We just thought you might be."

"I've more work to do now," said Chester. "I got another raise last month. They keep me pretty busy."

"That's great," said Jim heartily; "that's great for a young fellow. You're getting along great."

"You can't get anybody to clean right unless you stand over them all the time," said Abbie. "They simply won't do it and there's no use arguing."

Chester ran upstairs to dress and Abbie went back to the kitchen to talk again to the new cleaning woman. Together they made a tour of the house, Abbie pointing accusingly at corners and behind pictures, the cleaning woman, depressed and a little apologetic, agreeing with everything.

When Chester, dressed and freshly shaved, came down, Abbie and Jim were listening to the radio. Abbie said: "I'm coming over here the first thing in the morning and give this place a good going-over. Those curtains are a disgrace."

Jim held out his hands, palms upward, in genial tolerance. "I never saw anybody like Abbie for washing and scrubbing."

The next night, when Chester got home, there was a smell of soap about the place. Mirrors had been polished and the curtains were all down. Suddenly he felt a sense of obligation, of gratitude toward Abbie; a feeling of dependence upon her. Not only had Abbie cleaned his house, she had planned his dinner as well, and had left strict instructions with the servant. He went at once to the 'phone to call her, to thank her for what she had done, but Abbie answered seriously:

"Why, that's nothing at all, Chettie. I'd do the same thing for any of pappa's old friends. If we can't help each other here in the world, what can we do?"

He was a little disappointed and a little hurt at her casualness, a little off his guard. Abbie came every day for a week during his absence at the office, but she was careful not to be there when he arrived. But if he did not see her in that time, everything in his house reminded him of her, for Abbie left her stamp of orderly prettiness on everything she touched. His neckties were cleaned and pressed, his clothing repaired and arranged neatly. He found himself thinking about her more and more. She had given him her photograph months before. He got it out and had it framed. He placed it on top of his chest of drawers and each morning, when he awoke, the first thing that he saw was Abbie's sweet, childish face surrounded by her exact, golden curls. . . . One evening he knew that he wanted, more than anything in the world, to see Abbie again. He found her waiting, as if she had known that he would come.

After that he went to see Jim and Abbie often. They would spend the evening playing rummy or talking Often Mrs. O'Leary would come up. She ran a shop for seamen on the street level, just below Jim's rooming house. She was a large, comfortably made woman with rough, mottled skin and a white streak in her hair. Her arms were spread over with blue veins which resembled, in miniature, the delta of a swollen river. This July night she climbed the stairs laboriously, stopping at intervals to catch her breath. She came puffing into the room, fanning herself with a palm-leaf fan. She had once been a great beauty and she had never forgotten that fact: she dressed, in her old age, in absurd and antiquated finery, her cheeks and lips heavily rouged, her huge body corseted with stays to the point of agony.

"I closed up the shop," she explained. "I closed it up a little earlier than usual. There wasn't anybody in except a couple of boys from the *Eastern Moon* shaking poker dice with Sam. There wasn't a dollar and a half among them." She sat on the velvet couch, her back and arms braced with Abbie's sofa pillows. "I declare, Jim! You don't know how lucky you are to have somebody take care of you the way Abbie does."

"Yes, I do, Hattie. I know what a treasure Abbie is all right."

Abbie laughed gayly and lowered her head in confusion. "You mustn't pay me such compliments, Mrs. O'Leary."

Mrs. O'Leary sighed, her whole bulk heaving upward in unrest. "I wish my own daughter was more like you. I wish she was more of a homebody; but I suppose I can't blame her, at that. I guess she's got too much theatrical blood in her veins to settle down anywhere."

Abbie made a little, shivering gesture with her shoulders. "I

259

declare, I'd think she'd die of fright when she had to face all those strange people."

"It's in the blood, dear," said Mrs. O'Leary with pride.

"How's she making out?" asked Jim. "Have you heard from her lately?"

Mrs. O'Leary had brought with her clippings from newspapers in anticipation of this very question. She fished them from her tapestry bag and spread them out on the table.

"See," she said triumphantly. "They're printing her picture in the papers now. The critics give her good notices on her dancing and say her singing is adequate." Mrs. O'Leary made a wide, humorous gesture calculated to deflate all who criticize. *"Adequate,"* she repeated, winking her eye and raising the corners of her lips as if greatly amused.

"I've heard that it's hard for a girl to get a start on the stage in these days," said Jim.

But Mrs. O'Leary had saved her most important news. She took a letter from her bag, unfolded it and glanced down a page. "Lurline writes that she and her partner just landed a new job in a musical show opening next month. She's got a speaking part in this show and will have two specialty dances with her partner. The act is pulling down two hundred and fifty bucks a week!"

"That's great," said Jim. "We've got to have a drink of wine on that!"

"She'll be in electric lights before you know it. She'll be getting featured billing before next season, just mark my word. I never saw anybody go up like that girl has. . . . And I don't say it because I'm her mother."

Jim got up as if to go for the wine, but Abbie stopped him. "You sit still and talk to Miss Hattie. Chester and I'll go fix it."

Together they went to the kitchen and Abbie showed him the place where Jim kept his wine. "Here's the corkscrew. You open it while I fix some sandwiches and fruit cake." She looked about the room, her finger tapping her cheek, her face round and serious. "You better open two bottles. One may not be enough." She smiled at him and patted his arm. "You're a sweet old thing, you really are."

Chester began to feel very gay. He picked up a bottle and pretended to drop it, but he caught it just when it was about to strike the table. Abbie gave a muffled scream and placed her hands against her breast.

"Oh," she said, gasping. "Oh, but you scared me! I thought the bottle was broken that time, sure."

Chester laughed, too. A feeling of happiness came over him. He picked up two of the glasses from the tray and juggled them in the air, catching them safely just when it seemed inevitable that they would fall. And through it Abbie squirmed and giggled and gazed at him with adoring eyes.

But at last the bottles were opened and the glasses filled, and Abbie came over with the cake plate. She looked very cool and sweet in her white dress and there was a faint, delicate perfume about her. Something inside Chester began to ache. It was difficult for him to breathe. All at once he was obscurely angry.

"Jim shouldn't let women like May and Hazel live in the same house where you are. He ought to be ashamed of himself."

Abbie picked up the plate of cake and held it before her. Her voice became prim suddenly. "May and Hazel pay their rent regularly. So long as they do that, pappa hasn't any reason to throw them out."

She walked to the door, reached it, and looked roguishly over her shoulder. "Why are you so interested in them all of a sudden?"

She went into the next room and Chester followed her obediently. She put the wine and cake and sandwiches on the table quietly, so as not to disturb the conversation.

Mrs. O'Leary was still talking about her daughter. "Lurline's been after me to come to New York and live with her. Every letter she writes it's the same thing over and over: 'Mamma, come on up,' or, 'Mamma, I get so lonesome for you all the time,' but I tell her I've got a business here and can't leave it."

Jim said: "Well, we'd sure hate to see you go if you decided to do that, but I think you'd like it better in New York with your daughter."

"I guess I would, but my old theatrical friends are not there any more. Lord knows what has become of them all."

"You'd meet new ones. You'd have your daughter's friends, at first."

"Of course I might land an engagement, too," said Mrs. O'Leary. "I'm not an old woman. I've lost my shape and run down a little, but I can still play dowagers and do second business all right."

She picked up a glass from the tray Chester held before her. "Well, here's luck. May you live to eat the chicken that scratches on your grave."

Everybody drank with her except Abbie. Abbie did not touch wine.

After a while Mrs. O'Leary began to yawn, and not long afterward she said good-by and began her ponderous descent, stopping to rest occasionally on the stairs. Jim too, got up, announcing his intention of going to bed. Abbie got out a basket of sewing and put on the pair of horn-rimmed glasses which she used for close work. The glasses gave her face a sweet seriousness: She was like a little girl playing at being grown up. For the first time since their departure, Chester talked of Ruby and Bushrod, and Abbie listened sympathetically, nodding over her sewing. "You mustn't think that all women are like Ruby, though. Ruby is an exception to the general rule."

"*You* aren't like her, at any rate," said Chester earnestly. "You two are as different as the poles."

Abbie took a few slow stitches: "If I ever fell in love with a man, I'd devote my entire life to making him happy. I'd make him so comfortable that he'd never want to look at another woman."

Chester got up and sat beside her on the sofa. He took her hand, and Abbie laughed provokingly and drew back, but his head slipped down and rested against her bosom. "I'm so tired," he said. "You don't know how tired I am." She ran her fingers through his hair, stroking his cheek, and the cool touch of the thimble against his flesh sent a shiver through him.

"Will you kiss me?"

Abbie shook her head. "No, I'm saving my kisses for the man I marry!" She leaned forward and her curls fell over his face. "I've always regretted that time I let you kiss me in the garden. . . . Oh, I don't know what you thought of me."

"I thought you were wonderful. I still think you're the most wonderful girl I ever saw."

Abbie sighed. "I liked you from the minute I saw you. You've got such—such high principles." She looked at him for a time and then pressed her soft, sweet lips against his own.

The Whisperer

THERE was once a woman who had a bad son, but she deafened her ears that she might not hear the things others told her of him and covered her eyes with her hands that she might not see him as he was. "He is young and high-spirited," she said; "that is natural in the young. . . . He is willful, perhaps; but the things that he does are thoughtless. It is only his way."

But after her son had grown to manhood the evil in him came to the surface more strongly. He drank and whored and ridiculed his mother to his friends. He cursed her, when he chose, or beat her in his drunken moments; and he took from her everything that she had. When, at last, she was reduced to poverty, and too old to work any more, he strangled her coldly because she was no longer of use to him. . . .

So it was that this patient, sad-eyed woman came to be among the dead. But she could find no comfort in heaven, and she remained apart from the other shades, huddled against the rim of space in the place where rain falls. All day long she knelt there and looked downward at the earth, but when it was dark, and she could no longer see her son, she would go back and sit among her new friends, listening to their thanksgiving and their psalms, but apart from them.

For comfort she spoke aloud: "He was a beautiful baby. When I gave him his bath in the morning he would kick up his legs and laugh. I would kiss his knees and he would put his arms around my neck and hug me close. . . . He was an affectionate child."

But the other angels, intent on their songs, did not listen long. They only smiled and nodded and turned again to their harps.

Before the eyes of the old woman, at the center of heaven, was the high throne of God, incrusted with rubies and washed eternally with its own light. On it, in stern magnificence, sat the brooding God himself, while over His head flew angels. One night at dusk, in the silence between songs, the old woman got up and went to the throne. She prostrated herself and lay in that pure radiance which pours like a river from the mind of God, and at last God drew His eyes back from infinity and looked at the black bundle of her misery.

She spoke: "If he is a bad boy, as they say, it is because I have failed somewhere. The fault is not his;" and God gazed at her steadily, not understanding. Then the woman raised herself to her knees and rocked back and forth, pressing her face into her cupped hands:

"And now they blame him for what they say he did. They want to lock him in darkness with evil people."

She got up, emboldened by love, and approached the throne, tugging at God's white robes.

"He can't stand being alone! Even as a little boy he was afraid of the dark and of loneliness. . . . You must not let them do this cruel thing."

But God looked at her with eyes from which all passion had been drawn, not comprehending. He frowned and shook His head, and stared outward again across space. Above them the adoring angels fluttered in wide circles, like perturbed doves.

And so this old woman dwelt unhappy in Heaven, crowded all day against the edge of space, looking downward at the earth.

"God did not comprehend," she whispers through dry, anguished lips. "He did not understand what I wanted. . . . But do not despair, my son, for I have not forgotten you and I will find a way. . . . I will surely find a way to help you."

From the Diary of Sarah Tarleton

June 8, 1926. *Lillian and Evan came by to see us today. Evan was in Baycity recently and talked to his friend, Mr. Graham, about Chester. Mr. Graham gave a most enthusiastic report. Chester is doing well and is being advanced rapidly for a young man. Mr. Graham says that he has a remarkably keen business mind. Lillian thinks that Chester will be a partner in the business some day. Who knows. She loves the boy a great deal.*

29

On Sunday, during this season, the steamer which plied regularly between Baycity and the bathing resorts further down the coast was crowded. Chester was waiting at the gangplank, glancing anxiously at the street and occasionally looking at his watch. In' the distance, across the bay, were high, red bluffs on which pines and shrubbery grew; but between this eastern shore and the shore where the steamer was tied there were bayous and lesser bays; there were peninsulas and islands threaded through with small rivers and covered with marsh grass. (The bayous and the bays reflected the sky in its blue mildness. Marsh grass grew green, purple and yellowish blue and stood straight up in the morning air without motion.) It was early morning but already the band on board was playing; already couples were dancing, yawning a little, as if not quite awake.

Abbie was late. They had agreed to meet at half-past seven and it was now seven forty. In five minutes the gangplank would be pulled in and the steamer would sail. Chester walked up and down nervously; then he saw her coming toward him, her eyes sparkling, her yellow curls blown about by the wind. She came eagerly, half skipping, half running. On her arm she carried a basket which contained the lunch she had prepared. He went to meet her and Abbie placed her hand on his arm, looking up at him sweetly.

"If you say a word about my being late I'll sit down here and cry before everybody."

"I was worried about you, Abbie. I was afraid something had happened."

"You sweet thing! You old sweet thing, you!"

She raised her hand and touched his cheek. Chester looked about self-consciously, but apparently nobody was watching them. Importantly, he took the basket of lunch, and they went on board; but before they had found seats, the lines had been cast off and the steamer was on her voyage. The band was playing loudly, drowning out other sounds.

"It is sweet of you to ask me," said Abbie. "I've been dying to come over the bay all summer." She raised her pink, flat face, her eyes round and child-like, and pressed herself closer to Chester. They were out of the river, now, and were steaming down the bay. The sunlight sparkling on the water threw off a brilliant, almost a blinding glare. Chester raised his hand and shielded his eyes.

"Let's dance, Abbie."

She got up quickly, and he took her in his arms. They stood balanced for a moment, swaying a little to the music. They danced slowly, without words, looking at each other occasionally and occasionally smiling.

"Where did you learn all those fancy steps? I'll bet some young lady taught you those. You must tell me all about her."

"Nothing like that. I've been taking lessons."

"You try to make out that you're just an old woman-hater, but I know better. You can't fool me."

"Did I ever say a thing like that?"

"Well, no, you didn't exactly *say* it, but it's the way you act." She looked at him languidly with her round, yellowish eyes. The music had stopped and they went to the rail and leaned over the side.

"If you want to dance with any of those other girls," said

269

Abbie, "go right ahead. I won't mind at all. I'll just stand here and watch the water."

Chester squeezed her closer to him. "I wonder if you know how sweet you are?"

"It isn't that at all. I'd understand perfectly. It wouldn't make a bit of difference. We'd still be the best of friends."

"That's very unusual, just the same."

"Anyway, that's the way I feel, I hate people who try to—to *own* others, don't you?" She sighed tenderly, pressed his arm and looked away. The music started and they danced again.

They were still dancing blissfully when the boat reached its destination and tied up at the wharf. The crowd stood up, gathering its things together. Abbie looked at herself in her mirror. She twisted a yellow curl around her finger until it became perfect, exact. Then she shook her head, disarranging her hair again, and smiled, her tiny, childish teeth exposed. Chester picked up the basket and together they walked down the wooden wharf, between the rows of waiting people. The ship's band was silent, but in a pavilion, further away, another band was playing. The beach was covered with people playing in the water or lying idly in the sun.

"Let's hurry!" said Abbie eagerly. She stood still on the crowded wharf and clapped her hands like an excited little girl. "Let's hurry up and get into our bathing suits! Let's not waste any of our day!"

She turned and walked toward the bathhouse and Chester followed her, his eyes proud and eager. He was waiting for her when she came out. She threw off her bathing coat and lay beside him on the sand. "If pappa ever saw me in this suit," she giggled, "he'd absolutely shoot me." But Chester did not answer. He was speechless before the perfectness of her beauty.

In the afternoon they took a walk inland over the clay cliffs and among the scrub pines, and Abbie ran about gathering flowers. Presently they came to a deep gully, with sides of red clay, surrounded by green shrubs over which jasmine grew. It was here, in this remote, scented spot that they decided to eat their lunch. Abbie unpacked the basket and set out the dainty things she had prepared: the sandwiches cut into the shapes of hearts and stars and crescents; the little cakes baked in fluted molds.

Chester lay on his belly and looked over the edge of the gully, marking how red the clay appeared between the strips of new green which surrounded it. Far away he could hear the band which played in the pavilion and, occasionally, when the band stopped, the distant shouts of the bathers. Below him lay the calm, blue bay dotted with white sails, sparkling in the light.

"It's all fixed. Come to dinner," called Abbie.

Chester rolled forward and lay on his back, one arm thrown over his eyes to shield them from the sun. There was a bird flying far above his head. It rose higher and higher, and he watched it until it was swallowed in space, as if it had suddenly broken through the barrier of the sky and circled now above other worlds.

"Chester! Chester!" insisted Abbie with sweet petulance. "Why don't you come? Lunch is all ready."

"I'm not very hungry. I'd rather just lie here doing nothing."

"I fixed all this for you. I went to all the trouble I did just for you. . . . You ought to be ashamed, you really ought!" She began to lisp like a little girl, half in fun, half seriously.

Chester laughed contentedly. He put his hands under his head.

"I declare, I never saw such a person. All men are spoiled, but you're the worst I ever saw. . . . I guess I'll have to move everything over to you." She got up and moved the cloth, rearranging the food, chattering sweetly.

Chester turned and rested on his elbow and looked at the

food. Abbie was eating daintily, with quick, sudden movements. There was no fumbling with her fingers, no choosing. She knew precisely what she wanted.

"Of course you don't know how sweet you are," said Chester. "Naturally you haven't a mirror in your room."

Abbie moved over and sat beside him. "If you're too lazy to pick up your food, I suppose I'll have to feed you." She put her arm under him and lifted his limp body until his head rested against her shoulder. She became stern all of a sudden. "Eat this like a good boy, Chester."

He shook his head like a stubborn, willful child. "I don't want to."

"Very well, then. If that's the way you are going to behave, Mamma isn't going to take you with her next time." She pressed a tiny cucumber sandwich against his mouth, but Chester kissed the palm of her hand, and Abbie drew back, pretending to be alarmed. She laughed her high, childish laugh and pressed with her fingers against his jaws, trying to force them apart. Chester's head sank down and rested on her lap. He looked upward at her. She seemed very lovely among the green of the small pines, her yellow curls shining in the light.

"Eat this piece of cake," urged Abbie. "It's full of raisins and pecans. Eat it, or mother is going to be very provoked." Quickly she twisted her curls into a tight knot. She took her glasses from her bag and put them on, screwing up her face into a mock semblance of age, and in an instant her whole being seemed to vanish. She shook him angrily and he understood dimly that under her light playfulness there was hard reality, a will that would not be thwarted.

She said sternly, her jaw set: "You eat this cake or I'm going to send you away from the table. I'm not going to put up with your tantrums another minute, young man."

272

Instantly his langour vanished. He stared upward into her hard, bright eyes. There was no uncertainty there, no compromise. They were as cold and as fixed as the eyes of a cat. His own eyes wavered in confusion. He opened his jaws and obediently took the food.

Abbie bent down, all affection now, but still in character, and kissed him lightly on the cheek. "It makes Mother sad when her little boy won't obey her." Immediately she took off the glasses and unloosened her curls again, as if the joke had gone far enough. She laughed gayly and sprang up, her tiny, white hands fluttering up and down. Chester, too, got up and walked toward her, his eyes gleaming with excitement, but Abbie turned and ran through the pines.

He was surprised at her swiftness, at the way she dodged behind stumps and trees, always just beyond his hands, always eluding him. Their laughter rang out between the trees and echoed faintly in the gully, but they were terribly in earnest. At last, when they were both panting with exertion, he caught her.

Abbie slipped to the ground and Chester lay beside her, his arms holding her tightly, his flushed, laughing face close to her own. Slowly their smile faded, as if they knew that their play was ended and that this, at last, was the reality toward which they had both striven. He pulled her to him roughly and kissed her over and over, and Abbie did not resist him. She lay limp and defeated now, in his arms, her sweet, immature mouth puckered a little, her curls fouled with bits of leaves and pine straw.

"Don't take advantage of me," she said pathetically. "Don't make me a bad girl like May and Hazel."

He pressed his face against her warm, young breasts. "I want you to marry me, Abbie. I love you so much, and I want you to marry me."

They lay locked together for a long time, as if they would

never be separated, and Abbie smoothed back his hair and touched his eyes lightly with her finger tips.

"Let's not wait long," she said. "Let's be married very soon."

They caught the last boat that night. It was late and there were few people on board. They sat on the upper deck, their arms about each other, and watched a moon rise in front of them. The light spread like an opening fan upon the water; the steamer moved upon a gilded river; and in their wake the moonlight was shaken to golden coins by the movement of the vessel. They had not spoken for a long time, content merely to cling together, but at last Chester spoke, as if the very effort of speech cost him a great deal.

"When I was a boy I used to live on this same river, but father up, of course. That was a long time ago."

Abbie snuggled closer, a smile upon her lips. She was not listening. Her mind, at that instant, had room for nothing except her happiness.

On either side stretched the bayous and marsh land, and before them the slow, yellow river emptied itself into the bay, coloring the bay's water.

"I used to wonder where the river ended, and what Baycity was like, but I never thought I'd get here. It seemed too far away, in those days, for that."

He began to talk about his early life, about Mitty and his father and Hattie. He talked slowly, as if to himself, as if clarifying things in his own mind, for his own salvation. Later he talked of Sarah and Bessie and Bushrod; he spoke of the picture that he could almost see at times and how he wanted that picture tattooed over his heart. Abbie had heard those things before, but she listened patiently, her soft hand pressing his, her breath warm on his cheek. At last she looked up. "I think it is

274

very sweet about the picture. I can understand just how you feel about it."

Chester bent over and kissed her. "I think that this is the first time I've ever been happy in my life. I really mean it."

"We're going to be happy always, Chester. Nothing must ever come between us."

After he had taken Abbie home and had watched her climb the stairs, he stood on the deserted pavement, too excited for sleep. He walked about aimlessly, and then he found himself again by the river bank.

The moon had already set, its light withdrawn from the world, and below him the river was stealthy and oily and without sound, moving out of one darkness toward a darkness that was deeper. A few lights burned on ships anchored in the harbor, red and green lamps which seemed far away, and the east was black, with no wedge of first light breaking. Chester closed his eyes and leaned against a piling; he had not realized how tired he was, and there came to his nostrils the smell of ripe, slightly sour bananas blended with tar and old rope; the musty smell of marsh grass, spices and rosin. . . . His ears heard the river rocking and sucking at its pilings with a bubbling, definite sound which was almost a sigh. . . .

The sun was rising, and the bayous and the small bays were tinted with faint colors (aquamarines, lavenders and blues) washed over with the frailest pink; and between the bayous and bays marsh grass grew on the islands in variants of green, blue and yellow, all colors touching in perfection, a shimmer of pale, new light, lying indiscriminately upon sky, grass and water. . . .

Already stevedores were coming to work and Chester got up, brushed his clothes and walked away. He walked rapidly, in the direction of Abbie's house, hoping to catch a glimpse of her before he went to work.

30

THE wedding was set for August 5th. It was earlier than Chester had planned, but it was his twenty-third birthday and Abbie wanted to be married on that day and no other. With the decision once made, Abbie wrote a long, sentimental letter to Aunt Sarah, the sort of a letter that she liked to receive, and Chester broke the news to Bessie, Lillian Chapman and the other members of the family. After some days he received from Bessie a short note wishing him happiness, but doubting, nevertheless, that her wishes would come true. She regretted that she could not come to Baycity for the ceremony, but she was sending them a present, something for the house, which she hoped would be appropriate.

Lillian Chapman was more prompt and a great deal more cordial. She wired her congratulations and followed this up with a letter addressed jointly to Chester and Abbie. She had always delighted in weddings, particularly if she could have a hand in arranging them, and she was of the opinion that some member of the family should be with Chester "during this, the most important period of your life." She intimated, not too subtly, that she would be glad to undertake this responsibility, to assist in every possible way, to see that things ran smoothly. So Chester was not at all surprised when she showed up in Baycity a week before the ceremony eager to make everybody happy, to see that everything moved in the best tradition.

Lillian was looking extremely well, very smart and tailored. Her hair had been cut recently in a new manner which was most becoming: it clung in soft waves to her head. In her small, beautifully-shaped ears she wore jade pendants. Evan was prospering more than ever in his business and they were planning a tour of the Continent in the fall, unless something untoward occurred.

Chester met her at the station and drove her to the brick house. Lillian went at once to her room, took off her things and looked about her with preoccupied, calculating eyes. Already she was planning the wedding, already she had taken charge.

Chester said, in answer to her question: "Oh, it's going to be a smell ceremony with only a few people present. We hadn't thought about it very much one way or the other, but I guess we'll get married in the parlor at Abbie's place. I'd rather just go to the courthouse, or be married by a justice of the peace, but Abbie wants a home wedding, even if it's only a small one."

Lillian slipped her rings from her white, well-cared-for fingers. She poured water into the basin and washed her hands, turning the soap in her palms with a quick, decided movement.

"I quite agree with the young lady," she said positively. "I think she's entirely right. . . . A wedding never seemed sacred to me unless it is celebrated in church, or at home."

"Well, I suppose that's just a matter of taste, Aunt Lillian."

Lillian looked at her nails, breathing on them lightly. She picked up a buffer and brushed them quickly. "Taste, nothing. It's a question of right and wrong."

She was anxious to meet Abbie as quickly as possible. Sarah had already given Abbie an excellent recommendation, but Lillian trusted nobody's opinion in such matters except her own. Chester, who wanted to get back to his office, kept looking at his watch from time to time while Lillian expressed her views, on marriage, life and morals. He volunteered, finally, to telephone Abbie and ask if she could run over for a few minutes to meet her future aunt. Lillian thought this an excellent idea; she was surprised that it had not occurred to them at once. But Abbie must have anticipated such an event, and have been prepared for it: She was dressed and waiting to meet Lillian, she said, and she would arrive in five minutes.

The two women met downstairs in the tiny hall. They stood looking at each other, Lillian cool and assured, Abbie shrewd and slightly awed before such elegance. Abbie looked down at her hands and spoke: "I'm so glad you've come. There're so many things that I don't understand and want to ask you about."

She glanced up shyly. "I know I'm going to be an awful bother, but I'm going to depend so much on you. I do want everything to be correct." Abbie looked very small and helpless, as if she was frightened and would cry if she were alone. Her instinct had not failed her. She had got at Lillian at once. She was on familiar ground here.

Impulsively Lillian took her in her arms. "You poor child! Why, of course I will. I'll only be too glad to help in any way that I can." The two women lifted their faces and kissed each other. They sat down excitedly on the lounge, their arms still about each other, and began to make plans.

When Chester got home from work, the furniture had all been rearranged, and Lillian was supervising the preparation for dinner. She came into the hall to meet him, a faint drift of expensive scent in her wake, her blonde hair coiffed exactly, her cheeks delicately rouged. She was more animated than usual.

"I am very enthusiastic about Abbie. I have rarely met a girl who pleases me more. She's certainly refreshing in these days."

It seemed that Abbie had spent the entire day with Lillian. They had lunched together and they had arranged everything. Tomorrow they were going shopping for missing articles in Abbie's trousseau and for additional furniture for the new home. All plans for the wedding had been changed. It was now scheduled to take place in the brick house, in the living room, which could easily be banked with ferns and potted plants. An altar could be set up by the window with no effort at all and Lillian thought that an episcopal minister would be best, all things considered.

Chester looked at her seriously, but his eyes twinkled contentedly: "Have you decided who is to be invited?"

"Not entirely," said Lillian. "There are many things which we haven't had time to work out as yet." Dinner was announced and together they went into the dining room. "I hope you realize how lucky you are in getting a girl like Abbie. You're a lucky boy, is all I can say."

"We agree on that. You can't get an argument out of me there."

"Abbie has told me all about herself and her life," continued Lillian reminiscently. "It hasn't been easy for her, poor child. But she has come through everything so sweet and innocent. I think it's quite remarkable, but then, she's a most unusual girl in every way. She has great strength of character."

"There's nobody like her," said Chester. All at once his heart flooded with love. He got up, went over to Lillian and kissed her spontaneously for the first time in his life. "It's very nice of you to take all this trouble, Aunt Lillian."

"I am very pleased with you, too, dear," said Lillian. "Very pleased indeed." She put her arms about him and kissed him again. "You must try to be worthy of this treasure." At that moment she sounded so much like Aunt Sarah that Chester was startled at the similarity.

During the days that followed, Lillian often said she felt as if she were having the excitement and the happiness of her own wedding all over again. She bustled about the place, making arrangements with caterers and florists, or went shopping with Abbie. They arranged and rearranged the furniture, apparently never tiring and never quite satisfied with the results they obtained. Inevitably she met Jim but she was kind and gracious for Abbie's sake. Abbie had already explained her father, and Lillian had completely identified herself with Abbie. She went about defending her when there was no need for defense. "A person's character is the only important thing," she asserted; "that is all that really matters."

Aunt Sarah arrived with Evan Chapman the night before the ceremony, but Frank Tarleton could not come, after all. His rheumatism was bothering him again, and he was laid up in bed. But he sent his regards to his grandson, a small check, and his best wishes for a long, happy life.

At last the wedding was over and Chester turned and took his bride in his arms. She was very sweet and very beautiful in her flowing veil, which suited her, as if she had been born to wear a bride's attire. People were pressing about them offering congratulations, already a little tipsy on Jim's punch. Chester looked about, nervous, anxious to escape. In one corner he saw Aunt Sarah and Jim Saltis talking together and he wondered what topic they had found in common to interest them so. Aunt Sarah was waving her fan and leaning forward that she might see Jim's face better. She was wearing a new, black silk dress which she had made especially for the wedding, very long and very full with lace at the collar and cuffs. On her breast was the gold brooch, surrounded by seed pearls, in which her mother's face rested, a little yellowed, a little faded by time.

Lillian and Evan had given the married pair an automobile for a wedding present. They were driving to New Orleans for a short honeymoon and then, after a week, they "would be at home to their friends," as Aunt Sarah continuously stated. At last the guests had thinned out a little and Abbie and Chester went upstairs to change their clothing. They came down with their suitcases. The car was outside at the curb, awaiting them.

Everybody kissed Abbie again and pressed Chester's hand and they started off. Aunt Sarah stood watching them. "Are you sure you know the roads?" she asked anxiously. "It's so easy to get lost."

"We won't, though, Aunt Sarah," called Abbie. She laughed gayly and blew kisses. "We won't get lost, you can depend on that."

"She's such an intelligent girl," sighed Lillian, tired from her exertion of the past week and yet regretting, a little, that it was all over. "She has such a fine character. Chester couldn't have made a better choice. She's just what he needs."

"Sweet and dear," said Aunt Sarah. "Sweet and dear, indeed."

Evan Chapman came up. His face was flushed with too much punch. It gleamed with high lights as if it had been polished vigorously with a buffer.

"Chester has certainly changed for the better, it seems to me. . . . Well, it all goes to show you can't tell what way a cat is going to jump."

"He's not so repressed or self-centered," said Lillian. "He's going to be a fine, wholesome citizen yet.—I, personally, am very pleased with him and I don't mind saying so."

"Sweet and dear!" said Aunt Sarah romantically. "Sweet and dear, indeed."

The hotel register had been signed and the bags brought up, and at last Chester and his wife were alone in their room with the door locked against intrusion. Abbie did not take off her hat or her coat. She walked, instead, to the window and looked across the street at an office building where people were at work.

Chester said: "Well, we're man and wife now."

They were silent for a time, each ignoring the presence of the other, their eyes avoiding the bed on which they were soon to lie together.

"How large a city is New Orleans?" asked Abbie.

"I don't know exactly, but I'll find out for you."

"Oh, no," said Abbie in a small voice. "Oh, no!—That isn't necessary. I just asked out of curiosity."

There was a reading lamp which did not work and Chester got down upon his knees to fix it. He found that the cord was frayed at the point where it joined the plug. He sat down on the floor, took out his knife and fixed it. When he inserted the plug in the socket again, the light burned brightly.

"Are you going to read?" asked Abbie.

"Not now, darling. I'm going to wash my hands. I've got them dirty."

He went into the bathroom and began to sing a little, softly, to the accompaniment of the flowing water.

When he returned to the room, Abbie had taken off her hat and coat. She had fluffed out her hair and powdered her face. She stood again by the window awaiting him, looking pathetic and very young. Their eyes met and they walked to each other, saying no word. Their arms were locked, their cheeks pressed together.

"I love you so, Abbie. If I haven't said much it's because I can't talk about it." A feeling of tenderness came over him so strongly that he felt for a moment that he would not be able to breathe again.

"I'm going to make you very happy," said Abbie. "I'm going to make you so happy that you will never want to leave me."

Through the opened window the noise from the street came upward to their ears in a wave of blurred, unfocused sound, rising and falling like distant surf, with many noises mixed together and no noise distinct.

From the Diary of Sarah Tarleton

August 7, 1927. My grandnephew, Robert Chester Hurry, Jr., was married August 5th in Baycity to Miss Abbie (not an abbreviation for "Abigail" she tells me) Saltis. Thanks to Lillian Chapman, who was present with her husband at the ceremony, the wedding was very sweet and effective. The groom was twenty-three on the day of his wedding, but the bride will not be twenty until October. They make a very fine couple. We are all pleased with Abbie. Both Lillian and I agree that she is everything that a girl should be. She is sweet, pretty and sensible. She has a great respect for her elders and does not think that she knows it all, as is the case with most of our young people today.

A wish for the happy pair:

> *"May your hearts e'er be entwined*
> *In love as they are today.*
> *May you happiness ever find*
> *And sorrow come never your way."*

The only thing to mar the happy occasion was the absence of Bushrod from the ceremony. Poor boy, he was so fond of Chester and would have rejoiced in his happiness. I cannot help but worry about him. The bride's father, Mr. James Saltis, told me a great deal about him. We had a long, interesting talk and he begged me not to worry over Bushrod, saying that he could take care of himself, but I cannot get his plight out of my mind. Frank is calling me and I must go give him his medicine. His rheumatism is very bad again.

31

THE honeymoon was over and Abbie was settled in her new home. She pinned up her hair and began earnestly to be a wife. Her husband was making a fair salary and they were able to live in comfort, but Abbie was careful with money and she made every penny go a long way, bargaining sweetly for everything that she bought. For the first week or so she hired a cleaning woman to help her and together they went over the house, washing and scrubbing windows and baseboards, putting everything in immaculate order. But when her house was at last the way she desired it, she would not have a servant, preferring to do the work alone. She had brought all her pillows and knickknacks with her, and she made new curtains for the windows; but she was still not satisfied with the furniture that Chester and Bushrod had accumulated: It was too heavy and too gloomy for her taste. She would stand still in a room, a dust cap covering her curls, a smudge of dirt on her soft, pink cheeks and regard the furniture with speculative eyes, and in the end she would shake her head in despair. There wasn't much that could be done, after all: it was simply not to her taste.

After they were settled comfortably, Jim Saltis came over for dinner one night. He dropped in unexpectedly without invitation, as if his daughter's house were now his own, and when Abbie saw him, her face fell. She had other guests for the evening: two of the men from Chester's office and their wives, and she had not counted on them meeting her father, but with Jim dropping in this way, there wasn't very much that she could do, except set an extra place for him and pretend that she had expected him, accepting the embarrassing situation as best she could. Jim talked a great deal, as he always did. He talked about the sea, and the uncertainties of running a rooming house. Abbie tried every way possible to change the subjects which he brought up, but Jim, who was having a perfect evening, went on and on. Later he told about the unusual pieces of tattooing he had done in his time and Abbie laughed merrily, as if his words were not to be taken literally, as if they revealed a rare and perfect humor; that the things he spoke of were whimsical and unbelievable.

She was very vivacious and gay and Chester had thought that she enjoyed the evening, and that Jim's presence had made it so successful, but when they were alone in their room, their guests gone, Abbie threw herself upon the bed and clenched her fists angrily.

"Why did he have to come tonight of all nights, just when I was beginning to make an impression? Why did he have to come just when people were beginning to be nice to me?"

"Why, Abbie! What's the matter? What are you talking about?"

Abbie sat up and her firm chin trembled a little. "You know very well what I'm talking about. . . . What will people think of me? It seems that you'd be ashamed to have your wife subjected to such a thing." She got up and went into the next room to take off her clothes. She stayed there a long time and when she returned, her husband was in bed. She got in beside him and turned off the night light. She pressed her face against his chest and began to cry softly.

"Abbie! Abbie! What's the matter? What's wrong?"

"You're very stupid if you don't see what I mean."

Then, in the darkness, her husband's arms about her, she began to talk. She spoke of her early days when Jim still went to sea, of her mother, with whom he had lived when he was ashore. "I knew there was something wrong," said Abbie. "I knew it from the very beginning. Everybody on the block knew they weren't married. All the children I played with knew it, but what could I do?" When she was ten, her mother had died while Jim was at sea, and Abbie was put for a year in an orphan's home. Later Jim returned, claimed his daughter and moved with her to Baycity. With his savings he had opened the rooming house and Abbie had lived with him since that time.

"I don't blame pappa at all. Don't think I hold this against him. He did the best that he knew how. It was my mother's fault. He's not to blame because she was an immoral woman."

Chester sighed. It was pretty hard to tell who was right and who wasn't in this world. He had already discovered that.

"I've always wanted to know nice people. I always wanted to get asked to parties and things like other girls. You don't know how sick I was of living with pappa and seeing only sailors and women like May and Agnes."

"Don't let yourself get upset this way, darling. It isn't anything to worry about."

But Abbie couldn't be comforted. "I did hope, when I had my own home, that I could have some nice friends like everybody else, but I see now that I won't be able to do it."

"Of course you can. You can have all the friends you want. What's to prevent it?"

"You saw how it was tonight," said Abbie. "You saw how pappa was! . . . Mrs. Christensen won't ever come back again, I know she won't." Abbie began to sob again. "She was getting so she liked me. She had already said I ought to join their Wednesday afternoon bridge club."

Chester sighed again. "Well, I don't see what you can do, if they feel that way. After all Jim's your own father. He thinks a great deal of you, too."

286

Abbie did not answer. She snuggled closer to her husband, her body shaken with final, slight convulsions, and after a little while she went to sleep. But Chester lay for a long time watching her sweet, immature face. He noticed that in repose it did not look so soft or so helpless. There was a firmness about her chin and in the modeling of her cheek bones, and already there were strong, vertical lines between her brows. As he watched, a deep sense of tenderness passed over him. He bent over her and outlined with his finger the light, delicate sweep of her eyebrows, touching the wet lashes which swept her cheeks. "Poor little thing," he whispered; "poor little girl."

Abbie had always gone regularly to church, and she determined that even Chester's views of such things were not to influence her after her marriage. On Sunday morning she got up a little earlier than usual, cooked breakfast and placed the house in order. Afterward she went upstairs to fix herself for the services. At intervals she called down to Chester, but he answered her vaguely. Chester had promised to go with her this time, but he had not really meant it. Abbie came downstairs again and found him still in his bath robe, his feet propped on a chair, reading the paper. Her face fell when she saw that he was not ready. She made a hurt, disappointed sound.

She was wearing a pink dress, very full and lacy; her hair was up, with a cluster of curls hanging about her ears, and Chester thought, at that moment, that she looked very lovely. She came to him and sat in his lap, mussing up his hair. She was like a little girl again, and she talked in the lisp that she affected. "You're a bad boy to keep me waiting, you really are."

He put down the paper and took her in his arms. "I wonder if you know how sweet you are, darling?"

"We'll be late if you don't get dressed quickly," said Abbie. "You haven't a minute to lose."

Chester looked at her quizzically. He kissed her on her neck, rubbing his rough chin over her flesh.

"You've got to shave, too. You haven't even shaved yet!"

"Let's go next Sunday," he whispered. "Let's just spend today at home." But Abbie was insistent. She went upstairs with him and sat while he dressed, keeping up a quick flow of scolding, bird-like chatter.

That afternoon Jim called again. He was accompanied this time by Mrs. O'Leary. Abbie was very gracious and Jim followed her with adoring eyes as she moved about. Mrs. O'Leary wanted to see the wedding presents and Abbie took her upstairs while Chester and Jim sat below in the living room playing the radio.

Mrs. O'Leary walked heavily about, poking her fingers into chairs and couches, admiring everything, but Abbie went to the window and hid her face in the curtains, overcome by emotion.

Mrs. O'Leary said: "I declare, Abbie, I never saw a girl as handy with a needle as you are. I'll bet there's nothing you can't make."

Abbie did not answer and Mrs. O'Leary turned to look at her. She started to repeat her remark and saw that Abbie's back was trembling, that she pressed her handkerchief quickly to her eyes.

Abbie walked back to the bed where Mrs. O'Leary stood. "Thank you! Thank you very much." She smiled a little and then lowered her head quickly. "I made this dress I have on, too. Next week I'm going to make some shirts and pajamas for Chester. Things are so expensive when you buy them in a store."

Mrs. O'Leary stared curiously and then turned, grunting a little, to inspect the bed. It was covered with a rose-colored spread over which a lacy, hand-made drapery had been thrown. At the sides of the bed were two night tables, with two rose-colored reading lamps, and the bed itself was piled high with tiny pillows, arranged carefully: pillows fringed in lace, and in various patterns, pillows shaped like crescents, stars and hearts. In the center of the bed, and reclining against the bolster, was a doll with blonde hair and a vacant face whose long legs were tied into precise knots.

"I think the doll is awfully sweet, don't you, Mrs. O'Leary? . . . I didn't make it, though."

Mrs. O'Leary's ponderous mind had been working. She had not, really, been looking at the bed, nor was she now conscious of its lush daintiness. She said, hesitantly, after a pause: "I've known you for a long time, Abbie; if there's anything wrong between you and Chester, I think you ought to tell me."

"Why, there's nothing the matter with me," said Abbie in a weak, uncertain voice which denied her words. "Whatever made you think that? I'm perfectly all right."

Mrs. O'Leary spoke bluntly: "Is there anything the matter with your husband? What I mean is—well, I mean is there anything the matter with him?"

Abbie's embarrassment was painful. She got up and put her hand over Mrs. O'Leary's mouth. "Why, the idea! Why, the idea of such a thing! . . . It isn't that at all."

Mrs. O'Leary enfolded her with her arms. "Tell me what's troubling you, Abbie. I'll advise you just as if you were my own daughter."

Abbie began to sob, and for a while Mrs. O'Leary comforted her. "It isn't as if I didn't *love* pappa. It isn't as if I didn't appreciate all he's done for me." She began to talk rapidly in her childish, lisping voice and Mrs. O'Leary, stern and impregnable, patted her shoulder comfortingly.

"I've talked to Chester, but he doesn't understand how I feel. He thinks I'm just silly to feel that way."

"There now, Abbie. No man could understand that."

"And so you see," continued Abbie; "I couldn't hurt pappa's

feelings for the world. I'd rather cut off my right arm than to hurt him in any way."

"You sweet, helpless little thing! . . . You poor, sweet little thing." An idea occurred to Mrs. O'Leary. "I'll talk to Jim about things myself. I'll see that he gets the idea."

"No! No! He's my father, and I love him more than anybody in the world." Abbie caught herself: "More than anybody next to Chester, of course. I'd die if I thought he'd ever know I'd talked this way. . . . No, no, it's nice of you to want to help and I appreciate it, but you mustn't do that. He mustn't ever know."

"I won't mention your name in any way. I'll fix it so that he'll never suspect."

"Of course I can always come to see *him*. There's no reason why I can't do that."

Mrs. O'Leary laughed bluffly. She took her handkerchief and wiped Abbie's damp eyes. "So that's all that's been worrying you? Well! Well!—That can be fixed as easy as rolling off a log."

Abbie sat at her dressing table and removed all traces of her tears. She powdered her face and touched her cheeks lightly with rouge. She came down the steps with Mrs. O'Leary, their arms about each other. They were chatting together lightly. Abbie's eyes were bright and sparkling, her manner gay.

"I don't like to say it about my own daughter," said Jim, "but Abbie's the prettiest little thing in this town. She is for a fact."

Abbie came over to him, threw her arms about him and kissed him, as if already compensating him for the sacrifice that he was to make. She was very gracious to him, she made him the center of the group, laughing with delight at his words.

"Come, Jim," said Mrs. O'Leary at last. "We'd better be getting along. I think I'll open up for a while this afternoon even if it is Sunday."

Jim got up to leave. He kissed his daughter and shook hands with his son-in-law. He did not realize it at the moment, but it was to be the last time that he ever came to their house.

32

Abbie was happy in her home. She would rise early and fix breakfast for her husband, remembering just how he liked things prepared, and when he had gone to work, and she had kissed him good-by behind the green blinds that screened the door, she would sit down in front of the littered table and read the paper, turning first to the column on household hints. Afterward she sewed or cleaned her house over and over. In the afternoon she generally called to see some of her new friends, taking her sewing with her as a rule. All in all her life was placid and respectable. She asked nothing more. She was quite happy.

Upon Chester's return from the office, dinner was ready to serve, and Abbie was waiting to serve it, and at the first sound of his footsteps she would rush forward and open the door, before he had time to take out his keys. They would embrace there in the hall and Chester would whisper to her the extent of his love.

Abbie's evenings were equally pleasing to her. They entertained their friends or were entertained; went to the movies or sat quietly at home. And so the first year of their married life passed placidly, with only small events.

Chester had settled down to a calm, happy married life. He had put his early memories out of his mind; he was even beginning to forget Bushrod and Ruby. All that seemed to have occurred in the distant past, and in retrospect Bushrod and Ruby appeared somewhat grotesque, slightly out of drawing. His work kept him busy and Abbie made him happy. There was little else

292

to ask for. At twenty-four he was a silent, rather reserved man. His acquaintances thought him arrogant, and he was not very popular, but Abbie knew better than this. With her his mask of coldness disappeared entirely. When they were alone he laughed at her and teased her and acted generally like a boy, but it was Abbie alone who saw this side of his nature; it was something special, reserved for her. He enjoyed his happy marriage and his sweet, capable wife, and he might have gone on that way for the rest of his life, but his marriage was upset, at last, by a trivial incident; it was betrayed by Abbie's desire to know every part of him, to peer into every corner. . . . He had caught slight cold that spring and it had settled in his chest and Abbie hovered about him sweetly, fluttering with great precision.

"I'm going to rub your chest and throat with turpentine to-night and you may as well make up your mind to submit. There's nothing better in my opinion for breaking up a cold."

He caught her hand and held it. "All right, honey."

"If you're not feeling better by morning, I'm going to call up old Mr. Hallman and tell him you're sick and can't come to work. You've got to take care of yourself, Chester."

"It isn't anything at all, darling. It'll go away of its own accord in a day or so."

"I'm going to rub you just the same, and I think I'll give you a dose of castor oil besides."

And so that night Chester lay in bed with his pajama coat unbuttoned and Abbie went back and forth between the room and the bath with hot towels in her hand. He pretended that she was tickling him, and he squirmed about, laughing up at her.

"Lie still. I'll be through in just a minute and then I'll cover you up warm."

She dipped her hands into the turpentine and began to rub him again, but Chester caught her and pulled her face down to

293

his. She laughed gayly. "I declare, darling, you certainly are a responsibility."

"I love you more than anything in the world," he said.

"Silly," said Abbie. "Silly! Look out, I'll spill turpentine on you."

She pulled away from his arms and went on with her labors. "I've got to finish rubbing you before you take more cold." She began kneading his flesh again, but she worked more slowly now, more thoughtfully, as if pondering his declaration of love, as if doubting it for the first time. For a moment she stared thoughtfully at his thin, somewhat frail chest, but at last she bound him with a woolen cloth and buttoned his pajama coat, covering him warmly with a blanket.

Chester lay lazily and at peace. "I wonder if there's anybody in the world as happy as we are?"

Abbie did not answer at once. She moved about, putting her medicines and her towels away. She went into the bathroom and for a while there was only the sound of flowing water and a clock ticking faintly in the dim room. For a short time Chester dozed. He was almost asleep when he was aroused by his wife's voice. She stood above his bed, a thoughtful look on her face:

"Did you ever think of the picture you want over your heart?"

Chester was completely awake. He regarded, for a moment, Abbie's solemn, thoughtful face. "Why, I hadn't thought of that for a long time," he answered in surprise. "What made you ask that, darling?"

"Nothing, nothing at all—it isn't important. I was just wondering."

She sat before her mirror, combing out her yellow curls, humming a song under her breath. Abruptly the song stopped. She turned and half faced the bed. Her face was roguish and gay again, as if her doubts were dispelled. She smiled, showing her tiny, half-formed teeth, and came over to him. She kissed him impulsively.

"Are you sure it isn't *my* picture you want over your heart?" He laughed and pulled her down to him rumpling her curls. "I feel better already, honey. My cold should be gone by tomorrow." Abbie sat as if chilled, her smile faded and slowly her jaw locked in its stubborn line.

"I asked you a question, dear. . . . You haven't answered me yet." But Chester would not take her seriously; he continued to joke and to pull at her curls.

"Oh, I see," said Abbie finally. "I see. You don't want my face on you, after all."

"Darling! Darling! Don't be foolish. You know very well that I do."

She got into bed and lay beside him and he put his arms about her, but Abbie turned her back.

"Please let me alone," she said coldly.

Chester was puzzled. "Abbie! Abbie! What have I done? What's the matter with you, darling?"

"There isn't anything the matter with me. Just leave me alone."

Chester turned away and lay on his side.

"I'm sorry I even mentioned the picture," continued Abbie. "Please accept my apologies. I wouldn't have done it if I had known how you feel about me."

Breakfast was on the table when Chester came downstairs the next morning, and Abbie was seated ready to pour his coffee. He went over and kissed her.

Abbie spoke thoughtfully, the coffee pot held away from her. "If you really loved me, you'd want my picture on your heart."

"It isn't that at all, darling. You know very well that I love you."

"What is it then?"

He looked at her in distress, his brows drawn together. "I can't explain about the picture. It's something I can't explain, even to myself."

"That's awfully interesting. Awfully interesting, I'm sure."

Chester got up from the table abruptly. He put his arms around his wife, resting his cheek against hers.

"Oh, honey, you mustn't act this way. We said we weren't ever going to quarrel like other people."

"I'm not quarreling. I merely asked you to do something for me and you refused, that's all."

Chester sighed helplessly. He went back to his seat and began to eat, but he found it difficult to swallow. He felt unhappy and perturbed.

"It's such a simple thing," continued Abbie softly as if to herself. "Such an unimportant thing, after all."

He began, slowly, to explain about the picture, how the idea had come to him when he first saw Bushrod's tattooing. He realized that he was doing it clumsily, but the farther he went the more he entangled himself, and before he had finished Abbie began to cry. She shoved back her chair and ran out of the room. He followed her up the stairs and into their room only in time to see Abbie go into the bathroom. He rapped on the locked door and implored her to speak to him, but she would not. He could hear only the steady sound of her tears, and at last he went out of the house, to work.

"How did this happen?" he wondered unhappily. "How did this thing come about?" He was distressed and preoccupied all that day at his work.

For the first time since they were married Abbie did not meet him at the door when he came home from work. He was a little alarmed at first, his mind turning to fearful conjectures, and he went to look for her before he had taken off his hat and coat.

She was in the kitchen, and she was quite safe, but her face was white and strained. He came to her impulsively and tried to put his arms about her, but Abbie stood rigidly, without response. She was as cold and as hard as steel.

"I think you'd better let me loose now. The steak will burn."

He turned, feeling completely defeated, and went upstairs to prepare for the meal. They ate it under difficulties. Abbie answered all his questions politely, and listened while he told of the happenings at the office, but she did not speak of her own accord. She kept her eyes lowered, her firm jaw slightly forward. He could stand the strain no longer.

"We're being very silly to act this way over nothing. We're acting like children."

"Oh, you think it's nothing for me to find out that you don't love me any more."

"I do love you. You know very well that I do."

"You certainly don't act like you did."

"How can you say a thing like that, Abbie?"

"I ask you a simple thing, and you refuse it. . . . It's very apparent that you don't love me. I doubt if you ever loved me."

He sat facing her, not knowing what to do.

Abbie began to cry again. "I don't know what's going to become of me," she said piteously over and over. "I don't know what's going to become of me."

Chester became furious all of a sudden. It was not fair for Abbie to ask this of him; she was being unjust and unreasonable and she might as well understand that he was going to be the master in his own house. He had never asked anything of her, he had made no demands whatever. She had had her way in everything, his love for her the weapon that she held over his head. He was furious, thinking those things. He got up from the table. "Please understand once and for all," he said angrily, "that I'm not going to give in to you this time. You're acting like a child."

"Oh, so that's the way you prove your love!"

"Please don't ever mention the thing to me again."

And so for a few days the matter was not discussed, but it lay between them like a sword. Abbie continued to be polite to him, to see that he was fed properly and that he was comfortable, but beyond that she would not go. They were both silent, miserable and a little frightened that their happiness could be jeopardized by such a trivial thing, that their destiny could hang on such a trifle. Abbie grew colder and more remote, and one night he found that she had moved her belongings into the room which Bushrod and Ruby had occupied.

He said freezingly: "That wasn't necessary. I'll move into the next room, if you don't want to be with me any more."

"No, thank you. I'll be very comfortable."

She closed the door and locked it, and Chester lay alone in bed for the first time since his marriage, and tried to think calmly without anger or resentment. He surveyed, rapidly, his life with Abbie. She was certainly a good wife, and her love for him was not to be doubted. She made him comfortable, and she made him happy; there was nothing she wouldn't do, no sacrifice that she would not make to ensure his well being. Of these things he was positive. . . . But the price of all this was that he must be completely absorbed by her, must have nothing of flesh or spirit which she could not share. This was the price of his paradise. It wasn't reasonable for Abbie to ask what she did! If he gave in to her, if he bought her back on such humiliating terms, he would have no respect for himself again.

After a while he heard Abbie crying in the next room, and all his emotions were swallowed in his love for her. He wanted to kiss her, to hold her in his arms again. He got out of bed and went to the door.

"Abbie! Abbie, darling, I love you. You know I love you."

He got down to his knees, his lips pressed against the keyhole. There was a short silence before Abbie spoke in a small, blurred voice.

"Prove it to me then."

"I'll do anything for you except that. Please don't ask me to do that."

There came the sound of Abbie crying unhappily into her pillow. "If you really loved me, you'd *want* to do it."

And so things went for ten days. Abbie grew thin and lost weight. She would not go out of the house and she cried constantly. They went over and over the same ground, time after time. Chester tried to explain, to make her see his viewpoint, but Abbie always came back to her starting point. "It's such a little thing to ask. If you loved me, as you say, you'd want my picture over your heart."

Unexpectedly he gave in, as he had always known that he would. There was bitterness in his heart and contempt for himself as he stood waiting for her to unlock the door; but when she was in his arms, her soft body against his own again, he forgot everything except the present. He only knew that she was beautiful and that being away from her was not to be endured!

Abbie said: "I know, now, that you love me better than the picture; I know that you love me completely."

The next night he went to see Jim, and Jim tattooed Abbie's features over his heart. He made her face rounder and her hair curlier than they were in real life. He stretched her eyes enormously and her lashes were blue dashes as long as her nose. He put a precise, circular blush on each cheek; he gathered her mouth into a tiny pucker which was almost a heart, and he left a simper around her lips. Jim was proud of his daughter's beauty and he made the picture his ideal of all feminine loveliness.

Chester stood examining himself before the mirror in the workshop, sick and slightly ashamed. He thought: "The picture looks more like Abbie than she does in real life."

"That's as fine a piece of work as I ever turned out," said Jim.

But Chester did not answer, for he continued to stare at the reflection in the mirror and he was seeing Abbie with new, impersonal eyes. "Why, she's common and rather stupid," he thought with surprise. "She's only a cheap and a mean woman, after all. . . . How was it possible for me to be taken in so completely? Why didn't I see these things before?"

He turned from the mirror and buttoned his shirt, and at that moment he knew that Abbie was no longer of the least importance to him. He had an impulse to dig at her face with his nails, to obliterate it, but he realized that he could not. It was too late for that now and he would only make himself bleed. He put on his coat and went back to his house.

"I'd like to have a photo of that piece of work to put it in my showcase downstairs," said Jim.

Abbie had fixed an excellent dinner and she awaited her husband flushed and happy, now that she had won her final victory and the last barrier to her bliss had fallen. She had let her curls down for the occasion and she was wearing a thin, lacy dress, the one which Chester admired most. A fillet of pink ribbon was run through her hair. She was coy and roguish. Her golden eyes were bright.

He opened the door and came into the room and Abbie ran forward in her old manner, and threw her arms about him.

"I love you. You're so sweet to do this for me."

But Chester stood with his arms close to his sides, enduring her caresses, as if it were not polite to walk away.

"Are you mad with me, darling?"

"Of course I'm not. Certainly I'm not." He bent his head and kissed her dutifully.

300

"Are you tired?"

"I'm not tired."

Abbie had won her victory, but it was to be a costly one for her. It was her turn, now, to implore. She hung on her husband's words. She importuned, she did everything that he wanted, anticipated his least wish. She tried to be gay, to ignore the barrier between them, but she was never successful, would never be successful.

Chester spoke quietly, in answer to her fright:

"You've had your way. I've done what you asked. What more do you want of me?"

The old relationship between them was gone forever and Abbie could not yet understand what had happened. She felt that her husband was unjust to make so much out of such a little incident. It wasn't that important. But he would not talk about the matter with her again. He was very busy at the office and he found it necessary to work a great deal at night. Abbie tried for a while to take an interest in his work, to understand it and to discuss it with him. But he would only smile at her. He had covered his body with glass and Abbie could not get at him again; there was no place any more for her fingers.

Later they established another relationship of quiet acceptance of each other, inasmuch as they must live together, but Abbie was never entirely happy, although she accepted the inevitable calmly enough.

"Why didn't he say the picture meant so much to him, if that's the way he felt," she thought over and over. "It's his own fault for giving in to me."

During the fourth year of their married life, Mr. Hallman, senior partner of the firm, died. His widow was anxious to sell his interest in the partnership and Graham, the surviving partner, offered it to Chester. Chester went at once to Reedyville to talk to Evan Chapman. The result was that Evan endorsed his notes and a week later a new partnership under the name of Graham and Hurry was organized. Old Mr. Graham congratulated him. "You've gone a long way for a young man only twenty-six years old, but I want to say you deserve all the success you've had."

From the Diary of Sarah Tarleton

June 15, 1931. *Bessie arrived today. She is not looking well, poor child, and I'm afraid that she is living too fast a life in New York. I wish that she would marry some good man and settle down. She is a great comfort to Frank. She is his baby and, although I want to be fair, she was always his favorite child. If she could just turn all her misguided energy into some useful field, she could go a long way, but there's no use talking to her. Frank is feeling better already, now that she is here. I hope we can keep her with us for a long time, for his sake if for no other.*

June 20, 1931. *Had a long, nice letter today from Abbie. She has promised to visit Lillian Chapman a little later in the summer. We all hope to see a lot of her. Chester has become a fine, up-standing citizen and a credit to any community, and I think he owes most of it to his little wife. It was a fortunate alliance for him, and their marriage has been unusually happy. It is too bad that they have no children to make their home complete.*

The Whisperer

WHEN it lightened the drenched road and the countryside were revealed for an instant in the sharp, jagged light. . . . The fields lay covered in shallow water with the tops of old furrows showing through like the bones of immemorial monsters awash in ancient lakes. Water lay gray and undrained everywhere and the road itself was no longer recognizable as a road: It was a bog, a fen through which rivulets ran and emptied with a faint sound into ditches already swollen full.

The one man who walked this road shivered a little, as if he could feel the cold, and drew his coat closer about him. He stood still and surveyed the well-known countryside, his face lifting to the drenched land, his fingers raised in a tired gesture to his eyes. He stood silent there, turning from side to side, familiar with the country that he surveyed, knowing by recollection each tree, each outhouse, each foot of the rich earth.

Then he turned off from the road, down a lane, over a rotting stile. He stopped, finally, before a house and waited there patiently, his head lowered, as if he knew that the door would soon be opened to him. When the door did open a woman stood before him. Behind her there was a fire and a feeling of warmth.

The woman breathed quietly in her black dress, an old shawl clutched to her neck in one thin hand. With her other hand she held a lamp above her head, its light cutting sharply through the blackness; and in this puny wedge of brightness the rain swirled about, blown into circles, into tiny, impotent cyclones by unpredictable winds. In it the stranger stood revealed.

His skin was yellowish and soiled, with purple shadows beneath his eyes and sunken, purple circles in his cheeks. His hands were also soiled, as if he had but recently dug in the earth, and he made a moaning noise through blue, half-opened lips.

When the woman saw who he was her face set in patience and despair and she began to tremble. The light in her hand wavered with her emotion and threw uncertain, creeping shadows on the ground. . . . The wind had stopped now and the rain fell straight down again in round drops which struck the undrained pool beyond the steps, dotting it with a thousand up-springing dimples.

"You must go back," said the woman.

But the man before her shook his head and began to cry, his mouth wide open, his arms beating against his wet clothing.

He said: "I know a thing so terrible that your brain cannot comprehend it."

"Go back," said the woman. "Go back."

The man began to laugh with slow, terrible softness. "This is my message to you who yet live. This is what I now know: There is no quietness in death. It, too, is all noise and despair and confusion."

"Go back," said the trembling woman. "Go back. You cannot remain here."

33

BESSIE remained most of that summer with her family, but toward its close she wrote Chester asking if she could come down to visit him and Abbie for a few days, before she returned to New York. Chester showed the letter to his wife and she was delighted. She volunteered to answer the letter herself. She did so. She was very cordial and insistent, and the next week Bessie arrived. Bessie was a woman of thirty-five now, but she looked even older, possibly because she dressed so severely and made no effort to make herself attractive.

Chester went to the station to meet her and Bessie got off the train and strode toward him swinging her suitcases, her wide, high shoulders swaying in rhythm, as if she liked to feel heavy weights at the end of her arms. She put down the suitcases, caught him by the shoulders and swung him around, examining him. She was a little taller than he and he felt somewhat self-conscious.

"Well, if it isn't old Chester," she said vigorously. "The old boy himself!"

Chester laughed. "R. C. Hurry, in person: the wizard of fire insurance, rentals and real estate."

Bessie's face was brown and gaunt. She stooped a little, as if to negative her height. She wore no gloves and her hands were rough and capable-looking, her fingers stained with nicotine, her nails not too clean. She had been working on the farm all summer.

She began to talk in the dialect of the county. "Folks say as

307

how you're married, now: I hear tell that you're a family man, and all." She leaned over and kissed him impulsively.

"I'm afraid I am. I'm afraid it's all too true, Miss Tarleton."

Bessie stretched her eyes and pursed out her lips imitating Aunt Sarah's precise voice. "What a pity! What an unmitigated pity!"

She was in an excellent humor. In the taxi she laughed and told jokes and repeated all the gossip she had heard in Pearl County. When they approached the house Chester spoke, shrugging his shoulders.

"Abbie is inviting some people for tonight to meet you. I tried to stop it, but I couldn't."

"What sort of people?"

"Only the most respectable. Be sure of that. It will all be very refined."

"Well," said Bessie, "we'll live through it I suppose. You and I don't have to fool with them, do we? Can't we just go off by ourselves and talk?" She drummed on the window with her fingers. "What sort of a woman is your wife?" she asked abruptly.

"Oh, Abbie's all right. She's very sweet and womanly."

Bessie poked him in the ribs with her brown thumb. "I was afraid of that. I'm always leery when Aunt Sarah and Lillian are too enthusiastic. . . . My God, what did she do to them? You ought to run her for sheriff or some other public office." The taxi stopped and Bessie got out. She paid the driver herself, elbowing Chester out of the way.

Abbie was waiting for them in the hall. She came up to Bessie impulsively and kissed her, standing on tiptoes. "I've heard so much about you from Lillian and Aunt Sarah. We all are so proud of your success!"

"Success?" repeated Bessie. "Well, that's an angle I'd overlooked."

308

"We want your stay with us to be very happy, even if it is to be so short."

"I'll run up to my room and wash up a bit," said Bessie. "I'm grimy all the way down."

"Don't wear anything *too* elaborate tonight," sang out Abbie. "Just a simple evening dress."

Bessie stopped on the stairs. . . . "U-m-m," she said slowly. "Evening dress?— Now what would I be doing with an evening dress?"

Abbie stood with her mouth slightly opened, trying to cope with this situation. "Oh, of course, just wear anything that you please," she said hastily. And so it was that Bessie came to dinner dressed in a skirt and blouse. She had not bothered to powder her face nor to arrange her hair. It fell about her gaunt face and into her eyes like the hair of a terrier.

Abbie had arranged dinner for eight. Her table was very beautiful and she had got out all her best silver and the set of china which Lillian had sent her for Christmas. She surveyed it a moment, proudly, before they all sat down.

Bessie was talking to Mrs. Carson who sat on her left. "Oh, no, I don't fix my hair in this unusual way because I think it especially becoming, but you see it hides a bad scar." She raised her hair and there across her temple was a deep welt which ran upward into her hair line and was lost.

"Oh, you poor thing!" said Abbie sympathetically. "How in the world did that happen?"

"It isn't much of a story, I'm afraid.— I mean it hasn't much point; but I was speaking at a meeting down on the square one night. Somebody in the crowd threw a pop bottle at me and the first thing I knew we were all fighting. The cops came and one of them hit me with his club."

Mrs. Carson gasped and almost swallowed an olive. Abbie spoke quickly to cover the dead silence: "Have you seen the new car Isabel got for her birthday? She 'phoned me this morning and told me all about it."

But Mrs. Carson only stared, her eyes bulging a little. Nobody paid any attention to Abbie; their eyes were focused on Bessie alone.

John Prescott spoke slowly: "Do you mean that you are a communist, Miss Tarleton?"

"Why, of course," replied Bessie impatiently. 'What else would I be?"

"How very remarkable," said old Mrs. Prescott.

"What's wrong with that?"

Mrs. Carson laughed faintly: "It just isn't American, I'm afraid."

Bessie became excited. She pushed back her hair and began to talk with earnest zeal. She talked a long time, gesturing with her angular arms, the food on the table cold before her. There was a chilling and an absolute silence at the table when she stopped.

Abbie spoke to Louise Carson, touching her arm to attract her attention. "You must go with me to Sellings some day this week. I want to pick out a new coat for fall. I've always said you have such perfect taste in clothes." But Mrs. Carson smiled vaguely and turned back to stare at Bessie.

John Prescott laughed faintly: "I hate to think what would happen in the country if the communists took charge."

"It couldn't be much worse than it is now," said Bessie. She shook her wide shoulders angrily and pushed back her chair. She was aroused now, the light of battle in her eyes. She quoted statistics, cited examples of injustice and exploitation while her audience sat looking at her, their faces frozen.

When she finished old Mrs. Prescott spoke: "You may consider *yourself* as belonging to the lower middle classes, my dear, but I certainly will make no such admission."

"What class do you belong to, then?"

Mrs. Prescott breathed heavily through her nose. "I'm sure I haven't thought much about the matter one way or another, but I've always considered that I belonged to the very *highest* class."

"There are no class distinctions in America," said Bob Carson. "In Europe, yes, but in America every man is equal."

Bessie began to laugh. She shook her head a time or two and then discovered that there was food before her. She was hungry and began to eat quickly.

Abbie realized that her dinner party was spoiled. She was alarmed and resentful. When if these people thought that she shared Bessie's views? What if they thought—the idea almost took her breath away. She had planned a reception for Bessie the following afternoon and had already invited her guests, but she decided, at that instant, that Bessie would be much too tired, after her journey, to stand the party; that the excitement would be too much for her. She would get the people on the 'phone early in the morning and explain. . . . Possibly she could call most of them up tonight, for she had a feeling that her present guests would not stay long. And she was right. The party broke up early. When they had gone, Bessie sat back and lit another cigarette. She inhaled deeply.

"I think I made a hit with the old girl who belongs to only the best classes."

Chester laughed: "I think you played hell!" He reached out and gave her ear a yank.

Bessie threw out her arms and yawned: "Who cares?" she asked, indolently. "They thought I was terrible, of course. . . . Well, it's mutual on *both* sides, as old Addie Wrenn used to say."

"As a matter of academic interest," said Chester, "please don't think I fell for that story about the scar. I remember the time you jumped out of the plum tree and hit your head on a root."

"Do you remember how beautiful the plum thicket was in spring?" said Bessie quickly. "Do you remember the fig trees when they first turned green?"

In the hall Abbie could be heard telephoning steadily, but her voice was low and no word came through to their ears.

"I couldn't resist telling that old gal about getting beat up," said Bessie. "It made her whole evening."

When Bessie was undressed she shouted through the partition to Chester and he came into her room and sat beside her on the bed. He had not seen Bessie for more than ten years and in that time she had changed greatly. But those changes, he realized after a moment, were all superficial, all physical. Bessie had always been tender, abrupt and slightly malicious. She had never had any feeling for social contacts and would never have. She was, he realized, slightly exaggerated, slightly out of drawing like all of the Tarletons. Her only tenderness had been Brad Tallon, and, in a lesser degree, himself.

For a long time they sat talking together over the old days, laughing a little at the things their memories brought to the surface. Later Abbie came in. "Turn out the light in the hall when you come to bed. I'm going to sleep, dear."

"All right, Abbie."

She smiled, nodded to Bessie with just the right cordiality and went out.

"I hope I haven't upset your household," said Bessie.

Chester shrugged: "It doesn't matter."

"Poor little Chester! Women always did pick on you, didn't they? Especially Lillian and Aunt Sarah."

"You aren't being fair to Abbie. She's really very sweet, and you've seen only one side of her. She has her good points."

But Bessie had already dismissed Abbie from her mind. She flung out her shoulders. "Give me another cigarette."

She blew the smoke upward and spoke abruptly. "Do you remember the time Brad sent you to the creek to catch crayfish?"

"Of course I remember it. I was a simple child, I'm afraid."

"That was the first time he ever kissed me."

She leaned backward and closed her eyes. "I was very silly about his death but it took me a long time to realize that. A woman is a fool to waste her life grieving for something that can't be helped." She was talking rapidly but her face was quite steady, her voice calm. "I often think, why did it have to be Brad? What was the point in it? Who gained anything?"

"I hoped you'd got over all that, Bessie."

"I have, of course, long ago. There's no sense in remembering. . . . Do you remember the space between his two front teeth and the way he opened his eyes when you told him something that he didn't believe?" She broke off suddenly and began to play with the chain to the night light. "I haven't ever discussed him with anybody before. I wanted to talk to pappa and Aunt Sarah, but I couldn't do it. It was no use." She crushed out the cigarette and lit another.

"One Sunday afternoon I slipped away and went down to Pearl River where the boys swam. I'd never seen a naked man in my life, and I wanted to."

Chester laughed softly and Bessie laughed with him. "Oh, I know! I know! . . . poor little prurient maiden and all that, but I did just the same. I was about fifteen, I think. Anyway I hid behind that big live oak and watched until I saw Bradford come out of the water and stand on the bank. I never saw anything in my life as beautiful as he was that day naked."

She stopped quickly, overcome by emotion, but she kept her face calm, her voice quiet and matter of fact. "And now he's rotted away. His brown eyes have fallen out and rotted too." She laughed gayly and flung out her arms as if to negative her words. "Oh, Christ, oh, Christ Almighty, I don't see how I ever stood it."

Then as if fearing that Chester would offer her sympathy, she changed the subject.

"Do you remember old Professor Drewery and Aunt Sarah paying each other compliments, each of them trying to use nothing less than four syllable words? When I think of those days I have to stop and laugh."

"Those were the days when you were going to be a great opera singer. You were going to tour the world and have royalty at your feet, as I remember it now."

"When I think of him now I see first a picked skull with his teeth all intact in their sockets. Do you remember that space between his front teeth? . . . But of course you do. You've already said that you did! . . . How can people sit at home and think about dinner parties and automobiles and new dresses? When I remember Brad I want to go out and smash everything to pieces with an ax. . . . But I can't do it. . . . Not with an ax, I mean."

And so they talked of old times. It was daylight before Chester went to bed. The next night, to Abbie's relief, Bessie cut her visit short and went away. Only Chester had enjoyed it. The band between them was deeper than he had thought.

34

THE years passed placidly. Abbie had long been reconciled to her husband's coldness, to his lack of affection. He provided for her, he lived a respectable life and was getting along in the world. What more was there to be expected of life? He did the obvious things demanded of him, he was on the surface precisely like the husbands of all the women she knew. She was content.

The year before they had sold the brick house and had bought a bungalow in a new sub-division which had recently opened. Abbie had never felt right in the brick place with the grille work. It had always seemed a little odd to her. Besides, the fixtures were not modern, and it was inconvenient to her friends.

These things were very true, and Chester, too, was anxious to get away from the brick house. There were many painful memories connected with it which he preferred to forget. But he had always felt that the house really belonged to Bushrod and that some day he would return and claim it. He discussed this with his partner Donald Graham, but Graham thought it unlikely that Bush would ever return: he had been gone for eight years and in that time no one had heard from him. Chester realized that this was true, that he would never see his uncle again, and at last the transfer was made.

One night, shortly after the new move, he got a long-distance call from Sarah. The family, it appeared, had just received a telegram from a Doctor Carew in Athlestan announcing the death of Robert Hurry and asking if they would give the information to his son. Chester thanked Aunt Sarah for calling him and chatted with her for a moment. He came back into the living room where Abbie sat dealing herself bridge hands.

"It was Aunt Sarah. My father died this morning, but they didn't know how to locate me."

"Oh," she said sympathetically. "Oh, I'm so sorry."

Chester seated himself and began to read again. "I haven't thought of my father in a good many years. There's no sense in being a hypocrite, I suppose."

"Chester! Chester!" cried Abbie in distress. "How can you be so cold about such a thing? How can you be so hard?"

Chester leaned back and folded his paper. He was upset at the news, much more than he had thought possible and he thought of his childhood, so far away and so remote now, and a feeling of sadness came over him. He fought against it, trying to reason it out with himself, but he could not.

"You had better look up train schedules, dear. I think there's one around ten o'clock. I'll go pack your bags."

"Do you think I should go? Do you think they expect it?"

"Go? Why, of course you must. What would people think if you didn't go to your own father's funeral? . . . I'm surprised at you, Chester. I really am."

Chester went to the telephone and called Donald Graham, explaining that he would be away for two or three days. He came into the living room and looked out at the street. It was raining dismally and the wet asphalt gleamed like satin under the light. There was a party next door and he could hear occasionally scraps of talk and excited laughter. He had a moment of panic. He did not want to go back. He felt, dimly, that the experience would be too painful and for a while he regretted his decision. The idea of returning to his old home terrified him as it had terrified him when he was a boy during the early days with his grandfather, but he squared his shoulders and threw off his

316

fears. "It's something that must be done!" he thought. "I'll get it over with as quickly as possible."

Abbie came in with his bag and he went back to the garage to get the car. She insisted on driving him to the station herself.

"You'd better take your raincoat, too. The paper says this weather is going to keep up for a day or two."

He nodded and took the coat from its hanger. Later Abbie took him to the station, but she was silent and preoccupied during the drive. Chester thought, somewhat amused: "She's wondering if she should go into mourning for my father. She'll look it up in her etiquette book when she gets back to the house." At once he was ashamed of himself. "Why do I treat Abbie so unfairly?" he thought. "Why do I keep punishing her in little ways?"

He felt very tender toward her. He clung to her at the gate. He wanted to say: "Tell me not to go. It's a mistake to go. I feel that it is." But Abbie was kissing him, crying a little at this parting, as she always did.

"Good-by, darling. Telegraph me when to expect you and I'll meet you with the car. Be sure not to eat any fried food. You know it always disagrees with you."

He watched her standing there on the platform, looking slight and pathetic. He thought: "When I come back, I'm going to try to make it up to Abbie. There's no sense in our living this way."

Athlestan had changed little. There were the same wide streets with their double rows of oaks, the same somnolence, the same imperviousness to the outside world; but the oaks were dropping their leaves at this season and the houses stood out harshly behind them. The accommodation train pulled into the station and Chester got out, a little stiff and cramped, a little tired from lack of sleep. A man with a bald head and fat rolls which hung over his collar came forward to meet him. He extended a damp, soft hand. There was a curious shyness about him. He said: "You remember me?—Dr. Carew?"

"Yes," said Chester. He shuffled his feet and looked downward, not knowing what to do next. "You took care of me when I was sick."

Dr. Carew smiled. "You were a sick boy. I didn't think you were going to get well." He picked up Chester's bag and guided him to an automobile, sat at the wheel and adjusted a pair of spectacles around his ears. He started the car, leaning forward at an angle as if peering eternally at something just beyond his range of vision. "Yes, sir," he continued after a moment, "you were about as sick a boy as I ever had on my hands."

It was raining a little, a thin rain which fell steadily. People stood in the protection of doorways, looking at the muddy streets, their faces sullen and discontented.

"Athlestan hasn't changed much. It's about the same as it always was, isn't it?"

"We jog along," replied the doctor; "we don't go ahead very fast." He came to a corner, slowed down, put his hand out and turned. "How old are you now, Chester?"

"I'm twenty-nine."

Dr. Carew sighed. "Time gets away from us, doesn't it?"

"I see it's raining here, too," said Chester. "When I left Baycity the hurricane warnings were out."

"We'll get the tail end of it," replied Carew.

They reached the doctor's office and climbed the stairs together. Chester came into the consultation room and sat in a deep, leather chair; and the doctor sat before him, examining him with kindly, critical eyes. He spoke hesitantly: "I've known your father all my life. I knew your mother, too, and I was with her when she died." He got up, went to the window and looked

318

out at the fine, small rain. "Your father was always an unhappy man."

"What did my father die from?"

"A bad heart. He'd had it for a long time."

Again there was silence. Outside in the street was the strident sound of a horn, the voice of young girls laughing together and the noise of two automobile doors being slammed, with an interval of a second between them.

"He was a strange man," said Dr. Carew. "A strange, unhappy man." He came back and sat at his desk, playing with his watch fob, testing its weight in his open palm. "What I'm going to tell you is hard for me to do; please remember that. But I feel it's my duty to tell you before you go out there. It's better that way than for you to find out for yourself."

Chester spoke quietly: "It doesn't matter; don't try to spare my feelings. My father and I never got on together: you surely must know that."

Dr. Carew shook his head mildly.

"If it's about him and Mitty living together you needn't hesitate. I knew that even before I went to live with my grandfather."

"There are some children, too."

Chester put down the paper weight with which he had been playing. "Oh, I see," he said. "That never occurred to me. I don't know why."

"There's a whole houseful of them," said the doctor. "The oldest are almost grown."

"That's odd, isn't it? I never knew I had any brothers and sisters: I always thought of myself as an only child." His voice was impersonal, musing. He lifted his hand and rubbed the spot where his hair was beginning to recede slightly from his temples.

"Are they very dark? . . . Mitty, herself, is, you know."

"One of the little girls is quite dark."

Chester laughed quickly and the doctor looked at him. "That struck me as being funny," he explained; "the way you said it, I mean." He stopped laughing, and in the silence that followed he could hear a desk clock ticking behind him, and a man in the street below shouting to someone whose name was Charlie.

"Under the circumstances you can understand why no minister will bury your father." Dr. Carew lowered his eyes. "I don't think their attitude is unreasonable, from their standpoint, of course."

"Of course not. It's very natural that they should feel that way."

"I've arranged everything else," continued the doctor: "the burial permit, with the undertaker and all that."

"We won't have any religious ceremony."

He got up and drew on his gloves. "Everything is settled then? There's nothing for me to do at all?" The doctor had also risen. The thing that he had been dreading had passed off more easily than he had expected. He felt exuberant all of a sudden, and he spoke with bluff heartiness. "It's about lunch time. Let's go get something to eat."

Chester said: "All right; whatever you say goes with me." As they walked down the worn stairs he spoke again: "I want to tell you how much I appreciate all the trouble you've taken."

"It's nothing. I was the only friend your father ever had."

When they came out of the restaurant the rain had stopped, but the sky was leaden and cast over with clouds. There was little light from the sun, and over the town, and across the fields that lay beyond, was a fine, smoke-like mist.

They got into the automobile again and Dr. Carew started it.

"So you think the old town looks about the same?"

"Yes, sir," said Chester. Then, more slowly. "Of course, I don't remember it very well. Mitty used to bring me in sometimes on a Saturday afternoon but I was never here more than a dozen times in my life."

"The garages and the filling stations are new," said the doctor.

"Well, we've got to expect that. We got to go along with the times, I expect." They had passed the negro shacks which huddled on the outskirts of the town and were in open country. Fields, through which the pickers had gone, stretched on both sides of the road with the withered, brown stalks of the cotton still standing.

"What's the name of the little girl, the black one?"

The doctor thought a moment. "Ellen, I think. Yes, I'm sure that's right."

"That was my mother's name."

"I know it was."

He began to talk quickly, trivialities, as if anything were better than silence, but he knew that Chester was not listening to him. At last he stopped, defeated, and peered ahead at the misty road. Along its sides the leaves from trees fell steadily and drifted across the road. "I can drive you up to the door, if you want me to."

"No. No, that won't be necessary." He took out his bag and shook the doctor's hand again.

"Mitty's holding the funeral tomorrow morning, unless you want to change it."

"Oh, no! I don't want to interfere. The wishes of the widow should be respected, don't you think?"

"I'll come over for the ceremony," said Dr. Carew.

"Please don't," said Chester quickly. "Please don't do that."

The doctor stared at him strangely. "You're under a strain right now. I've been watching you for the past couple of hours and I know just how upset you feel."

"You're wrong this time, doctor. I was never calmer in my life."

"I'll give you something to put you to sleep if you think you need it."

Chester laughed harshly and swung his bag out of the car. "I'll drop in to see you again before I leave. Thanks for all you've done."

He walked through the grove of oaks and up the brick walk that led to the house, but before he reached it he stopped. "By God, Mitty got the place painted, after all," he said. "She was always talking about it." He put down his bag and surveyed the old house. The porch had been straightened and the rotted boards replaced; creepers had been pulled away from the veranda and there were brick flower beds laid out. Behind the house were a series of chicken runs, clean with white paint. The whole place looked well cared for and somewhat prosperous.

An early dusk was coming and the pine grove was already wavering in its softness. Trees and outhouses were losing their sharp outlines, blurring and mellowing a little. Above his head rain frogs croaked and locusts began to sing in strident, sustained voices. When they stopped there was a strange hush, deeper than any mere lack of sound, as if the saturated earth and this decaying house exhaled a silence of its own: a silence too pure and too profound for the ears of mankind.

As he turned his head from side to side surveying the familiar scene, he saw Mitty for the first time. She was standing behind a tree, half concealed in the shadow. She stood there humbly, her head slightly lowered. He looked at her and smiled. She ran toward him and threw her arms about him. "Baby! Baby!" she said. . . . "Baby!"

Chester stood rigid. "How do you do," he said. "How do you do, Mitty."

35

THE inside of the house was very clean and its woodwork had been repainted recently, but the great living room, which had once been so magnificent with carpets and chandeliers, was bare now of all furniture. The floor had been painted white and it was lined with a series of incubators and brooders. It was here that Mitty hatched eggs and kept the young chickens until they were old enough to be put outside in the pens. The incubators were not working now, but there clung to the room a sweet-sour smell of wet chicks just emerged from their shells.

Chester walked through the familiar house, from room to room, with Mitty beside him, her eyes following him eagerly. She stretched out her hands as if to touch him and then pulled them back to her sides.

"Are you still a single man?" she asked.

Chester said, not turning, "Oh, no. I've been married a long time."

"We never knowed that. Your pappa and I never knowed."

"What difference does it make, one way or the other?"

"I'd have sent you a present, sugarpie."

He turned and looked at Mitty, seeing her really for the first time, and he was conscious of how she had aged. Her tight, nappy hair was turning gray at the sides and her throat, which he had remembered as being firm and straight, was stringy now and fallen a little. There were thread-like lines around her eyes. When she smiled, he saw that some of her teeth were missing.

"I should have sent you an invitation to my wedding. I didn't think of it at the time."

They came into the kitchen again and he sat on the old, worn bench beside the stove. It was almost dark and Mitty lowered the shades.

"Can't I fix you something to eat, baby? You've got to eat to keep your strength."

"No, thank you. No, I don't think so."

"Just a cup of coffee," she begged. "Supper won't be ready for two hours yet. Just a cup of coffee. It won't take a minute."

"All right. All right, if it isn't too much trouble."

He looked at the old wall clock and saw, to his surprise, that it was only four o'clock. He had thought it later.

Mitty put water on to boil and got out a clean, linen rag which she fitted over the pot. She sat down on a stool opposite him and spoke bitterly:

"It ain't my fault you never heard from us after you left. I'd have wrote, baby, but Miss Sarah told me I couldn't do it. Everybody looks down on me for what I done. Everybody say I'm a dirty woman."

Chester said: "It doesn't matter to me. Please remember that, Mitty."

"Everybody thinks I'm low and no-account. Everybody thinks that. You think that too in your heart, honey."

"I haven't any feeling about it one way or the other."

"Lord God! Lord God!" cried Mitty in despair. "Nobody knows what I went through. Nobody knows the trouble I've had."

She rocked back and forth, her black hands covering her face. She raised her head, her eyes humble and piteous. "Ellen knows. Ellen knows what I went through. She knows my heart is pure. She knows that what I done never pleasured me any."

But, even in her emotion, Mitty did not forget the coffee. The pot of water was boiling now, and she went to it. She poured it slowly over the grounds which filled the linen sack.

"What else could I do? What else could I do for Ellen except what I done?"

Chester spoke casually. "Dr. Carew said there were a lot of children. Where are they now?"

"Don't worry, baby. I sent them down the road a piece to stay until after the funeral is over." She reached over humbly, and touched his hand. "They won't shame you none, baby. You won't even see them, while you're here."

"Are they very dark?"

"Come on, little Chester! Drink your coffee. Come on, I'll pour it out in the blue cup you used to drink out of when you was a little boy."

"Are they very dark?"

Mitty sighed. "The little girl is dark."

Chester sat at the table, drinking the hot coffee. It warmed him a little and he felt better. He was conscious that his head had been aching all morning.

"Six children I had in all," said Mitty. "Four boys and two girls. The oldest boy and girl ain't here no more. Your pappa sent them up north, to study. . . . He had his faults, Chester, but he was good to his children. He never denied them nothing that he could give." Again she rocked back and forth, overcome with memories, covering her face with her hands.

A tired feeling came over Chester. He put down his cup and closed his eyes. "He never took very much interest in me as I remember it."

"Baby! Baby! Your pappa is dead: you mustn't speak ill of him!"

"All right. All right, Mitty."

He brushed his face with his hands with the rough gesture which had been habitual with his father. "Soon I must go up-

325

stairs and look at him," he thought. "I don't want to do it, but I must. It's something I can't avoid much longer."

Mitty was rocking back and forth, her black face twisted up. "I'm just an ignorant woman, but I done the best I knew how. I done what I thought was right."

Chester went to the window and looked out. It was raining again thinly and mist still rose from the drenched land. Through the haze he saw Jim's cabin, a fire shining through the window.

"What became of Hattie and Jim?" He realized, all at once, that he had forgotten about them. He had not even asked about them or thought of them since his return.

"They're still on the place, baby. They're still here, but that Jim gets more no-account every day. God knows what makes me go on feeding 'em, like I do."

Chester pulled the shade down and went into the hall to put on his coat. "I think I'll go over and see them for a little while."

Mitty was hurt. "What you want to do that for? Why don't you stay here and talk to me while I cook supper?"

"I won't be gone long."

"You haven't told me hardly anything at all. There's so much I want to hear, baby."

"I'll be back for supper."

"All right," said Mitty. "All right, then." She held the door open for him. "Don't get your feet wet. You know how easy you take cold."

Jim was stretched before the fire and Hattie was sitting behind him, peeling potatoes and dropping them into a pot at her side. Chester opened the door and came in and Jim sat up, his anvil head thrown back, his mouth open; but Hattie, when she saw who the visitor was, got up excitedly, came to him on her lath-like legs and kissed him loudly, her arms close about him.

"I knowed you wouldn't forget your old Hattie. Jim said so,

but I knowed you wouldn't. I knowed all the time you wouldn't."

She pulled up a chair and Chester sat before the fire, feeling its warmth, his legs stretched wide. Hattie and Jim were both past sixty and he realized, with a shock, the changes which time had made in them. Jim had become fat and he was almost entirely bald, with only a fringe of thin, nappy wool growing above his ears and on the back of his head. He pulled away from the fire slowly, grumbling a little, as if it pained him to disturb his old bones.

Hattie had taken Chester's coat and his hat and was hanging them up. "Lord God!" she exclaimed. "This here coat lined with silk. Look here, Jim! Look here a minute."

"I don't care nothing about coats."

"Are you a rich man?" asked Hattie. "Mitty say she bet you is."

"Oh, no, I'm far from that, Hattie. Far from it."

Hattie sat down again and went on with her work. There was a pause. They sat thinking, trying to find a topic in common.

"How are things here? Is Mitty making anything with the chickens?"

"We has good years and bad ones, baby," said Hattie. "Good and bad ones."

"They're mostly bad," said Jim.

Hattie had dried up with time. Her arms and legs were frail in their brittleness and her flat, high buttocks were even more exaggerated than when she was younger.

"Do you remember a coon you used to have named Buck?" asked Chester. "I've often wondered what became of him."

"I had a hound named Buck, once," said Jim. He frowned in an effort to recall the past. "I don't recollect no coon by that name."

327

Hattie poked him with her shoe. "*Sho* you do, Jim! That was the one that got killed by the Eldridge dogs one night."

"Maybe I remember. Maybe so."

Hattie had finished her potatoes. She put them on the stove to boil, and began washing collard leaves.

"Ain't them collard greens played out yet?" asked Jim. "I'm tired of eating collards."

"It takes a good hard frost to kill collards," said Hattie.

She turned to Chester. "I expect you're married by now, baby."

"Oh, yes."

"I expect she's a sweet thing."

Jim was mumbling to himself: "What makes folks come saying I had a coon named Buck. I don't recollect no coon named Buck. . . ."

Hattie's potatoes were boiling briskly and she came back from the stove. "Do you tote your wife's picture about with you? I'd sho like to see her, baby. I'd sho like to see that sweet white girl."

Chester got up upon sudden impulse and took off his coat and vest. He unbuttoned his shirt and removed that too. "Oh, yes, I carry her picture wherever I go. I'll be glad to show it to you."

Hattie and Jim looked at Abbie's childish, beautiful face with its red circles for blushes and its blue, fat curls. Hattie was entranced. She came over and touched the picture in amazement.

"Is she really that pretty and sweet-looking?"

"I'm afraid she is. I'm afraid she's even sweeter." But his bitterness was lost on Hattie. Another part of his brain kept saying, "You're not just; you're not fair to Abbie."

"That sho was a thoughtful thing to do, having your wife's picture put on you where you can see it every night and every morning the first thing."

328

"It was her idea," said Chester. "I don't want to take any of the credit."

"It was nice though," said Hattie. "It was real thoughtful." Chester put his hand above his heart and tightened his flesh, and Abbie's eyes and lips rose upward into an idiotic, angelic smirk. He released his skin and pulled downward, and instantly Abbie's face took on a sour, disgusted expression. Jim lay on the floor and laughed until he was helpless. "Lord God!" he groaned. "Lord God Almighty." Hattie, too, began to laugh, slapping her flat, wide thighs.

When Mitty closed the door behind her and went out of the room, Chester walked to the bed where his pinched, dead father lay and drew back the sheet that covered him. He stood there quietly, surprised at his father's inoffensive mildness; for Robert's grayish hair had been brushed and parted neatly and he wore a black, new suit; a black, ready-made bow tie, adjusted inexpertly by the unaccustomed fingers of a woman. His eyes were closed precisely in their small, veined caverns and his mustache was trimmed, as if Mitty had sought, at last, to make him attractive to death. He seemed small and unimportant in death, as if something within him, which had made him a man in life, had shrunken now and withdrawn into itself. He rested rigid and composed, the way death had caught him, with mottled and waxen hands folded at last in peace. He was only a small, pitiful old man, after all, and he could harm no one. Chester drew up a chair and sat down beside the still form. He thought: "How could I have been afraid of this pathetic dead man? How could he have hurt me? Why have I hated him all my life?"

He felt a rush of strange emotion which shook him and left him weak. He wanted to apologize to his father. It seemed so senseless now, such a waste. Everything seemed senseless and mixed up. He reached out and touched his father's cold cheek

329

with a hand which was also cold. "Forgive me," he whispered. "Please forgive me." He touched also the thin, graying hair, but very gently; and he saw that his hands were jerking and he felt hot tears on his cheeks. He got down upon his knees beside the bed and rocked his head from side to side, a feeling of suffocation in his breast. He cried soundlessly.

"Who am I to have judged you? . . . God knows I've done nothing with my own life." He bent above his father, as if to impel him to listen, but the dead man was beyond hearing or caring in the strange place to which he had gone. He lay stiff with straight limbs, his eyes closed forever to this world, his brain blotted out in silence. Chester took his father's hand and held it: "You were always puzzled and frightened and alone and I understand, now, that it is too late. . . . Listen, listen to what I say: I, too, am puzzled and frightened."

Beyond the barrier of the wall he could hear Mitty moving about and speaking to someone, and a moment later there came a tap at the door. "Chester," she called softly; "little Chester, are you still there?"

"Yes, what is it?"

"The coffin's done come, baby. You better go in your old room while we put him in it."

He walked into the hall where Mitty and the men stood, his face averted, so that they could not see that he had been crying.

Mitty touched his arm in comfort. "It won't take long. You go in and lie down."

Obediently he went into his old room, but he did not make a light. He lay on the bed fully clothed and stared upward at the dim ceiling. The voices of the men continued, but he could distinguish no word that they said. Again he saw his father's face and his shrunken, rigid form.

"We might have meant a great deal to each other. We might have given each other happiness," he whispered. "That was a loss. That was a great loss." He turned on his side and gave way to his grief utterly, his body racked and shaken, his hands making futile gestures in the air.

There came to him, then, through the still air, the myriad sounds of the autumn night; sounds too faint and too vague to be heard individually, and existing only as a part of a larger sound. There was the despairing cry of a swamp rabbit caught in a trap, the scream of a bird in a hawk's claws; there were red leaves breaking from their stems and falling to earth with a dry rustle; there were wild pigs grunting and turning uneasily in their pine straw; the falling of infertile eggs from old nests and the breaking of frail, speckled shells. Then, too, there was the frightened piping, whispering and scraping of insects alarmed at the brisk air, knowing, if vaguely, that their summer had ended and was gone.

Mitty entered the room. "Don't worry, baby; don't grieve. Everything going to be all right."

36

THE undertaker's assistants arrived early the next morning. There were two of them, both dressed in dark clothes and wearing dark gloves. They brought with them a wreath of autumn leaves and chrysanthemums from Dr. Carew and another larger and more elaborate design, mounted on an easel, above which rested, with outstretched wings, a white, stuffed pigeon. Stretched across this design was a purple ribbon with the words: To Father From His Loving Son, stamped in gold.

Mitty looked at the design, turning it in her black hands. "It was kind-thoughted of you, Chester, to get flowers for your pappa."

"I didn't. Dr. Carew must have sent that one too."

Hattie said: "I want to go up and see him once more befo' they screws the coffin lid down."

"Possibly the wreath isn't from me at all. Possibly it came from my brother up north."

"Baby! Baby!— There's bitterness in your heart against me."

The undertaker's assistants were smoking on the porch, whispering together in hushed, stricken voices. The buzz of their speech came through the door blurred and indistinct, rising and falling like the hum of bees.

"Dr. Carew tried to get a preacher to come," said Mitty, "but n'ere one would do it. We got to bury him without one, I expect."

Chester went onto the porch and the undertaker's men threw away their cigarettes and settled their faces as if they had been caught in an act disrespectful to the dead. They became solemn, tender and inexpressibly sad.

Chester spoke to the older man. He had a red face and tiny eyes as colorless as water. On the back of his neck and across his cheeks were festered places, or the pits left by such pimples. "We are ready for the funeral."

The undertaker nodded. "Whenever it is convenient to you, we are at your disposal."

It had stopped raining and the day was warm and close. Against the horizon were dense, low-hanging clouds supported by the tops of the pines, and the sun, already high, shone with a sickly, wan light, as if its rays came to the earth filtered through yellow smoke. In their pens the chickens were listless and silent, huddled together.

Chester said: "My father was not a religious man. There won't be any service at all."

But the older assistant looked at him with his sad, small eyes. "We are prepared for all emergencies," he said. From the pocket of his coat he took a book bound in morocco. He smiled discreetly, and spoke: "I will gladly read the burial service for you." He stretched out his hand as if to touch Chester's sleeve, as if to say: "I know the situation. You needn't hide anything from me. The dead do not need lies, for they cannot feel shame. I have only sympathy and understanding."

Chester pulled away and the undertaker came onto the porch. He looked at the sky and nodded to his two assistants. For a moment they all whispered together, their faces drawn and aching. The undertaker spoke to Chester: "You had better remain inside until the body has been taken to the grave."

Chester went again to the kitchen where Mitty, Hattie and Jim awaited him. "They are going to bury him at once," he said. He sat down on the bench and in a few minutes he heard the undertaker and his men going upstairs. They returned stealthily, speaking to each other in whispers, the old stairs creaking. From their slow steps and their whispers one would have known that they carried a coffin.

"It's stopped raining," said Hattie. "That's a good thing."

"Let me make you a cup of coffee, baby," said Mitty. "I got hot water all ready."

Chester shook his head. "What sort of chickens beside white Leghorns do you raise?"

"That's all, baby. Just Leghorns."

"Leghorns is the best layers," said Hattie.

"A buff Orpington has sweeter meat, though," said Jim. "A buff Orpington is a better eating chicken."

But they were silent when the undertaker came into the room and told them that everything was now in readiness.

Jim had dug the grave in the family burial plot which lay to the left of the house, amid the grove of oaks, and Robert was to lie next to his wife at last.

Chester and Mitty came out first; Hattie and Jim followed a moment later. They stood while the undertaker's assistant read the service, their feet sinking a little into the sodden, spongy earth. He read slowly, getting from each word, each phrase, its full value and adding a significance of his own. The casket lay exposed in the gray light before them with upturned, dripping earth about it, its black, lustrous surface stained prematurely with mud. On it rested the flowers, already faded a little, already withering at their edges.

Mitty drew close to the grave side, upright and arrogant, her finely chiseled, hawk's nose held proudly. There was no grief in her face or in her bearing, no sign of any emotion. Chester, too, stood silent but he was not listening to the words; he was willing that his mind should not hear them. He turned his head and looked at the familiar landscape and there, a long way off, behind the shelter of the chicken runs, he saw Mitty's four children watching. All at once the smallest child broke away from the group and ran toward them. When she reached the grave she began to cry, but Chester took her hand and held it and she pressed her trembling body against him.

Mitty glanced with fury at the weeping child and she bent down to dry her daughter's eyes. "I'll whup you within an inch of life when I get you at the house," she whispered. "I'll whup you so bad you can't walk."

But the undertaker and his men pretended that they did not see the black child; that they had not heard Mitty's furious words. They went on with the service, pretending that the interruption was a natural thing, a thing always to be expected at funerals.

The last prayer was being offered and Chester stood thinking. "This will be all over Athlestan by tonight. Everybody will hear about it and laugh." He closed his eyes, too weary for bitterness, no longer caring if people laughed or not. When he opened them again the men had lowered the coffin and the first spadeful of mud fell upon his father with a hateful sound. Chester and Mitty went back to the house, to sit in the kitchen, by the fire.

"You're not to punish her in any way."

Mitty answered: "I told Ellen to stay where I put her until after the funeral was over with, and she didn't pay me no mind. My chillun got to do what I tell them to do."

"Just the same you are not to punish her. I won't have it."

He went outside where the black child waited in fear. "So your name is Ellen, too? That was my mother's name."

"Yassuh," she said. She reached out and touched his sleeve, to convince herself of his reality, broke away and ran to join her brothers and sisters waiting for her behind the chicken house.

"How can I manage my chillun when you go upsetting things?" asked Mitty in a hurt voice.

The clouds against the horizon were becoming darker in color and there were strange, lemon-colored markings in the sky. A mist, like thick steam, arose from the saturated earth and wavered, obscuring the sharpness of things. It was difficult to breathe in the close, thick air. Far away dogs began to bark. The chickens huddled together in their pens, their feathers ruffled, their heads under their wings, and in the barn a mule brayed nervously and kicked its heels against the wall with a sound like distant artillery.

Mitty sat down upon the steps and Chester sat beside her.

"This place is all yours now. Everything belongs to you, little Chester."

"I don't want it. Keep it for your own children."

But Mitty continued patiently: "What you think I've been working and slaving for all these years, trying to get the place in good order? What you think I done that for?"

"I don't know."

"I done it because I wanted you to have something, baby; that's why I done it."

"I don't want it," said Chester. He got up and walked into the house and Mitty followed him. She sat down on a stool and raised her face upward. All at once she was broken and old and confused. She began to cry fiercely and without restraint. It was the first time that Chester had ever seen her cry, and he was astonished at the vastness of her emotion. She rocked back and forth, her hands pressed against her face.

"If you loved me, baby, you wouldn't say that," she said. And she would not be comforted.

But Chester stood above her, regarding her coldly, in possession of all his emotion. He was thinking suspiciously: "This grief can't be real. She's only acting, and she has a purpose. There's something back of it."

He was restless and that afternoon he went for a walk. The air had cleared a little, but over the land there hung a delicate wetness, not quite rain and not quite mist but possessing the qualities of both. The earth about him was drenched and dead and the cotton fields resembled, in miniature, the destruction of the world by water. Sheets of still water lay undrained across them: gray water, reflecting nothing, from which the bare, hard stalks, like dead forests, stood up.

He skirted the flowing fields and walked through the woods to the river. Clouds lay everywhere close to the earth, unmoving, windless. They touched the even tops of the pines, resting upon them.

It was gray in the woodland and only a faint, unreal light sifted itself through the trees. He walked aimlessly through the woods, stopping for no reason at all to stare upward. A strange, disturbed feeling came over him. "I'm sick," he said in surprise. "There's something strange the matter with me." He walked on and on through the wood, his shoes crushing into the moss and leaves that carpeted it.

At last the wood stopped and he saw before him the yellow river, swollen with rain and high between its banks. He lay flat on his belly, watching the river. Beside him was an old log with decayed, peeling bark in which insects worked; and growing from it, in a sparse cluster, were white, unhealthy things which resembled the fingers of a dead man. Chester broke off one of the fingers and held it in his hand, regarding it with curious eyes. Then, angrily, he twisted it in half, and a puff of brown, stinking powder blew upward, choking him. He threw the finger from him in disgust and began rubbing his hands in the wet earth to rid them of taint.

Before him the river flowed sluggishly or whirled, in spots, into sullen eddies. At these agitated places the water was beaten into lacy, golden foam, like the whipped whites of eggs stained

337

with chocolate. Chester turned on his back, heedless of the cold earth, and stared upward at the grayness above him.

"I never asked much," he said aloud; "I never wanted much." He closed his eyes as if in pain, frowning a little.

A feeling of despair, unreasoning and deep, came over him: an understanding of the cold cruelty which underlies everything and which will outlast everything that lives. These things came to him less definitely than thought, deeper than thought or reason, with the overwhelming sadness of music. He sat upright on the bank and looked again at the trees, the gray sky and the ceaseless river, as if to fix them in his mind forever. "What is it I want?" he asked over and over. . . . "What is it?"

Before him, on the opposite side of the river, a red monolith of clay stood up cut off from the rest of the bank, isolated and undermined by the waters. As he watched, he saw it tremble and collapse from within and fall into the current, its peak toppling first, its sides running in long shivers to the river. . . . For a time there was a yellow dust hovering above the place where the cliff had stood but gradually that, too, drifted beyond the trees into nothingness.

The Whisperer

THERE was once a writer who became tired, finally, of himself, his friends and all the things he had done. And so he went that spring to a cabin where he could rest: where he would be away from everything that was familiar to him. He had wanted to go alone, but his daughter, knowing his helplessness, had come with him to see that he ate properly and that he did not set himself on fire while smoking in bed.

The cabin was built on the side of a mountain, close to its summit; and below was a valley, fresh with the first greenness of spring, through which a river flowed. Beyond was a stretch of hills against the horizon, but softened somewhat with distance: from this height even the valley was blurred and a little indistinct, all outlines blending and flowing into each other, and the wide river was merely a band of silver flat and shining between willows.

The writer spent his days lying under a tree, watching the scene below him. It was beautiful at all times, but he liked it best in early morning, when the sun first touched the meadow, for then the river glistened like silk and delicate mists rose up-ward, mists so radiant and so shot with light that they were like rainbows whose colors had run together.

He was still a young man but there were crow's-feet around his eyes and his lips were marked with the harsh lines of sorrow. He had planned to work on a new book that spring, but he found that he could neither remain indoors nor concentrate his thoughts. Every morning when he got up he would say to him-self: "I will start work at exactly 9 o'clock. Nothing shall stop me today." But instead of working he would lie under his tree and look at his limp, empty hands until his daughter's voice would ring out, and the writer would answer: "Yes, yes, my dear. I will start tomorrow. I will work tomorrow."

One morning as he lay under the tree he looked for a long time at the sky before him and he saw that it was deeply, evenly blue, with white clouds piled against the horizon. At first the clouds appeared stationary, as if they were painted against the sky (they were so calm, so motionless) but as the man watched he saw, in reality, that this was not true. He saw that the clouds moved eternally, changing a little as they moved, but so grad-ually, so imperceptibly, that no man could tell wherein their pat-terns varied. His discovery excited him. He turned and rested his chin in his cupped hands. "This is strange," he thought; "this is very strange."

His daughter was now awake. Inside the house he heard her singing a song which tied his memory to many painful things. And so he lay for a while listening to his daughter's voice and watching the scene before him. Then, inexplicably, a consciousness of the world's beauty and its unending sadness came over him in an emotion so complex and so profound that it almost stopped his breathing. Wave after wave of this rich feeling passed through his body. He stood up and lifted his arms to something eternal, identifying himself with the clouds and the meadows and the stream. He thought: "Since the beginning of time all things have been shaping and reshaping themselves in different patterns, against different lights, and this is the instant of their perfection." A strange feeling of power came over him, a feeling that he was wider than space, that he was more enduring than time, and he spoke aloud, his whole body trembling.

"I will put into words this beautiful, simple feeling that I have. . . . I will catch the meadow and the clouds and the river as they are now so that man may have one perfect thing forever."

He took pencil and paper and began to write, and when he

had finished he lay back again, for he was very tired. His ecstasy was gone and he was again only a weary and an impatient man a little past his first youth. He picked up his notebook and read the words he had written, but even before he had finished he threw the book away. His eyes closed and his face twisted with pain. "Nothing that is true will ever be said," he whispered over and over. . . . "Nothing of the least importance can ever be put into words."

37

CHESTER lay staring at the yellow river, thinking disturbing thoughts, until there was a crackling of twigs behind him, a scraping movement of branches, and he looked up and saw Mitty a few feet away. She raised her head and peered anxiously in both directions, and stood breathing quietly, listening. Her skin was stretched tightly across the bones of her face. With her high-bridged, jutting nose, her full, half-veiled eyes, she resembled somewhat the arrogant, mummified head of an Egyptian queen.

"Chester!" she called. "Chester!— Where you at?"

He got up and stood before her.

"Hattie told me she seen you come this way. I figgered I'd find you here by the river sommers." She noticed his clothes, saw that they were muddy and stained. "Lord God, Chester. Haven't you got no more sense than to lie on the damp ground? Do you want to catch cold, sugarpie?"

It was getting darker gradually. The sky was low and overcast and thick clouds hurried across the horizon, but where they stood no wind blew, no branch stirred: it was as calm here as those chiseled and waiting regions that lie beyond death.

Mitty pulled her man's hat farther over her eyes. She spread her shabby coat on a log and they sat down, side by side. She took his hand.

"It's going to storm. Don't go back tonight, baby. Stay over and spend a day or two."

"I've got to get back to my work."

Mitty's voice was full of gentle reproach: "You haven't even told me what kind of work you doing. I don't know the first thing about you any more."

Chester began to talk of his present life, but almost at once a feeling of its triviality came over him and he stopped.

"Wasn't there somebody else on the place besides Hattie and Jim when I was a boy?"

"Iffen there was, I don't remember him, baby."

"There was, though. There was somebody else, Mitty, and you know it."

"Let's go down to the bar and get sand," said Mitty. "It's going to storm before night."

The wharf had entirely gone and there was nothing left now except a few blackened pilings leaning unsteadily away from the current. There was no breeze but the surface of the water was somehow agitated, as if beneath its depth there was unrest. Sticks and refuse whirled in the current and there passed, at intervals, wide islands of water hyacinths torn from their beds in some clogged lagoon and floating now toward the Gulf.

"It hasn't changed very much, after all."

"I expect it's changed more than you think," said Mitty. "I expect it's changed a good deal."

Birds still sat upon the rotting pilings, rubbing their beaks against the oil sacks at the base of their spines, clinging to the posts with their sharp claws while they lifted their bodies upward and beat at the air with their wings.

"Tell me about your wife. Hattie say she's a pretty thing."

"There isn't much to tell. She's very sweet. She has all the usual virtues."

"Is she a good housekeeper? Does she take care of you well?"

"Oh, yes, she does that excellently."

Mitty narrowed her eyes shrewdly: "Then why don't you love her? Have you got ere a grudge against her?"

344

He was irritated under this cross-examination and he spoke harshly. "No. . . . She's all right, she's a fine woman. If our marriage hasn't been as happy as it should, it's my fault. I'm willing to take the blame."

"Look out for moccasins in that grass," said Mitty.

They went to the bar together and scraped up the wet, golden sand, and dumped it into the baskets which Mitty had brought. And as they knelt there, a flock of gulls with spent, battered wings flew up from the south. They circled wearily above the pilings, contemplating rest, but rose again in regret, straightened out and continued on their way, screaming with piercing purity, following northward the course of the river. The river birds, preening on their pilings, became alarmed, and they, too, made shrill sounds, but they would not leave the security of their posts.

Mitty said, squinting up at the sky: "We better hurry home, baby; it's getting ready to blow."

She would not stop to rest when they reached the bluff again for the rushing clouds seemed closer now, heavier against the horizon, and they stifled the sky with their weight. Between the frame of the imminent, pressing clouds the enlarged sun broke feverish and red and hung above the unreal river. There was a sick light on the water and the trees and the land itself was dying with a wan, unearthly blight.

They found the path, lifted their baskets of sand and walked away from the river through the still woods. Before them wild, lean pigs were running, squealing and snapping at each other in senseless terror. Swamp rabbits, as gray and as quick as ghosts, hurdled the underbrush in long, slow leaps, their ears flattened with the force of their own movement, and squirrels came out from their nests to stare at the menacing sun, and twitch their sensitive tails; for there was unrest in the woods and each thing fled its disaster.

Chester and Mitty walked rapidly, arm in arm, speaking rarely,

345

until they came, at length, to the fields which marked the boundary of the Hurrys' land. They circled the fields to the left, that being the shorter way, and approached the house from the rear. Before them in a thicket of elderberries was a cabin which had fallen to pieces with the years, its roof already caved in, its door hanging broken on broken hinges, and as Chester examined the ruined place a strange, excited feeling came over him. There was a singing in his ears and his throat felt hot and dry. His memory was reaching backward to grasp but there was a door which would not open to his hands.

"Who lived in that cabin, Mitty?"

Mitty took a step forward and touched his arm. "Come on, baby," she begged. "Come on; let's get indoors."

But Chester's face broke up. He raised his arms in the air and the basket that he carried slipped from his uncontrolled fingers and fell, the sand spilling before him.

"What was his name? What was his name, Mitty?"

The first, tentative puff of wind came and Mitty's skirts bulged upward a little. Her apron made a small shelf before her. "His name was Baptiste, if you must know, baby."

All at once Chester felt despair and a strange weakness, as if his bones had become water and were too fluid to bear his weight. He swayed back and forth unsteadily. There was something coming into his mind; a door was being opened, releasing the banished past. He heard the ticking of a clock and saw a pendulum spinning crazily back and forth.

"Baby!" said Mitty in alarm. "What ails you?"

He cried: "I won't remember it, Mitty! There's no sense in remembering now," and the thing that was crowding into his mind faded again, slowly the door ceased to move.

The puffs of wind were coming at quicker intervals now and their force was stronger. The two wreaths lifted from Robert's grave and blew over the fence that surrounded the burial plot.

They slid across the ground for a few feet and then raised upward again before the wind's power and rolled like hoops through the grove of oaks. Mitty leaned forward in a half-circle, her body strong against her blown clothing. She spat with wry lips.

"Can't you forget the way Baptiste twisted on that rope? I'm sorry I ever taken you to see him, baby."

Then something lifted Chester up and flung him face downward among the dead cotton. He thrashed about in the field, tearing up the stalks with his hands, making a sharp noise which resembled, somewhat, the increasing whine of the wind, but at last he lay quiet, his body passive, his face pressed into the muddy earth. He was hot and uncertain. He shook his head weakly, beating at his temples with his open palms. Vague, frightening things floated before him and he shivered, confusing the terror of reality with the terror of dreams, not separating them, unable at this moment to distinguish between his terrors, but gradually actuality drew away from the unreal content of his mind, leaving sharp and unclouded the thing that must be faced.

Mitty was lifting his head, wiping the dirt from his face with her apron. She rested his head in her lap, rocking him back and forth. "Baby! Baby!" she pleaded. "Don't act this way."

Chester raised himself upward and stood with Mitty, their arms about each other for support. "I done the best that I could," she cried. "I done the best that I knew how." But he broke away from her and ran toward the house, stumbling and falling and moving forward again, and Mitty came behind him on her old legs, moving slantwise against the force of the wind. Her battered, man's hat was pulled far down upon her head, her coat held together with black, frightened hands. When he reached the yard he stopped and held onto a young sycamore tree, sheltered somewhat by the frame of the house.

"Go inside!" shouted Mitty. "Go inside quick, baby!"

But he shook his head at her.

Then the sky dipped downward toward the land and the wind came with senseless fury, bending the trees and ripping at fences and outhouses, shrieking and screaming, as it tore at the earth. The chicken runs were overturned and the white hens flew wildly about, beating their wings against the wire mesh, seeking their freedom. In the distance he saw Mitty's four children emerge in single file from the grove. Their arms were locked about each other's waists and they moved slowly toward the security of the old house, a small, frightened group in need of shelter.

Chester turned then and ran down the brick walk and when he reached the road he continued to run borne along by the force of the wind, faster and faster. His face was twisted with pain and his hands pressed together in agony. "I'm very amusing," he shouted over and over; "I'm essentially a comic character!" but his words were lost in the larger sound of the world's fury.

From the Diary of Sarah Tarleton

October 25, 1933. *Today is my seventy-third birthday and I thank my Heavenly Father for preserving my life so long, for giving me health and happiness. I do not feel so old and I hope that there are many more years left to me yet, but if my Master calls me home I shall respond to the summons with a peaceful heart. What is all this unrest in the world? The discontent, the worry and the running about from place to place? My nephews and nieces and their children consider me a stupid old woman, in fact, Elizabeth told me as much frankly when she was here. This is not true, but assuming that she is right, merely for the sake of argument, I would like to respectfully ask what she, Jesse, Lillian and Chester have gained by their intelligence. Are they happier than I? I think I can answer that question firmly in the negative. My long life has taught me one thing: we must accept with humble heart whatever comes our way and we must not expect too much. But I must stop all this philosophizing and get to work. Mrs. Herman Outerbridge has got the books of the Pearl County Ladies' Auxiliary in a fearful tangle and it is up to me to straighten them out again. It does seem that a mature woman, a high-school graduate, could write a few short paragraphs without misspelling most of the words or do simple sums in addition and multiplication, but alas, such is not the case! I do not know how this county would get along if it were not for me.*